CW01540366

WALTHAM FOREST LIBRARIES

CLASS AND CONSEQUENCE

By the same author:

Seventeen Years in Obscurity: Memoirs from the Back Benches, The Book Guild, 1996

CLASS AND CONSEQUENCE

David Watkins

Book Guild Publishing
Sussex, England

First published in Great Britain in 2007 by
The Book Guild Ltd,
Pavilion View
19 New Road
Brighton
BN1 1UF

Copyright © David Watkins 2007

The right of David Watkins to be identified as the author of
this work has been asserted by him in accordance with the
Copyright, Designs and Patents Act 1988.

All rights reserved. No part of this publication may be reproduced,
transmitted, or stored in a retrieval system, in any form or by any means,
without permission in writing from the publisher, nor be otherwise
circulated in any form of binding or cover other than that in which it is
published and without a similar condition being imposed on the subsequent
purchaser.

All characters in this publication are fictitious and any resemblance to real
people, alive or dead, is purely coincidental.

Typesetting in Baskerville by
IML Typographers, Birkenhead, Merseyside

Printed in Great Britain by
Antony Rowe Ltd, Chippenham, Wiltshire

A catalogue record for this book is available from
The British Library.

ISBN 978 1 84624 053 9

Let not ambition mock their useful toil,
   Their homely joys, and destiny obscure;
Nor grandeur hear with a disdainful smile,
   The short and simple annals of the poor.

   Thomas Gray: *Elegy in a Country Churchyard*

Chapter 1

He was born in the early afternoon of a cold, wet day in March 1890, at Pembroke, in the 'little England beyond Wales' in the far west of the principality. He was his parents' ninth-born. All the children had survived. That was a matter of comment, sometimes admiring, sometimes jealous, among neighbours. Few of them had been so lucky. Infant mortality was high.

'I hope the poor little mite lives,' was the comment of the midwife who helped deliver him.

'They breed like rabbits,' was the dinner-table comment of the doctor who had perfunctorily visited the pregnant mother, having pocketed his fee, minuscule for him but substantial for the ever-growing family. He was speaking at a dinner party at the house of one of his more profitable patients, one of the local squirearchy.

His wife chimed in. 'The dear Queen had nine children,' she said. She pronounced it 'the deah Queen'. She herself had just become pregnant again. Her three young children were safely at home in the capable care of the housekeeper.

Dr Jones froze. His wife never seemed to think before she spoke. He would be having words with her when they got home.

'You can hardly compare the Queen with people like that,' he said coldly. 'She had a duty to ensure the continuation of the royal line. And what a splendid example to us all,' he added.

Even as he said that, he regretted it. He had intended to flatter his host, whom he knew to be one of only two children but who had already fathered four, but it suddenly dawned on him that the Queen's splendid example could just as easily be said to apply to those lower orders with their large families.

'This is a very good wine, Squire,' he said hastily. He didn't really know anything about differentiating between wines, but it tasted good and he was desperately anxious to change the subject.

'Not a bad claret at all,' said the squire. 'Recommended to me by my brother-in-law, last time we visited them in London.'

Squire Hatherly really knew little more about wine than the doctor, but he had been told it was good by his brother-in-law, who did know about such things. It was useful to be able to boost his standing among these local people through being thought of as something of a connoisseur. It was also a useful opportunity to remind them that he was a regular visitor to distant London. Privately, though, his brother-in-law's superior knowledge rankled badly. In fact, his brother-in-law rankled badly for a number of reasons.

He was a wealthy Conservative Member of Parliament. He was English and the owner of numerous coal mines, some in the north east of England, some in south Wales; he also held lucrative directorships in other industrial concerns. When the squire's sister had announced her engagement, the family was aghast.

The fellow was not a gentleman. He had not even had the manners formally to ask her father for his consent. He had no family background and had not been to a decent school. He spoke with strong traces of what they understood was called a Geordie accent.

But perhaps what rankled most of all was that, with all those faults, he was self-evidently more intelligent than any of them. He was as sharp as a razor and very quick at learning about everything, including picking up social graces that a fellow from his background ought not even to aspire to. The squire's sister was over the age of consent and had stood firm, so the marriage had gone ahead.

There had been some confused talk about disinheriting her but the family had been unexpectedly disarmed by her husband making a generous settlement on her in her own name. She had been able to use part of that to help the family, whose estate had suffered from the great slump in agriculture in the later decades of the century. It all added to the squire's gall that he needed his sister's help to sustain his very well-heeled style of life, while hating the source of the money.

'Are you likely to be going up to London again soon?' asked the doctor, mightily relieved that the conversation had taken a new turn.

'We shall be going again next month,' said the squire. 'It's so easy now that the Pembroke and Tenby's nine-thirty train from Pembroke Dock carries through carriages which are transferred to the Great Western at Whitland and go right through to London, through that Severn Tunnel they opened a few years ago.' Although contemptuous of trade, he liked to display his knowledge of such things.

'We shall be going to the Savoy Theatre,' he added, further to impress his guests. 'There's a new opera, a great success I'm told. It's called *The Gondoliers* and it's by Gilbert and Sullivan.'

'Pair of damned radicals, if you ask me,' said Colonel Mulholland. The fact that no one had asked him, or was likely to, did not feature in the colonel's thinking.

He was the oldest of the squire's guests, another local landowner, retired from the army. He was known to have inherited considerable wealth and was the only person present to whom the squire felt he ought to defer.

'Oh, I don't know,' said the doctor's wife. 'Sir Arthur Sullivan was knighted by the dear Queen seven years ago.'

The doctor frowned. He was increasingly concerned. Over recent months, she seemed to be getting to show signs of independent thinking that were unsuitable for any woman, leave alone the one who was his wife.

'A well-deserved knighthood,' said Squire Beauchamp, another guest, 'and I don't think Gilbert is really a radical. More of a Conservative satirist, I should think.'

Squire Beauchamp was also a local landowner, minor but believed to be of very ancient lineage. His name, pronounced Beecham, was thought to indicate direct descent from the Normans, who had colonised south Pembrokeshire in the eleventh century, thereby creating the little England beyond Wales. But his politics were considered suspect. The colonel's view of him was succinct: 'Damn Whig, if you ask me.' The colonel had never become accustomed to Whigs becoming Liberals and Tories becoming Conservatives. It also annoyed him that Beauchamp had one of those aristocratic names that were pronounced differently from the way they were spelt.

The conversation was starting to take a turn that was beyond the comprehension of most of the guests. It was the doctor to the rescue again.

'Is your brother-in-law likely to be joining the government?' he asked the host.

'No!' said the squire, rather more emphatically than was

necessary. 'He is too busy with his – er – financial interests.' He could not bring himself to say 'trade interests'. His explanation was accurate, but he was annoyed that the idea could be entertained that someone like his brother-in-law should even be considered by Lord Salisbury, the Prime Minister, as a potential minister.

'Glad to see that young Balfour is taking a firm hand with those bloody Irish,' the colonel said, 'if the ladies will pardon my language.' In reality, he couldn't care less whether the ladies pardoned his language or not.

Arthur Balfour, the Prime Minister's nephew, had been given responsibility for enforcing his uncle's Irish policy of 'twenty years of resolute government' and was thought of as one of the rising stars of politics.

'Good chap,' said the squire. Then, 'I'd like your advice Colonel. I'm thinking...'

But the colonel was in full flood, slightly flushed from the claret and from the white burgundy that had preceded it.

'Damn Catholics causing trouble in Ireland,' he said. 'Damn chapel ranters stirring up the working classes in all the coalfields. And that bloody fellow Gladstone encouraging the lot.' Everything of which the colonel disapproved was either bloodstained or destined for hell, sometimes both. His hatred of the Leader of the Opposition knew no bounds. But now he paused, slightly surprised at having expressed himself coherently on no less than three subjects but also, for all his ego, slightly concerned that he might be going too far.

'You want my advice, Hatherly?' he asked his host.

'Yes' said the squire, 'I'm thinking of putting my youngest into the army when he's old enough. Of course, he's only two now. My eldest will succeed me in charge of the estate and the two girls will of course marry. What would you advise?'

'Good thinking,' said the colonel. 'Send him to a good school. Rugby, where I went myself and sent my boy, or somewhere like that, then get him a commission.'

By that time, they had all finished eating. The squire's wife stood up. No word was spoken, but all the women guests also stood up. The men did likewise out of courtesy. Led by the hostess, the women then silently left the room to leave the men to port, cigars and conversation deemed unfit for the ears of women.

Back in the crowded little house in Pembroke, they decided to call the new baby Hugh, Hugh Hughes. This was in accordance with a Welsh custom. The child would grow up with contemporaries such as Evan Evans, William Williams and David Davies. For the Hughes family, though, it was a first. The names painstakingly inscribed in the family bible, over three generations, held no precedent. There were recurring Johns, Fredericks, Thomases and Josephs, but never before a Hugh. Nor was there ever a David, strange perhaps in Wales. But then, this was the little England beyond Wales.

Within three years, the family would be completed, with the births of two more girls. Only then would the mother's child-bearing days be over.

She had been born Leah Abigail Davies, the last of seven children, two of whom had not survived infancy. Like all her brothers and sisters, she was given names from the Bible, her father insisting that they all be given what he called proper Christian names. She was married when she was eighteen to the handsome young Joseph Thomas Hughes, her brother Matthew's best friend, who had come courting when she had just turned seventeen. He was just a year older. Both families approved the match. Not least among the reasons for her father's approval was that his prospective son-in-law had proper Christian names.

Both young people felt strong sexual stirrings which aroused and excited but also frightened them. The only thing they had been taught about such things was that they were wicked. In so far as they had learned anything more, it had been through sniggering conversations among friends. Their pre-marital activities never moved beyond kisses and cuddles of the most chaste kind.

Their approach to marriage was straightforward. Pleasure in family life could only come from companionship and having children. Men had certain desires which women had a duty to meet, but they could only possibly do so in marriage. The result was children, and marriage had been ordained by God for what was called the procreation of children.

Any idea that pleasure could be obtained through the act of procreation was sinful and blasphemous. No notion could be entertained that husband and wife should derive pleasure and happiness from the union of their bodies. Any feelings of enjoyment they ever felt were cancelled out by feelings of guilt.

All their children had been conceived in 'the missionary position', although they did not know that it was called that by more sophisticated people or that there were alternatives. It had all been done under blankets in the dark, with Joseph's rough nightshirt and Leah's scarcely less rough nightdress never removed but just pulled up to their waists.

They went to church after every birth, to give public thanks, to God for giving them the child and to seek forgiveness for their sin in procreating it. They were not stupid and the contradiction between thanking God and, at the same time, seeking his forgiveness for the action he had ordained, mildly puzzled them. But they had been brought up to believe that it was the right thing to do, and that it was not for the likes of them to question such things.

When they were first married, they had lived with Leah's parents. There was room because she was the youngest of the family, and her brothers and sisters had by then gone elsewhere. Their tiny bedroom provided their only privacy. Before the birth of their second child, they moved to the house in Pembroke; quite an adventure, the costs of which had caused them much worry.

Life was hard. Money was always short, but Leah was astonishingly skilled at handling it. Meals were frugal; both parents sometimes went without so that the children did not. Fortunately, feeding them was eased because there was a large garden behind the house, where Joseph grew vegetables to supplement the bread and cheese and cheap cuts of meat which otherwise provided their staple diet. He also grew flowers, so that for most of the year, house and garden would be a blaze of colour.

Their father's gardening skill had contributed greatly to most of the children growing up reasonably healthy. The only exception was Albert, the sixth, who was sickly from the start. They had thought that he would not survive but, with devoted care, he had.

Clothing the children was done through the simple expedient of handing down to the younger ones as their brothers and sisters grew older. Shoes were repaired time and again until they virtually fell apart. Leah never stopped cooking, cleaning, mending and darning. The house was always spotless.

For all their problems, Joseph and Leah loved each other. Neither of them ever looked to another man or woman. When a brash young man had made advances to Leah, shortly after her marriage, she had sent him packing pretty sharply. They loved their children and grew increasingly proud of their large family, although they were not averse to admitting that the children were often more of a trial than a blessing, and all were brought up in the strict discipline of a Victorian household. Chastisement was always on hand for misdemeanours. In practice, in that household, it was rarely used.

It was written on little Hugh's birth certificate that his father worked as a porter on the Pembroke and Tenby Railway. Their house was some distance from Pembroke station, where Joseph worked, so that he had a longish walk to and from work. But that was no problem. It was something he had been used to all his life.

When they married, he had been a farm labourer, like the majority of his contemporaries. Some of his mates had left the area to go elsewhere to work, mostly in coal mines or iron works. He had thought about doing that but the experience of his friend Matthew had abruptly changed his mind.

Matt, as they all called him, was Leah's elder brother by a year and a half, making him a little older than Joseph. They both worked on the same farm. It was through Matt that Joseph had met Leah. But Matt was a restless soul, who hankered to move on.

'There's better money to be earned in the pits, Joe,' he said more than once.

'I don't know,' Joseph would reply. 'There's terrible stories of what hard work it is. And very long hours. And about children working there.'

'Well, we were only boys when we started here,' Matt would retort. 'And we work long hours. Well before daylight and well after dark in the winter. And don't try to tell me it isn't hard work, especially on the potatoes and the haymaking.'

Joseph could not disagree. Getting the early potatoes out of the ground and sacking them up to be taken away in the early summer was back-breaking work. So was it at haymaking time. For that matter, it was long, hard work at every season of the year, but he was a more cautious soul than his friend. Better the devil you knew than the one you didn't.

But Matt's mind was made up. A month before Joseph and Leah were married, he left the farm and went off to work in the pit at Begelly, ten miles or so away, on the road to Carmarthen.

Farmer Haskins, for whom they worked, tried to dissuade him. The farmer was a kindly man. His wife had died in childbirth, many years earlier, when their only child had been born. He ran the farm with his now married daughter and her husband. He worked as long and as hard as any of them. In some ways, he looked upon the two young labourers as the sons he had never had.

'Don't go, Matt,' he said, 'It's terrible in those pits and you'll have to work all the hours God made, in terrible conditions.'

'We work all the hours God made, here,' Matt replied.

'I know it's hard,' said the farmer, 'but here, at least, you're in the fresh air with all this lovely country and the animals all around you – far better than working in the pitch dark under the ground.'

But Matt could not be dissuaded and duly left.

Just over a year later, when Leah was expecting her first baby, a letter came, to say that Matt had suffered a terrible accident. He had been trapped in a roof fall in the mine. They had to cut off his left leg above the knee. He was in constant pain. The pit manager had told him that they would no longer employ him because they only wanted able-bodied men.

'Dear God, what are we going to do?' asked his mother.

'There's no choice except to bring him home,' replied her husband grimly. 'There's no way I'm going to let them put him in the workhouse or in one of those terrible charity hospitals.'

'But how are we going to get him here? Even if we fetch him by train, it's a long walk to the station at that end, like it is here, and he can't walk.'

Joseph took the sad news to Farmer Haskins, who was visibly upset. 'I begged him not to go there,' he said. Then, after a moment's thought, 'I'll take you over there in the pony and trap and we'll fetch him.'

They set out early on the following Sunday. Helping Matt was more important than the normally obligatory churchgoing.

When they eventually found the cottage where Matt lodged, Joseph was mildly surprised to see that it stood in quite a large and well-cultivated garden. A man and woman were working in the garden. It struck Joseph how ragged they looked. Two small, barefoot children were playing, and chickens were clucking around.

'Excuse me,' Farmer Haskins said. 'Is this where Matt Davies lodges? We've come to fetch him.'

'Aye,' said the man. 'We wondered if you'd be coming. Matt had a letter yesterday. I don't read myself but he said to expect you. Come in.'

The cottage was a low, whitewashed building with an amateurishly thatched roof, a smoking chimney at one end, a single door and two small windows. When they went inside, it was a shock. There was only one room, dimly lit from the two small windows and from the fire at the end. It took their eyes some time to become accustomed to the gloom after the bright sunlight. Then came another shock. The floor was bare earth.

But the greatest shock of all for Joseph was the sight of his best friend, lying on a blanket on the floor in front of the fire. Matt now looked at least twice his real age. The stump of his severed leg was swathed in dirty, bloodstained bandages.

Joseph was too choked to speak. He could not keep the stinging tears out of his eyes. They somehow managed to get Matt upright; he supported himself on a crude, home-made crutch. The two friends embraced, neither able to speak for some time. They knew it was not the sort of way men were supposed to behave, but their emotions overpowered their sense of male correctness.

'We've come to take you home, Matt,' Joseph finally managed to say.

'Why aye,' replied Matt. It was a frequently used Pembrokeshire colloquialism, usually spoken with spirit, to indicate agreement, but now Matt spoke it with utter listlessness. That upset Joseph all the more. He sensed that the high spirits he had so admired had gone out of his friend.

'We've done our best,' the miner's wife said, 'but we can't do any more for him.' She said it with the fatalistic air of someone who had seen it all before and fully expected to see it again.

Between them, they got Matt into Farmer Haskins' trap. Matt did not complain, but it was clear from his involuntary wincing at every movement and, later, as they struck rough patches in the road, that he was in pain. It was after dark when they got him home.

His mother made up a bed for him in the living room. He was only able to hobble around a little when he left it. The doctor came occasionally, but they could not afford regular visits and he only came when it was clear that Matt was taking a turn for the worse. A nurse came from time to time to dress his leg, but whereas it should have been done every day, it was done only occasionally. Leah and his mother did their best to help but, lacking expertise, their efforts were of little avail.

Matt, who had been so bright and talkative, now spoke little. It was clear that he was deteriorating all the time. The lack of proper attention to what was left of his leg caused gangrene to set in. He died shortly after Leah's first son was born. One of his last conscious actions was to cradle the newborn baby in his arms. They named the baby Matthew.

As they lowered the cheap coffin into the grave, Joseph felt an anger he had never known before. For all the joy of his marriage and his firstborn child, he felt empty. It was his first encounter with death at close quarters. Someone he dearly loved was gone for ever. A young life had been cruelly taken and, outside his family and close friends, nobody cared in the slightest degree, either about the loss or the brutal circumstances that had brought it about.

It was not long after Matt's untimely death that they moved to the house in Pembroke. Leah was pregnant again and their second child, a pretty little girl they named Mary, was born at the new address, as would be all their later children. Joseph left the employment of Farmer Haskins when they moved, because the new home was too far from the farm. The farmer was genuinely sorry to see him go. To Joseph's surprise, on his last pay day, an additional five gold sovereigns were pressed into his hand. He could think of no other employer who would have done that. It was the largest amount of money he had ever seen.

He had obtained a job nearer to the new home, as carter for a grocer and general provisioner in Pembroke. The hours were still long. Grooming the horse was among his duties, and it was his farm experience that had helped get him the job.

Now he travelled extensively round the local countryside, delivering to the houses of the local gentry. He was soon catching glimpses of a way of life totally removed from his own experience.

Always, he would go to the tradesmen's entrance at the back, usually to be received by a housekeeper or cook. As they got to know him better, he would sometimes go away with gifts of food, with strict instructions not to let anybody see. He would also pick up fascinating bits of gossip. Mrs Phillips, the cook at Squire Hatherly's, was always a good source of information.

Mrs Phillips, he learned, was not a Mrs at all, but was given the title as a matter of courtesy. He never encountered either Squire or Mrs Hatherly and was under Mrs Phillips' strict instructions that should either of them happen to come into the kitchen, he must silently and respectfully keep his distance. Should he accidentally meet them outside, he must immediately doff his cap.

One day when he was in the kitchen, he was witness to a conversation between the cook and the butler, Mr Jevons, a very grand man who always ignored him. They talked as if he was invisible.

'He's coming down this weekend,' said Jevons, with evident distaste. 'Not our sort at all. Can't for the life of me understand why she married the likes of him.'

'Money, of course,' said the practical Mrs Phillips briskly. 'They wouldn't be able to keep this place up the way they do without his money.'

The reference was to the squire's sister, who had married the mine-owning Member of Parliament. Joseph noted the 'not our sort'. It was entirely in line with what he had discovered elsewhere on his rounds, that some of the more senior-ranking servants in a rigidly hierarchical society were even bigger snobs than their masters. It was part of the same order of things that Jevons, who was never called Mr, and the woman, who was always called Mrs although she was not a Mrs, could discuss such things in front of him as if he did not exist.

The biggest of the houses at which he called was Colonel Mulholland's, set at the end of a long drive through thick woods. Joseph had a countryman's joy of the beauty of nature and he always found pleasure in going up that drive, above all in the spring, when the woods were thick with bluebells and the sun, shining through the trees, was making beautiful patterns on the ground and giving promise of the summer to come.

Goings-on at the colonel's were even more intriguing than at the squire's. There was a pert, pretty little housemaid, who somehow always managed to appear when he called, but he carefully kept his distance from her.

'Bit of all right,' remarked Bert, one of the footmen. He winked. 'Likes it too. Reckon young master's been there as often as I have.'

Not very long after that, both footman and maid disappeared. No one there would tell him anything, so he asked at Squire Hatherly's.

'Where are Bert and Molly, over at the colonel's?'

'Sacked,' said Mrs Phillips, in her usual brisk way. 'He put her in the family way.'

She lowered her voice. 'At least, that's what we've been told,' she said. 'On my reckoning, it was just as likely to have been the young master. Trouble was, Bert couldn't keep his trousers on when she was around and she didn't seem too sure herself who the father was, so it was easy to blame Bert.'

'Where have they gone?'

'Don't know. They're going to make him marry her.'

'But if it's not his baby ...'

'No matter. There was no way the colonel would have it that his son could be the father. There was a terrible row.'

Rather unwisely, Joseph, eager to learn more, passed the gossip back to the colonel's, on his next visit there. It was a fatal mistake not to take account of how his own words might be passed on and twisted in the process. When he collected his wages at the end of that week, the shopkeeper told him angrily that he was sacked.

'Don't expect to tell lies about my customers and get away with it,' he shouted.

'But it's not lies. The servants in all the big houses know it's true.'

That made the shopkeeper even angrier. He became red in the face. 'Don't you dare accuse the gentry of lying on the basis of lies told by servants,' he shouted, his voice rising to a near scream. 'Get out! And don't come back here. You can count yourself lucky I'm paying you this week's wages.'

Joseph felt like throwing the meagre money in the man's face, but a wiser inner counsel prevailed. He just walked away. He had learned another lesson about the world in which he would have to fight all his life to earn a living, as well as about the people who inhabited it.

The dismissed Bert and Molly, although in difficulties initially, proved in the longer run to be extraordinarily lucky. After their hurried marriage, they found themselves blacklisted in all the local country houses. Eventually, however, they obtained posts in the household of a wealthy iron master who had just retired to Tenby. He was a childless widower who took a liking to the young couple. There were inevitable rumours that Molly was not averse to giving him what were called favours. Within a few years, Bert and Molly were respectively butler and housekeeper, with a healthy young son who looked remarkably like a Mulholland grandson.

Fortunately for Joseph Hughes, he was soon able to get a job as a porter on the Pembroke and Tenby Railway. It was the height of the railway age and, humble though his job was, he felt proud to work in this new industry that was transforming the whole country and to wear the ill-fitting but distinctive uniform it required, complete with collar and tie.

He could remember how, as a small boy, he had marvelled at the great gang of navvies who had descended on the countryside to build the railway, making cuttings, embankments, bridges, tunnels and stations.

Then there had been the official opening, when the entire town of Pembroke had seemed to be on holiday, with the church bells ringing and the main street, from the old castle to the new station, decorated with flags, streamers, flowers and greenery. With his father, he had been one of a huge throng who had seen the official train leave for Tenby, packed with privileged passengers and departing to a great roar of cheering and clapping, which the engine driver had acknowledged with blasts on the whistle. How he would have loved to be that engine driver.

The extension of the franchise in the 1884 parliamentary reform act gave him the vote for the first time. He did not know much about politics but felt strongly that he must fulfil his new civic duty. He thought Mr Gladstone was a good man, so he made up his mind to vote Liberal. Had he had any doubts, they would have been dispelled by an encounter during the election campaign.

He was at the back of the house when there was a knock on the door. The children came shrieking 'Daddy, Daddy, there's a strange man at the door.' He opened it to find himself face to face with the shopkeeper who had sacked him a year earlier. There was instant mutual recognition but the grocer stated his business.

'I see you're on the electoral register,' he said, 'I'm canvassing votes for the Conservative Party.'

Joseph did not raise his voice. His tone was deadly. 'Get out of my house,' he said, very slowly. 'Don't you ever come calling here again,' And he slammed the door, feeling distinctly pleased with himself and confirmed in his politics.

He was disappointed that the Liberals were beaten by the Conservatives, but he gathered that it was something to do with disagreements among the gentry about Ireland. He supposed though that it wouldn't change his life to any great extent.

Chapter 2

'You pay proper attention and learn your lessons,' Joseph said to Hugh, as the boy set off for his first day at school. 'I never had the chance you are getting.'

By then, there was a national system of free education. It was rudimentary, but it was a big step forward for families like the Hughes. As he sent his youngest son off that day, Joseph could not help recalling his own schooling.

He had been lucky to have lessons provided through the charity of the church. As well as being taught to read and write, he had learned elementary arithmetic. Above all, he had been taught that the absolute truth of Protestant Christianity, as taught by the Anglican Church, could not be challenged. Nor should anyone challenge the nature of the God-given system of society in which they all lived.

As he grew older, he had come to enjoy reading. He followed the local weekly newspaper and there were copies of *Oliver Twist* and *David Copperfield* in his house. He enjoyed these books because they described life as he himself knew it. He found the plots a bit complicated and he had problems with quite a lot of the words at first, so he also bought a dictionary and a book about grammar, both soon well worn from constant use. He encouraged the children to read and he was determined that they should all have an education.

At about the time when his firstborn, Matthew, had become of school age, attendance was made compulsory, but he had to pay for him and for the other older ones. Now, for his younger children and for the middle ones still at school, it was free; a great relief for his very tight family budget.

Little Hugh was nervous at the prospect of school, made the more so by stories told him by his older brothers and sisters. His nervousness was not eased by his first experience. With the other newcomers, he was paraded before the assembled older pupils, who included, at the top end, his brother Albert, who would be finishing school within a few months and, in the middle range, his sisters Edith and Winifred. The head of the school walked up and down at the front, swishing a cane and looking for someone to choose from among the new intake. He stopped in front of Hugh.

'You, boy,' he said, poking him with the cane, 'what's your name?'

'Hugh Hughes.'

'Say "Sir" when you speak to me. And in this school, you will be known only by your surname.' Then, raising his voice, 'Remember that, all of you. I am Mr Kendle and you always address me and your other teachers as "Sir". Now, boy, what's your name?'

'Hughes, sir.'

'That's better.' He swished the cane menacingly. 'Any nonsense, any disobedience and any failure to learn your lessons and I shall put this little chap to good use. That is the first lesson for all of you to learn.'

Mr Kendle held the view that the strictest discipline was required in all schools, just as it had been enforced in the one he had gone to. He had seen a colleague dismissed because he could not control his class. That was never going to happen to him. A class or, for that matter, a school without discipline could become a mob, and the only way to enforce discipline was through fear of corporal punishment in this world and fear of burning in hell in the next.

He moved along the line, asking each his or her name in the same way. Then he stood back.

'Have you all learned your first lesson?'

'Yes sir.' It was a dispirited chorus.

Mr Kendle was in his mid-thirties, a dark-haired, dapper man with a carefully trimmed moustache. He had convinced himself, but nobody else, that he had eliminated all traces of his Welsh accent. It was a foible which made him much mimicked among his pupils.

He came from Cardiff, the younger son of a solicitor, who had paid for him to attend a grammar school and then sent him away from home to a college in Manchester. He had had no real plans about his future and at first worked in his father's office, but he found the work unattractive and turned to teaching.

His first post had been as an assistant teacher at a school in the mining valleys. There, he had met and married the daughter of a local tradesman of some substance. It was a matter of disappointment to both of them that they had failed to produce any children.

The local School Board who appointed him to the post in Pembrokeshire had been impressed. They had felt that he possessed the qualities to instil the necessary discipline, fear of God and right amount of knowledge as was suitable for the future hewers of wood and drawers of water who would be his pupils, without giving them ideas above their station.

In reality, Mr Kendle was a more complex character than he appeared either to the board or to his pupils. He had an independent mind which his own education had actually sharpened rather than dulled. That sometimes made him prey to conflicting thoughts that worried him.

He believed implicitly in the greatness of Britain and her mighty empire, but there were aspects that concerned him. During his college days in Manchester, he had observed some of the people who worked in the 'dark, satanic mills' of William Blake's poem. He had felt disturbed, not only at the conditions in which they lived and worked, but also by the fact that the vast majority of them were illiterate. That was when the first seeds were sown of his interest in education.

When he was teaching in the Welsh coalfield, the mine owners and their like had done their best to ensure that they controlled the School Board, but they had faced strong opposition. The board had to be elected every three years in open public election and the elections were always contested. Edward Kendle was an instinctive upholder of the established order, and there was one candidate who seriously worried him.

It was 1889 and parents still had to pay for their children's schooling. The candidate advocated free education, free school meals for children who needed them and technical education. Kendle agreed with all that and he was particularly attracted to the latter proposition. There had been a distinctive, technical background in the teaching at his college in Manchester and he had long concluded that the ever-developing technology of British industry needed not just illiterate miners and factory hands, but skilled and literate craftsmen in large numbers.

Unfortunately, the candidate putting forward these very acceptable views was, himself, entirely unacceptable. He was a publicly declared Socialist, and had written in his election address:

I would remind you that the Board School is used for the

children of the poor only; it is not good enough for the children of the rich; some day I hope it will be good enough for all.

For Edward Kendle, that was dangerous and subversive talk. It was the privately educated classes, of whom he was proud to be one, who had made Britain so great. The Duke of Wellington himself had said that the Battle of Waterloo was won on the playing fields of Eton. Kendle had dismissed with contempt someone whom he once heard retort that, equally, the charge of the Light Brigade was lost there.

Discussing the board election with his wife, he said, 'The fellow has got some good ideas but other ones that are quite mad. Every sane person knows that a state education system for rich and poor alike would undermine the very foundations of the country. It won't happen in a hundred years.'

'Of course not, dear,' his wife replied, looking up from her embroidery.

'If I were a betting man,' he said, 'I would put money on it not happening.' He was not a humorous man any more than he was a betting one, but he could not help adding whimsically, 'But then, I shan't be around to collect my winnings in the nineteen eighties and nineties.'

Of course not, dear,' said his wife, who also lacked humour but was strong on wifely duty.

Her husband really did feel that it was a great pity that a candidate who put forward some very sensible policies had put himself completely out of the running with others which were so dangerous. But to his astonishment, not only was the candidate elected, he topped the poll. It was then that he first decided to start looking for a post elsewhere, and so it was that he arrived in Pembroke.

The School Board there was different. Most of its members regarded the triennial elections as, at best, an inconvenience and, at worst, a dangerous experiment. The difficulty was resolved in the event because, somehow, it invariably worked out that there were never more candidates than there were places to be filled. Almost all the board members firmly believed that their first duty was to ensure that the education for which they were responsible was provided with as little cost as possible to the ratepayers.

Mr Kendle stood in front of the class. On the wall behind him was a large map of the world. It was a hot day in June 1897, the year of Queen Victoria's diamond jubilee. There were to be great celebrations and it was even rumoured that the Prince of Wales would visit Wales. Mr Kendle had decided to give an appropriate slant to the geography lesson.

'Who can tell me why so much of the map is coloured red?' he asked.

A number of hands shot up. He chose one of the girls.

'Please sir, that's the British Empire.'

'Good.' He thought a moment. 'Can anyone tell me what this projection of the map is called?' He did not expect any of them to know that, but one hand was raised.

'Yes?' he asked.

'Please sir, it's called Mercator's projection.'

'Very good.' He was surprised. 'How did you know that?'

'Please sir, I read it.'

'Good. Let that be a lesson to all of you. Learning is not something that only takes place in school.' He was a great one for pointing out anything that should be a lesson to them.

The boy who had answered was called Robert Snape. Mr Kendle knew already that he was the brightest boy in the class, one of the brightest in the whole school. But he also knew only too well that the prospects for his abilities to be stretched and developed properly were negligible. It was one among those involuntary thoughts that he found so worrying.

Snape was the most ragged and almost certainly the poorest boy there. His father had abandoned his mother, himself and his two small sisters to go off with another woman. Before that, he had regularly beaten his wife and children. Mrs Snape, haggard and old before her time, tried desperately to maintain a home. She managed to earn a tiny income by working long hours in various houses as a charwoman. She was desperately afraid that she would die before the children became old enough to support themselves, and they would have to go into the workhouse.

Because of his ragged clothes, Snape was nicknamed 'ragged-arse Robert'. Once, but only once, he had been an object of the attention of the class bully. The bullying stopped abruptly, because Robert was as tough physically as he was mentally. He had a resilience built up through numerous beatings from his father, who, on one occasion, had beaten him nearly senseless when he tried to intervene to protect his mother. The would-be bully had sustained both a bloody nose and a black eye. Both boys had duly been beaten for fighting.

Mr Kendle, for reasons not unconnected with his next question, had not thought it necessary to point out that Mercator's projection caused certain land masses to appear much larger than they actually were. Now, he used a pointer to pick out one of the very largest of the red areas.

'What country is this?' he asked.

A number of hands were raised, including, of course, Robert Snape's, but Mr Kendle picked someone else, who told him that it was Canada.

'One of the greatest dominions of the British Empire,' the teacher said.

Now, Hugh raised his hand and was called to speak.

'Please sir, I've got two aunties who live in Canada.'

'Do you know where in Canada they live?'

'Yes sir. It's in the prairie, about a hundred miles west of Winnipeg.'

Ah,' said Mr Kendle, 'pioneers of the British Empire. People to be proud of. They are the sort who are making our great empire even greater.'

The two aunts were Hugh's father's two younger sisters. They and their husbands had emigrated in 1888, two years before Hugh was born. His eldest brothers and sisters remembered them clearly, and they exchanged letters from time to time with his father. Hugh had been told many times of their departure.

When they left Pembroke on the train, the whole family had assembled to see them off, knowing that they were highly unlikely ever to see them again. Their few possessions had been put in the guard's van. His father had accompanied them on the train to Swansea and seen them off on the ship which took them to Halifax, in Nova Scotia. From there, they had made a very long train journey.

They had left Wales because of abject poverty throughout the British countryside. There were promises of a better life in Canada. They did not really understand the situation but, with no prospects ahead of them at home, they took the promises at their face value, especially as each emigrant family was to be freely given a whole square mile of land to farm. However, the reality proved to be very different from anything they had expected.

In the first place, there was the journey. They had spent the best part of three weeks crossing the Atlantic in miserable conditions in the steerage of a slow, mixed cargo and passenger ship. Then had come days and nights on end in the scarcely less miserable conditions in the train, which finally left them in what appeared to be a virtual wilderness.

Among the things they had not understood was that the Canadian Pacific Railway had not long been completed and that, to make it profitable, it was necessary to populate and cultivate the prairie across which it ran. There was another irony which escaped them. They were there to grow wheat in competition with the already developed prairie in the nearby USA, and it was American wheat pouring into Britain which had helped so much towards the destruction of agriculture at home, creating the poverty which had caused them to go to Canada.

As for the square mile of prairie, they had to clear it themselves and build their own wooden home. They found winters of, to them, unimaginable severity, followed by hot summers with plagues of mosquitoes. Initially they had been terrified by the appearance of 'Indians', but they had proved to be friendly and helpful. The families were eternally grateful for their help, without which they might well not have survived.

None of that was ever mentioned in the sisters' letters back to their brother. Had they known what they were going to, they would not have gone. Having arrived, they were too poor to go back. It was the way, as Mr Kendle put it, that the great British Empire was being made even greater.

The actual anniversary of Queen Victoria's accession came some days after the lesson. The children were granted a day off school to witness the celebrations. Each was given a small Union Jack flag on a stick to wave, donated by local tradesmen.

On the great day, the streets were decorated with flags and bunting and there were pictures of the Queen in most of the shop windows and in many of the houses. A detachment of soldiers, splendid and sweating in ceremonial uniforms, marched from the barracks in Pembroke Dock to the station in Pembroke, a military band leading the procession. The streets through which they marched were lined with cheering people. At the station, the soldiers boarded a special train which took them back to Pembroke Dock.

As the soldiers entered Pembroke, they had to march up a short, sharp incline. At the top, near the castle, where Hugh and his schoolmates were duly assembled, the soldiers stopped to rest and to partake of refreshments provided by local publicans. On forming up again, before they set off for the final stretch, the band played 'God Save The Queen'. Everyone stood to attention and most joined in the singing. Immediately they finished, a group of twenty or so men started singing another anthem, in Welsh. They were at once approached by police. They only had time to sing one verse, before they were hustled away.

Hugh's father was standing in the crowd, anxious to see his children taking part in the ceremonies. That evening, Hugh, puzzled by what he had seen, asked his father what it was about.

'Dad, who were those men?'

'They were Welshmen, from the north of the county.'

'But aren't we all Welsh?'

'Yes, but we are different from them.'

That puzzled Hugh even more. 'What were they singing?' he asked.

'It's called "Land Of My Fathers" and it's supposed to be the Welsh national anthem.'

'Why did the police stop them?'

'They were taken away for causing what's called a breach of the peace. I don't think anything was done to them. They were let off with a caution.'

Hugh was still puzzled, more so if anything. 'But what's wrong if it's the Welsh national anthem?'

Joseph was getting a little impatient.

'It's not the proper national anthem; he said. 'That's "God Save The Queen" and it was an insult to the Queen to sing it.'

Hugh was still puzzled. He had felt a boyish surge of pride and patriotic feeling, generated by the music of the band and the great crowd of people singing 'God Save The Queen', in perfect harmony, as only a great Welsh crowd could. But he had found the other song not only more tuneful but more moving, even though he did not understand the words. And why was he different from those who had sung it? So he turned to his schoolmate Robert Snape. He had struck up a friendship with Robert, who always seemed to know more than most of them.

'Why are we different from people in the north of the county?' he asked.

'Dunno,' was the answer, 'but I'll try to find out.'

It was several weeks before Robert had the answer. 'It's because hundreds of years ago, the Normans invaded here' he said. 'There's a line they call the Landsker, which runs across the county. That was as far as they got. It's all Welsh north of that.'

'What do you mean by a line? Is it drawn on the ground?'

'No, silly, it was a line of fort – fortifi – fortifications.' Even Robert had problems with long words of whose meaning he was not entirely aware.

Hugh was impressed by his friend's superior knowledge, but it all seemed a bit stupid to him. They all lived in Wales; surely that made them all Welsh?

By now, he had two younger sisters, the last of the family. They were called Alice and Myfanwy. Giving a Welsh name to their last-born, like giving the name Hugh to their ninth, was an innovation for Leah and Joseph. They had been inspired by the song of that name as well as by the beauty of the name itself. Neither of them understood the Welsh words of the song, but Joseph had read a translation in the local newspaper. It was a bit disappointing that the English words did not fit the lovely melody, but they loved the line that read 'may the blushing red rose of health dance a hundred years upon your cheeks'. They did not know, but, subconsciously, they were reflecting a growing sense of Welsh awareness, which was as potent in their little England beyond Wales as in the rest of the country.

As in all large families, the older ones tended to be closer to each other than to the younger ones, and vice versa. But Hugh felt a particular affinity with this older brother Joseph, the fourth-born, who was nine years his senior. Joe, named after their father, was the sportsman of the family. He had introduced Hugh to kicking a football around at an early age, as well as playing with a rugby ball, and he had given him an insight into the rules of both games. He had also tried to teach Hugh to swim, but not very successfully.

Joe had become a strong, self-taught swimmer while still at school. Hugh, Joe and a group of friends, including Robert Snape, used to bathe in the estuary of the Pembroke River, at a spot not far from where they lived. The sessions were brought to an abrupt end, though, by the police, when a scandalised lady who happened to be walking on the river bank complained about naked little boys bathing in the river. Her attitude was very different from that of the young girls who, unknown to the boys, were in the habit of gathering, giggling, behind nearby bushes to watch them.

Always fascinated by water, Joe, when he left school, became a deck hand on a small steamer that traded between Pembroke and other places within the extensive Milford Haven natural harbour. He then conceived an ambition to swim from Pembroke Dock to the town of Milford Haven, a distance of some five miles. And, in the summer after Hugh's ninth birthday, he did it, properly attired, of course, and followed by several rowing boats, in one of which Hugh and his father were passengers.

There was quite a lot of excitement, including a report in the local paper. Hugh basked proudly in glory reflected from his big brother.

'I gather, Hughes,' Mr Kendle said, 'that your brother, who used to attend this school, has achieved quite a sporting success.'

'Yes sir.' By now becoming sophisticated in schoolboy conduct, he experienced a strong temptation to say 'sah' in mimicry of Mr Kendle's carefully cultivated accent but, fortunately for him, resisted it.

'I could wish that he had devoted as much effort to his lessons when he was at school.'

The year was drawing to its close. A war had broken out in South Africa against some people called Boers and it seemed that it was not going too well. Everyone felt, though, that the Boers could never defeat the might of the British Empire, once it got properly mobilised.

Mr Kendle told his pupils that they were on the threshold, not just of a new year but a new century. Once the war in South Africa was over and the Boer republics, which had foolishly declared war on the British Empire, had been defeated and incorporated into the empire, the children would live into a century of unparalleled progress.

Chapter 3

For Colonel Mulholland, at Bellwood House, the new year seemed to pile tragedy on tragedy. In the autumn of the old year, his wife had died. Their marriage had been one of convenience for dynastic reasons but, although loveless, it had been by no means unhappy. An heiress, she had added to the already large Mulholland fortune and they had settled into a happy companionship. He was wont to reflect that, after all, most marriages were of convenience one way or another, and most of those entered into for love had, in his experience proved unhappy or downright disastrous. His only regret was that there had only been one child from his marriage.

He missed his wife sadly and the New Year's Day ball which they had always given for the tenantry and neighbouring gentry, normally one of the glittering occasions of the local social calendar had been overlaid with an inevitable air of gloom. She had always been the driving force behind it, and it was the more poignant because the ball had been intended to be even grander than usual because it marked the turn of the century as well as the year. He had fiercely resisted suggestions to cancel it. Dammit! Traditions had to be observed, whatever the circumstances.

Then, within weeks, he had received an official telegram to inform him that his son, Captain Richard Mulholland, had been killed in action in South Africa, at the Battle of Spion Kop. The local press was fulsome, referring to the hero's death of the son of a distinguished local family with a long history of military service.

Views in military, as well as in family, circles were more ambivalent. It had long become apparent that Richard was unlikely to reach any great heights. He had achieved the rank of captain solely because of his background, and he had been stuck at that rank for sufficiently long to indicate that he was unlikely to make the jump from junior to senior officer. He had not married and had acquired a reputation as a womaniser.

With the loss of his only child, the colonel, getting on in years, had no direct heir. His nearest relative was his sister, who had no sons but two married daughters. Whatever happened, his estate would pass out of the Mulholland name. He suddenly felt sad, lonely and old.

His father and his grandfather before him had both been in the army. Before that, his ancestors had built up a great fortune in the West Indies, from which he still derived a large income, added to by his late wife's inheritance. All knowledge of the fact that both fortunes had been built up on proceeds from the slave trade had long since been banished from the collective family mind. The problem of to whom he was going to pass on the inheritance worried him.

Within the passage of only a few weeks, the problem suddenly became more acute. He had been settling down for an after-lunch nap when his butler came to announce that 'a gentleman and three persons' were at the front door, asking to see him. The butler handed him a visitor's card, on which was the name of Mr Henry Black, from an address in Tenby.

The butler, an old family retainer, was agitated. Among the 'three persons', he had instantly recognised Bert and Molly, the former footman and maid who had been dismissed many years earlier. He did not know the elderly gentleman they were accompanying and whose card he had brought to the colonel, but the sight of the youth who was the third of the 'three persons' had shocked him, for the youth looked beyond any doubt to be a Mulholland.

Colonel Mulholland did not know any Henry Black and had no idea who these people could be.

'Did they say what they wanted?' he asked.

The butler seemed embarrassed. 'Er – no sir,' he said.

'I suppose you had better show them in then, so that we can find out.'

The group entered the room, led by the elderly gentleman, Mr Black. The youngest member of the group stayed well back. Even so, the colonel felt a sudden numbness as soon as he saw him. No wonder the butler had seemed unusually ill at ease.

'I am sorry, Colonel, to call on you without notice,' Mr Black said, 'but I would wish to introduce my butler and housekeeper, Mr and Mrs Flowers.' He motioned to the youth to step forward. 'And this, he said, 'is Mrs Flowers' son. May I introduce Master Albert Mulholland Flowers.'

The colonel found himself confronted with a youth who looked exactly like his own son at that age. He realised, with something akin to horror, that he could be looking at his illegitimate grandson. The butler thought he was going to have a heart attack.

Ever loyal, the butler spoke first. 'Will there be anything else, sir?'

'No, you can leave us.'

'Shall I bring tea, sir?'

'No!'

The colonel recovered himself. 'You had better sit down,' he said to the visitors. 'And what is your business?'

Shaken though he was and surmising only too well why they were there, he resolved at once to stonewall. He was not an old soldier for nothing.

Mrs Flowers spoke. 'You will no doubt remember,' she said, 'that seventeen years ago, you dismissed my husband and myself because I was pregnant with Master Richard's child. This is him, your grandson. We were all most sorry to hear of Richard's sad death, but we thought it necessary to come here to claim Albert's inheritance.'

'His what?'

'His inheritance. He is your grandson.'

The colonel was at a loss. He could only bluster. 'Are you seriously asking me to believe that your bastard is my grandson?'

'Yes. You've only got to look at him to see that he is.'

Mr Black intervened. 'There really is no doubt about it, Colonel,' he said. 'I know the full story of Bert and Molly's dismissal from your service and your refusal to recognise that your late son could be Albert's father. But I put it to you in all seriousness, especially now that I have met you and can see for myself. You only have to look at him to see the family resemblance.'

'And is this boy's father registered on his birth certificate as my son?'

Molly stepped in quickly. 'No,' she said. 'My Bert agreed to give him the protection of his name. We were married before he was born. But we have given him the middle name of Mulholland in honour of his real father.'

Honour! thought the colonel bitterly. Then he said with heavy sarcasm, 'I seem to recall that, at the time, there was some doubt about the boy's parentage, even in your own mind.'

'Oh yes,' said Mrs Flowers, showing all the pert verve of the young Molly she had once been. 'It's true that I was in both Bert's and the young master's bed at the time. But just look at him again. We saw it from the day he was born. You can see the resemblance, not just to Richard, but to you too. Besides,' she added, with the air of someone indisputably saying the last word, 'Bert has never been able to give me any children.'

Mr Black stepped in again, 'Mrs Flowers' conduct at the time may have been regrettable –'

'Regrettable!' roared the colonel. 'Damned immoral. That's why I sacked them both.'

'Nevertheless,' said Mr Black, 'you only have to look at the boy to see his parentage.'

'Are you seriously suggesting, sir, that I should accept this – this – this boy as my grandson? I suppose he's some illiterate little brat from some board school.' The colonel was floundering and he knew it.

'No,' said Mr Black. 'As a matter of fact, I paid for his education. He has been taught at Llandovery College. No doubt, you recognise that as one of the leading Welsh public schools. He's as fluent in Welsh as in English, with a fair knowledge of French too.'

'Welsh! – and bloody French,' exploded the colonel. 'Is that supposed to be good?'

The hitherto silent Mr Flowers now spoke for the first time. He spoke in the cultured tones of a well-trained butler, but without deference and with sarcasm dripping from every syllable.

'I think sir,' he said 'that those are accomplishments to which perhaps you yourself might not wish to lay claim.'

'Don't you dare speak to me like that. You remember your place.' It was the only thing he could think of to say.

The uncannily Mulholland–looking youth now spoke for the first time. 'I'm sorry we've upset you, sir.'

'You shut up!'

There was a pause. The colonel knew that he was losing the game and it was dawning on him that, horrific though the thought was, this really was his grandson. 'And what,' he asked, directing himself to the youth's mother, 'do you mean when you talk about claiming his inheritance?'

'Well, we know that following Dickie's sad death –'

'Don't you dare refer to my son in that familiar manner.'

'Well, I'm sorry, but I did know him rather well.' She giggled. 'We know that you have no immediate heir. We only want you to do the right thing.'

'You are not, I assume, seriously suggesting that I should make him my heir and leave my estate and property to him.'

'We are only asking that he receives something in recognition of his parentage.'

The colonel was suddenly very weary and anxious only to terminate these awful proceedings. 'I shall have to think about your allegations,' he said. Then fiercely, 'But understand, I am not accepting any of your claims and I am making absolutely no commitments.'

'I think,' said Mr Black, realising that the time had come for a judicious intervention, 'that we can leave things at that for the time being. With your permission, sir, we will leave now. I hope we may hear further from you. You have my card.'

'You certainly had better leave.' He rang the bell which stood on the small table beside his chair. The butler appeared with an alacrity that suggested he might have been hovering close enough to the door to be within earshot.

'These people are leaving. Show them out.'

After they had left, he sat down, bruised and angry. His world was shattered, his wife dead, his son killed, no immediate heir to his estate. And now the reappearance of that little slut with the boy who was unmistakably the product of his son's seduction of her all those years ago. The more he thought about it, the more depressed he became.

He dined alone that evening, immaculately dressed for dinner, as always.

'I suppose, Talltree,' he said to the butler, 'that that boy's appearance did not escape your notice.'

'No sir.'

'I imagine that the entire staff are already in a state of some curiosity.'

'To a certain extent sir. May I say that all the staff are sorry that you clearly have a lot on your mind following Mr Richard's sad passing.'

What he really meant was that the entire staff were agog with excitement and speculation. Some of them, like himself, remembered the sacking of Bert and Molly, as well as the great row that had taken place between the colonel and his son.

'My own son lied to me,' the colonel said. His voice was desolate. 'He denied absolutely having had anything to do with that girl.' He became bitter and scathing in a way the butler had never heard before. 'The word of an officer and a gentleman!'

The butler remained silent. Many years of service had made him deferential to the point of obsequiousness, but now he felt something akin to pity for the man he had deferred to for so long.

Colonel Mulholland spoke again. 'And on the basis of lies told by my son, we dismissed that girl and the footman.'

Talltree tried to comfort him. 'She was – er – not entirely innocent so far as Flowers was concerned,' he said.

'That is true, but it doesn't alter the fact that my son fathered her child and lied to me about it. I seem to recall, too, that there was a delivery man who also lost his job for talking about it.'

'Yes Colonel, I believe his name was Hughes.' It was Talltree's turn to feel twinges of guilt, aware that he had played his own part in getting Joseph Hughes sacked, by complaining to his employer that he was spreading malicious gossip about the young master.

For a week, the colonel pondered. Then he wrote to Mr Black, inviting the young man, whom he referred to as Mrs Flowers' son, to come and visit him, unaccompanied. The youth duly appeared, and the gossip in the kitchen was frantic.

'How old are you exactly? the colonel asked.

'I'm sixteen.'

'Still at school, I gather, Llandovery College.'

'Yes sir.'

'Any idea about what you mean to do after school?'

'Mr Black, who has been so kind to me, has talked about my going on to university, possibly Oxford or Cambridge.'

'And after that?'

'I haven't really thought about it, but Mr Black – although he is retired he still has wide business interests and, as he has no son of his own, he has spoken about my taking those over eventually.'

'Damn lucky, aren't you. When were you first told,' picking his words very carefully, 'that it was possible that you might, just possibly, be my grandson?'

'It was when we read of your son's death in the papers.'

'And how long had Mr Black known about this?'

'He had known for many years. When you sacked my mother and my – er – that is to say – and her husband, they were unable to get jobs in service until after I was born. My – er – Mr Flowers worked as a labourer while they looked for other work. Then Mr Black retired and went to live in Tenby and advertised for a married couple as servants. They applied and he took them on. They told him the truth from the start. I think he took pity on us. Mr Black is a real gentleman.' He emphasised the word real a little more than was perhaps either necessary or tactful.

The emphasis did not escape the colonel, but he decided to let it pass. 'How old is Mr Black?' he asked.

'I think he is in his seventies.'

'And no family?'

'That's right. He is a widower with no children.'

'You do realise, my boy, that there is a great stigma attached to being the child of unmarried parents?'

'I do, sir.'

'And that if I were to recognise you as my grandson, all the world would know that you are illegitimate?'

'I do, sir. But it is not my fault that my parents were not married.'

This was said with some spirit, and it was becoming clear to the colonel that he was talking to an intelligent and articulate young man. Damn sight brighter than his father, he thought bitterly. I fathered a cad, and the cad, with a servant, fathered a child worth twice his father.

He felt that it was time to end the interview. 'Thank you for coming,' he said, in a tone more conciliatory than he would have dreamed possible before the meeting. 'The pony and trap that met you at the station will take you back there to catch the train.'

After the youth had left, he set to thinking again. There was no alternative that he could see to accepting that this was his grandson and he would have to do something for him. If only he weren't illegitimate, there could be no doubt that he would be his natural heir. As it was, with Richard dead, his will was invalid. Most of his estate would have gone to him, with a bequest to his sister and various other, smaller bequests. Now, if he did not make a new will, his sister would be able to claim everything. He did not like the thought of that at all.

Anger welled up in him as he thought bitterly of his dead son. If only he had told the truth. Instead of sacking the girl and the footman without, as he now realised, justification, he could have provided for the child. It was easy to be wise after the event but, he mused, he could even have forced his son into marrying the girl. It would have been a terrible scandal and she would probably never have fitted into their world, but at least he would have had a legitimate grandson, probably several grandchildren – and a good, solid stock to provide for the future of the family.

His thoughts turned again to the youth. What an extraordinarily lucky little bastard, he mused, choosing the word very deliberately. The boy was already in line to inherit from that fellow Black, and now, possibly in line to be his heir too. But if he did make him his heir, there would be ructions from his sister, as well as from several cousins. It was all so complicated and painful.

He would have to give it all a lot more thought, a process to which he was not accustomed.

For the young Hugh Hughes, the new year brought no such potential for good fortune as it did for the young Mulholland Flowers. For the Hughes family as a whole, though, it was a happy year, for it saw no less than three family weddings, those of Hugh's eldest brother, Matthew, and his two eldest sisters, Mary and Elizabeth, known in the family as May and Lizzie.

Matthew was fourteen years Hugh's senior. He had left school even before Hugh was born and, like most boys in the rural areas, he had been put to work on a farm. It was a degrading process. On a date publicised in advance, the school leavers, aged twelve, together with older unemployed men and boys, gathered at a prescribed place in the main street at Pembroke, and local farmers who were looking for workers came to take their pick.

In accordance with custom, Matthew would work for a trial period of six months. He would live at the farm, board and lodging provided. At the end of the trial period, the farmer would decide whether or not to give him a permanent job and how much to pay him for the six months. It might be that he would decide to pay him nothing and even dismiss him then and there. There was no redress.

Fortunately, Matthew had been lucky. He was picked by a farmer who owned a small farm, which only he and his wife worked. They were finding that they needed help. They had no children but they had an adopted daughter who was already helping on the farm. She was a year older than Matthew.

It soon became apparent that Matthew was a born farmer. He took to the work with interest and enthusiasm and, as he and the adopted daughter grew through adolescence to adulthood, they, too, took to each other with growing interest and enthusiasm. They were married in the spring of 1900 and, shortly afterwards, the farmer and his wife, who warmly approved of the match, made Matthew the heir to the farm. There would be no great fortune – indeed, only a hard-won living – but by then Matthew was already looking at the possibilities of acquiring or renting adjoining land and so extending the farm.

Hugh's eldest sister, May, the second-born of the family, had not taken up any employment on leaving school, staying at home to help her mother with the ever-growing brood of younger sisters and brothers. She had met and in due course become engaged to John Burrows, a young workmate of her father's on the railway.

Joseph approved of the young man but when John announced that he was going to leave the railway and move to the valleys, to work in the mines, he was filled with misgivings. Clear in his memory, and instantly recalled, was the agonising death, after a terrible accident in the pit, of Matthew Davies, his wife's brother and the best friend of his youth.

John sought to ease his worries by explaining that the pit he was going to, not far from Swansea, was a different proposition from the pit at Begelly, where Matt had worked. To start with, the seams were much wider and there was not the water in the workings. More important, there was now an Act of Parliament which controlled working conditions and compelled regular inspection of the pits. Above all, the miners had a trade union to protect their interests and to see that the Act of Parliament was properly observed.

Joseph was not entirely convinced and remained uneasy, but he liked John and did not object to the marriage, which took place in the summer, a couple of months after Matthew's.

The third wedding, in the autumn, was between Lizzie, Joseph and Leah's third-born, who was Hugh's senior by nearly eleven years. Lizzie's husband, Raymond Jones, was a worker in the naval dockyard at Pembroke Dock, a time-served craftsman who was considered a 'good catch', so much so that they could afford to rent a small house of their own to start their married life, rather than living with in-laws, as did most of their contemporaries.

For Joseph, with three family weddings, it was an expensive year, modest though the ceremonies were, but he was happy that his three eldest children were all getting settled into their own lives. For all his and Leah's love for their children and pride in their large family, they both felt relieved that there could now be no more children and that, with all of them growing up, the future looked easier. They were happy, too, at the prospect of becoming grandparents in the not too distant future.

By 1901, only Hugh and his younger sisters, Alice and Myfanwy, were still living with their parents and still at school. One cold, January day, at the end of morning lessons, Mr Kendle assembled the entire school. He was wearing a black tie and, normally so strict and unbending, he seemed strangely emotional. Most of them already knew what was in the morning newspapers.

'I have to tell you,' he said in his very best quasi-English accent, 'that Queen Victoria has passed away peacefully and surrounded by her loving family. The passing of the Queen marks the end of the longest and greatest reign in the history of our country. It goes without question that we, like the entire nation, share in the grief of the royal family.'

He paused, then added, loudly and theatrically, 'The Queen is dead. God save the King.' He lifted both arms to indicate that he expected a response.

'God save the King,' the children chorused. They knew their place.

In the playground, Hugh's friend Robert Snape expressed more down-to-earth views.

'I don't see what difference it's going to make to any of us because a very old lady who was Queen has died and there's now an old man who is King.'

That was more in tune with the feelings of those he was speaking to than Mr Kendle's oratory. With the short average life expectancy of those times, many of the children had experience of deaths in their large, extended families and, hardened, they took it as a matter of course. The death of a remote old lady whom they knew only through being drilled in deference, meant little to them.

'My mam,' Robert went on, referring to his mother, as they always did, in the Welsh way, 'is still going to have to skivvy all day and me and my sisters are still going to have to go on working in the fields out of school and all through the summer holidays so that we can make enough to live.'

Robert was by then generally recognised as the brightest boy in the school and the view he expressed was typical of the sort of things he said regularly to his friends. Such views might have brought punishment if heard by his teachers and they would not have qualified as examples of what Hugh's Sunday school teacher meant, when he told his charges about words of wisdom coming out of the mouths of babes and sucklings.

Hugh knew that many of the things Robert said were supposed to be wrong. The trouble was that he almost always found himself in agreement.

That evening, he said to his father, 'Dad, it's not going to make any difference to us that the Queen is dead and that there's now a King who is an old man.'

'You mustn't say wicked things like that,' his mother said.

'But it's not wicked.'

'Don't argue with your mother,' his father said. 'The new King is now the head of the country, like the Queen used to be, and we must all look up to him.'

Hugh's parents had never known a time without Queen Victoria. They had lived through decade after decade of deference. It simply did not occur to them that royalty should be anything other than the object of deference and reverence.

Joseph was now in the prime of life. Leah could still see him as the good-looking boy who had come to court her so many years ago, notwithstanding that he was becoming portly and his hair was greying and thinning. In the fashion of the times, he had grown a handsome moustache, which suited him. His job was still a humble one, but they were respected by all their neighbours and friends, not least because they had successfully brought up a large family and had never lost a child. A dignified photograph of the two of them had an honoured place on the mantelpiece of their living room. They had both learned a great deal in what Joseph was wont to call 'the university of life'.

He was starting to wonder about the future for Hugh, who would be twelve the next year and so at the end of his schooldays.

Hugh would leave school at the Easter break 1902. He was no great scholar but he was fully literate, able to write grammatically in the clear, legible, if standardised hand he had been taught. He enjoyed reading and was reasonably numerate. His knowledge of geography and history could only be described as vague, due entirely to the inadequacy of how he had been taught. He was a lively, healthy boy with the thick, dark hair he had inherited from his father.

So far as starting work, his father was wondering what to do about it. There weren't many prospects and the only option he could see was that the boy should be put to work on a farm. But Joseph hated the idea of his youngest son going, as had his eldest, to what he called 'the cattle market', to be paraded and bought at the whim of any farmer, as if he were no more than another animal or piece of equipment for the farm.

In the event, he decided to visit the farm where he had himself worked all those years ago, to see if there might be any prospects there. He had acquired a bicycle and, one afternoon shortly before the boy's birthday, having finished an early shift at the station, he cycled to the farm. Farmer Haskins was now dead and the farm was run by his daughter and son-in-law, Maggie and Bill Kramer. They recognised him at once and he was welcomed with tea and cakes.

After mutual enquiries about health and reminiscences of earlier days, Joseph came to the point.

'My youngest boy, Hugh, is about to leave school. I'm wondering if there is any chance of you taking him on.'

Bill Kramer thought a moment, exchanging glances with his wife. 'Times are difficult,' he said slowly, 'but we might be able to manage it. We run the farm with our boy Jim. He's seventeen now. Our daughter, Ellen – you will remember her as a little girl – she's married and living in Haverfordwest.'

'The other side of the water,' Joseph said.

Those who lived on the opposite side of Milford Haven Harbour, which ran deep into the county, were always referred to by south Pembrokeshire people as being on the other side of the water.

'Her husband is a baker and keeps a shop there,' Bill Kramer said.

'Any children?'

'Not as yet, but we're hopeful.'

'You think you could take my boy on?'

'Ye-es. He will have to come and live in. I'll pay him pocket money every week and we'll review things at the end of the usual six months.'

Joseph realised that it was no great deal and it worried him as to how Hugh would get on, leaving home at such an early age. But then, he had confidence in the boy and the situation was no different from that faced by plenty of others his age, including his own older brothers in their time.

'I'm grateful,' he said. 'If it suits you, I'll bring him here straight after Easter.'

'That'll be fine.' They shook hands and Joseph went home.

He still had nagging thoughts. Had he really done the right thing? Would Hugh take to farming? What worried him especially was the thought of the boy being so suddenly separated from the family and the home. He decided to speak to him.

'Well my boy, you'll be leaving school soon.'

'Yes Father.' Hugh sensed that this was going to be serious, hence his using 'Father' rather than the usual 'Dad'.

'Have you thought about what you might be doing?'

The anticipated answer duly came.

'No.'

'I've been out to Round Pond Farm, to see Mr Kramer. That's where I started work. He's prepared to give you a job for a trial period of six months. You ought to take it. There's not much work about.'

'Yes father.'

Joseph continued rather more doubtfully. 'He wants you to go and live on the farm. What do you think about that?'

'I suppose it will be all right.' Hugh was not, in reality, at all sure, but he had been brought up to obey his father absolutely, and if his father said he had to do it, then he would have to. He had not, as he had said, given any thought to what he was going to do when he left school and he knew only too well that there was very little choice for boys from his background.

'I'll buy you a bike,' his father said, 'and you'll be able to come home on your days off.'

'Yes Father.'

That ended the conversation. Hugh told his friend Robert about it the next day.

'At least you've got a job,' Robert said. 'I don't know what I'm going to do.'

Robert did not know it, and would have been surprised if he had, but the question of his future was exercising Mr Kendle's mind. The teacher was only too aware that Robert, although often troublesome, was too good to be wasted on a menial job. There was, in Mr Kendle's view, every possibility that he would end up as a member of what he thought of as the criminal classes. He had no father to guide him and, even if he had been available, his father could only be a malign influence. He called Robert to see him after school.

'Snape,' he said, 'you'll be leaving school soon. Have you given any thought to your future?'

'No sir.'

Schoolboy rebellion welled up inside Robert. He thought it was a stupid question. What was the point? He would have to take any job that came along; the only imperative was that he should earn something, even though he knew it was only likely to be a pittance, because he had to help his mother and his two younger sisters, both of whom were pupils in the school.

'They are taking on labour at the naval dockyard in Pembroke Dock. Have you thought about going there? In two years' time, you could get an apprenticeship and that would set you up to be a skilled craftsman.'

'But I would have to leave home – and I must help my mam and sisters.'

Mr Kendle felt strangely moved by the response. There really was more good in the boy than he had thought, too much to be allowed to be thrown away.

'You would be able to help them,' he said. 'You would have to start as a labourer, but you would earn more than on a farm. Why not think about it?'

'Yes sir. Thank you sir.'

Robert was astounded. Apart from his mother and Hugh's mother and father, it was the first time any adult had ever spoken to him in a kindly way. That old bugger Kendle, of all people, he thought.

Hugh was waiting for him. 'What did he want?' he asked, half expecting, by no means without reason, that his friend was in some sort of trouble. Robert told him what had happened.

'Will you try and get in at the dock?' Hugh asked. Then, with a sudden burst of inspiration, 'My brother-in-law, Ray, works there. He might be able to put in a word for you.' He took a delight in referring, in a grown-up manner, to his newly acquired in-laws.

'I'll have to think about it.'

Robert was a not infrequent visitor to the Hughes household, where his family circumstances were well known. He had gone away with more than one cake baked by Leah and with more than one bag of vegetables from the garden.

That same day, Hugh spoke to his father about his conversation and, when his sister and brother-in-law came to tea the following Sunday, in a by then established family ritual, the matter was raised again.

'I could put in a word for him,' Ray said. 'It's true, they are taking on labour at the yard.'

'He's a bit younger than me,' Hugh piped up. 'He won't be leaving school until the summer break in July.'

'That's no problem,' Ray said. 'I reckon too that we might be able to take him in as a lodger. We've got room and we'd only charge him very little.'

Hugh carried the news to Robert, who, after much thought and discussion with his mother, applied in due course for work and was taken on at the yard. He then went to lodge with Ray and Lizzie. By then, Hugh had been several months at Round Pond Farm.

Chapter 4

Shortly before Hugh left school, his father took him into Pembroke and bought the promised bicycle, boy size to suit his stature. Hugh had mastered the art of riding it by the time they got home. It was the most expensive present he had ever been given and he took instant and intense pride in keeping it perfectly cleaned and oiled. He would have liked to show it off by riding to school, but there was no provision there to store it.

His father also bought him a new pair of wellington boots, which would be essential for working in the mud at the farm. But, as the time approached for him to start, he became increasingly uneasy at the prospect. His parents had the same feelings, his mother especially, although they carefully concealed them from Hugh.

'I am worried, Joe,' Leah said. 'He's very young to be leaving home.'

'He's no younger,' Joseph replied, 'than any other boy leaving school. Besides, look at Matthew. He started in the same way and it worked out fine.'

'But that was a long time ago and Matthew was lucky. Hugh is different from Matthew and it doesn't mean that things will work out the same for him.'

'I can't see why they shouldn't. Matthew had to take his chance in the hiring at the cattle market. With Hugh, I've got the job for him and at the farm where I started work myself.'

More than he recognised, he had been influenced by nostalgia for times in his youth. He did not appreciate that those times had not been so happy as they appeared in complacent retrospect.

'Remember how kind Mr Haskins was to us,' he said.

'But Mr Haskins is dead and there's no saying that the Kramers are likely to be the same sort of people.'

'What else is there for him to do? You know as well as I do that times are hard.'

'I don't remember any times when things were not hard,' Leah said. 'But you could have tried the railway. I'm sure they would have listened if you had spoken for him. If he got a job there, he wouldn't have to leave home.'

It was rare for her to argue with her husband and it was the mark of her concern that she did.

Joseph was starting to get irritated. The truth was that his own doubts had grown over what he had done without considering other possibilities. He knew there was reason in Leah's concern, but he could not bring himself to acknowledge it.

'The railway!' he said. 'There's nothing there and no future. All the years I've worked for them and what do they think of me?'

'Well, there must be something nearer home, so that he wouldn't have to go away to live.'

'Like what?'

'Isn't there anything in Pembroke, like a shop or something?'

'No!' He said it with some heat. 'Have you forgotten how I was treated? And that bloody shopkeeper who sacked me is now lording it as a bloody Tory on the Council.'

She had provoked memories of a different sort, which still rankled after so many years. All sorts of mixed emotions were welling up inside him. It was very rare for him to swear in the house and he regretted it immediately. He was losing his temper and it was time to control himself. But he had a stubborn streak. He felt that his authority as head of the house was being challenged. He had made a decision and would not back down. Besides, he had entered into a bargain.

'I've made an agreement with Mr Kramer,' he said, 'and I can't go back on it.'

He was a fundamentally honest man. For him, it was inconceivable that, having given his word, he should not keep it.

'I'm sure it will work out,' he said in a more conciliatory tone. 'After all, we had a struggle against some pretty bad things ourselves.'

That might not have been entirely relevant but it struck a mutual chord and they both knew it ended the argument. It was certainly true. With very little except their own common sense and with no alternative except to learn as they went along, they had survived and provided for their large family in a society where everything was designed to crush them. Joseph still believed in 'the university of life' because, in practice, it was the only place of learning that had been available to him.

But he knew that things were no longer as simple as they had seemed when he was younger. Now, he knew that things were happening that shaped all their lives and which were beyond any influence he could exert.

To come to terms with that, he had taken on a certain measure of fatalism, rooted in what he had been taught as a small boy. He had come to think that, whatever happened, it must be ultimately for the best. It was not his fault that he had never heard of Voltaire, or of his naive hero Candide and Candide's mentor, the absurd Dr Pangloss, with his doctrine that everything was for the best in the best of all possible worlds.

Hugh duly finished school at Easter, sent on his way with his fellow leavers with valedictory platitudes from Mr Kendle.

They were setting out on their greatest venture. The school had done everything it could for them. They must do nothing to disgrace the school. They were the generation who would be carrying on the great traditions of their country. Every one of them had a duty to King and country to do their best.

'Bullshit!' was Robert Snape's comment. 'Do your best for King and country! What about doing something for yourselves? King and country won't.'

Robert would never have admitted it but, for all his toughness, he was saddened at parting with his best friend.

'We shall still be able to see each other,' Hugh said. 'I shall be coming home on Sundays and I'll get my mam and dad to invite you. Besides,' he added slyly, 'Myfanwy will be there.'

It had not escaped his notice that Robert could not keep his eyes off his youngest sister, three years their junior. A little maliciously, he was pleased to see that Robert blushed. At last he had found a chink in his friend's armour-plated personality.

Robert was already adept at changing the subject when it became embarrassing.

'And why,' he asked, in a near perfect mimicry of the head teacher, 'does Kendle speak in such a silly way, to try to hide the fact that he is Welsh?'

'I think he does it as much as anything to impress the other teachers,' Hugh said.

There was more truth in his remark than he realised. The

assistant teachers were as much in awe of Mr Kendle as were most of the pupils. Mr Kendle knew that and considered it as much a part of his duty to keep his handful of assistants under control as it was to control the children.

On the appointed day, Hugh cycled to the farm, accompanied by his father. His few small effects were packed in a cheap attaché case, strapped on the back of his bicycle. Also included were a pen, ink and a supply of writing paper, envelopes and stamps. He was under strict instructions to write every week.

He had to wear the new wellingtons, because there was no other way to carry them, which did not make for comfortable cycling. The nearer they got to the farm, the more apprehensive he felt.

'I'll pay him two shillings a week,' Mr Kramer said, 'and, of course, we'll provide his board and lodging.' He said it with the air of a benefactor conferring massive largesse.

'And you'll consider his position after six months, in the usual way?' Joseph asked.

'Yes. But that's a long way off and we'll think about it nearer the time. I'll attend to it on the Michaelmas quarter day at the end of September.'

Joseph addressed himself to his son. 'You be a good boy and do as Mr Kramer tells you. We'll see you on Sunday.'

'I'm not sure that will be possible,' Mr Kramer said. 'We're very busy here and I can't guarantee that he can have every Sunday off.'

Joseph was a little taken aback. 'But I thought the Good Lord himself decreed that Sunday was to be a day of rest.' It slipped out involuntarily. He could have bitten his tongue as soon as he said it. It was the nearest he had ever come to sarcasm.

'The Good Lord,' Mr Kramer replied crushingly, 'did not have to work this farm.'

Mrs Kramer had been standing by. 'You can bring your bike through and leave it in the dairy,' she said, echoing the tone of her husband, as if conferring a great favour. 'I'll take you up to your room.'

'I'll say goodbye for now, son,' said Joseph.

'Goodbye Father.'

His father mounted his bicycle and rode away. There was no parting handshake; handshakes between parents and offspring were not part of their culture. Nor was there any parental hug. They both felt that such a display should not be made, especially in front of this cold couple.

The farmhouse was fairly substantial, stone-built with a slate roof. The ceiling of the living room was hung with cured sides of bacon. Hugh quickly found that, apart from an occasional rabbit and an even more occasional chicken, the bacon was the only meat they ever ate. There was a parlour, which was quite grandly furnished but hardly ever used, where the furnishings included a piano which nobody ever played. Due to the smallness of the windows, all the rooms were gloomy. At the back was a large kitchen, where they ate. The kitchen led into another large room which was called the dairy, where the stone walls were not plastered and where butter was made and much other work was done.

There were three bedrooms. One of them, much the smallest, was allocated to Hugh. The only furnishings were a single bed with a chamber pot under it, and a small chest of drawers on which stood a china washbowl, jug, towel and soap dish, together with a candlestick, candle and box of matches. Toilet facilities were the outside privy, but that was normal in Hugh's experience. Water was drawn from a pump situated in the dairy.

'Put your ordinary shoes on and bring your wellingtons downstairs,' Mrs Kramer said without further explanation.

Dejectedly, he unpacked his few things and changed his footwear. Then he went downstairs, shy, bewildered and very unsure of himself. Mrs Kramer was in the kitchen, her husband had disappeared.

'Come out here,' she said 'There's some bread and jam and a cup of tea on the table. Put your boots by the door of the dairy. You'll need them when you go out. Mr Kramer will be back soon with Jim – that's our son. Before it gets dark, Jim will show you round the farm.'

Jim Kramer turned out to be a gangling youth, taller than his father, even more scruffy in his working clothes, with his father's ruddy complexion and his mother's brown hair. On being introduced, he looked down at Hugh without speaking.

'Hello,' Hugh said and good-naturedly held out his hand, which Jim ignored.

'Take him out and show him round,' Mr Kramer said. 'Put your boots on, boy. You'll need them outdoors.'

He was shown the farmyard with the barn, pigsty, chicken run and cowshed, all with their inhabitants settled for the night. Then he was taken through the fields. The Round Pond, from which the farm took its name, was situated in the field where the cows were turned out and was much appreciated by them. Another field was planted with potatoes. He already knew about Pembrokeshire early potatoes, an important source of income for local farmers. Throughout, the taciturn Jim grunted rather than spoke explanations. By the time they returned to the farmhouse, it was almost dark.

Mrs Kramer had prepared a meal of cold ham and warmed-up vegetables, for which they all sat round the large kitchen table. The three Kramers exchanged conversation about farming matters that was largely incomprehensible to Hugh. He sat silent, until Mr Kramer addressed him.

'That's your brother Matthew over at Old Oak Farm,' he said. 'Lucky too, marrying the Leemings' adopted daughter. Got the makings of a good farmer, though.'

It was the introduction to what Hugh soon discovered, that every farming family knew every other for miles around. Soon, too, he was to discover that there was a sort of camaraderie, so that when extra help was needed, as at potato picking, haymaking and harvest, everybody helped everybody else, which of course saved any of them from having to take on extra paid labour. But the camaraderie did not mean that there were not also feuds and enmities.

'Time for bed,' Mr Kramer said. 'We've got to be up early in the morning. I'll knock you up. You'll have to get up earlier here than you've been used to.'

'There's water in your room for you to wash,' Mrs Kramer said. 'From tomorrow, it'll be up to you to replace it from the pump – and to make your bed.'

'And don't take too long about getting up,' said her husband. 'We've got plenty of work to do. At least, at your age, you won't have to spend time shaving.' This was said with no hint of any twinkle in his eye.

Hugh, face to face with the reality of a new world, went to bed thoroughly depressed. He did not sleep at all. Even so, it seemed no time before Mr Kramer knocked on his door. It was still dark.

'Time to get up,' he said. 'Breakfast in fifteen minutes.'

So began a period of unremitting, back-breaking, all day toil. The only breaks each day were mid-morning, usually in the fields, and at twelve noon, when they all took their main meal. Otherwise, it was an endless round of taking the cows to their field, mucking out, bringing them back, learning to milk and generally doing any number of other jobs. It was always evening before the working day finished, and the longer the days became as the year advanced, the longer became the hours of work. If he had not been able to sleep that first night, he became so tired at the end of each day that the problem did not repeat itself. At the end of each week, Mr Kramer presented him with his due two shillings.

He did not get away on that first Sunday nor on the next. The new bicycle remained untouched in the dairy. He wrote a short letter to his parents on each of those first weeks to say that he could not come because there was too much work to do. He wrote no other comment on his situation.

A couple of days after the second Sunday, as they were finishing the midday meal, a young man rode into the farmyard on horseback, dismounted and walked into the kitchen. Hugh was delighted, it was his eldest brother, Matthew. Spontaneously, he left the table to greet him. Apart from anything else, it was the first time he had ever seen any member of his family on a horse.

'Hello young Hughie. How are you doing?'

'I'm fine.'

'Looking well. Getting some colour in your cheeks, I see.'

Matthew addressed Mr and Mrs Kramer. 'Hello Bill, Maggie. Pretty busy, I take it?'

'You know how it is,' said Mr Kramer.

'Too busy to let Hugh go to see his mam and dad on Sundays, I gather. I was down seeing them last Sunday and they were a bit concerned. I hope it will be possible for him to go there next Sunday.' It was said very pointedly.

'I'll have to see how we are fixed.' Bill Kramer spoke in a surly manner. He did not like Matthew and resented what he considered an interference in his domestic business. His son Jim scowled silently. By that time, there was already no love lost between Hugh and Jim. Maggie Kramer sat silently. She did not offer Matthew a cup of tea from the large pot on the table. But Matthew had clearly come with a purpose and was not to be put off.

'I know there's always a lot to do,' he said, 'but we usually manage to find some time off work on Sundays.'

'I dare say,' said Maggie Kramer, 'but this is a bigger farm and it takes us all our time.'

'I know that, but I still think my brother is entitled to have time to see his parents. He is, after all, only twelve. Oh, and by the way, talking about bigger farms, you know that big field next to us: I'm negotiating to buy it. It belongs to Squire Hatherly and he's prepared to sell.'

Bill Kramer scowled almost as much as his son. 'You've got the advantage,' he said. 'Your father–in-law owns the land over there at Old Oak Farm. It's a different matter here. Hatherly owns the land and we've got to find his rent every quarter day, as well as keeping ourselves.'

'Yes,' Matthew said, 'I know that. I hear that Hatherly has his own problems. If it wasn't for that rich brother-in-law of his and his sister, they'd be in trouble. Well, I'll be off. Hope to see you on Sunday, Hugh. I shall be going to see mam and dad. Good day to you, Bill – Maggie – Jim.'

He had been careful to assert the purpose of his visit in his final words, whilst also making reference to Squire Hatherly, a figure of mutual dislike.

Hugh got to see his parents that Sunday. It was a joyful occasion, with Matthew and his wife Lydia there. So was Robert Snape, who, when not chattering away with Hugh, telling him all the latest school news, was clearly no less interested in Myfanwy. She, in turn, now with nearly all of ten years behind her, clearly found his unspoken attention agreeable. Hugh cycled back to Round Pond Farm a good deal more cheerful than he had been since first going there. The new bicycle was lovingly cleaned before he went to bed.

Visits to his parents went on, although on an irregular basis, as the year moved into high summer. By then, his knowledge of country matters was growing apace and he was becoming reasonably proficient at the hard work, although far from happy with it. The Kramers did not treat him badly, but they were never friendly. They tolerated rather than welcomed his presence, while taking full advantage of the cheap labour he provided. Not least among the reasons for their attitude was disappointment in their son Jim. Although it was Jim who was the farmer's son, it soon became clear that Hugh was brighter and more adaptable. Between Hugh and Jim, there was a mutual dislike which became steadily more intense.

Occasionally, Matthew would ride over and that always increased the tension. All three Kramers disliked Matthew, mainly because he was a young man who was clearly more successful at farming than they were. Hugh came to learn, from gossip picked up from neighbouring farms, that Round Pond was not as well farmed as it had been in the days of Maggie Kramer's father, Mr Haskins. He wondered if that was part of the reason they always seemed so miserable. He also realised that his brother's visits, intended principally to ensure his own wellbeing, were a mixed blessing, because they always made the Kramers even more unfriendly.

The first week in August arrived, the bank holiday weekend. The Kramers had insisted that he work on the Sunday, as a condition of having the whole of bank holiday Monday off. He cycled to Pembroke straight after the usual early breakfast. Later in the morning, his sister Lizzie and her husband Ray arrived from Pembroke Dock. They were accompanied by his friend Robert, who had just left school and gone to lodge with them. He was due to start work the next day at the dockyard. Robert was bubbling with excitement. Hugh felt a strong pang of envy, the first time he had ever felt like that about his friend. What a contrast to the way he had felt when he started work – and still felt.

His mother and Lizzie, together with his two young sisters, were preparing the meal, while the men sat and talked. As Robert spoke excitedly about starting work, Ray intervened.

'There's plenty of work at the yard,' he said. 'There's a new government programme to build more warships because the Germans are building up a big navy.' He turned to Joseph.

'I don't suppose, Dad,' he said, 'you've thought about leaving the railway? They want riveters and you could train very quickly. The money would be much better than on the railway.'

Joseph was not unresponsive to the suggestion. He was becoming increasingly dissatisfied with his job. If a chance came to better himself, he would take it.

By then, the little Pembroke and Tenby Railway had been absorbed into the mighty Great Western. He had seen the line relaid, practically rebuilt, to bring it up to the higher standards of the new owners. The old locomotives and carriages had been replaced by the smart green locos and the brown and yellow 'chocolate and cream' carriages of the GWR. But, apart from new uniforms, he had seen no improvement in the wages and conditions of the workers and he could not see any chance of promotion.

'It's a longish journey to make every day from here to the dockyard,' he said doubtfully.

'There are houses available in Pembroke Dock,' Ray said. 'Reasonable rents and quite close to the yard.'

'It would be a big change to make. I shall have to talk it over with Leah.'

You've only got the two girls at home now,' Ray said. 'They could be transferred to school in Pembroke Dock.'

'Oh, well, we'll have to see about it.'

The conversation jolted Hugh. He could see that his father was interested. Nor did it escape his notice that Robert's eyes lit up at the mention of his two younger sisters moving to Pembroke Dock. He thought, Lucky sod, got a job he likes, going to live with friends, got a sweetheart who will also be close by. It made him sulky. He was mostly silent for the rest of the day and went back to the farm feeling miserable.

He felt a sudden outburst of boyish rage against his father. He put me on this bloody awful farm, he thought. If Robert could get a job at the naval dockyard, why couldn't I have had the same chance?

His father was troubled by not dissimilar thoughts. Hugh's suddenly going quiet had not escaped his attention. The boy didn't say much or write much in his regular letters, but he had a strong feeling that he was not happy, and he had not forgotten the Kramers' cold attitude when he took him there. Might it not have been better to have tried to get him into the dockyard instead of on a farm? Perhaps, if he himself got a job there, he might be able to get him in. Hugh's six months' trial period at the farm was already two-thirds over. He was now uneasily aware, too, from what Matthew had said, that the Kramers were not noted among their peers as particularly good farmers.

He and Leah talked at length about his changing jobs. She sensed that, to some extent, he wanted her to help make up his mind for him, which she did. He applied for a job and was taken on straight away as a riveter. Almost immediately, they moved to Pembroke Dock, to a bigger house close to the dockyard. They both felt some sadness at leaving the little house where they had lived so long and brought up their family. But, now, for the first time in his life, Joseph had only a short walk to work and he was happy that the house had a good garden, so that he could continue his much loved hobby and provide all the vegetables and flowers they needed.

Hugh's first visit to the new house was in mid-September. May, his eldest sister, and her husband John Burrows were also visiting that weekend from the valleys. They had come to see the new house and also to bring the news that May was pregnant, so that Joseph and Leah would soon have their first grandchild. This news was received with joy and, after it had been discussed, the conversation moved on, as it always did, to various other family matters before turning to the subject of Joseph's new job.

'It's very busy,' he said, 'especially with this new naval building programme.'

'There's plenty of work in the pits, too,' May's husband added.

The conversation moved on again. The subject of the newly expected baby came up repeatedly. No one thought to ask Hugh about his job, which annoyed and depressed him. As he cycled back to the farm, a whirlwind of mostly angry thoughts was going round and round in his head.

He was sad that the little house in Pembroke, the only home he had ever known, had gone out of his life for ever. He would never be able to look upon the new house in Pembroke Dock in the same way, and he did not like the journey; there were steep hills, both ways, up which he had to push his bike. And he did not want to stay on the farm. They might solve that for him by not allowing him to in any case. But there was no way he would go to his parents' new home.

His brother-in-law's remark about plenty of work in the pits flashed into his mind. He had spent very little of the 'pocket money' he had been paid. There was precious little chance to do so. He had enough to buy a train ticket to Penduffryn, where John and May lived. He would go there and get a job in the pit.

It did not enter his thoughts, but what was happening was that a combination of circumstance and emotion was forcing him to grow up at an early age and was pushing him inexorably towards the first big decision he would have to make about his own life. He decided that he would tell no one what was in his mind but, at the end of the six months he was bound for, which was now only a couple of weeks away, he would steal away from the farm. He did not care what his father, the Kramers or anybody else might feel about it. And he did not really care about whether he received the back pay due to him or not, but at least he would have a go at getting it.

A couple of weeks later, when Michaelmas Day came, he approached Mr Kramer timidly, but boyishly determined that he must stand up for his rights.

'Please sir,' he said, 'my six months are very nearly up.'
'I know that. What about it?'
'W-will you be paying me my back money?'
'Your what?'
'My back money.'
'What the hell are you talking about? What back money?'
Hugh's timidity was rapidly being replaced by rising anger.
'When my dad brought me here, you said you would pay me two bob a week pocket money and then look at it again when today came.'

'Well, I am looking at it. And I'm looking at you, you insolent little brat. How dare you question me. Get out there and get the cows out into the field.' His voice rose and his normally ruddy complexion became near purple. 'I've got enough money to pay out today as it is. Don't you know it's quarter day and Squire Hatherly's manager will be here to collect his rent? Now get out and bloody well get on with your work or I'll take a strap to you.'

By the end of that diatribe, Hugh was shaking with anger. He was so angry that he could not speak. This is as much as I'm going to take, he thought, as soon as he regained control of himself. I'm getting out first thing tomorrow.

He had calmed down somewhat by mid-morning. He was in the field which faced the farmhouse across the road and saw three people arrive on horseback. He recognised Squire Hatherly's estate manager, who always came to collect the rent, usually alone. This time, he was accompanied by an older man, the squire himself, and a boy whom Hugh judged to be a couple of years older than himself. They tethered the horses and went into the farmhouse. Then the boy came out again. He caught sight of Hugh and walked towards him.

'Hello,' he said, 'Who are you?' He spoke in what Hugh called a toff's voice.

'My name's Hugh Hughes. I work here.'

'Pleased to meet you. I'm Jeremy Hatherly, Squire Hatherly's younger son.'

He held out his hand. Hugh was surprised. He was not used even to being noticed by the gentry, leave alone being invited to shake hands. He wiped his hands on his trousers and automatically took off his cap before offering his hand. He noted the other's smart clothes and polished riding boots, vastly different from his own dress.

'I'm afraid my hands are dirty,' he said.

'So what? You can't do honest work without getting your hands dirty. What's it like, working on a farm?' He could not possibly realise what an explosive question it was at that particular time.

Hugh controlled himself. 'It's all right,' he said shortly. 'What do you do?'

'Oh, I'm at school. Rugby, up in England. I'm here for a few days, staying with the pater.'

'The pater?' Hugh was puzzled.

'Oh, sorry, that's my father.' It was said without condescension, almost apologetically, as if he realised he was talking jargon which his listener would not understand. Where he might have put Hugh down, he put him at ease and, in doing so, unknowingly relieved some of the tension inside him.

'I suppose,' Hugh said with just the hint of a smile, 'that the time will come when it'll be you who will be coming to collect the rent.'

'No, not really, that'll be my elder brother, Edgar. He'll be taking over the estate after the pater. I shall be going into the army.'

Across the road, the squire and his estate manager came out of the farmhouse with Farmer Kramer, who was suitably obsequious in the presence of gentry. The squire shouted, 'Come here, Jeremy. It's time to go.'

Jeremy shook hands again. 'So long,' he said. 'Good luck. Hope to see you again some time.'

'I hope so.'

Jeremy joined his father and the estate manager.

'I thought I'd told you before,' the squire said to his son, 'about being over-familiar with servants.' He had a secret dread that some disastrous liaison might occur in his family as it had in Colonel Mulholland's.

'I am getting old enough to decide for myself who I'll speak to,' was the reply. That did not please the squire but he judged it prudent not to engage in argument with his son in front of the lower orders.

Jeremy mounted his horse. As the three rode off, he quite deliberately turned and gave Hugh a friendly wave. Hugh warmed to him. He sensed something of a fellow rebellious soul.

Farmer Kramer was not pleased. 'You remember your place in the presence of gentry,' he said as he replaced his cap. Hugh ignored him.

Neither Hugh nor Jeremy could know about the conversation concerning Jeremy's future in the army that had taken place at his father's dinner table, just a few days after Hugh's birth and which, to some extent, had been sparked by Dr Jones's supercilious reference to that event. And neither of them could possibly foresee the terrible circumstances in which they would meet again, when they would both be in their twenties.

For the rest of that day, there was an icy silence between Hugh and the Kramers. His mind was made up that it would be his last day there. That night, turbulent thoughts kept him from sleeping just as they had done on the first night there but, this time, he was glad, because he intended to be up very early and feared to oversleep.

Everything was worked out. On finishing work, he had washed his wellingtons under the pump. On retiring, he waited until all was quiet, with everyone in bed, then he stole silently down and took the boots to his room. He figured that had he taken them up earlier and been noticed, someone would have wanted to know why he was taking them from the usual place at the door, where the outside footwear was always left. Back in his room, he packed his few possessions into his little attaché case and managed to tie the boots to the case.

Very early in the morning, he silently went down to the dairy. He strapped the case and boots onto his bike, went outside without making any noise and rode away. The first light was just showing. As he cycled along the narrow lane, the tension in him seemed suddenly to melt away, to be replaced by an immense exhilaration. The tune of 'Land Of My Fathers' came into his head. He burst into song. He did not know the words, so he sang 'La lah – la la la lah – '

His immediate destination was Pembroke station but, as it was so early, he went into the town. He tried to make himself as inconspicuous as possible but he wanted to be in sight of a clock. There was a train shortly before eight o'clock and it was crucial that he should not miss it.

When he presented himself at the ticket office, the clerk recognised him.

'You're Joe Hughes' boy, aren't you?'

'Yes. I want a single ticket to Penduffryn and to put the bike in the guard's van.'

'You don't want a return?'

'No!"

The booking clerk looked at him a little oddly but made no comment. 'I know you're under fourteen,' he said, 'so it's half fare. Change at Whitland and again at Port Talbot. Oh, and remember me to your dad. I suppose you're off to see your sister at Penduffryn.'

Chapter 5

There were a number of people waiting for the train. He was worried that someone might recognise him and ask where he was going on his own and why, or even perhaps try to stop him. No one did, but when the train came in and he put his bicycle in the van, the guard, echoing the booking clerk's curiosity, asked him, 'Aren't you Joe Hughes' youngest boy?'

He regretted that his father had worked on the railway. Everybody who worked there seemed to recognise him. But now he had his answer ready.

'Yes, I'm going to my sister's at Penduffryn.'

'Taking your bike?' Pause. 'And your wellingtons?'

'Yes.'

'Oh well, I suppose it's none of my business.' He could see that the boy was not going to be communicative but his tone indicated that he clearly thought it *was* his business.

Hugh had never travelled outside Pembrokeshire, and even in the county his travels had been limited. It was the third train journey he had made. Both the previous ones had been to Tenby, on August bank holidays, with his parents and some of his brothers and sisters. When the train reached Tenby, he found himself recalling those happy days.

The children had paddled in the sea and he had marvelled at the bathing machines drawn up at the water's edge as well as at the dress of the people emerging from them gingerly to enter the water.

Some of the gentlemen – it went without question that they must be gentlemen, not mere men – had looked like giant wasps, in black and yellow costumes. He had been even more intrigued by the ladies, who seemed to be wearing almost as much to enter the water as to stay on dry land. Some of them even wore stockings. He had not been able to resist comparing them with himself and his friends bathing naked, much more sensibly, he thought, in the Pembroke River until the police had stopped them.

The Tenby stationmaster was standing on the platform just outside his compartment, resplendent in frock coat and braided cap. 'Whitland train,' he shouted, 'Change at Whitland for the London train.'

The London train! He wasn't just going into new and unknown territory. He would be going on nothing less than the London train. The very thought put a spring in his step when he alighted at Whitland.

'Over the bridge,' the guard told him, 'to the main up platform. Walk back along the platform to be near the guard's van.'

On the main line platform, a finger-post was already in position to announce the expected train. 'Carmarthen Swansea Cardiff Newport London' was painted on it. To the untravelled Hugh, they seemed like magic names. As he waited, another local train drew into the adjoining bay. It was from Cardigan, and most of the people who alighted were speaking Welsh. He recalled the group of men in Pembroke for Queen Victoria's diamond jubilee who had been stopped by the police from singing the Welsh national anthem and whom his father had described as being different because they were Welshmen from the north of the county. Looking now at his fellow passengers, he couldn't see that they looked any different from the sort of people he had known all his life.

When the train came in, it seemed altogether bigger and more impressive than any he had seen before. The carriages even had corridors, along which you could walk the length of the train. The guard, who, to his relief had obviously never known his father, told him to get into a compartment close to the van, because there would only be a short stop at Port Talbot and he would not have much time to retrieve the bicycle.

His sense of adventure was growing. By that time, they would have long discovered his absence from Round Pond Farm. Settling into his seat, he wondered how they were reacting.

The first stop was Carmarthen, where the train reversed, so that he was then at the front. By then, all the seats were taken and people were standing in the corridor. Shortly after leaving Carmarthen, the train came onto the sea wall at the mouth of the River Towy.

He realised that, across Carmarthen Bay, he was looking back towards Pembrokeshire, and he found himself wondering vaguely if he would ever again go back there to live. The train, now at speed, left the sea wall and ran through sand dunes before stopping at Llanelly.

For a country boy born and bred, his first sight of an industrial town was a shock. Steelworks and other factories belched smoke and fumes over mean little streets. By the time they reached Swansea, by far and away the largest town he had ever seen, there seemed to be nothing except factories, railway sidings and smoke, with rows of houses terraced up the hills behind.

Again the train reversed direction, so that he was once more at the rear. The ticket inspector came round, struggling to get through the crowded corridor.

'Change at Port Talbot,' he told Hugh.

Port Talbot proved to be a grim and grimy station, gateway to a grim and grimy town with factories, steelworks and houses set on a narrow strip of flat land between docks and what seemed to him to be towering mountains. Deposited on the platform, he wondered what to do. He approached a porter. At least, no one here would know his father.

'I want the train to Penduffryn,' he said.

'Stay on this platform. You've got an hour to wait. Hugh noted that his accent was different from that of Pembrokeshire people.

The hour passed quickly. He was fascinated by trains passing through the station, mostly slow-moving loads of coal in one direction and empty coal trucks going the opposite way to return to the pits. When his train arrived, it seemed small and shabby compared with the main line express. The last lap of his journey was a slow one, by way of tortuous curves and steep gradients, the little engine seeming at times to be almost at its last gasp.

Penduffryn was the end of the line, a large mining village near the top end of a valley. Houses, shops, pubs, chapels and railway lines all lay in close proximity. The colliery was the most prominent feature, with an overhead pulley system to take large buckets of waste up to the slag heap perched on the mountain.

Outside the station which, like Pembroke, had just one platform but was nothing like as clean, Hugh was suddenly at a loss. He had no idea how to find his sister's house. Besides which, it was now afternoon and having had nothing to eat all day, he was feeling very hungry. The sense of adventure which had sustained him was evaporating. He spotted a post office near the station. What better place to ask for directions?

The postmistress, a stout, well-bosomed lady with pince-nez glasses, was chatting in Welsh with another lady. She broke off when Hugh entered and said something to him in Welsh.

'I'm sorry,' he said, 'I don't speak Welsh.'

The two women looked at him with a mixture of sympathy and contempt.

'How can I help you?' the postmistress asked.

'I'm looking for my sister and brother-in-law,' he said. 'May and John Burrows. Can you tell me how to get to their home please?'

'You're May's brother?' asked the postmistress. 'You're a lot younger than she is. You'll be from Penfro, although I suppose you call it Pembroke.' She paused. 'Little England beyond Wales.' The sympathy in her voice showed how sorry she felt for him, coming from such parts.

The other lady intervened. 'They live at fourteen Upper Terrace,' she said. 'I live at number seventeen. I'll take you there.'

It was a short walk to the house, mostly uphill. They had to cross the railway, which ran into sidings beyond the station. Upper Terrace was a row of miners' cottages, looking across the valley and over the roofs of the equally unimaginatively named Lower Terrace. Immediately across the road in front of Lower Terrace were railway sidings, where a shunting engine was noisily marshalling coal wagons. There was a fine view of the slag heap on the other side of the valley, with the colliery below it.

'Is May expecting you?' the lady asked him, looking curiously at the bicycle he was pushing, with the small case and boots strapped on the back.

'No,' he said.

'Are you coming to stay?'

'I'm not sure, but I expect so.'

'Well, here we are.' They stopped at the door, neatly painted and with a spotlessly scrubbed step, like all the others in the street. The lady knocked at the door, then pushed it open.

'Hello May! It's Aggie Evans. I've got a visitor for you.'

May appeared in an apron. 'Hello Aggie,' she said. She stopped short at the sight of her little brother.

'Hughie!' she said. 'What on earth are you doing here?'

All the tension inside Hugh suddenly exploded. The words came out of him in a torrent.

'I've run away from that farm,' he blurted out. 'I can't stand it any more. And I can't go home. Dad would never understand. He'd send me back. Please take me in. I want to get a job in the pit.' Suddenly and uncharacteristically, he was sobbing uncontrollably.

May took him into her arms, not far off tears herself. 'There, there,' she said, 'of course we'll take you in.' She turned to the lady who had brought him. 'How did you come across him?'

'I was talking with Miss Evans the post and he came into the post office to ask how to get to your house and, as I was just coming home, I brought him.'

'Thank you so much, Aggie. I can see we've got something to sort out here. The men will be coming off shift from the pit soon and I'll have to talk it over with John. We'll have to see what's to be done.'

Mrs Evans left for her own house, a few doors along the street. May addressed Hugh, now more in control of himself and inwardly angry and embarrassed because he had allowed his emotions to get the better of him.

'Put your bike inside the door,' she said. A thought struck her. 'You surely haven't cycled here?'

'No, I came on the train.'

A twinkle appeared in May's eye. 'Brought your wellingtons, I see,' she said.

'I wasn't going to leave them there for the Kramers.'

'Better take your case off the bike. At least, we've got a spare room where you can sleep. But you can go up there later. I suppose you're pretty hungry. We'd better put that right first. We'll have a proper meal when John comes in, but you'd better have some bread and dripping and some cake straight away.'

She took him through to the kitchen. He ate ravenously what she put in front of him. May was busy, in and out of the kitchen. A cooked meal was in preparation on the kitchen range. There was another room behind the kitchen, with a door to the small yard at the back of the house. As he finished eating, he heard someone come in through the back door.

'Hello love.' It was John.

'Hello sweetheart,' she replied. 'There's a surprise waiting for you in the kitchen.'

If it was a surprise for John to see Hugh, it was an even greater surprise for Hugh to see John, For John was black from head to foot, covered in coal dust and with his dust-impregnated working clothes exuding what Hugh would later come to recognise as the distinctive smell from the pit.

'Hugh!' John exclaimed. 'What are you doing here?'

'He's run away from that farm,' May explained, 'and he wants to get a job at the pit.'

'Good God!' John said.

'Before we talk about that, or anything else,' May said, 'you go straight back to the scullery and have your bath. It's all ready for you. There's plenty of hot water.'

The scullery was the room behind the kitchen. It was clear that John was not allowed anywhere else in the house until he had cleaned up. The sound of vigorous washing could soon be heard. In due course he emerged, changed into clean clothes.

'Well now, Hugh,' he said, 'what's all this about?'

Hugh related his experiences at the farm and why he had left, adding that he remembered what John had said about there being work at the pit.

'Mm – yes,' John said. 'You won't be able to go underground until you're fourteen, but there's also work on the surface – lamp room, engine room or, if the worst comes to the worst, sorting the slag from the coal.'

May interrupted. 'The first thing we must do is let Mam and Dad know he's here. They may know already that he's run away and they'll be worried sick. I'll go to the post office in the morning and send a telegram.'

That night, Hugh slept far more comfortably, more welcomed and more at ease, both with himself and with his surroundings, than for months. Only the shunting of the trains disturbed him from time to time, but that was something in time he would not even notice. Quite early in the morning, his sister took him to the post office.

'Good morning, Blodwen,' she said to the postmistress. Hugh suppressed a giggle. Blodwen struck him as a funny name but he thought that if anyone looked like a Blodwen, it was certainly the postmistress. May wrote out the telegram to let his parents know that he had arrived safely and that a letter would be following.

'That'll be one and threepence including the address,' Blodwen said, counting the words. 'They'll have it within a couple of hours.'

'I've got some shopping to do,' May said as they left the post office. 'All the shops are close by. I want to go to the co-op for some groceries and to Evans butcher.'

Hugh was intrigued. 'Why do they call people names like Evans butcher and Evans the post?' he asked.

May smiled. 'It's because there are so many called Evans here – and Jones as well – that people give them those nicknames to tell them apart. Oh and by the way, although we are the only Burrows in the village, they call John "Johnny Penfro" because he's from Pembroke. You'll probably get called "Hughie Penfro". You'll soon get used to it.'

He had no doubt that he would get used to it, but one thing already fixed in his mind was that, whatever anybody else called the stout postmistress, for him she would always be Blodwen post.

Shortly after they arrived home, a telegram was delivered. It was from his father, inquiring if he was there. The smartly uniformed telegram boy was about his own age and eyed him curiously. He already knew who Hugh was and what the contents of the telegram were. Blodwen post saw no more harm in divulging the contents of telegrams than in reading what was written on postcards.

The news that Hugh had run away had reached his parents some hours after the event, via the guard who had seen him onto the train at Pembroke and off at Whitland. All day, it had nagged the guard that something was amiss, so, since he lived close by, he went straight to see them on finishing his shift. The two girls, Alice and Myfanwy, were home from school but Joseph was still at work. Leah was shocked and worried at the news.

'Oh dear,' she said, 'Joe won't like this.'

Joseph came in shortly afterwards and he certainly did not like it.

'What am I going to say to Kramer?' he demanded angrily. 'I made an agreement with him and it's been broken. I shall have to go and see him at once.'

'You might think about the boy before your wounded pride,' Leah said. 'I'm not surprised myself. It's obvious he hasn't been happy there from the start.'

Joseph was taken aback. He was essentially the Victorian husband who did not expect to be questioned by his wife about how he treated their children. Yet the nagging doubts that had haunted him for months had proved correct. Leah could see that he was troubled.

'Don't go there tonight,' she said. 'Why not go and see Matthew first? He knows the Kramers better than we do. Let things calm down for a day or so, then go with Matthew to see them.'

He knew she was right. 'I'll go to Matthew's as soon as I've had something to eat,' he said. A thought struck him. 'We should make sure he really has gone to May's,' he said. 'You'd better go to the post office in the morning and send them a telegram.'

He bolted down his meal and cycled to Matthew's. The two girls were agog with excitement. By the next day, the whole school would know about Hugh's precipitate departure.

Matthew was startled by his father's unexpected arrival but not entirely so by his news.

'I haven't heard anything,' he said. To Joseph's chagrin, he went on to repeat Leah's reaction. 'I can't say I'm altogether surprised. The best thing would be for you to come here tomorrow. We'll go over to Round Pond. I don't think you ought to go on your own. Kramer can be a nasty piece of work. Oh, by the way, I've just bought a pony and trap. We'll go over in that.' He was secretly revelling in the knowledge that the Kramers would be infuriated by their arrival in his newly acquired means of transport.

While Joseph was at Matthew's, Leah went to see their daughter Lizzie, to tell her the news. Lizzie's husband Ray was by then a chargehand at the dockyard and on the way to becoming a foreman. Robert Snape was also there, avidly interested.

'Tell Dad to take the day off,' Ray said. 'I'll see that it's all right. I'll let his foreman know that there's some unexpected family trouble that he's got to see to.' That made things easier for Joseph. It also ensured that by the next day, a sizeable number of the staff at the Royal Naval Dockyard also came to know about the situation, not least from Robert.

With an unexpected day off, Joseph was able to go to the post office himself to send the telegram to May. Her telegram to him arrived not long after he returned. So, by the time he arrived at Matthew's, he knew that Hugh was safely at Penduffryn.

He found it quite a pleasure to be driven to Round Pond Farm in a pony and trap, mentally noting that things couldn't be going too badly for Matthew to be able to afford such a conveyance.

From the moment they arrived, it was clear that Bill Kramer was in a bad mood. He came storming out into the road and did not wait for them to alight from the trap, the very sight of which, as Matthew had calculated, made him even angrier.

'I've been wondering when you were going to show up,' he shouted. 'Why haven't you brought that little bastard back?'

That made Joseph really angry. 'Don't you dare call my son a bastard,' he shouted back.

Matthew intervened quickly. 'My brother has gone to my sister's in the valleys. We only found out where he was a few hours ago.'

'The ungrateful little swine. Letting me down after all I've done for him.'

Matthew put a restraining hand on his father's arm. 'Like what?' he asked.

'Like what! I've taught him farming, gave him board and lodging for six months, and paid him.'

'Two bob a week, as I understand it,' Matthew said coldly. 'And it takes a lot more than six months to learn farming.'

Bill Kramer turned to Joseph. 'I've a good mind to make you pay me back that money.'

'Don't talk such bloody rubbish,' Matthew retorted. 'You've had six months' work out of him at far less than he ought to have been paid.'

'You know as well as I do that I'm under no obligation to pay him anything for that six months unless I'm satisfied with him. And look what he's cost me in board and lodging. What are you going to do about it?'

'Nothing,' Matthew said. He gathered up the reins, well aware of the advantage of talking down from the trap to the man on the ground. 'Come on Dad, we've done all we need to here.'

'I'll have the law on you,' Bill Kramer shouted as they left him standing in the road. But they all knew that it was an empty threat.

For Joseph, as he was driven back to Old Oak Farm for a welcome cup of tea and slice of cake before cycling home, there was a new reality to ponder.

His younger offspring might still be children and subject, apart from the rebellious Hugh, to his will, but it was his eldest son who had handled a difficult situation much better than he himself would have done. Then there was Lizzie's husband, Ray who had saved him from the embarrassment of asking for time off work. Both young men represented the new generation who, inevitably, would be taking over from him, and indeed, were already starting to do so. At the same time, he felt a sense of relief. He had to admit to himself, although he never would to anybody else, that he had made a mistake. Now, thankfully, the episode was behind them all.

Shortly after Hugh's arrival, his brother-in-law John arranged to take him to see the colliery manager, William Yewsley. It was well known that the manager always insisted on seeing all applicants for jobs instead of leaving interviews to underlings. John warned Hugh that they must remove their caps before entering his office and hold them in their hands. Mr Yewsley must be addressed as 'sir' and they must not speak until they were spoken to.

The mine manager was part legend, part hate figure. He was in his late forties, a smallish, sharp-featured man with a pointed nose. He lived in what was, for the miners, a grand house close to the pit, but his domestic arrangements had by no means always been like that. He had started working life as a pit boy, and there was a grudging admiration for him for having made his way in the world. He knew coal mining backwards. Having qualified in the Rhondda Valley, he had been appointed manager at the Penduffryn colliery ten years earlier.

Almost immediately, he had been confronted with the 1893 national lockout of the miners who, newly unionised, had resisted the mine owners' demand for a twenty-five per cent cut in wages. The lockout had lasted from July to November. It had been violent and bitter. In some places, the military had been called out and, in Yorkshire, they shot two men dead and wounded sixteen others.

Nothing so serious had happened at Penduffryn, but there had been one occasion when police reinforcements were brought to deal with demonstrations at the pit and outside the manager's house, where all the windows had been smashed.

Trapped inside, William Yewsley feared for the safety of his wife, young son and two daughters. He had taken them upstairs, loaded the shotgun which he regularly used against birds and rabbits, and taken up a position on the stairs, facing the front door. He anticipated that the sight of the gun would be sufficient to deter any attack if the house should be broken into, but he was determined to fire if he was rushed. Fortunately, no break-in occurred.

Outside, though, the miners had built barricades across the railway line and across the one road that led to the village, in anticipation of the arrival of police reinforcements or soldiers or both. The wives and children had collected stones and taken them to the barricades to be used as ammunition. When police reinforcements arrived, a number were injured by well-aimed stones, and a number of miners, as well as wives and children, were injured in baton charges.

The national dispute had eventually been brought to an end by the intervention of the Prime Minister, William Gladstone, and the employers had been compelled to let the miners return to work without any reduction in wages. It had been a great victory for the miners but had left a long legacy of bitterness.

The then newly-appointed William Yewsley would have liked to have denied employment to a dozen or so whom he considered as ringleaders. He had not been able to do so, but what he had done was to bide his time and then dismiss them one by one for supposed disciplinary offences. Some of the miners had wanted to strike in their support, but although victorious, the union had been so weakened that a strike was not possible.

Most of the sacked men had eventually gone elsewhere. Two or three older men had stayed behind, denied work for life, dependent solely on the goodwill of relatives and neighbours. They died within a few years, their lives shortened not only by many years of hard labour followed by unemployment, but also by the coal dust in their lungs.

When Hugh and John were shown into the manager's office, he was reading through some papers from the several piles on his desk. Hugh's eyes were drawn from the desk to the walls, which were covered in plans of the pit workings. Mr Yewsley continued looking at papers, apparently ignoring them as they stood before him. It was a favourite ploy, designed to make their inferior status clear.

'So, Burrows, you want to put this boy to work at the pit?' He only knew John's name because it was written on one of the pieces of paper in front of him. He did not look up.

'Yes sir.'

'I gather that he's your brother-in-law.'

'Yes sir.'

'Usually, I get fathers bringing their sons looking for jobs.' He did not add that it could well be the worse for any father who did not bring sons of working age to supplement the workforce. He looked up at last and spoke to Hugh.

'So you want to be a miner?'

'Yes sir.'

'Not from these parts, are you?'

'No sir, from Pembroke.'

'Like your brother-in-law.' He looked them both up and down, comparing their size and ages. 'I suppose I should say "like your big brother-in-law".' He was not without a sardonic sense of humour and there was almost the ghost of a twinkle in his eye.

'What have you been doing up to now?'

'I've been working on a farm, sir."

'So you know something about animals.' He made a note. He always made notes about anything he thought might be useful at some later stage.

'Start Monday morning, first shift. You'll be sorting out the dirt from the coal.'

John spoke up. 'I was hoping sir, that there might be something in the lamp room or on the winding gear.'

'There isn't. See that he's at the pit head on Monday morning on time.'

They both knew they had no choice except to leave.

Hugh's new job was hard and dirty and the long hours sent him home very tired. He did not complain; it was his own choice. Several clichés occurred to him. He had burnt his boats; he had made his bed and he would lie in it. Only too glad to, he would think whimsically as he struggled to keep his eyes open after returning from work. Now, though, in contrast to what he had known at Round Pond Farm, his new home gave him warmth, understanding and affection, and that made a huge difference.

In the spring, John and May's child was born, a boy they named Luke. It tickled Hugh that he was now an uncle, but there was a disadvantage as, like the doting parents, he was deprived of much-needed sleep by Luke's constant exercise of his clearly very healthy lungs.

The question arose of introducing Luke to his two sets of grandparents. The first opportunity was not until the August bank holiday weekend after he was born, when it was decided that they would all go to Pembroke. By then, Hugh had been at Penduffryn for the better part of a year.

Letters from his father, at first cold and admonitory, had gradually become warmer. He noted the greeting changing from 'Hugh' to 'Dear Hugh' to 'My Dear Son'. He guessed, correctly, that the change was the result of his mother's influence. He was nervous, though, as to how he might be received. In the event, he was greeted cordially; his mother had seen to that in advance. His parents were as pleased to see him as to meet their first grandson. There was other good news in that another grandchild was on the way, for Matthew's wife Lydia was pregnant.

However, there was news of another expected grandchild that was not considered at all good. Hugh's brother John, the fifth-born of the family, who was seven years his senior, had become enamoured of a local girl. She had returned his attentions with enthusiasm and both of them, consumed with youthful ardour, had thrown convention to the winds in a series of clandestine but hugely enjoyable sessions of lovemaking. The inevitable result was that the young woman had become pregnant.

The news had already reached Penduffryn by letter. The most informative letter had come from Hugh's friend, the irrepressible, irreverent and now rapidly maturing Robert Snape. May and John had been suitably shocked at the nature of the news and mildly shocked that it should be a matter of such frank discussion between two boys of such tender age.

By that August weekend, the young couple had disappeared. 'Sent into exile in the salt mines' was how Robert put it to Hugh when the two friends joyfully renewed their acquaintance. But the scandal was still at boiling point.

Leah and Joseph had been profoundly shocked when they learned what had happened from a sheepish John. But the reaction of the young woman's parents was even more outraged. They were prominent and active members of a particularly strict chapel. The girl's father had stormed round to Joseph's to announce that he was ordering his daughter out of the family home. He wanted the young couple to appear in the chapel, where they would be publicly denounced 'for bringing a child into the world without The Lord's command', after which, his daughter 'would never darken his door again'.

Joseph and Leah, with their solidly Anglican upbringing, refused absolutely to have their son publicly humiliated in what they considered such an unchristian way in a place of worship of which they were highly suspicious. But they insisted that the two must be married without delay and that the best thing would be for them to go away.

The minister at the chapel was no less unforgiving than the girl's father but more intelligent. He announced that he would spend a whole day in prayer to seek divine guidance as to whether he should or should not marry the couple. The outcome of his meditation left him not sure whether he did receive divine advice or whether he had come to a conclusion through his own consideration of the facts. The only possible course of action in such a dilemma was to give divine guidance the benefit of the doubt. So he agreed to marry the couple in a quiet ceremony. He also contacted a fellow minister in a suitably distant valley in east Wales, who agreed to find a home there for them.

All this had been accomplished shortly before that memorable bank holiday. The two were united in what Robert Snape gleefully called 'a shotgun wedding' and departed to their new home without delay. John, who had worked as a farmhand, became the third member of the family to become a coal miner and the first to provide his parents with a granddaughter.

Chapter 6

Having passed his fourteenth birthday, Hugh applied to work underground. He knew that the work would be even harder, dirtier and much more dangerous than his job on the surface, but the pay would be better and it would be more of a man's job, which, with growing adolescent ambition, was what he wanted. He expected that he would have to apply again to the mine manager in person but, in the event, he had to see Dai horses.

Dai's real name was David Jones. There was a problem in the abundance of men called Jones and it was made even more complicated because so many of them were also called David. No man with that first name was ever called by it; he would be Dai or Davey – the anglicised Dave was never used. Some had been named with the Welsh Dafydd but, with one exception, they were all called Dai. The exception, who considered himself a cut above everyone else, wanted to be known by the Welsh Dewi. Since the English phonetic pronunciation was Dowi and since he was the local pastry cook, he succeeded, to his mortification, in getting himself known as Dowi Doughy.

Dai horses was in charge of the pit ponies, the unfortunate animals used to haul the coal from the face to the bottom of the pit shaft for lifting to the surface. Dai's brother Ioan, who was a farmer further down the valley, had a contract to supply ponies to the pit.

Since the ponies had to be replaced when they grew too big, there was a continuous demand and it was a lucrative contract, from which Dai received many a backhander. As for the animals, when they became redundant, the lucky ones would be sold to farmers and hauliers who might need them. The most unlucky would be sent to the knacker's yard while, occasionally, some would be turned loose on the mountains, which meant that, never having had to fend for themselves in the wild, they soon died anyway.

'I know why you're being put on the ponies,' John said to Hugh.

'Don't you remember that when you told Yewsley you had been working on a farm, he made a note of it.'

'But that was over a year ago – a year and a half.' A year and a half was an interminable period in the life of a fourteen-year-old.

'No difference, he always makes notes of things he thinks he can use to his own advantage in the future.'

'But I don't want to go back to mucking out and looking after animals.'

'You'll also be leading them to and from the face,' John told him. 'It's better than working with a pick and shovel. Besides, you've no choice.' They both knew he was right.

Dai horses personally took him down the pit the first time. It was a salutary experience. The descent in the cage was unnerving in itself. Then, keeping their heads low to avoid the roof, they travelled to the coal face on the trolleys pulled by ponies. There was silence and utter darkness in the seemingly endless tunnels, fleetingly lit only by the miners' lamps, while, at the face, it was very hot and noisy from the combination of men, black from head to foot, hacking away with picks and shovels, and the coal being loaded into the trucks. All around, the dust was like a fog.

As Hugh became accustomed to his new duties, he came to realise that everyone in the pit had a job to do and had to know how and when to do it. If they did not do the right things at the right time, a situation disastrous to life and limb could very easily and quickly develop. The tragedy was that such situations developed all too often, leaving miners dead and injured and families to mourn the loss of breadwinners. And there was the all-pervading dust, always there to enter lungs and leave men struggling to breathe for the rest of their shortened lives.

It was not surprising that such conditions created a united and determined society above ground as much as beneath, a vibrant, politicised society with a strong culture of its own that threw up its own leaders, articulate, self-taught men of considerable learning. The trade union lodge, affiliated to the South Wales Miners' Federation, played a major role in the community. The chapels did so even more strongly, because they also brought women into active participation. In both institutions, men of personality and determination were leaders, acquiring a dignity and standing that was wholly denied in their employment.

There was a male voice choir, a colliery band and a rugby team, all known throughout the coalfield; no mean achievement given the strength of the competition.

John Burrows was a keen rugby player, a regular in the first team, and he lost no time in partly coaxing, partly arm-twisting Hugh into joining the juniors. Hugh, recalling his introduction to the game by his brother Joe, was happy to do so. He was no great player and never expected to make any impression, but he enjoyed the rough and tumble, notwithstanding that, as often as not, it sent him home bruised and sore after a match. The experience made him a lifelong follower of the game.

One thing he soon became aware of was that the game was unexpectedly classless in Wales. The colliery manager's son, Will Yewsley junior, was a valued player in the first team, and his father regularly turned out to watch matches, joining miners and their families standing round the field in a way he would never have dreamed of doing in working time. The team captain was the local doctor and there was a good representation of other professional people.

For Hugh, born and brought up in a community of rigorous class distinctions, it seemed puzzling. It was Dai horses, a man of more perception than most, who explained things.

'You see boy,' he said, 'in Wales, rugby is a religion, not just a game. With all the pits being sunk and the steelworks and all the other industry growing up, it brought Wales out of the dark ages. Rugby was a sort of religion that brought all classes together to express our national identity.'

'How about in England?' asked Hugh. 'I thought that, like cricket, they invented it as a game for toffs, at a school called Rugby.'

'That's balls,' snorted Dai, not a man to miss out on an appropriate expletive. 'There were games played in villages all over England and Wales – and I should think Scotland and Ireland too – where you had to run with a ball, long before that toffee-nosed lot claimed to invent it because somebody picked up a ball and ran with it, instead of kicking it. He broke the rules but, of course, being English toffs, they changed the rules and claimed they'd invented a new game.'

'You sound as though you don't much like the English,' Hugh said, half laughing, as he was sure he was meant to.

'Not at all, boy. I don't dislike the English. There are some of them working in this pit and in plenty of other Welsh pits, decent lads like ourselves, who've come here to work because there's no work for them in England. It's toffs I don't like, whether they're English, Welsh or any other nationality. All the same, though, Wales was Wales before England was England, and although we were the first to be colonised by the English, they haven't beaten us yet.'

Where religion was concerned, Hugh had been brought up in the Anglican tradition, because that was how his parents had been brought up. But he was no great believer. Much of what he had experienced in church services and at Sunday school had been incomprehensible. His mother had always told him that there was 'one above us' and his general, vague perception was that you had to be good because of this all-seeing one above. Being good meant being obedient to your parents and kind to others, which seemed reasonable. But being good also seemed to mean being obedient to people like Farmer Kramer and everyone above him in the social hierarchy, which did not seem anything like so reasonable.

He had been taught nothing about any of the other world religions with their adherents all round the globe. As far as he understood it, those people were all heathens, and where the British Empire ruled their lands, kindly missionaries worked to turn them into Christians and also into enthusiastic subjects of the great white queen/king across the seas.

In church, you had to be sure that you sat suitably towards the back, because the front rows were reserved for the gentry and those in the middle for the people who ranked below the gentry but above the likes of the Hughes. It might well be easier for a camel to go through the eye of a needle than for a rich man to enter the kingdom of God but, whatever the situation might be in heaven, in that earthly house of God, all the advantages were with the rich men.

John and May, who had also been brought up in the same tradition and for the same reason, had left the Anglican church and joined the local Wesleyan Methodist chapel, not for reasons of any conversion but simply because that was what almost everybody else did. They had persuaded Hugh to attend, and the experience proved to be decidedly different.

The place of worship was no longer a beautiful, centuries-old building, but an austere, mid-Victorian stone box which seemed even colder in winter. In the chapel, no gentry attended and you sat wherever you found a seat, which might not be easy if there was a preacher who was noted for his oratory and you were not in good time.

In church, you had been harangued by robed clergy who came from very different backgrounds from your own, who talked differently from you and talked down to you. The whole atmosphere seemed to be summed up in the hymn the children sang regularly at Sunday school, claiming that the Lord God had made all things bright and beautiful as well as all things wise and wonderful, including

> The rich man in his castle,
> The poor man at his gate,

whom God had made 'high or lowly, and ordered their estate'.

By contrast, in the chapel, you could be harangued by a lay preacher dressed like yourself in his Sunday best, who could well be a respected fellow worker in the pit and an official in the union. There would still be much that seemed incomprehensible, with plenty of hellfire and brimstone, but Hugh found these preachers by and large more inspiring than any he had heard before. Their general theme was much more acceptable: that all men were equal in the sight of God and that it was evil that the great majority were ruthlessly crushed and exploited for the profit of the few, above all by the mine owners.

Quite often, the sermons also included strong denunciations of the evils of drink and of the brewers, who, he gathered, ranked only slightly below the mine owners as exploiters and degraders of the people. He noticed, though, that such denunciations never seemed to stop the pubs being filled on Saturday evenings by men who went to chapel the following morning.

Although it was a Welsh-speaking area, there were a fair number who did not speak the language, so the services were always conducted in English. There was a small number of older people who spoke Welsh only, remnants of the time before compulsory state education and its determined efforts to stamp out the Welsh language. There were few, in that dawn of the twentieth century, who could foresee that, by the twilight of the century, Welsh would be a subject in the successors to those same schools, in an attempt to teach the language to a large and reluctant majority who had no wish to learn it.

Within a year or so, Hugh was beginning to understand some of the language, although he knew that he would never acquire the ability to converse in it and he abandoned all attempts to read it.

'I hear,' his sister said one Sunday morning when they were walking back from chapel with their neighbour Aggie Evans, whom he had met that fateful day when he had arrived, 'that Johnny Onions will be here this week.'

'That's right, Miss Evans the post told me yesterday. They're expected on Tuesday.'

'I see that Blodwen wasn't in chapel this morning. Unusual for her.'

'She's got a bit of a cold. Thought it better to stay home.'

'No wonder Dai horses looked a bit disappointed.'

They all sniggered. The relationship between the bachelor Dai and the spinster postmistress was a matter of some merriment throughout the village. He was clearly much taken with her but she, equally clearly, was not responsive and he lacked the boldness to make any approach to her.

'I want to buy from Johnny Onions,' May said. 'Perhaps you'll be kind enough to help me out with them.'

'Of course I will.'

When they got into the house, Hugh, whose curiosity had been aroused, asked his sister, 'Who is Johnny Onions?'

'Oh, there's several of them,' she told him. 'They're Frenchmen who come here to sell onions.'

'What do you mean by asking Mrs Evans to help you out with them?'

'It's because she can talk with them. They speak a language very like Welsh.'

'But how do they speak Welsh if they're from France?'

'They come from a place called Brittany, in the west of France, where there's a language called Breton, which is very similar to Welsh. And they sell very good onions.'

The onion sellers duly arrived, men wearing berets and navy blue and white horizontally striped jerseys and with the suntanned, weatherbeaten look of men who were both farmers and seafarers. They were very much at home with the Welsh speakers, some of whom, regular customers over the years, welcomed them like old friends.

Hugh had been two years in Penduffryn when, one Sunday morning, the minister announced at the end of the service that he would shortly be leaving to move to another chapel. There was nothing unusual in that; it was the normal practice of the Methodist Church to move the ministers every three years or so. But the final sentence of the announcement caused a distinct frisson of excitement.

'My successor, who will be arriving in about a month's time and whom I know you will welcome most warmly into our fellowship, will be the Reverend Gwynfor Morgan.'

Outside, the congregation gathered in groups to discuss this news.

'By golly,' said Bill Evans, Aggie's husband, 'Yewsley won't like this.'

'Yewsley won't half be taking some stick from this pulpit now,' said Dai horses.

'Why is that?' asked Hugh's brother-in-law John. 'And why all the excitement?'

'It goes back to the '93 lockout,' explained Dai. 'Gwynfor worked at the pit. He wasn't much more than a boy then but he was one of the brightest there and very prominent in leading the opposition to the owners. Yewsley had it in for him from the start and a few weeks after it was all over, he sacked him, just before Christmas. There were some who wanted to strike to support him, but the union was too weak after the lockout, and with everybody so poor and it being Christmas, there wasn't enough support. Yewsley timed it exactly. He knew what he was doing all right.'

'So what happened then?' asked John.

'Gwynfor left these parts soon after and we lost track of him. There was no family; his dad actually died during the lockout, not due to that but because he had the dust in his lungs, and Gwynfor's mam had died several years before that. All that had made him very bitter, even though he was really a very good-natured boy. I did hear later that he had got into theological college in Cardiff and trained as a minister.'

'It looks as if we shall be in for some exciting sermons,' John said.

'You bet!' Bill Evans agreed.

He spoke with a pleasurable expectancy which seemed to be generally shared. Everybody was chatting cheerfully and amicably. There were even some who claimed to have seen Miss Evans the post smile at Dai horses but that he, poor man, had been too overcome to respond.

In the New Year of 1905, the owner of the colliery was knighted 'for public and political services', becoming Sir George Robson JP, MP. He was the Conservative Member of Parliament for a constituency in the north east of England, from where he originated and where he owned a number of collieries. He had got himself elected twenty years earlier, not least by presenting himself as 'Geordie' Robson, the friend of the miners, and succeeded in holding his seat in successive elections, although sometimes by only narrow margins. He owned a number of pits in south Wales and had extended his 'public service' to that area, having been appointed a deputy lieutenant of the county of Monmouth and a magistrate in Glamorgan.

He had married the sister of Squire Hatherly of Pembrokeshire, a controversial marriage because his wife's family looked down on him as he was not a 'gentleman'. If they held him in contempt, he held them in even greater contempt, very conscious that they were kept in the style which they took to be their natural right only because of the money he had settled on his wife.

In south Wales, he used his marriage to a daughter of the Welsh gentry as much for public and political purposes as he used the name Geordie in the north east of England. His social climbing knew no bounds. To his immense satisfaction, his daughter, only shortly before his knighthood, had married into the English aristocracy, becoming no less than a countess. He also had a son, whom he hoped would follow him into Parliament.

Squire Hatherly, in Pembrokeshire, was almost incandescent with suppressed rage at the news of his brother-in-law's knighthood and scarcely less churlish over his niece's marriage.

'Don't know what the country's coming to,' he confided to his old friend Colonel Mulholland.

'My views exactly,' the colonel replied. 'These damn middle classes seem to think it's they who ought to be running the country, even buying up land and pretending to be gentry.'

The colonel had his own problems of class and property. He was five years on from being forced to recognise his illegitimate grandson, sired, as he put it, by his dead, caddish son, foaled by a servant girl and already heir presumptive to the wealthy industrialist Henry Black. The colonel had still not been able to make up his mind over what to do about changing his will. He was now seventy and aware that time was not on his side.

'By the way, Hatherly,' he said, 'how's that younger boy of yours doing, the one going into the army?'

'Oh fine, he'll be leaving Rugby this year and I've arranged for him to enter Sandhurst to train for his commission.'

'Good show,' said the colonel.

Sir George Robson had decided that, especially with a general election in the offing, it would be a good thing if his knighthood were to be celebrated at all his collieries. Accordingly, instructions were sent out to all managers to close each pit on days to be arranged, preferably in the summer. He would personally visit each pit on its chosen day, and the day off, unpaid of course, would give 'his' miners the chance to display their gratitude, not only for the day's holiday and his knighthood but also for his generosity in providing their livelihood.

William Yewsley, like his fellow pit managers elsewhere, received these instructions with grave misgivings. He was instructed that on the appointed day, Sir George and Lady Robson would arrive for lunch at the manager's house. There would be no need to worry about the catering. Professionals would be brought in from Swansea; they would decide on the menu and the wines, and the company would pay. The miners were to be instructed to assemble, and would be expected to applaud their employer as he arrived and again when he left.

'There is bound to be trouble,' Yewsley said to his wife. 'Depriving them of a day's pay and expecting them to celebrate. It's madness. We shall have to have extra police called in. And if he expects me to call for three cheers for him, he can forget it as quick as he likes. Just imagine what the response to that would be.'

His wife's mind was already on other aspects of the visit. 'We shall have to have the house specially cleaned,' she said, 'and I shall have to get a new dress.' Her husband sometimes wondered if she ever really listened to anything he said.

His twenty-year-old daughter Margaret spoke up. 'Why don't you get in touch with the union,' she said, 'and see what can be done to avoid trouble.'

Her father nearly exploded. 'The union! We don't recognise any union. You ought to know better than to make such a stupid suggestion.'

'Well, you'll have to see somebody who can influence the men.' She thought for a moment. 'Why not see that rather good-looking Methodist minister, Mr Morgan? He exerts a lot of influence.'

'Morgan! I sacked that troublemaker years ago. Now he's got the nerve to come back here, preaching sedition from his pulpit!' A new worry struck him: his daughter referring to that chapel ranter as good-looking. What did that mean – especially as the fellow wasn't married?

'Steady dear,' Mrs Yewsley said. It always worried her when he got angry.

'I'll have to go to the police station,' he said, 'Get them to put on a show of strength to discourage any trouble. And as for any ringleaders, I'll deal with them afterwards, as I did with Morgan and his like.'

Margaret was not to be put off. 'That was a long time ago,' she said. 'Besides, as a man of the cloth, he might well be looking, himself, for a way to avoid trouble. I know he's not our church, but he is an ordained minister in his own church, and it's the church most of the miners go to.'

'It might be worth thinking about, dear,' Mrs Yewsley said. 'As Margaret says, he might also be looking for a way to avoid trouble.'

'Why not ask him to come here to talk about it?' Margaret said.

'Do you seriously think I'm going to have him in this house?' He roared the words. 'Hardly twelve years ago, he was with a mob smashing in the windows. I had to be ready to use my shotgun to protect you and your mother and sister and brother.'

'Well then, get him to come to your office.'

'I'll see him in hell first.'

Yet, for all his rage, he was not a slow thinker and the truth was dawning on him that he would be as damned if he did not see the minister as if he did. It horrified him that Sir George's ill-judged visit might be met by an angry, possibly stone-throwing crowd. For his own sake, as well as for everybody else's, that had to be avoided at all costs. The news of the impending 'celebration' was already all round the village and an ugly confrontation was in the making. After a couple of days' agonised thinking, he swallowed his pride. A message was sent to the minister asking him to come to the colliery office.

The meeting was not cordial. The two men did not shake hands. They were old enemies meeting face to face for the first time, each wary of the other, each bitterly opposed to everything the other represented, yet both knowing that, even if their motives were different, they had a strong interest in a common objective and that a great deal depended on that objective being achieved. And, in each, there was an unavoidable curiosity to see what the other would be like at close quarters.

William Yewsley opened the conversation. 'Good morning,' he said grimly. It was as hostile a greeting as any he had ever given. He did not rise from his chair and he did not offer Morgan a seat. It added to his discomfiture that the fellow was, as his daughter had said, rather good-looking – and with something of a commanding presence.

The greeting was as hostile as any that Gwynfor Morgan had ever received. No change in attitude, he thought, not even the manners to offer me a seat. As though I'm some supplicant he is condescending to speak to, instead of somebody he's desperately anxious to meet. Aloud, he said, reflecting Yewsley's manner and putting something like contempt into his voice, 'Good morning.'

'I believe you are aware, Morgan, of Sir George Robson's impending visit.'

'I am, Yewsley, and I am also aware that as I am an ordained minister, I expect to be addressed as "Mr Morgan".'

Yewsley swallowed hard. 'Very well, Mr Morgan,' he said, 'and I expect to be addressed as "Mr Yewsley".'

'Of course, Mr Yewsley. Now that we understand each other, can I help you?' It was deliberately condescending and, to add to the effect, he took a chair that was standing by the wall, pulled it forward and sat down. Yewsley, although suppressing his feelings with difficulty, decided not to respond in kind.

'I am most anxious,' he said, 'that there should be no trouble when Sir George comes here. I also know that you exert much influence, and I would hope that, as a minister of religion, you would be prepared to exert that influence to avoid violence.'

'I share your anxiety to avoid violence, but it is singularly silly to deprive the men of a day's pay and expect them to cheer the man who is depriving them of it, to say nothing of the way they have been treated in the past – and for that matter still are.'

'I am not going to enter into any discussion about anything except means to stop violence. And as a precautionary measure, I shall be arranging for police reinforcements to be here.'

'I have no doubt that you will. I hope you are aware that the presence of large numbers of police will, in itself, be provocative.'

'I will ask that their presence be as discreet as possible.'

Gwynfor Morgan thought hard. 'It is impossible to forecast what may happen,' he said. 'Tempers are already running high. The very last thing I want is for anybody to get hurt. I will do everything I can to prevent bloodshed, but understand one thing very clearly: there is no way that people in this village, outside a few sycophants, are going to applaud Sir George Robson.'

There were no further exchanges and Morgan left. The request to meet Yewsley had come as a surprise and, recalling the lockout all those years ago, he had not forgotten being beaten with a police baton and left bleeding in the gutter, then being dismissed, forced to go elsewhere to earn a living and finding that he was blacklisted in every colliery he applied to for work. But he also knew that the very last thing he wanted was to witness more violence.

Like the mine manager, he had his own difficulties and, no less, he wanted to find a way out. In his case, he wanted the miners and their families to be able to show their disapproval of the coal owner but without causing a disturbance in which they would be the ones to lose out. He thought long and hard and, because he was a sincere religious believer, he prayed for guidance. Finally, and after consulting with the most influential members of the chapel and with the union representatives, who were in several cases the same people, all of them as angry as he at the mine owner's action and equally anxious to avoid trouble in the streets, he decided to preach a sermon drawing on the sermon on the mount.

The lesson would be taken from the verses referring to the fowls of the air, who sowed not, neither did they reap nor gather produce into barns. He would go on to the lilies of the field, who toiled not, neither did they spin.

Following up on those sentiments, in his sermon he would castigate 'this man who is coming among us' who gathered only profits made from the toiling of those who laboured in the bowels of the earth with so little reward. He would also denounce him because he sat in Parliament to make laws to oppress the toilers, yet now came expecting to be cheered for doing such things. But he would point out that, also in the sermon on the mount, they were taught that blessed were the merciful and that you should turn the other cheek to whoever should strike you.

To end, he would tell them that he, himself, would be in the street when the man visited. He would show his disapproval of the unchristian conduct of the man and his minions in a wholly

Christian way, by remaining still and silent. He would most earnestly hope that the entire village would join him and do likewise.

As the day for the sermon approached, everyone knew that it was going to be exceptional. The chapel was crowded to capacity, with people standing round the sides and at the back. Among those at the back, duly noted with curiosity and no little suspicion, was Margaret Yewsley, accompanied by her brother. Her father had been furious when she announced her intention to be there but, faced with her implacable determination and realising the value of a first-hand account of the proceedings, he had not prevented her from going, so long as her brother was with her.

The minister was on his finest form. Those who were expecting the blaze of Welsh oratory, much in vogue in those times, were not disappointed. Had they not been in church, there would have been a roar of applause at the end. The irony of the choice of closing hymn was no less appreciated.

> Fight the good fight with all thy might,
> Christ is thy strength and Christ thy right.

Chapter 7

Sir George Robson arrived top-hatted and frock-coated, accompanied by his wife, in a chauffeur-driven motor car, the first that had been seen in the village. For all the exhortations to turn out and greet him, whether from the chapel or from the colliery management, a number of the miners and their families stayed at home. In some houses, the curtains were drawn, as if for a funeral. A fair number did gather near the manager's house, including the Reverend Morgan with leading figures from the chapel. A little way off, another gathering displayed the union banner.

Mr and Mrs Yewsley, the latter resplendent in her specially purchased new dress, together with the dozen or so invited luncheon guests, greeted the visitors at the door. The group was seen into the house in stony silence, notwithstanding that Sir George turned towards the bystanders and raised his top hat. Hugh, John and May were there, with little Luke.

'His wife is that Squire Hatherly's sister, from Larkfield Lodge, near Pembroke,' John told Hugh.

'I didn't know that. I saw Hatherly collecting the rent from Round Pond Farm – my last day there – and I talked with his son.'

'How did you come to be talking with his son?' May asked, surprised. Hugh explained his encounter with Jeremy Hatherly.

'Friends with the gentry, eh,' May said. 'By the way, Matthew has bought some land from Hatherly. Seems to be doing all right.' There was a touch of sisterly envy in her voice.

Down the road, the pawnbroker's shop window was entirely covered with a large, hand-painted poster stating 'BALFOUR PERSECUTES JEWS'. It was the work of Hymie Ginsberg, the pawnbroker and the only Jew in the village. As a youth, Hymie had been brought from Russia by his parents, refugees from the anti-Jewish pogroms in that country. Although quite young, he was, given the nature of his business, known inevitably as 'Uncle'. He was well regarded, not least because he was always lenient and ready to extend credit to those in genuine difficulties, a reaction born from vivid boyhood memories of poverty and oppression in the country of his birth.

From the post office, a few doors along the street, Blodwen Evans had seen Hymie putting up the poster. Puzzled, she asked him what it was about.

'It's a protest against the Aliens Act, which Balfour's government has just passed and which Sir George Robson supported in Parliament,' he explained.

'What is the Aliens Act?' Like everyone else in the village except Hymie, Blodwen had never heard of it.

'It's to stop refugees from the anti-Jewish pogroms in Russia, like my family, from coming to this country.' There was a degree of passion in Hymie's voice that Blodwen had not heard previously.

'Oh! Why have they passed it?'

'Balfour said in the House of Commons that a large Jewish population would not be to the advantage of the civilisation of this country. He also said that evil had fallen on parts of the country because of alien immigrants who were Jewish.' He paused. 'Do you think that I have brought evil to this valley?'

'No, of course not,' Blodwen said. An entirely new subject had been brought into her consciousness. She knew only too well that there were families whose survival from week to week depended on Hymie's business. She thought a moment. 'After all, we've got people who've come here from England and Ireland to find work.' She spoke as if she regarded those countries as being scarcely less foreign than Russia.

Sir George could not fail to notice the large poster in the window under the three brass balls. At the manager's house, he raised the matter over the drinks which preceded lunch.

'I suppose,' he said, 'that the pawnbroker is some Jewboy who is on about the Aliens Act.'

'Er – yes,' Yewsley said. 'I don't really know much about him.' He was at a loss and as mystified as Miss Evans had been, because it was really the act about which he did not know anything.

His daughter chimed in. 'What exactly is the Aliens Act?' she asked. She was less concerned to conceal her ignorance and anxious to learn. If there was a slight edge to her voice, it was because she felt that it was not polite to use the term 'Jewboy'.

Margaret's impetuosity worried her father. He and Mrs Yewsley had devoted much thought as to whether any or all of their offspring should be included in the guest list, not least because of Margaret's always lively and frequently unpredictable behaviour. Ultimately, they had decided to include them, in order to show off their family to Sir George. Now, her question seemed to justify her father's worries.

'There are far too many refugees coming into this country,' Sir George said, 'and the purpose of the act is to stop them.'

'And is Mr Balfour a persecutor of Jews?'

'Certainly not, but he believes – very properly in my view – that the Jews should be sent to Palestine, not come here.'

At that moment, to the relief of both Mr and Mrs Yewsley, the conversation was cut short by the hired butler announcing 'Ladies and gentlemen, luncheon is served.'

They all sat down to a lunch which, provided by the outside caterers, was easily the most lavish seen by either the host and hostess or the majority of the guests. Most, not excluding the Yewsleys, were bemused by the complicated array of cutlery and glasses. They only came to terms with it by covertly watching and following Sir George and Lady Robson. Sir George was very aware of and happy with their attention, which he took as gratifying evidence of his social superiority.

William Yewsley was worried that Sir George would raise the subject of his cold reception. To his immense relief, the matter did not come up. Robson had of course noticed, but he knew that it denoted wider problems than could be resolved by any chat round that lunch table. This was the last of his visits to his collieries. His reception at every one had been cold and, at more than one, openly hostile. He was shrewd enough to gauge that it was more than antipathy simply because he was the colliery owner, an indication, among other straws in the wind, that feeling was running against the government he supported. There was unrest everywhere. The government itself was deeply divided between those who supported free trade and those who wanted preference given to imports from the territories of the British Empire. The omens were not good.

When the party emerged after the lengthy lunch, there was still a crowd outside in the warm summer sunshine. Many had brought sandwiches, although a not inconsiderable minority had eaten nothing, while the official party had regaled themselves inside the house. There was the same stony silence as before.

Gwynfor Morgan, for all his' self-control, could not keep down his anger as he compared the pinched, poorly-dressed people in the crowd with the well-fed revellers, flushed and garrulous from their lunch. In a sudden, impulsive gesture, wholly unpremeditated, he turned his back to them. Those closest to him promptly did the same and, in a sort of domino effect, so did everyone else as they became aware of what was happening.

'We turned our other cheeks,' thundered a lay preacher subsequently, blissfully unaware of the double-entendre and mystified for life by the suppressed giggles in the congregation.

Sir George ignored the demonstration, shaking hands with Mr and Mrs Yewsley and the guests. He and his wife entered the motor car to be driven back to Swansea, there to entrain for a short visit to Squire Hatherly before returning to their London home. The crowd dispersed, satisfied that they had made their point. With the departure of the motor car, the extra police who had been brought in also departed, having had the sense to stay at a discreet distance as requested. Hymie Ginsberg stood outside his shop, glaring, waiting for the car to pass before taking down his poster.

'I must say, Margaret,' William Yewsley told his daughter disapprovingly, 'that I thought you were a little forward towards Sir George.'

'The old boy didn't seem to mind,' said Will junior. 'I reckon he even fancied Marg a bit.'

'Really Will,' his mother remonstrated. 'That is no way to talk about either Sir George or your sister. Please try to behave in a more gentlemanly way.'

'Well,' Margaret said with some spirit, 'if I hadn't asked about the Aliens Act, nobody would have had the faintest idea what he was talking about. Somebody had to say something that wasn't entirely sycophantic.'

'Don't talk in that tone,' her father said. 'We all owe our livelihood to his enterprise.'

'Enterprise rewarded with a knighthood from His Majesty,' her mother remarked. 'It's the first time I've ever met a real knight, and in our own home, too.'

'Reward for enterprise in the shape of exploiting all of us so that he can make huge profits while he toils not neither does he spin,' Margaret retorted.

'Don't you quote the Bible at me, miss,' her father said. 'I should never have allowed you to go to hear that Methodist preacher.'

Margaret seized the opportunity. 'Did you see how Mr Morgan turned his back? And how everybody else did the same when they caught on?'

'Disgraceful conduct for a man who is an ordained minister, even in that church.'

'I don't know. Given the grievances the men have, I think it's entirely understandable. What's more, if it had not been for Mr Morgan's sermon last Sunday, things could have been a lot worse.'

'Don't you argue with me about things you don't understand. That's the end of the matter.' He was getting annoyed. What were things coming to when a daughter could speak to her father in such a manner?

Both Margaret's parents were worried about their elder daughter. She was a good-looking girl for whom they had high hopes of a good marriage. They had in mind the son of the manager of another nearby colliery, who was already a qualified mining engineer with every prospect of a successful career ahead of him. Several meetings had been engineered between the two and it was clear that the young man was smitten, but Margaret, who had a mind of her own, had not responded. Her parents would be really alarmed if they knew that she was already turning over plans in her mind as to how she might meet 'that preacher' again.

A few days later, a letter from Margaret was delivered to the minister's lodgings. She wrote that she had appreciated his sermon and the part he had played in preventing any violence. She asked that if he wished to reply, would he do so in the form of a poste restante letter which she would collect from the post office as her father did not know that she was writing and would be 'upset' if he did. She was not prepared to admit, even to herself, but the spellbinding sermon had stirred up an attraction such as she had not before felt towards any man, while, her nature being what it was, her father's hostility had served only to strengthen her feelings. Her father did not understand her sufficiently to realise that he was producing the opposite effect to what he wanted.

Gwynfor Morgan was agreeably surprised to receive the letter and replied immediately to thank her. She had been pointed out to him that Sunday morning in the chapel and he had been intrigued. He had also seen her standing in the background when Sir George Robson had departed from her father's house and, when he turned his back on the mine owner, he had found himself regretting that he was also turning his back on her.

He reflected, when he posted the letter, with other mail, that he could have saved the stamp by handing it in at the post office, but he knew that such a course of action would set tongues wagging, and the last thing he wanted was to cause any embarrassment to Miss Yewsley. Unfortunately, he reckoned without the eagle-eyed Miss Evans. She recognised the writing, and within days it was around the village that Mr Morgan was writing 'secret' letters to the mine manager's pretty daughter.

Inevitably, the news reached her father through his eager network of informers, and he confronted her at the breakfast table.

'I have reason to believe,' he said, 'that you have been exchanging letters with that Methodist preacher.'

'I wrote to thank him for his help in preventing trouble when Sir George and Lady Robson were here,' Margaret said, 'and he wrote back, like a proper gentleman, to thank me for my letter.'

'I forbid you to have anything whatever to do with him.'

'I won't be forbidden from doing anything,' she replied, reddening.

'Oh yes you will! You remember, miss, that until you are twenty-one, you are in my care and my control.'

'Well, I shall be twenty-one in a few months, so you had better get used to not ordering me about.'

Mrs Yewsley intervened, hoping to calm things down. She was as alarmed as her husband at the conduct of their headstrong daughter, not least because, for her, any association between a young, unmarried woman and a young, unmarried man ought to be strictly chaperoned and could not take place in any context other than as a prelude to marriage.

'Really Margaret,' she said, 'it's not proper for you to associate with a man like that. He's not only a chapel person but, not many years ago, he was just a pit boy.' If it was an attempt to pour oil on troubled waters, it was more akin to throwing a match on petrol.

'I know it was before my time,' Margaret said angrily, 'but there was a time when father was just a pit boy.'

Her father shouted, 'I've spent all my life working so that my family should have something better than I started with, not for my eldest daughter to throw herself away on some penniless preacher.'

'Mr Morgan has also bettered himself and he had to contend with being unjustifiably put out of work by you and being blacklisted on your instigation in every pit in the coalfield!'

'Go to your room, miss,' her father shouted. When he was really angry with his offspring, he always addressed them as 'miss' or 'sir'.

'No, I won't. I'm tired of being ordered about and having my whole life arranged by you. I'm not one of your miners.' She flounced out of the room, but certainly not to go to her own.

A greater altercation was only avoided because her father had to leave the house to go to his work, but a rift had been opened between father and daughter which could only deepen, much to the distress of the mother.

The Reverend Morgan's lodgings were at the substantial home of Mr and Mrs Thomas Jones. Mr Jones, a pillar of the Methodist Church, was the proprietor of a successful drapery and outfitters. The Jones had a daughter whom they had named Marigold Miriam. Both mother and daughter were supremely good seamstresses, whose skill brought customers from throughout the valley. It was to them that Mrs Yewsley had gone for her new dress for Sir George and Lady Robson's visit.

With the arrival of the unmarried young minister, Mr and Mrs Jones had started to entertain hopes that a match might be made between him and their daughter. As thrifty tradespeople, they always took money into account and they reasoned that although Mr Morgan would never be well off, that would not be an impediment because Marigold could look forward to a modest income from the business.

Marigold had a brother, who was heir to the business. He was named Abraham Lincoln Jones, after the assassinated American president, whom Mr Jones admired as one of the greatest Christian gentlemen and martyrs of the nineteenth century. The name was an embarrassment to the young man, who was called Abe by his friends and went to great lengths to conceal his middle name. Many of his friends were in the rugby club and they included the mine manager's son, Will Yewsley.

Will's attention had been attracted to the talented and nubile

Marigold. He had devoted much effort to using his friendship with her brother as a means to strengthen his acquaintance with her but with no success. Part of the problem was that Mr Jones senior did not approve of the Yewsleys. His son's acquaintance with the younger Yewsley via the rugby club was one thing but it was a very different matter where his daughter was concerned.

Mrs Yewsley's decision to order her very special new dress presented an opportunity her son lost no time in exploiting. He quickly offered to accompany her to the shop to discuss the order and for the several subsequent fittings, thereby establishing acquaintance with both Marigold and her mother. He directed all the charm of which he was capable towards both and, to his delight, Marigold seemed responsive. Her response did not go unnoticed by her mother, who, shortly after Sir George Robson's visit, raised the matter with her husband.

'I believe, Tom,' she said, 'that Marigold is quite attracted to that young man and, I must say, he seems a nice boy.'

'I've seen how he has been doing everything he can to attract her,' replied her husband, 'and you too, for that matter. But that doesn't alter the fact that he is a Yewsley and his father is a very unpleasant man.'

'Well maybe, but after all, Mrs Yewsley is a good customer. That dress was the most valuable single order we've ever had. Besides, there are the two daughters and, who knows, Mr Yewsley himself might want a suit made at some time – and so might Will.'

'Really Caroline, you almost seem to want to encourage him. What about Marigold and Mr Morgan?'

'Well, for all our efforts, I can't honestly see that Gwynfor and Marigold really have any special feelings for each other. Besides, young Mr Yewsley's financial future is likely to be much more promising than Gwynfor's.'

'Oh, have you been making enquiries? What work does he do, anyway?'

'He is a qualified mining engineer, like his father. He studied at college in Swansea and works at one of the pits down the valley – goes every day on the early train.'

'I'm surprised he isn't at the pit here, with his father.'

'His father wouldn't have him here, thinks it's much better for him to be at another pit, owned by another company.'

'Hm, so that he can learn to ill-treat the miners independently of parental influence, I suppose.'

'I know, Tom, that you are very suspicious but I was thinking that we might ask Abraham to bring him here for tea next Saturday afternoon. They've got a rugby meeting to talk about next season's matches and they could come here afterwards.'

'I believe he's a regular player in the first team. At least that's a point in his favour, but I am not happy about him coming here.' He could see, though, that there was a glint in his wife's eye and a note in her voice that he knew of old. 'Oh well, all right if you insist, but I shan't be here.'

So it was that Will achieved an important advance, welcomed into the Jones household, warmly by Marigold and her brother, cautiously by her mother and not at all by her father, who absented himself on more urgent business at the shop, not unreasonably, since somebody had to be there on the busiest day of the week. Mrs Jones took good care to ensure that the Reverend Morgan was also there, so that she could gauge her daughter's attitude to both young men when both were present.

Marigold handed round the tasty home-made Welsh cakes upon which her mother prided herself, while Mrs Jones poured the tea.

'I do hope, Mr Yewsley,' she said, 'that your mother was happy with the dress we made for her.'

'She was very happy,' he replied. 'The dress suited her beautifully and Lady Robson herself complimented her on it.' Mrs Jones simpered, as wild but unattainable visions flashed through her mind of future orders from Lady Robson.

'I do hope,' Gwynfor said, with genuine feeling, 'that your father is not still angry over the reception Sir George received.'

'He's not very happy but he'll get over it, and I doubt if Robson was altogether surprised. In fact, it seems that he had much rougher receptions at some of his other collieries.'

'I expect you know,' Gwynfor said, 'that your sister, Miss Margaret, was kind enough to write to me to thank me for the sermon I gave.'

'Yes, I do know. I'm afraid there was a terrible row with my father over that. They are still hardly speaking to each other.'

'I am so sorry,' Gwynfor said, obviously concerned. 'The very last thing I would ever wish is to be a cause of friction between father and daughter.'

'Oh, there's more to it than my sister's letter to you. It was an explosion that has been waiting to happen for some time. Margaret does not see eye to eye with my father on a lot of things – and he is a hard man.'

'As I know from bitter experience,' Gwynfor said sharply. Then, changing to a more conciliatory, tentative tone, 'I – er – suppose that it would not be advisable for me to intervene?'

Mrs Jones detected what she thought was almost a wistful tone in his voice. Oh dear, she thought, we've got something more complicated than I thought. Marigold is not interested in him but obviously interested in young Yewsley, and Gwynfor is interested in Margaret Yewsley.

Aloud, she said, 'Perhaps you might like to visit us again, Mr Yewsley, and bring your sister.' She said it rather unthinkingly and the complications such an invitation could create dawned on her as she spoke. 'I shall, of course, have to speak to my husband,' she added hastily. 'I am afraid that he does not like your father and – er – I believe your father – er – dislikes Mr Morgan.' Her voice trailed off.

'Even more complicated than Romeo and Juliet,' Will said cheerfully.

'I'm sorry.' She looked blank.

He realised he had blundered and tried to retrieve the situation. 'Shakespeare,' he said, 'Young lovers, hostile families.'

It did not help. Mrs Jones knew little about Shakespeare, and what little she knew, she did not like. She had been brought up on Dr Thomas Bowdler's *Family Shakespeare*, in the firm belief that Shakespeare in the original was too coarse and indecent to be read by God-fearing, decent people. She found the expression 'young lovers, hostile families' quite disturbing.

Gwynfor intervened. He had been lodging long enough at that house to know something of Mrs Jones's reading habits and views on literature. He did not want the possibility of meeting Margaret Yewsley to slip away because of an argument that he saw as basically absurd.

'Romeo and Juliet is a deeply moving story of human relationships in tragic circumstances,' he said. 'A great, tragic piece of theatre, but it is a play, a work of fiction, which we should not relate too closely to our own, real life experience.'

'I hope,' Mrs Jones said, 'that it does not contain the sort of thing that Dr Bowdler drew attention to.'

'Not to my knowledge,' said Gwynfor, who, like all of them, had neither read nor seen any performance of the play. 'But it has to be pointed out that there are some parts in the Holy Bible itself which could well not meet with Dr Bowdler's approval.'

Will was trying not to smile. Marigold intervened quickly. 'I do hope that you will come again, Mr Yewsley, and I would love to meet your sister.'

'Me too,' said Gwynfor, just a shade too hastily. 'That is, of course, subject to Mr Jones's agreement.'

'I will of course speak to my husband,' Mrs Jones said, thankful that the conversation had come back to respectability, 'but I am sure, Mr Yewsley, that he would join me in welcoming you here again and with your sister.'

'You are all most kind,' Will said. 'I am afraid that I must be leaving. Thank you so much, Mrs Jones, for your hospitality and kind invitation to come again and to bring my sister and thank you, Abe, for introducing me into your home. Mr Morgan, it has been a real pleasure to meet you. I look forward to seeing you again and I know my sister will be delighted to meet you. Miss Marigold, I look forward to seeing you again. Thank you, everyone.'

The speech was a master stroke. It left everyone happy. Gwynfor decided then and there that he would take 'Thou shalt love thy neighbour as thyself' as the text for the sermon he had to prepare for the following day.

Margaret's twenty-first birthday brought things to an explosive climax.

By then, her relations with her father had deteriorated almost to vanishing point and the situation was a matter of serious concern to a troubled Mrs Yewsley. Margaret had taken to regular attendance at the chapel services, as well as to visiting the Jones household, always accompanied by her brother.

Mr and Mrs Yewsley were privately agreed that Marigold would be by no means an unsuitable match for Will. They thought that, although it might be socially unpalatable for him to marry into a Nonconformist family, it was something they would be able to live with, provided, as Mr Yewsley said, that his family would not have to be subjected to the attentions of 'Bible punchers'. They themselves, were nominal adherents to the Anglican Church but far from regular attenders at services or any other church functions.

But the idea of Margaret marrying Gwynfor Morgan was anathema. In her father's view, the fellow was nothing less than the dangerous agitator he had always been. He actually called himself a Christian Socialist. Furthermore, he could never expect to have an income coming anywhere near to what they had always envisaged as being earned by Margaret's future husband.

Ironically, there was one unexpected spark of light. The young man whom they had in mind, the son of a fellow colliery manager, disappointed by Margaret's lack of response to him, had rebounded by showing a lively interest in her sister, and Alice, two years Margaret's junior, had shown that she was by no means uninterested.

The young man was present at the twenty-first birthday celebration, held at the Yewsley home. Marigold Jones was present but, unsurprisingly, and to Margaret's suppressed fury, Gwynfor Morgan was not. For all the congratulations and good wishes, the atmosphere which should have been so jolly seemed tense and unreal. When they finished eating, Mr Yewsley rose to propose what proved to be a very perfunctory toast to his daughter. She was very nervous as she made what was obviously a carefully rehearsed reply. It was delivered slowly and deliberately, not so much for effect, but because she was anxious to make it word perfect.

'I want to thank my mother, especially, and my father for all they have done for me,' she said, 'and to thank everyone for their lovely presents.' There was a long pause before she continued. 'I do hope that what I am going to say will not cause distress. Yesterday, the Reverend Gwynfor Morgan proposed marriage to me and I accepted him.'

She sat down to a stunned silence, finally broken by her brother

'Congratulations,' he said in a strangled voice,' I do hope you will be happy.'

'Oh my dear,' her mother said, 'I do hope you know what you are doing.'

Her father rose from the table. 'I suppose I should have expected something like this.' He was shaking with anger. 'You could scarcely have chosen a worse time publicly to insult me in my own home. You will pack your things and leave this house. You can go to your paramour.'

He left the room. For perhaps the first time in his life, he knew that he had lost a battle where victory meant everything to him.

Will, galvanised, spoke up. 'You go too far, Father,' he shouted after him. 'Mr Morgan is no paramour. He is a Christian gentleman of the highest standards.'

Mrs Yewsley got up to follow her husband, not because she wanted to demonstrate any sharing of his feelings but because she knew that he needed to be comforted. She recognised that beneath the fury and, as he saw it, humiliation, he was profoundly sad. Her instincts were right. When she found him in another room, for the first time in all the years she had known him, she saw tears in his eyes.

Back in the dining room, the young man whom they had once had in mind as Margaret's future husband said, 'I think that it will be best if we leave.' It was clear that everyone agreed, deeply shocked and embarrassed.

Will escorted Marigold out of the house. 'I'll take you home,' he said.

'We could take Margaret in,' she offered. 'As you know, it's quite a large house and I'm sure I can persuade my parents to agree.'

'I can only apologise,' Will said, 'My father's conduct was inexcusable. I am so sorry that you should have to witness something like that – and at what should have been a happy occasion.'

'That's all right. I know that your father is very upset – and, after all, it wasn't the best way for Margaret to behave. Oh Will! I am so sorry.'

He could see how upset she was. There was suddenly a hugely increased bond between them and they moved mutually into each other's arms. It was not the first time he had kissed her but it aroused her strongest and most prolonged response. Suddenly, he felt in another and better world.

'Will you marry me?' he asked breathlessly.

'Of course I will.' They engaged in an even more emotional embrace.

'I shall have to ask your parents, especially as you're only nineteen.'

'Fine,' she said. 'Let's ask them straight away.'

Her father opened the door to them. Her mother was standing behind him in the hall, both of them surprised at seeing the couple.

'Why are you so early?' her mother asked. 'We had not expected you for at least another hour.'

'I am afraid,' Will told her, 'that the evening has been a terrible disaster.'

'Oh dear, what has happened? You'd better come in and tell us.'

Will and Marigold, although bursting to tell their own news, recounted the events at the birthday party.

'Oh my dear,' Mrs Jones said to her daughter. 'What a terrible business. Of course Margaret can come here, at least temporarily. But we had no idea that Gwynfor had proposed to her. We saw that things were moving that way but I know Gwynfor was hoping that something like this could be avoided. I am sure that he will have been looking for a way to speak to Mr Yewsley. He's out on chapel business at the moment but he'll be very upset over Mr Yewsley's reaction.'

'I'm afraid he's not the only one,' Will said grimly. Although well aware of his father's strong feelings, he had been shocked at his reference to Gwynfor Morgan as Margaret's paramour, which he knew to be totally unjustified. He thought that Margaret, strong-willed as she was, ought not to have made her announcement either at the time or in the way that she had, but that, in his view, did not justify his father's slur on her and on Gwynfor.

'We've got some good news for you,' he said, taking Marigold's hand.

Marigold could contain herself no longer. She burst out 'Mam and Dad, I want to marry Will. He has just proposed to me and I have accepted him. Please give us your blessing.'

'Please sir,' Will added at once, 'I would like to ask your permission to marry Marigold.'

Although her parents had been expecting something of the sort in due time, the suddenness took them by surprise. Allowing for the fact that their quiet evening had been interrupted by two dramatic and life-changing announcements within minutes, they behaved with remarkable aplomb. They exchanged glances. Mrs Jones gave an approving nod. Everyone knew then that the matter was as good as settled. Recovering from his initial surprise, Mr Jones decided that it was essential to behave in the correct manner.

'I take it, Mr Yewsley,' he said, 'that you can keep my daughter in the style to which she is accustomed.'

'I'm sure I can, sir. I am a qualified mining engineer, and I would hope in due course to become a pit manager.'

'Less dictatorial than your father, I would hope. Well, Mrs Jones and I have seen how things have been going between you two and I am happy to give my permission. My wife and I would, however, wish you to wait a while, until Marigold is twenty.'

'Of course, sir.' The two men shook hands. Marigold embraced her father and her mother, and Mrs Jones allowed Will briefly to kiss her cheek.

Margaret moved into the house the following day, but living in the same house as Gwynfor, notwithstanding that nothing of the slightest impropriety occurred between them, was untenable. It was instantly a matter of at best sniggering and at worst scurrilous gossip. She moved again in a few days to other lodgings, found for her by Mr Jones through the good offices of a fellow member of the congregation.

Accompanied by Gwynfor, she went to her old home to collect such belongings as she had not been able to carry when she left. They thought it best to go when they knew her father would be at the pit. There were tears from her mother and sister, but they were civil enough, if awkward, towards Gwynfor. He left a letter for her father, formally announcing their betrothal. When her father came home, he read the letter and tore it up.

Since she was more or less penniless, Mr Jones offered her a position in the shop. She had never gone out to work and found it hard, especially as, having no experience, she could be little better than a general dogsbody. But she accepted the position gratefully, fully aware that it was not without value as experience for the very different new life she had chosen. The shop also provided a suitable place for regular contact with her mother and sister. Her father remained adamantly aloof. That was hurtful and disappointing for her and Gwynfor but it served to strengthen their love for each other.

Neither of the two weddings announced on that traumatic evening could take place for some time. Will and Marigold's marriage was delayed for months because of the agreement that she would not marry until she was twenty, Gwynfor and Margaret's because they felt that it would not be proper for it to take place too quickly after its tumultuous announcement.

There was also the question of where Gwynfor and Margaret would live. It was considered only proper that a married minister should have his own house, usually rented from the church at a nominal rent. As no such accommodation was available, Gwynfor instituted enquiries about moving to another location but, given the relatively short time he had been at Penduffryn, the church authorities could not see their way to move him for at least another year.

Not long after the birthday party, a letter arrived asking William Yewsley to go to Cardiff to meet Sir George Robson to discuss a new appointment. The letter was not specific but the tone suggested promotion. He duly met his employer at one of the best hotels in the city. Robson opened the conversation.

'You have now been manager at Penduffryn for twelve years.'

'Yes, Sir George.'

'And you were with this company for quite a long time before that. You have worked your way up the ladder with commendable success.'

'It has not been easy; ours is a hard business, but I have stuck at it.'

'And you have produced good profits at Penduffryn, even when things have been difficult.'

'I have always tried my best to serve the company's interests.'

'You know that I own seven pits in south Wales and half a dozen more in the north east of England.'

'Yes, I am aware of that.'

'I also have a number of other business interests and it takes up a lot of time. I want to devote more time to family and social matters, especially as my daughter is now the Countess of Cottingham and moves in society, so I am going to delegate more. I am appointing an area mines manager in the north east and another in south Wales. You will be taking the Welsh post.'

'I shall be honoured to accept, Sir George.'

'It will mean moving to Cardiff,' Robson continued. 'All the Welsh managers will report directly to you. There will be a substantial improvement in salary, and a good house will be provided for you in a good part of Cardiff.'

'When do you wish me to start?'

'Straight away. I have someone in mind to take your place at Penduffryn, and you will start organising the new arrangements so that you will be here in Cardiff by Easter of next year. I'll take you now to the new office, where your secretary is already in place and awaiting your instructions. Then, before you leave, we'll go and have a quick look at your new house.'

Yewsley's pleasure at this substantial promotion did not prevent him from reflecting sardonically that there was no question of asking if he would accept, or if he had any questions. All the arrangements had been worked out in advance and it was simply a question of telling him. If he did not accept without question, he would most likely be out altogether. The higher you climbed, the further you had to fall, unless you owned the ladder.

He had, of course, long forgotten the interview in his office, three years earlier, but the situation, although at a higher level in the hierarchy, was not entirely different from when he had peremptorily told Hugh Hughes that he would start work by sorting the dirt from the coal.

'So that's settled,' Sir George said. 'I understand that you are having some trouble with a wayward daughter.'

'I was not aware that you knew about that.' Bitterly, he added, 'But then, everybody in the coalfield seems to know about it by now. But I would not want, Sir George, to trouble you with my domestic problems.'

'Pretty girl,' Robson said. 'I remember meeting her at your house. Bright, too, as I recall.'

'It is a matter of deep distress that she insists on marrying so unsuitably.'

'I believe the fellow was an agitator in the 1893 dispute.'

'The fellow still is an agitator. Now preaches agitation from a pulpit. Actually admits, as if it was something to be proud of, that he is a Socialist.'

Sir George spoke sharply. 'This damn socialism is spreading all too far. We've got to stamp it out. You know, there is actually one in the House of Commons. Scotsman called Keir Hardie, elected for Merthyr Tydfil here in Wales. A jumped-up ex-pit boy.'

It did not escape William Yewsley that the description might equally be applied to himself. Arguably more so, since he received a salary, whilst Keir Hardie was not paid as a Member of Parliament.

'I have heard of him,' he said. 'He seems to be a hero among the miners.'

'Some hero,' Robson said. 'When the King's grandson was born – our future King Edward VIII – he actually opposed sending a message of congratulations to Queen Victoria. Actually said, among other things, that the boy would grow up to be unfit to reign and that there would be rumours of a morganatic marriage.'

'I recall that royal birth.' Yewsley was not entirely able to keep a measure of irony out of his voice. 'It was the same day as the explosion in the pit at Cilfynydd, when over two hundred miners were killed.'

'I do hope you can sort something out concerning your daughter,' Robson said, turning the conversation back to what he considered to be more important.

'I doubt it. She is absolutely determined to go ahead with this marriage and as she is twenty-one, I have no power to stop it.'

Sir George Robson suddenly became uncharacteristically ruminative. 'Funny thing, love,' he said. 'You know, when I married, my wife's family were dead against it. They despised me because I was not "a gentleman". My wife was a spirited girl, though, like your daughter. She was over twenty-one and she stood out against them. Even then, I could have bought them out and, even now, if it wasn't for the settlement I made on my wife, they couldn't live in the style to which my money has accustomed them. Bastards!'

William Yewsley was non-plussed and not a little annoyed. 'I would not wish to draw any parallel between my daughter and Lady Robson,' he said stiffly.

Robson backtracked hastily. 'Of course not,' he said. 'I did not mean to make any comparison. It's just that my wife's family always bring out the worst in me. I apologise.' It was an exceptional occasion. He rarely apologised to anybody for anything.

Yewsley returned to Penduffryn feeling pleased with himself, to start the complex business of winding up one job, moving house and preparing for his new post. He reflected that he had probably reached the zenith of his career, but how sad that it coincided with all the trouble with his daughter. Strange, he thought, how Sir George had brought up the circumstances of his own marriage.

As for Sir George, he shortly afterwards found himself with even more time to devote to his family and his ambitions in high society than he had anticipated. He was swept out of Parliament in the great Liberal landslide of 1906, whilst the hated Keir Hardie was triumphantly re-elected at Merthyr to become leader of a new, twenty-nine-strong Parliamentary Labour Party.

Gwynfor and Margaret's wedding took place shortly before he was moved elsewhere in the coalfield. The timing was considered ideal because there had been a suitable interval since the announcement of their engagement and also because it was appropriate for him to take up his new appointment as a married man. There was a large turnout of well-wishers for the wedding and widespread regret at his departure.

Margaret's father refused to attend the wedding, leave alone give her away, and she was led down the aisle by her brother. By that time, her father had left to take up his new post in Cardiff. There was no more regret at his departure than welcome for his successor, an equally hard man transferred from another of the Robson collieries.

Marigold reached her twentieth birthday a few weeks afterwards and she and Will were then married. Gwynfor and Margaret were among the guests, Will's father was also there but he refused to speak to either of them. Will and Marigold moved down the valley to live near Will's work. Marigold's skill as a seamstress was much missed by her parents.

Chapter 8

Twenty-first birthdays were important occasions. This was decades before the term teenager entered the language with all its connotations, and twenty-first birthdays were the time of 'coming of age', the time of full, responsible and independent manhood or womanhood, the time when you were given the key of the door, so that you could, in theory, come and go as you pleased. But you were much less likely to have such a privilege conferred if you were a newly adult woman than if you were a man. In other aspects, too, the fullness and independence of your life, male or female, was more a matter of theory than of practice.

By the time Hugh Hughes came of age, in 1911, he was an experienced miner, respected as good at his job by his workmates, always the most searching judges of the competence of colleagues. There was even talk that in due course he would take over from Dai horses when Dai retired. But Dai's retirement was a long way off, so there was little scope there for fulfilment.

In the eyes of his employers, he was no more than an anonymous 'hand', part of the necessary equipment to run the colliery as cheaply and profitably as possible and easily dispensed with if they thought fit. He could be dismissed and left to his own devices if an accident disabled him and made him unprofitable. There was a workmen's compensation act, but in practice it was little more than useless.

Accidents happened all the time, although the pit was supposed to have a good record because only a small number of men and boys had been killed there. In the year before he became twenty-one, nearly a hundred and fifty had been killed in a single day in a pit at Whitehaven in north west England. The year before that, nearly a hundred and seventy had died in an explosion in a pit at Stanley, in County Durham.

The threat of damage to the lungs through prolonged breathing of the dust in the pit was ever present. It was something of a mystery as to why some were affected and others not. Some seemed to be unscathed through a lifetime of work, others became badly disabled, gasping to breathe, incapable even of walking any distance, old before their time and dead before their time.

Protests were dealt with severely. Six months before his coming of age, six hundred police had been sent from London and put under military command to attack striking miners. Penduffryn had not been involved but, not far away, there had been ten days of fighting and a miner had been killed. At Tonypandy, the miners had been rounded up by soldiers with what the commanding officer, General Neil Macready, described as 'a little gentle persuasion with the bayonet'.

So much for the fulfilment and independence of adult life.

By and large, Hugh took such things in his stride with all the confidence of youth. But as he had grown through adolescence, there had been other, more personal things that had troubled him. There had been those worrying erotic dreams, wet dreams as they were called. He slept in his underwear, the normal practice, and it embarrassed him that his sister, who did all the clothes washing, could not avoid seeing the stains on his underpants caused by his involuntary ejaculations.

There was also the disturbing, although sometimes exhilarating way his penis was liable to become erect without warning. There was no shortage of girls in the village, some of them pretty, and he had walked out a few times with several of them. He had not formed any particular relationship with any, but it alarmed him that his penis was always liable to become erect in the presence of a pretty girl, and she would subsequently feature in those embarrassing dreams.

No one, of course, had told him that such things were a normal part of growing up, to say nothing of nature's means of ensuring the continuation of the species. You never discussed such things with any member of the family or, for that matter, to any extent with anybody else. His sister May made occasional remarks about getting himself 'a nice young lady'. She obviously meant with a view to marriage, but he had no desire to marry any of the girls of his acquaintance.

Sex was an unfailing, if uninformed, topic of conversation among his workmates. There were those in his age group who constantly boasted about their alleged conquests. He came to the conclusion that those conquests existed almost entirely in their imaginations.

Sometimes, he reflected with amusement that his brother John really had made such a conquest, with the result of his accidental fatherhood, hurried wedding and banishment.

When he was sixteen, a young man had come to the village as an assistant to the barber. There was a certain air of effeminacy about him and he had a disconcerting habit of running his fingers through Hugh's hair rather more than seemed necessary.

'Lovely hair,' he said at the second time of cutting it. 'Lovely and thick and so dark – really black.'

'Yes,' Hugh said innocently. 'I inherited it from my dad. All my brothers have it too.'

'I bet you've got hair on your chest as well,' the barber said. There was a suppressed excitement in his slightly lisping, rather high voice and it made Hugh uneasy.

'Yes, I have,' he said, a little uncertainly.

His emotions were mixed. His brother-in-law, John, had remarked jokingly about it when they were taking their baths after coming off shift one day, as one of the things that separated the men from the boys. There had been something slightly disturbing about the way he said it but Hugh, although mildly embarrassed, did not take exception. It seemed to fit in entirely with the sort of 'man's talk' he was accustomed to in the pit. But he did not like the way the barber was talking. Then the barber did something to which he really objected. He put his hand on Hugh's groin.

'I bet you're big down there too,' he said.

'You can stop that as quick as you like,' Hugh said sharply. 'Get on and cut my hair.' His voice was sufficiently raised to cause several of the customers sat waiting in the shop to glance up from their newspapers and magazines.

'Oh, sorry I'm sure,' the barber said. 'No offence meant.'

Sitting in the other chair in the shop and being attended to by the proprietor was Dai horses. Hugh's haircut was finished first.

'Before you go, Hughie,' Dai said, 'hang on outside a minute. There's something I'd like to have a word about.'

Hugh waited outside. He had a great respect for Dai, who knew so much more and was so much wiser than most. He was like an older version of Hugh's knowledgeable school friend Robert Snape and had become something of a mentor to him.

'I saw what happened there,' Dai said. 'Don't worry about it, he won't trouble you again.'

'What's the matter with him?' Hugh asked.

'Oh well,' Dai said, 'he prefers boys to girls. He can't really help it. It's just the way nature has made him. I think he's harmless enough though.'

'He'd better not try anything on with me again,' Hugh said.

'He won't. He knows when to take no for an answer and he knows that he could go to prison for that sort of thing. Have you heard of Oscar Wilde?'

'Oh - yes.' Hugh. had heard of Wilde as the butt of obscene jokes.

'He was that way,' Dai said. 'Sent to prison for it – hard labour. I doubt if he had to labour any harder than the men in the pits but, coming from his background, I don't suppose he had ever done any manual work before in his life. Terrible tragedy, brilliant writer ruined. After what happened, it'll be decades before his greatness comes properly to be recognised.'

By his late teens, Hugh had dropped out of attendance at the chapel and had taken, instead, to Sunday morning rambles on the mountains with like-minded workmates. He had lost interest in the chapel when, with the departure of the Reverend Gwynfor Morgan, a less charismatic minister had arrived. He felt more responsive to the fresh air and to the glories of the mountainous countryside than to the confines of the chapel, with its mostly tedious preaching.

When you spent so much of your life underground, it was marvellous to walk on the mountains, whatever the weather. It was a steep climb from the valley but the view from the top on a clear, sunny morning was superb. There were mountains all round, stretching north eastwards to the Brecon Beacons, which towered over the others, rising from the industrial haze of Merthyr, Aberdare and the Rhondda Valley. To the south, the waters of the Bristol Channel sparkled in the distance. It all exhilarated and inspired him, although he would have found it difficult to explain exactly why.

There had been great celebrations to mark his birthday with his sister, brother-in -law, neighbours and friends. Then he had gone to Pembroke Dock to stay a few days for further celebrations with his parents. With all but two of his elder brothers and sisters now married, he found himself with a bewildering array of young nephews and nieces. His two younger sisters, Alice and Myfanwy, were both engaged, Myfanwy to Robert Snape, her childhood sweetheart and Hugh's oldest friend.

Robert, just a few months his junior, was nearing the end of his apprenticeship at the dockyard and the wedding was planned to take place when he was twenty-one and became a journeyman receiving an adult wage.

The resourceful Robert had found another source of income. Always fascinated by everything around him and fond of writing, he had submitted a short article to the local weekly newspaper. To his surprise it had been accepted and, after submitting a further piece, he had been invited to write a regular short column.

The articles were written under a pen name and were commentaries on life in the county as he saw it. Their radical nature frequently aroused the ire of establishment-minded and letter-writing readers of the paper. One reason for disguising his identity was to protect himself from the victimisation he would have experienced in his job if he had been known to be the controversial columnist. He was lucky to have an unusually enlightened editor who, apart from having a dearth of writers and with space to fill, saw him as an asset in selling papers.

Although the payments were modest, they more than doubled his meagre earnings as an apprentice. He had been able to set something aside towards his forthcoming marriage as well as to help his deserted mother and, until they became wage earners, his two younger sisters.

His mother, who had worked so hard and for so little return as a charwoman, had achieved her ambition, modest in its way but immense to her, to live long enough to see her children become self-supporting and freed from the danger of having to enter the dreaded workhouse if she died prematurely. All trace had been lost of the husband who had beaten her and the children and then left them for another woman.

The dockyard was working flat out, as Robert explained to Hugh.

'It looks as if there's going to be a war,' he said. 'The German Kaiser is building up a big navy and, although we've already got the biggest navy in the world, we are building it up still bigger to warn him not to make trouble.'

But if there was some measure of what passed for prosperity at the dockyard, the situation in farming was desperate after four decades of agricultural depression. Hugh made a quick visit to his brother

Matthew at Old Oak Farm and was disturbed by what he found. Matthew no longer seemed to be the protective big brother who had stood up for him against the surly Kramer family when he had been a farm boy.

The earlier owners of Old Oak, Mr and Mrs Leeming, who had employed Matthew as a boy and whose adopted daughter Lydia he had married, had both died, leaving the farm to Matthew. He, a born farmer, had improved and enlarged the farm in the face of all the difficulties of the times, not least by several purchases of adjoining land from Squire Hatherly. Matthew was now the father of three children – a son, the eldest, and two daughters – and a fourth child was on the way. The two eldest were already at school.

'How do you work what's now becoming quite a big farm?' Hugh asked. 'I don't see any sign of any farm workers.'

'Farm workers! You won't see any sign of any of those. I can't afford to pay wages. I'm not made of money! Lydia and I and the children do the work between us.'

'But the two eldest are at school.'

'Yes, but they get up early and work on the farm before going to school and work when they come home. Even the little one, Angela, who hasn't yet started school, does her bit.'

To Hugh, it seemed shocking that young children should be used in such a way, to save the cost of employing labour, but he could see that to his brother it seemed to be a perfectly normal state of affairs.

'Round Pond Farm is going downhill all the time under the Kramers,' Matthew said. 'It's really sad when you consider how well run it was in Mrs Kramer's father's time. I reckon that within a few years, they'll be selling up. It'll go cheap and I shall be in the market to buy it.'

'Where will you find the money?'

'I'll probably take out another mortgage on this place. The bank ought to be all right, they know my credit is good. The thing is, though, that I shall want to buy the land as well, from Hatherly. That'll cost more.'

Hugh felt depressed. This hard, calculating individual seemed so different from the Matthew he remembered from earlier times.

At a higher level in the social hierarchy, things were not easy for Squire Hatherly. The land he had sold to Matthew was one of several sales he had made. For the most part, the land had been unproductive and was sold cheaply to farmers like Matthew who would put it to better use. What worried the squire was that almost all his tenant farmers were in financial difficulties, endangering his rents.

Fortunately, he had the continuing financial support of his sister. The settlement made on her by her husband all those years ago when they had married had been successfully invested and had grown considerably in value, producing an increased income. But it infuriated the squire that his despised brother-in-law was not only getting even richer but was now a knight of the realm. It was little less galling that his niece, the despised brother-in-law's daughter, was now no less than a countess.

The squire and his wife were still regular visitors to Sir George's London house, but they found themselves ill at ease in the sophisticated London society in which the Robsons now seemed to move with ease. They were more than suspicious that some of these haughty, self-appointedly superior people laughed at them behind their backs.

His only confidant in these matters was his old friend and neighbour Colonel Mulholland. The colonel, too, had his problems, mainly arising from prolonged indecision over what to do about his will in relation to his illegitimate grandson, Albert Mulholland Flowers.

The young man's benefactor, the wealthy retired iron master Henry Black, was now dead and, true to his word, he had bequeathed the bulk of his fortune to the young man, who, now in his late twenties, was master of substantial and profitable industrial concerns. With a successful inheritance behind him and every sign of further successful money-making before him, he was now on the lookout for a wife. His sole motivation was to father a family to succeed him. He did not intend to die childless like his benefactor.

Colonel Mulholland had maintained contact with his ambitious grandson. After a decade of indecision and only too conscious that he was now an old man, the colonel was more than ever exercised by the matter of the succession to his estate. The only other subject that exercised him was fury at the policies of the Liberal government. If there was one thing above all others he liked about his grandson, it was that his views on that subject were identical.

Henry Black had died in 1908, the year when the government had introduced old age pensions at the princely rate of five shillings a week to those over seventy, and seven shillings and six pence to married couples, well aware that relatively few lived to or beyond seventy. Albert Flowers's reaction, shaped by his new responsibilities as a considerable employer of labour, had pleased the colonel.

'Depriving the working classes of incentive to save for their old age,' he had said.

By the time the National Health Insurance Act was working its way through Parliament, with its proposals to make it compulsory for workers and employers each to contribute a few pence a week, Albert was a fully established industrialist of some importance.

'An impossible burden,' he had declared. 'This government is putting ever bigger burdens on industry and weakening our ability to compete in world markets.'

Colonel Mulholland, notwithstanding an innate contempt for middle–class trade as opposed to what he felt to be divinely ordained aristocratic landowning, had warmed towards his grandson and had conveyed those remarks to Squire Hatherly.

'Yes,' the squire had said, 'my brother-in-law confirms that exactly.'

'Damn government,' the colonel said, 'pampering the working classes. Do a damn sight more good if they made those bloody trade unions illegal.'

The Lloyd George budget of 1909, with its new taxes and death duties on the rich, raised the colonel's ire more than anything else and played its part in finally making up his mind about his will. With his hatred for David Lloyd George exceeding even that he had felt in earlier times for William Gladstone, he calculated that if his grandson inherited from him, at least he would have other income to maintain the house and the estate.

His sister, who had been the main obstacle to his intentions, had died. Her two daughters, for whom she had fiercely sought a share of the family fortune, had both made good marriages and so became a lesser factor in what the colonel saw as his difficult equation. A relatively minor bequest to each of them would square the circle, he thought, wholly unconscious of mixed metaphors. Then, another thought came to him. His grandson needed a wife, so that the line could be carried on. He had someone in mind.

'Do you expect your elder daughter to be marrying soon?' he asked Squire Hatherly, well aware of the expected answer.

'No, I am afraid not,' the squire replied. 'It's rather disappointing. As you know, my younger daughter is married, but I don't see any prospects for Alice. Unfortunately, she's not the best-looking of girls, but I hate the thought of her becoming an old maid.'

'I believe she is just a year younger than my grandson,' the colonel said.

The squire's eyes lighted up as he realised the line the conversation was taking. 'Yes,' he said, 'that is so and, of course, they have met several times when your grandson has been visiting.'

'I think we might arrange something.'

'But we don't know what either of them might think about such an arrangement.'

'That ought not to be an obstacle,' the colonel said. He went on in what he thought of as his characteristically forthright way. 'My grandson wants ability to breed rather than looks.' In a more ruminative tone, he added, 'My own marriage was largely arranged by my parents and it worked out well enough.' He paused. 'And I still do so miss my dear wife, even after all this time – and losing my son so shortly afterwards.' His voice trailed off in genuine sadness.

'My marriage was also really an arranged one,' the squire said, 'and it has worked out pretty well too.'

'I'll invite the boy down,' the colonel said. 'I'll give him some encouragement.'

'The boy' was duly invited. His mother and stepfather, who had also benefited from Mr Black's will, were not invited. But then, they never had been, since that traumatic day when they had first brought Albert to the colonel's home.

'I have decided,' the colonel told him, 'about my will. Apart from some fairly small bequests, I propose to make you my heir.'

'Thank you sir.' He had not been able to get out of the habit of addressing his grandfather as 'sir'. He regarded him as an increasingly doddering old buffer and not particularly bright, but wealthy and to be cultivated. He had waited a long time to hear this.

'There will, however, be certain conditions,' the colonel said.

'May I ask, sir, what they will be?'

'In the first place, you must legally change your name. I know your middle name is Mulholland but I want that perpetuated as your surname. I also want you to take your father's first name, Richard, which goes back generations in the family.'

'I see what you mean, sir.' He hesitated and went on with a note of compassion in his voice which the colonel had not expected but for which he felt a sneaking admiration. 'But I cannot abandon my mother's married name, nor my stepfather's, who gave me the protection of his name when I most needed it.'

He thought a moment, his brain working, as always, faster than his grandfather's.

'I know,' he said, 'How about Richard Albert Mulholland-Flowers, hyphenated?'

There was a silence as the colonel thought long and hard. Dammit, he decided, the boy knows what he's about. Must say, it sounds rather good.

Aloud, he said, 'Very well, we can agree on that.'

'Do I gather, sir, that there might be further conditions?'

'Yes, one other. You must marry. I have someone in mind.'

'Oh!' There was a pause. When the young man replied, there was a noticeable element of sarcasm in his voice. 'May I ask who is the young lady you have in mind? Do I by any chance know her?'

'Yes, you do. You've met her several times. It's Squire Hatherly's daughter Alice.'

'I see.'

The young man had not expected to be confronted so bluntly. His mind, as always, worked rapidly. He did not like being bounced into something so serious, and he did not feel any particular attraction to the young woman, who wasn't very good-looking. But then, he thought, I have been thinking about marriage and the old bugger knows it. And all this money at stake. Mentally, he took a deep breath. After all, if it doesn't work out, a chap can always find consolation elsewhere. He was more the son of his philandering father than he realised.

The colonel was speaking again. 'I have invited Squire and Mrs Hatherly to dinner tomorrow evening,' he said. 'Alice will be accompanying them. You will have the opportunity to propose. Her father has spoken to her and she will be expecting it.'

Thus the marriage came about. The proposal was one of the least romantic ever made and was accepted in the same spirit. The wedding, shortly afterwards, was a magnificent affair in the parish church at Pembroke, followed by a glittering reception at Bellwood House, one of the few properties in the area large enough to host it. Among the guests was the mother of the renamed Richard, splendidly dressed and accompanied by her husband Albert, magnificent in morning dress. Both were completely at ease in the exalted company and revelling in returning as important guests to the house from which they had been so ignominiously dismissed all those years earlier.

'I trust you are well, Talltree,' Albert said to the now aging butler, as he took a glass of champagne from the proffered tray.

'I am very well.'

Albert held the glass up to the light. 'Nice colour,' he said with the assured air of a man who was a connoisseur and knew it. He added casually, without taking his eyes off the glass he was inspecting, 'When I was Mr Black's butler, I always made a point of addressing his guests as "sir" or "madam".'

Talltree gritted what teeth he had left. 'Yes sir,' he said.

'Why, Talltree,' Mrs Flowers said, 'you've hardly changed at all.'

'Thank you – madam.' He made it the most icy expression of gratitude he could muster.

Sir George Robson made a point of talking to the bridegroom, his newly acquired nephew-in-law.

'I believe, Richard,' he said, 'that you have extensive interests in steel making and in engineering.'

'Yes Uncle George, that is so, although not maybe as extensive as yours in coal mining.'

'I also have interests in engineering. When you get back from your honeymoon, I would like to talk. Sooner or later, there's going to be a war, and there will be a big demand for armaments and plenty of profit to be made. Perhaps we might consider a partnership.'

Richard recognised a kindred spirit. 'As soon as I get back,' he said, 'let's arrange a meeting.'

According to the Greenwich Observatory, the summer of Hugh's twenty-first birthday was the hottest and driest in the seventy years they had kept records. South Wales sweltered and Penduffryn was stifling. The Sunday morning walks on the mountains had never been such a relief. High up, there was always a cooling breeze. The breeze, the scenery, the chat among friends, usually ribald, often lewd, all contrived to give a marvellous sense of release.

The chat revolved almost exclusively around happenings at the pit; the night before in the pub or in the miner's club; gossip about local people; whether such and such a local girl was worth pursuing; the, to them, hilariously long and undeveloped relationship between Dai horses and Blodwen Evans the post; the victories or defeats of the rugby team in the last season and its prospects for the next; whether the choir would get anywhere in competition with its numerous rivals; or the colliery band, something of a joke because its players, although dedicated, were more enthusiastic than competent.

This was their world, vibrant but limited nevertheless, and under the boisterous exchanges, often witty and penetrating, there was an underlying dissatisfaction. It arose from the narrow parameters within which their lives were conducted; from the restricted relationships between the sexes; from their dirty, dangerous and underpaid work; from the cramped little houses in the mean little streets they inhabited; from being at the bottom of a heap they had no hope of climbing.

Beneath the sunshine of that hot summer, they were part of the vast majority in the 'land of hope and glory' who had little share in the wealth and grandeur of the mighty British Empire. They were actually getting poorer – and they were increasingly aware of it.

Close to Penduffryn, there was a natural amphitheatre in the mountainside, a place with perfect acoustics, used from time to time for public gatherings. On one occasion, Keir Hardie had come there to speak. Almost the entire village seemed to be there, augmented by several hundred who had come from elsewhere in the valley.

Hardie was thunderously applauded. He had given them a vision of a future that could be made so much better, but only if they themselves had the will to make it so. Hugh went home moved and inspired; he was unable to sleep that night, kept awake by the turning over and over in his mind of what he had heard and the vision it had inspired. His attitude was shaped for life towards the society in which, like his father before him, he knew that he would have to fight all his life to survive.

He was a staunch member of the union, the South Wales Miners' Federation, although he was often disappointed that the local officials, his elders and betters as they were generally recognised and respected, seemed less enthusiastic for action than he and most of his mates. He supported the newly created Labour Party, although he had no right to vote. He was not one to get up and speak at meetings, but he had a strong sense of solidarity with his fellows. His work with the ponies took him to every part of the pit and had brought home to him that the conditions in some parts, where there was water and more slag in the coal, made it impossible for the miners to earn as much as others in less difficult locations although they had, if anything, to work even harder.

When a ballot was taken in every lodge throughout Britain for a strike in support of seeking a minimum wage of five shillings a day for underground workers, the vote was three to one in favour and he was one of the majority. When all efforts at negotiations with the mine owners broke down in the face of blank refusal, he was one of a million on strike throughout the country. It was the first time he had been involved in direct action, the first time there had ever been such a national stoppage.

'We've got to be prepared for anything,' said William Williams, the lodge secretary, known universally as Williams the union. 'If they send in the army, we may have to think of putting up barricades.'

'The last time we did that was in the '93 lockout,' said Dai horses. 'Here we are nearly twenty years later and, if anything, things are worse.'

Dai was management and not involved in the strike, but his sympathies were well known. Blodwen Evans the post, the apple of his eye, was not sympathetic. It was rumoured, although more maliciously than accurately, that she supported the Conservative Party, the ultimate sin in the eyes of the majority, and it was speculated, again without evidence, that that was the reason her relationship had never blossomed with Dai.

'They may not use troops,' said Williams. 'That Churchill, who was so fond of using them, has been moved from the Home Office to the Admiralty.'

The government, desperate to end the strike, drove a bill through Parliament, supposedly to force the mine owners to accept a minimum wage, but it was meaningless, with no reference to how much the minimum wage ought to be.

Hugh, with many others, felt angry and betrayed and, in a second ballot, he voted to stay on strike, ignoring the advice of the lodge secretary to vote for a return to work. Williams was a respected lay preacher as well as lodge secretary and wielded strong influence in the community. He was also a staunch Liberal.

'Look boys,' he told a crowded meeting in that natural amphitheatre in the mountain side, 'we owe it to our government to end the strike. They have put a bill through Parliament in only ten days to establish the principle of a minimum wage.'

It was one of the few occasions when Hugh was moved angrily to speak at a meeting.

'But they haven't put anything in it to say what the minimum wage ought to be,' he said. 'The Labour Party opposed it at every stage.'

Williams was crushing. 'The Labour Party, Hughie Penfro, is a bunch of agitators. They haven't been educated to govern. It's the Liberals and – although I hate their guts – the Conservatives who are born and educated and fitted to run the country.'

Hugh reddened, annoyed by the put-down. He could see any number of objections to what Williams had said, but he knew that he would get confused if he tried to voice them. It was clear, though, that there was sympathy for what he had said among many in the gathering.

In Wales, the majority, in tune with Williams's advice, voted to end the strike. In the country as a whole, a majority voted in favour of continuing, but it was judged insufficient and the strike ended, with little accomplished. Once again, Hugh, with many others, was left angry, frustrated and disillusioned.

His feelings were deepened the following year, when there was an appalling explosion in the pit at Sengenydd, not far from Penduffryn, the greatest pit disaster of them all, killing over four hundred, virtually wiping out the manhood of an entire village. The news was received in Penduffryn with dumbfounded shock. People gathered in little groups, shocked beyond measure in eerily silent streets.

'Dear God,' Hugh's sister May said, 'what have we done to deserve this?'

'We've allowed them to get away for too long without proper safety precautions,' Hugh replied. 'That's what we've done.'

'I suppose it's the will of God,' May said.

'Will of God be damned,' Hugh retorted, his feelings at boiling point. 'It's the bloody will of the bloody mine owners. Those bastards couldn't care less about the men as long as they're making money out of them.'

'Really, Hugh,' May said, 'I never thought to hear you use language like that.' It was something of a defining moment for both of them, the realisation that he was no longer just her little brother, but a grown man in his own right with his own opinions.

A special service was held at the chapel to mourn the dead. The austere building was packed to capacity. Hugh accompanied May and John. It was the first time he had attended in years. He was not there from any belief in any almighty, but solely to show respect for the dead and for their grieving relatives. It all added to the general sense of frustration and dissatisfaction he was coming increasingly to feel about life in general.

He had lost interest in his job. Each shift, he went through the motions mechanically. Outside work, he found it difficult to feel involved in anything. He was moody and depressed. What, he found himself wondering, is the point of it all? Farm boy to miner, full stop. It was not entirely surprising that, when Germany invaded Belgium and Britain declared war, he was caught up in the wave of jingoism that swept the country.

It confused him that, two days after war was declared, Keir Hardie made a speech in his nearby constituency, denouncing the war. He was not surprised that Hardie was shouted down and had to be protected by his friends from an angry mob. For his part, he was more in agreement with another famous Socialist, the writer H.G. Wells, who had said of the Germans that the time had come to be done for ever with this drilling, trampling foolery in the heart of Europe.

Hugh wanted to be a part of ending it. Everybody said it would be all over by Christmas. It gave promise. of adventure and a sense of purpose that he had never known before. He handed in his notice, went to the nearest recruiting office and joined the army.

He gave his next of kin as his father at the address in Pembroke Dock. His brother, Joe, the one who had always been fascinated by water, was by that time a deck hand on the trawlers working out of Milford Haven. He handed in his notice and joined the navy.

Joseph and Leah, their parents, felt a confused mixture of patriotic pride and uneasy dread of the consequences of their sons' precipitate action. It was a feeling not confined to those in their stratum of society. Squire and Mrs Hatherly, who were far greater stakeholders in that society, felt greater patriotism but a very similar anxiety for their younger son, now Lieutenant Jeremy Hatherly of the Royal Field Artillery. But Colonel Mulholland, nearing his eightieth birthday, had no doubts.

'Time to put down those damn Huns,' he said, reflecting the sentiment of H.G. Wells in less elegant language. 'They supported the Boers, who killed my son. That bloody Kaiser ought to be hanged after it's all over.' It was the first time in his life that his views had been ahead of those that would later be held widely among his fellow countrymen.

Richard, his grandson, already pleased because his plain wife was pregnant, felt even more pleased at thoughts of the profits likely to be made from armaments. His wife's uncle by marriage, Sir George Robson, with whom he had by then entered into a business partnership, looked forward to an increased demand for coal and to the war being an aid to keep those stroppy miners in their place.

In their different ways, Hugh and his brother, together with Sir George and his nephew-in-law, reflected the weight of feeling in a country which had never been more bitterly divided by its social system but was suddenly united in its determination to protect that system from a foreign enemy.

Chapter 9

Induction into the army proved to be very different from anything Hugh had expected – in so far as, in his innocence, he had entertained any realistic expectations at all. He was provided with an uncomfortable and ill-fitting uniform. The words of the quarter-master-sergeant in the clothing store lingered in his memory.

'If it fits, hand it back – it must be somebody else's.'

So far as the uniform was concerned, the winding of puttees round his lower legs proved to be one of the most difficult parts of getting properly dressed.

For preliminary training, he had been sent to Salisbury Plain, the first time he had been out of Wales. At the training camp, he had been bullied and abusively shouted at as if he was a criminal aiming to destroy his country rather than a citizen who had volunteered to lay down his life to save it.

He had not opted for any particular regiment and was drafted into the artillery, after an illuminating interview with a second lieutenant younger than himself, who had all the snotty superiority of the early twentieth century public schoolboy of the less intelligent kind.

'What did you do in civilian life?'

'I was a miner, sir.'

'You mean you actually hewed coal underground – with a pick and shovel?'

'No sir.'

'What did you do then?' It was asked with an underlying tone of 'Are you questioning my authority? And if you are, it'll be the worse for you.'

'I was a driver, sir.'

'A driver? What do you mean? What did you drive?'

'The pit ponies, sir, between the coal face and the cage.'

'What is the cage? Are you telling me that there are ponies in the mines and that they are kept in cages?'

'No sir. The cage is what takes the coal to the surface. The ponies are used to haul the coal from the face to the cage so that it can be taken to the surface.'

There was a pause, during which it was possible to imagine little wheels turning inside the lieutenant's head, rather like miniaturised versions of the pit-head winding gear, as he struggled to grasp what he had been told.

'So you have some experience with horses?' He pronounced it 'hawses'.

'Yes sir.'

Another pause, while the officer wrote something. It recalled Mr Yewsley, the mine manager, making a note when Hugh had told him that he had worked on a farm before seeking work in the pit.

'You'll be going into the field artillery. There's a need there for horse drivers.'

'Yes sir.'

The dim lieutenant had succeeded, accidentally and against all army tradition, in more or less putting a round peg into a round hole. It seemed that Hugh's father's decision to put him on a farm all those years ago was to shape his destiny as much in the army as it had in the pit.

For the first time, he now came into contact with young men of his own generation from all parts of the United Kingdom. He had difficulty with some of their accents, especially those from Clydeside and Tyneside, some of whom he found to be almost incomprehensible. He soon got used to being called Taffy or, more intimately, Taff. Soon, they all developed a universal camaraderie, contemptuous of the commissioned officer class and almost as full of hate for the regular army non-commissioned officers who were their trainers as for the German enemy.

From Salisbury Plain, he was sent to Ireland for further training in gunnery and horsemanship for, although he had more or less grown up with horses, he had always led and groomed them, never actually ridden them. At his initial attempts, he suffered several nasty falls. The NCOs responsible for his training were not amused.

'Who the fuckin' 'ell gave you permission to dismount?'

'No one, sergeant.'

'Then fuckin' well get back on that horse and if you dismount again without permission, you'll be in real trouble. Understand?'

'Yes sergeant.'

'And before you come back on parade, get that mud cleaned off your uniform and get those puttees wound properly or you'll be put on a charge for being improperly dressed. You're supposed to be a soldier in charge of horses, not a bloody, stupid, improperly dressed little prat rolling in the mud.'

The camp was situated somewhere to the west of Dublin, in what seemed to be the perpetually wet Irish countryside. In his rare off-duty hours, he sometimes went with his new-found mates to the nearby village.

'Village' was an exaggerated description of the place, for it consisted of little more than a collection of hovels, a couple of forlorn little shops, a pub and a church. The church and all the people were Catholic, another thing entirely new in his experience. The people seemed to have a habit of crossing themselves constantly, for no apparent reason. They also seemed in awe of the priest, who appeared in the village from time to time and who was not friendly towards the soldiers.

What shocked Hugh most of all was the all-round evidence of abject poverty. His own life had not remotely been one of any luxury, but he was appalled at what he saw now. The countryside was dotted with single-storey houses, pitifully small, grossly overcrowded and with bare earth floors. Their inhabitants, from children to grandparents, mostly wore no shoes and stockings. It seemed to be a normal part of the way of life for poultry and small farm animals to be in and out of the houses.

Not far from the village was a Georgian country mansion. It was owned by an English landowner who was absent for most of the year and who, the soldiers soon came to learn, was universally hated. He was currently in residence and the officers of the regiment were always welcomed at the house. The rank and file did not entertain any expectations of being invited even into the grounds.

Whenever the soldiers were in the village, there were always military police present. When the soldiers ventured into the village pub, they were met with a mixed reception. Few of the customers showed any friendliness and there was a general impression that their money, little as it was on a mere shilling a day, was more welcome than they were. One Saturday evening, an argument developed into a tragedy and brought home that the military police were not only there to keep the soldiers in order.

Hugh was there as one of half a dozen. A similar number of young

Irishmen came in and their hostile attitude became clear immediately.

'English bastards!' one of them said in a loud voice.

The soldiers instinctively gathered closer together but did not respond.

'English bastards! Get back to fuckin' England. You've done enough damage here already.'

'Who the fuckin' 'ell do you think you're calling an English bastard?' asked one of the soldiers in his broad Glaswegian accent.

'Or me, a Welshman for that matter?' Hugh added.

The Irishman turned on the Scot. 'Fuckin' Scottish Orangeman, I suppose,' he said. He stepped forward and spat. The Scot promptly hit him and there was a violent fight in progress within seconds.

It was broken up by the sudden appearance of two armed military policemen. One of them, a corporal, stopped the fight by the expedient of firing his revolver in the air, bringing down part of the pub's flimsy ceiling.

He shouted at the soldiers, 'You lot get back to camp. Now!'

He turned to the ragged group of young Irishmen. 'And you lot get back to whatever hovels you've come from. You ought to be in the army fighting for your King and country, not attacking these boys who are.'

'Bollocks!' said the ringleader who had started the affray. 'Fuck you and your fucking King and country.'

'You'll apologise for that or I'll arrest you on a charge of treason.'

'Just try.'

The military policeman lifted his revolver. 'I'm warning you,' he said.

With one accord, the Irish group tried to rush him. Without compunction, he shot the leader in the chest. The young man, his eyes filled with a mixture of disbelief and hatred, fell dying to the floor. The bullet, at point-blank range, had gone right through his body.

The military policeman and his companion pointed their guns menacingly.

'You lot get out of here and back to the camp,' he shouted at the soldiers. 'We'll accompany you for your own safety.' Having seen them outside, the two police backed out to join them.

'For God's sake,' Hugh said, still wiping a bloody nose, 'what are you going to do about him?'

'Nothing. Fenian bastards. Let them look after their own.'

It was a subdued group who made their way back to the camp, escorted by the military policemen. Hugh, who had grown up in a tough environment where it was far from unknown for striking miners to be shot at or beaten up by soldiers, was nevertheless deeply shocked by what he had witnessed, which he saw as little less than cold-blooded murder. It was a traumatic introduction to the conflict in Ireland that had gone on for centuries before he was born, would continue throughout what would prove to be his long life and would go on long after his death.

He assumed that it would be left to the unfriendly Irish priest, who seemed to rule everything in the neighbourhood, to give the dead man's family such comfort as he could and to arrange the funeral. No charges were brought against the soldiers but they were thereafter confined to camp. The two military policemen were quickly moved to another posting, in England. No reports of the shooting appeared anywhere and no evidence ever emerged that any inquiry had been conducted.

Hugh was sent home for Christmas, with orders to report at the end of his leave to a depot on Salisbury Plain, for transhipment to France.

By then, it was only too clear to all except the perennially naive, of whom there was no shortage, that it was going to be a long war. The great German offensive, which was supposed to encircle Paris and overwhelm France in a few weeks, had been fought to a blood-soaked standstill and the line of trenches to which he was to be sent stretched from the Belgian coast to Switzerland. He was trained, albeit perfunctorily, to fire a rifle, ride and control horses pulling field guns and to fire artillery pieces.

He arrived at Pembroke Dock in the dark evening of Christmas Eve, weary, fed up and weighed down by his greatcoat and his kitbag. His father was waiting for him at the station.

'Hello Hugh.'

'Hello dad.'

They shook hands. It was the first time he had ever shaken hands with his father. It had something to do, he felt sure, with the fact that it was the first time his father had seen him wearing uniform.

His youngest sister, Myfanwy, was also there with her husband, his old friend Robert. Everyone was muffled up against the cold, but from Myfanwy's appearance, it was clear that there would shortly be another Snape, yet another niece or nephew for Hugh. Myfanwy hugged him.

'Got a bun in the oven, I see,' he said. He had picked up the expression from other soldiers. He saw that the vulgarity startled his father, but Myfanwy laughed.

'About six weeks to go,' she said.

'How's the army?' Robert asked.

'Oh, all right.' He was aware that he did not sound entirely convincing.

'I thought about joining up,' Robert said.

Myfanwy quickly interrupted. 'I wouldn't let him, not with the baby on the way.'

Robert opened his mouth to speak but then didn't. Hugh could not recall ever having seen that before and he sensed that the army was a subject of some contention between husband and wife. He turned to his father.

'How's mam?'

'She's fine, looking forward to seeing you.'

'How's Joe, in the navy?'

'He's all right. He writes regularly. He's somewhere at sea and can't be home for Christmas.'

They walked to the house. Several neighbours were at their doors to greet him; some clapped their hands, which embarrassed him. Leah was at the door. Behind her, the house was brightly lit and decorated for Christmas. He guessed that there would be a huge meal ready and was not disappointed.

'Oh Hugh,' his mother said, 'I do feel proud of you but I pray to God every day that he will protect you and save you. Joe, too, in the navy.'

'Try not to worry, Mam. We'll be all right.'

Alongside the treasured photograph of Joseph and Leah on the mantelpiece in the living room, there was now a photo of his brother in his sailor's uniform. His father saw that it caught his eye.

'We want one of you, too,' he said. 'I've arranged to take you to the photographer before you go away again.'

Awaiting his arrival was a Christmas card with a long letter from May and John, saying how much he was missed at Penduffryn. So many of the younger miners had gone to the army that pressure was now being exerted on those left not to join up. The colliery management was concerned about a damaging loss of labour, especially as the war was increasing the demand for coal.

Good, he thought. Anything that makes those buggers worried must be good. Must be the first time they've ever shown any concern over the miners.

What really surprised and amused him was saved for the final page of May's letter. To the total astonishment of the entire village, Dai horses and Blodwen the post had suddenly announced their engagement and were to be married in the spring. 'Just shows what changes the war is bringing,' May wrote. Hugh could not stop himself from laughing out loud and had to explain to the others what he was laughing at.

'I reckon he deserves a pension after courting her all those years,' he said.

Christmas Day and Boxing Day passed incredibly quickly, crowded with family reunions. Apart from Joe, in the navy, May at Penduffryn and John in the east valleys, all his brothers and sisters came to see him. The house was full of their children, Joseph and Leah's ever-growing family of grandchildren, Hugh's ever growing family of nephews and nieces.

There was, though, a jarring note struck with Matthew, his eldest brother. Matthew and Lydia now had a second son and she was pregnant again, which would make their family up to five children.

'Another pair of hands to work on the farm, whether it's a boy or a girl,' Matthew said. Hugh assumed that it was meant as a joke, but quickly came to realise that it was not.

'The war,' Matthew went on, 'is going to make a world of difference to farming. There'll be a big demand for home-produced food and real money to be made at last.'

Hugh bit back the words on his lips. While Joe and I and hundreds of thousands of others are laying our lives on the line, he thought. Aloud, he said, 'Are the Kramers doing any better at Round Pond?'

'They won't be able to cope with this new, wartime demand. I've already spoken to Hatherly's estate manager about buying the farm – and about buying the land as well.'

'What did he say?' Hugh asked.

'He's quite happy about it. They don't want bad farmers as tenants. In fact, I might be able to buy the land before the farm and then I could put the Kramers out. Be much cheaper than buying the farm outright.'

Hugh was saddened. He had no love for the Kramers, but how different Matthew now was from the brother he had once been grateful to and had looked up to. He turned away and did not pursue the conversation. It did not escape Joseph and Leah that a widening gulf of disaffection was growing between their eldest and youngest sons.

The special photograph proved to be splendid. Hugh, standing with one foot resting on a low stool, bandolier in place over his shoulder, was holding a swagger stick in front of him. Suitably serious, he was looking straight into the camera, so that his eyes followed you from whatever angle you viewed the picture. His father insisted on paying for a number of copies, including an enlarged one to be framed to stand on the living room mantelpiece.

Hugh had to leave on New Year's Day. The day before, there was one last visitor to see him. It was George Penfold, the guard on the train to Whitland all those years ago when he had run away from Round Pond Farm and who had informed his parents of his departure. George was now no less than a stationmaster.

'I've never forgotten you, Hughie,' he said.

'I've never forgotten you, Mr Penfold. You were very kind to me that day.'

'It seemed appropriate to me that I should come to see you again, as you are going away once more to travel, under God's guidance and protection, into an unknown and dangerous world. My wife and I, as a token of our regard and our prayers for you, would like you to accept a small but priceless gift.'

Hugh recognised the tone and manner of a lay preacher. He was not surprised that the small gift was a pocket-size bible. Written on the flyleaf was *Hugh Hughes from G. and M. Penfold. Be a good soldier of Jesus Christ.* The bible was newly published by the British and Foreign Bible Society, to be given to the soldiers of the prince of peace and heaven as they they went to war and hell at the western front.

Hugh read the inscription. It occurred to him that German soldiers were quite likely receiving similar tokens, God having been enlisted to fight on both sides.

'Thank you, Mr Penfold,' he said. 'I will do my best.'

His entire family seemed to be at the station to see him off. A number of other soldiers were also leaving and the platform was crowded. George Penfold, resplendent and self-important in braided railway uniform, had kept a seat for him and instructed a porter to place his kitbag on the luggage rack for him. His father shook his hand.

'Be sure to come back to us, boy,' he said. There was a break in his voice that Hugh had never heard before. His mother embraced him; she was too choked to speak.

As the train pulled away, he hung out of the window until they were all lost to sight in swirling smoke and steam. His mother's will power had broken down and she was in his father's arms, crying. He took his seat in a sombre mood, which seemed to be shared by the other passengers in the compartment. They included another soldier. Hugh wondered if he too might have one of those pocket bibles. It seemed the natural thing to speak to him, but the train was past Tenby before anyone spoke.

The letter he received from his father and read in a dugout in June 1916 shocked him profoundly. It contained the news that his brother Joe had been killed in action. The letter stated simply that Joe had been killed at the Battle of Jutland and lost at sea.

What it did not say, because it had not of course been disclosed in the official telegram to his father, was that Joe had been blown to pieces when his ship, HMS *Queen Mary*, had exploded, the second British warship to be so destroyed within the space of an hour by accurate and effective German fire from better-designed ships. There seemed to be 'something wrong with our bloody ships,' as Admiral Beatty had said to the captain of his flagship.

Hugh sat down in the dreary, muddy dugout to write home, completely confused as to what to put in his letter. He pictured his father and mother receiving the dreaded telegram. They would have known instantly what it contained, that either he or Joe had been killed. He found himself wondering stupidly how many such telegrams Blodwen post, now Mrs Dai horses, must have received and read in Penduffryn post office before dispatching them to the bereaved next of kin.

Memories welled up of Joe teaching him the rudiments of rugby and football as a schoolboy and of Joe's love of water and ships that had led him into joining the navy. He recalled Joe's epic swim from

Pembroke Dock to Milford Haven. Now, what remained of him was somewhere in the cold waters of the North Sea.

By this time, he was already nauseated by the war to which he had gone so gaily nearly two years earlier. He had first seen action at the Battle of Loos in the autumn of 1915. There, he had found himself on a battlefield of slag heaps and destroyed mining villages with which he could not help but feel an affinity, although the gently undulating countryside was very different from the Welsh valleys he knew so well.

The opening artillery barrage, which was supposed to destroy the German defences and make way for a breakthrough, had not worked. Thousands of infantrymen had advanced with perfect discipline to their deaths at the hands of the German machine gunners. For the first time, the British had used gas, some of which had blown back onto their own lines. He himself had been affected, fortunately only mildly and disabled for just a few days, but sufficiently to be left with a troublesome cough for years to come.

The cough was not helped by the habit of smoking he had picked up. He had not smoked before but, in the army, it was encouraged because it was thought to calm the nerves. In the days of his training, there had been an occasion when the soldiers had been paraded to receive 'Princess Mary's gift', which turned out to be a small packet of Woodbine cigarettes.

Situated close to the training camp he was sent to after crossing the Channel were a couple of brothels. At the first of them, the charges were low, to cater exclusively for the lower-ranking soldiers. The second establishment catered exclusively for officers, charging more for the same services in more congenial surroundings with drinks included.

Having heard enthusiastic accounts from those who had savoured the pleasures of the other ranks establishment, Hugh had ventured there with two others. All three were virgin. In their generation, it was not unusual for young men to be in their twenties before losing their virginity. To Hugh's future grandchildren, it would seem strange and, to their children, laughable.

All three soldiers were fired by a heady mixture of arousal, curiosity and anticipation but, when it came to the crunch, all three approached the venture with trepidation. Hugh had almost dropped out on reaching the door, acutely conscious that he had no idea of what would be expected of him. His nervousness was only overcome by the knowledge that to back out at that stage would mean lasting ridicule.

Both the proprietress and the experienced prostitute to whom she allocated him had instantly recognised the situation. These were by no means the first soldiers they had encountered who were without previous experience. They were eager to serve them, not least with a view to encouraging return visits. They were, after all, business women.

Even so, 'the French landlady', as the soldiers called the proprietress, was a more caring person than they realised. She believed, not unreasonably, that she was providing a necessary and morale-boosting service. She had a son of her own, the product of one of the encounters of her earlier career, now a young conscript invalided out of the French army because his left leg had been shattered. She felt an almost motherly sympathy and pity for these British soldiers who would so soon be marching into the same sort of horror. '*Beaucoup de morts beaucoup de blessés*', as she found herself saying ever more frequently.

As soon as Hugh and the not uncomely girl who had been chosen for him had entered the little private room, she took off her few garments, causing his eyes almost to pop out of his head.

'Tommee like me?' she asked, but he was too tongue-tied to do anything other than nod his head in appreciation. She at once set expertly to work to help him undress.

'Tommee nice,' she said, 'and 'e iss ready.'

She indicated that he should lie on the bed and when he had done so, she squatted on him and used her hands to help him enter her. It was all over very quickly and, in no time, he was dressed again and being ushered out to make way for the next client.

The three soldiers, secretly disappointed because it had all ended so quickly, nevertheless felt exhilarated. They exchanged raucous and exaggerated accounts of their new experience as they walked back to the camp, none admitting that it was a first experience and all planning further visits.

His confidence boosted, Hugh visited the brothel a second time. He was served, more satisfyingly, by the same girl. He was starting to establish a rapport with her and looked forward, a little guiltily, to a third visit. In the pidgin French he was beginning to pick up he asked her name. She told him to call her 'Miss Fifi', which he realised was highly unlikely to be her real name.

'But Tommee will 'ave to pay more to 'ave more time viz me,' she warned him.

In the event, he was saved any additional expense because no further visits took place. He was posted, at short notice, to the battlefield. He went, with the sense of adventure he still felt at that stage towards the war, heightened by his new sexual experience. The battle front quickly brought an appalling awakening to reality.

He was in the same gun crew as his two comrades who had accompanied him on that first visit to the brothel. One of them was quickly killed, the other badly wounded. They were manhandling a field gun into position when an enemy shell scored a direct hit on the gun. Hugh was a short distance away, attending to the horses which had been unharnessed from the gun. The blast threw him to the ground but the horse he was handling took the shrapnel, saving his life.

The animal was writhing on the ground in agony, neighing piteously. She was the lead horse, which he had ridden. He had developed an affection for her and named her Myfanwy, after his sister. Now, there was only one thing he could do. He took his rifle and shot her through the head. Her terrified eyes, as she looked at him for the last time, haunted him for months afterwards.

He staggered through the carnage to do what he could for the other soldiers. That nothing could be done for the dead man was immediately apparent. He lay covered in blood, his head half severed from his body. There were several others who were wounded in various degrees. He did what he could to help. Others came running to assist. They responded automatically, with no thought other than to help fellow beings. None of them considered their action to be in any way heroic, notwithstanding the continuing enemy fire. The stretcher bearers arrived to take away the wounded and the dead man. Then, Hugh's legs suddenly buckled under him. He leaned on the wreckage of the field gun and was sick.

As part of the great build-up of men and armaments in preparation for the Battle of the Somme, he was subsequently moved to that sector of the front and it was there that he had received the news of his brother's death.

Moved there at the same time was a newly promoted captain who became his company commander. Hugh recognised him instantly as Jeremy Hatherly, whom he had met when they were both boys, on his memorable last day at Round Pond Farm.

A few days after writing back to his father, he was attending to the horses when a voice behind him asked 'Driver Hughes?' He turned to find himself facing the captain. He saluted automatically.

'I was most sorry to hear of your brother's death in the navy,' the captain said, after returning the salute as automatically as it had been given.

'Thank you sir.'

'I had to see your letter to your father, as part of the censorship. I noted the Pembroke Dock address. I thought I would have a word, as I am from Pembrokeshire myself.'

There was a dawning recognition in his eyes. 'We've met before, haven't we?'

'Yes sir.'

'Can you remind me where?'

'Yes sir. Round Pond Farm, near Pembroke, Michaelmas Day 1902.'

'Of course. You were working on the farm. Interesting that you can remember it so precisely. Did you go on working on the land until you joined the army?'

'No sir, I left shortly afterwards and went to work in the pits in the valleys.' He thought it neither the time nor the place to say why he remembered it so precisely nor to say just how shortly afterwards he had left.

'You seem to be very good with the horses. Far too many of those who have been put in charge of them don't know anything about them. That's why I assumed you must have gone on being a farm worker.'

'Actually sir, I was a pit pony driver.'

'Ah, I see.' He paused. 'I did try to get you compassionate leave in view of your brother's death in action but, at present, no one can be spared from the front.'

Hugh was briefly at a loss for words. He had by then been well drilled into the concept that he must always be unquestionably subservient to officers, to whom he must never speak unless spoken to first. He realised, though, that the friendly, upper-class youth of long ago had matured into a more sympathetic and insightful officer than the majority of those he had so far encountered.

'Thank you sir,' he said.

Within days, the bombardment started. For a whole week, the German lines were subjected to a huge artillery attack. Then, at half past seven on a fine sunny July 1st, the guns fell suddenly silent and the infantry advanced across no-man's-land onto what they had been told would be the destroyed German trenches. All they had to do was go forward at a walking pace, mop up or take prisoner any remaining enemy soldiers, take over their trenches and wait for the cavalry to come up from the rear to make the breakthrough that would win the battle and end the war.

Hugh's unit was only a short way behind the trenches and they had a clear view of what was happening. Within hours, minutes even, it was evident that the battle could not be won. The advancing infantry were being mown down by merciless machine-gun and rifle fire. As the German artillery found their range, shelling was added, and it soon extended to those units like Hugh's, which were immediately behind the trenches. They were returning the fire but to little apparent effect.

Captain Hatherly was observing the scene through field glasses.

'Dear God!' he shouted above the deafening noise. 'The bombardment has hardly damaged their defences. Our troops are being slaughtered. This isn't warfare, it's sheer massacre.'

He turned to his immediate superior, Major Verrey-ffaire.

'For God's sake sir, get the message back to HQ. Tell them what's happening and get them to stop it.'

The major was shocked, not by the casualties and the course of the battle, but by the attitude of the captain.

Gerald Verrey-ffaire, the most inappropriately named man in the British army, was a tight-lipped, humourless man with a carefully clipped moustache. He wore a monocle in his right eye, not because of any ocular defect but because he thought it added gravitas to his demeanour. The one solid achievement of his life was in mastering the art of keeping the monocle in place in all circumstances.

'I shall send no such message, Captain,' he shouted back sharply. 'I am surprised that you should even think of such a thing.'

'But sir, we are just throwing lives away uselessly.'

'There are bound to be initial casualties. Our job is to maintain the assault and make the breakthrough.'

'But we're not making any progress at all. This is madness.'

The major turned on him angrily. 'May I remind you, Hatherly,' he shouted, 'that our duty is to obey orders, not to question them. And may I further remind you that to do so under fire is a very serious court martial offence.'

Jeremy wanted to shout 'It's the bloody fools who have planned this who ought to be court martialled'. But he knew that he had to defer to his superiors in rank, however inferior they might be in intellect. He remained silent, with half-recalled lines from Tennyson flashing into his mind. Something about soldiers having no right to reason why, only to do and die, for how were they to know that someone had blundered.

'It's pretty obvious that someone has blundered here on a colossal scale.' He said it involuntarily but, fortunately, not loud enough for the major to hear him over the noise of battle.

A train of thought took him back in a split second to pre-war conversations in Pembrokeshire with his father's old friend, Colonel Mulholland. He regarded the colonel as an arrogant old bore, but he knew that as a young subaltern he had served on the staff of Lord Raglan, the commander-in-chief in the Crimea War, scene of the disastrous charge of the Light Brigade, about which Tennyson had written those lines.

The colonel had recounted how Raglan, who had been on Wellington's staff at the Battle of Waterloo, where he had lost an arm, referred constantly to 'those damned French' and was apt to become angry if reminded that the French were now his allies. Jeremy thought that Raglan must be a leading contender for the title of most blundering British commander in history, a title for which there was very strong competition. Now, surveying the death and destruction all round him, he thought bitterly that tradition was being well upheld.

Within two hours, twenty thousand British soldiers had been killed or wounded; by the end of the day, nearly three times as many.

Chapter 10

The assault was kept up for week after week and month after month, resulting in several kilometres of devastated land and a few small, destroyed and strategically unimportant villages being captured. The German line did not break, it just wavered back a little in good order, continuing all the time to inflict heavy casualties on the British.

Hugh's unit was close behind the infantry throughout and, like them, under constant fire. He would be the last to lay any claim to bravery but, for the most part, he found that fear was cancelled out by sheer tiredness and lack of sleep. Fear seemed a stronger emotion during occasional lulls in the battle, when the uproar that had become normality seemed to change to almost eerie quiet and there was time to think.

Eight weeks into the battle, he was wounded. Shrapnel hit him in the leg. He tried to remain standing but he lost his balance, fell and became unconscious. When he came to, he was on a stretcher, his uniform cut away and his steel helmet removed, and a stretcher bearer was doing his best to staunch his wound with field dressings.

'Not to worry, Tommy,' the stretcher bearer said. 'As soon as we can get an ambulance here, we'll get you to hospital.'

But it was long hours before the ambulance arrived and every hour brought more wounded and several dead. One of the ambulance orderlies who carried him on the stretcher to the vehicle was a large man probably twice as old as most of the other soldiers. In conversation with the other stretcher bearer he spoke with a cultured, educated voice. Hugh's curiosity was aroused.

When he and the others had been placed in the ambulance, the big, older man went round to the front to sit with the driver. The other orderly, who, Hugh noted, called the big man 'Bob', stayed in the back with the wounded.

'My name's Steggles,' he said in an unmistakeably Cockney voice.

He produced a mouth organ. 'It's going to be a bit of a rough ride, boys,' he added. 'I'll give you a tune or two, just to pass the time.'

He proved to be an accomplished performer, with a wide repertory of wartime and pre-war music hall tunes. The wounded men, in pain from every jolt of the vehicle, found it far more valuable than merely passing the time. When they eventually arrived at the field hospital, the big man came round to help get them off the ambulance.

'Nice selection of tunes, Harry,' he said to the other orderly.

As the big man moved away to help elsewhere, Hugh's curiosity overcame him. 'Who's that chap?' he asked.

'Oh, I call 'im Bob,' Harry replied. There was a twinkle in his eye. 'Actually, 'is name's Ralph, although 'e insists that you say it "Raif". That's why I call 'im Bob.'

'He's a lot older than any of us.'

'Yes, 'e is – and as you can tell by the way 'e talks, 'e's a toff. But there's nothin' stuck up about 'im, 'e's a real gent, far different from most of those snotty officers.'

''ow come 'e's just an ambulance orderly?' The dropped Cockney aitches seemed to be catching.

'Well, when the war started, 'e volunteered like I did and I suppose you did. 'e's over military age but 'e felt 'e 'ad a duty to join up, somethin' to do with goin' to one of them public schools, as they call them, I think. He was at Cambridge University too – and the Royal College of Music.'

'He's a musician?'

'Composer actually. Quite famous too, 'is name's Vaughan Williams.'

'Sounds like there's something Welsh about that.'

'Well, Taff, I don't know about that, but 'is ancestry might be in Taffy land.'

'You seem to know him pretty well.'

'Yes, I was in the unit a bit before 'im and because 'e was older, 'e needed an 'and with 'is uniform and diff'rent things, so I 'elped 'im. We've been friends ever since.'

Hugh was impressed by this obvious camaraderie between two people from such widely differing backgrounds. But Captain Carmichael, the medical officer who operated to remove the shrapnel from his leg, was far from impressed by such friendships.

It genuinely shocked the captain that a man with as high a social status as his own, and of creative talent into the bargain, should be serving among the lower orders. Surely the fellow must, like himself, have had influential friends in the War Office who would see to it that he was commissioned.

The captain came from an elite medical background. His father was a distinguished Harley Street specialist who, as he never tired of telling his fellow officers, was consulted by members of the royal family. After qualifying, the captain had become a junior partner in his father's practice, where his patients consisted exclusively of the wealthy and the titled.

Fired with patriotism, he had joined up at the outbreak of war, eager to do his bit and convinced that it would be all over by Christmas. With no experience outside his own privileged station in society, it had simply not occurred to him that he could have patients who were not officers and it had come as a shock that most of those he had to attend to proved to be from the lower ranks.

His attitude towards non-commissioned medical staff was as condescending as towards his patients and he fitted exactly into the category described by Harry Steggles as 'snotty'. He took what comfort he could from discovering that there were some among the female nursing and support staff who were volunteers from 'good families'. Several of those, as disturbed as he was by the trauma of the war and not without an eye to post-war or even wartime marriage, had been prepared to grant him sexual favours, which he accepted with gratitude but without commitment.

As the war went on, he became increasingly depressed by the sheer scale of the casualties. Whatever his social failings, he was a fine surgeon and it horrified him that he had been turned into something of an automaton, dealing more or less mechanically with an endless stream of patients who had become only statistics, simply to be patched up where possible for return to the fighting.

Hugh's recovery progressed quickly, helped by his naturally wiry constitution, so that he was soon able to leave his bed and sit outside in the fresh air. With the aid of a stick, he was able to walk. From outside the hospital, a bugler could regularly be heard practising, somewhere in the distance. Several times, Hugh saw the big orderly, the composer, listening and making notes. Without knowing it, he was witnessing the genesis of a 'pastoral' symphony that would reflect the horror of the war in its own poignant and very original way.

'You'll be back at the front in no time,' Captain Carmichael told him. If it was meant to be encouraging, it fell understandably flat.

Soon afterwards, he was sent on home leave to complete his recovery, still walking with the aid of the stick, which proved to be something of a badge of honour, marking him out for respect and attention.

The journey was tedious. First, to Calais by rail in a cattle truck adapted to carry the wounded. Then a late-night crossing to Dover, the ferry blacked out against submarine attack. Then another train journey, first to London on the South Eastern and Chatham Railway, the SECR, the 'Slow, Easy and Comfortable', as the soldiers called it, slow because of the pace to London, easy and comfortable because they travelled in passenger carriages as opposed to the cattle trucks in France.

He had not visited London before and felt some trepidation at crossing the cosmopolitan city where more than three times as many people lived as in the whole of Wales, but a friendly woman porter on the Underground at Charing Cross station saw him onto the right train for Paddington. He was naively impressed at seeing famous names like Piccadilly Circus and Oxford Circus as he passed through the stations. At Paddington, he was in time to catch the last train of the day with through carriages for Pembroke Dock and just had time to send a telegram to tell his parents the time he would be arriving. Again, he found friendly porters, anxious to help him and find him a seat, in which he slept for most of the long journey on the crowded train.

It seemed as though most of his family were at the station to meet him, both his father and mother, Myfanwy with her two-year-old son and husband Robert, as well as two other sisters. Even the station master, Mr Penfold, who, with no offspring of his own, felt an avuncular interest in his old friend's son, was there to welcome his 'good soldier of Jesus Christ'. It was an emotional occasion.

Not once during his leave did his mother mention his brother Joseph's death in action, although his father and others referred to it, but never in her presence. She had, temporarily at least, blotted it out of her memory. She did, though, raise another matter.

'I'm so proud, Hugh,' she said, 'to think that you played your part in inflicting that heavy defeat on those Germans.'

She saw that he was puzzled and did not understand why. 'On the

Somme,' she said. 'Just a minute.' She went to a drawer and produced a newspaper cutting.

Headed 'A Slow Push Sparing In Lives', the article, described as the semi-official review of the first day of the Somme Battle, stated that it had been very satisfactory and rich in promise. It was a slow, methodical push, sparing in lives, that would cause the enemy's resistance to crumple at some point. The article declared that the first day of the battle 'permitted developments to be awaited with confidence'.

Hugh, recalling the slaughter he had witnessed on that terrible first day, to say nothing of the subsequent days and weeks until he was wounded, read the cutting in disbelief. He contained his thoughts with difficulty.

'Yes mam,' he said. 'It's very hard – but we shall win in the end.'

By that time, conscription had been introduced for single men. The only one of the family to be affected was his brother Albert, five years older than himself. Albert, the sixth-born of the family, was the only one who had never enjoyed good health and he had failed to pass the army medical examination. He was living with Matthew on the farm, where it was felt that working in the open air would be good for him.

Hugh was more cynical. Being exploited like Matthew's children, he thought. Being worked towards illness more than good health.

Robert Snape was now a foreman at the dockyard. He had been exempted from military service, both as a husband and father and because of the national importance of his work. Robert was not entirely happy about the situation. He really wanted to be in the army and he felt inferior to those who were. But, with his sharp mind, he realised that the situation at the front was very different from the propagandised way it was reported.

'Are you still writing for the local paper?' Hugh asked him.

'No,' Robert said sharply. 'They didn't like everything I was writing about the war. All they want is cheerful stuff about how well it's going, when any idiot – apart from those running the war – can see from the casualty lists that it's not going well.'

'There were some terrible letters in the paper,' Myfanwy added, 'saying that he ought to be out there fighting, not attacking the boys who were.'

'Ignorant, jingoistic bastards!' Robert said angrily. 'I never wrote anything attacking our boys. Just some pretty mild remarks about the loss of life.'

'It's a good job he always used a pen name,' Myfanwy said, 'otherwise we should have had stones through the windows.'

'Mam showed me a cutting reporting on the first day of the Battle of the Somme,' Hugh told them. 'It was a pack of lies, nothing like what I saw for myself.'

'How long is it going to go on?' Robert asked.

'A long time yet. It's deadlock at the front.'

Myfanwy changed the subject. 'Matthew is buying Round Pond Farm' she said. 'I gather the Kramers are retiring. He's going to buy the land and all from that Squire Hatherly.'

'Funny how things work out,' Hugh said. 'Hatherly's son Jeremy is my captain. You remember I told you, years ago, how I met him on that last day at Round Pond Farm.'

'Have you been up to the farm to see Matthew?' Myfanwy asked.

'Not yet. I thought he might have been down to see me. After all, it's me who is home wounded from the front.' Nothing more was said; pretty well all the family knew by then about the coldness between the brothers.

He had to report for medical examination at the local barracks and, within a couple of weeks, the walking stick was taken away from him and he was declared fit to return to active service.

Returning to the front was deeply depressing, with the ever-present thought that he might never see home again. There were constant replacements for casualties, but at least one bright moment occurred when one of them turned out to be 'Jock' Mackay, his old comrade from the days in Ireland in the early months of the war.

Jock was the Glaswegian who had been spat at in the Irish pub, provoking the fight that had resulted in the cold-blooded shooting of the Irishman. Neither Hugh nor Jock had ever expected to see each other again. They greeted each other in trench-speak gallows humour.

'Och aye, y' Welsh bastard.'

'Why aye, y' Scotch prick.'

'So this is where ye've been enjoying ye'self all this time,' Jock said.

'And where have you been hanging out on the old barbed wire?'

'Och, I've been up near Ypres.' Like all the soldiers, he pronounced it 'Wipers'. 'Reckon we shall all be going there soon. They say there's another big offensive on the way.'

He was right. Within a few weeks, the battle that would come to be known as Passchendaele started. It was stopped after little more than a week because of unseasonably heavy rain, but it was to be restarted as soon as reinforcements could be brought up and the weather improved. The unit to which Hugh and Jock were attached was to be part of those reinforcements.

Major Verrey-ffaire briefed the junior officers. 'We shall march to the railhead, then entrain for Etaples, where the troops will have a week's training in readiness to go to the front. Any questions?' His tone indicated that questions would not be welcome.

'Yes sir.' It was Captain Hatherly. The major groaned inwardly. Always that fellow. Why couldn't he just do what he was told!

'Yes captain, what is it?'

'Why is it thought necessary for our troops to require training to go to the front? After all, they are at the front now and they've been there for a long time.'

The major had no idea of the answer to such a sensible question. 'Our orders,'; he said stiffly, 'are that the troops will have a week's training in readiness for the new offensive. We shall, of course, carry out all orders that we are given.'

When the news reached the troops, the reaction was emphatic. Etaples, a very large training camp on the French coast, had a reputation for appalling food and accommodation coupled with exceptionally brutal training. Newly conscripted troops were sent there for final training before going to the front. For seasoned front-line soldiers, it was an insult of a high order to be sent there.

'Eatapples!' roared Jock Mackay, using the soldiers' pronunciation, 'I was sent to that fuckin', God-awful place last year. Run by bloody officers, NCOs and redcaps who've never seen the front line – and they're supposed to train us for the front?'

He lowered his voice. 'You know,' he said, there's a large crowd of deserters close by. There's Aussies and New Zealanders and, I'm glad to say, some Scots, running their own place in the woods and sand dunes close to the camp. Those boys from down under just won't stand for it. They can teach us a thing or two. D'you know, they get paid four times as much as we do – and there's no death penalty in their armies. You mark my words, there's going to be big trouble in Eatapples before long.'

To most of those listening, the disparity of pay and disciplinary methods between the British army and the Australian and New Zealand Army Corps came as a revelation but even the least informed was aware of growing opposition to the war.

In Russia, the whole army was in a state of mutiny. There had been a revolution and the Tsar had been forced to abdicate. There were stories of mass refusal to fight in the French army, stories that the soldiers had declared that they would of course defend France against the hated 'Boche' but they would not take part in any more suicidal offensives planned by stupid commanders from the safety of headquarters behind the front line. The Americans had entered the war, but there was widespread cynicism about their motives.

'Waited to see who was likely to win and then came in on the winning side,' Jock had said.

He was voicing the cynical view of many soldiers of all ranks, to say nothing of war-weary civilians. Back in Pembrokeshire, it was a sentiment shared by a social spectrum stretching from Hugh's mother and father to Colonel Mulholland.

The unit was soon moved on its way towards Ypres. The troop train arrived at Etaples station several hours behind time. There had been frequent unscheduled stops on the way, leading to all sorts of rumours, among them that there had been a German breakthrough. It was a hot Sunday evening in early September and by the time they eventually arrived, everyone was tired, hungry and fed up. The soldiers were ordered to detrain and assemble on the platform.

That something was seriously wrong was immediately apparent. Soldiers and military police were drawn up within and around the station, as if in preparation to fight off an attack. Beyond the station, there was a hubbub as if there was fighting in the streets. The sky was lit up as if by bonfires or burning buildings.

Major Verrey-ffaire addressed the troops. 'There is a change of plan,' he said. 'We shall not be stopping at Etaples, but continuing straight to the front.' There was a murmur of dissent.

'With respect sir.' It was Sergeant Major Lantlin. 'The troops have had little to eat all day. Shall we not be at least stopping for a meal?'

Sergeant Major Lantlin was a regular soldier of the old school, who had been in the front line almost continuously since the outbreak of war. He had been wounded three times and had been decorated with the recently instituted Military Medal for bravery in the field. He was greatly respected. Even Major Verrey-ffaire recognised that he could not slap down such a man for daring to question him without permission.

'That will not be possible, Sar'nt Major,' he said. 'There have been developments – disgraceful developments – at Etaples which make it undesirable for us to go there at all. The train will be stopping beyond Etaples and a meal will be arranged.'

'With respect sir, what sort of developments are there? Is it true that there has been a German breakthrough?'

'No, there has not.' The major seemed to choke on his words. 'There has been a – a – disturbance at the camp and in the town.'

The murmur of dissent among the soldiers grew noticeably louder.

'Silence in the ranks,' shouted the sergeant major, but, for once with little effect.

'It's happened,' said Jock Mackay excitedly. 'I knew it would sooner or later. I reckon there's a right mutiny going on there.'

The troops were ordered back onto the train. They obeyed but there was dissent among them. Jock and a few other hotheads were for refusing and breaking out of the station to join in whatever was happening in the town.

'Don't be so bloody stupid,' Hugh told him. 'Do you want to finish up facing a firing squad?'

Jock wisely took his advice. The train moved off but, beyond the station, there were amazing scenes. Hundreds of jeering soldiers were lining the tracks, some were trying to move heavy pieces of army equipment onto the line to block the passage of trains. They were not in time to stop that particular train but, as it passed at a walking pace, many of the soldiers on board cheered and waved encouragement. A few opened the doors of the cattle trucks and jumped onto the track to join them. Hugh physically stopped Jock from doing so.

Passing through Etaples on that crucial Sunday evening, all too many of them could all too easily have become part of a revolt of thousands of ill-treated soldiers, a full-scale mutiny that would last a week and result in the General Officer Commanding at Etaples being relieved of his command. But it was a mutiny which the British army would not admit, even after it was confirmed to have taken place in the answer to a question in Parliament more than six decades later.

The troop train rolled on towards the front, taking Hugh towards the battle that would remain in his memory even more vividly than the Somme. He would count it little short of a miracle that he got through it alive and not wounded, apart from the intensely painful condition called trench feet, caused by being constantly more than ankle-deep and often knee-deep in liquid mud.

For at Passchendaele, the slaughter was added to by the effect of unremitting rain. As far as the eye could see, the battlefield was an utterly destroyed wasteland of mud and water.

There were soldiers who drowned in water-filled shell craters, in addition to those killed by enemy action. There were wounded who were left to die because the stretcher bearers could not get to them.

Often, it was impossible to get the field guns into position because the horses could not get through the mud, whereupon dozens of soldiers, floundering knee-deep, had to try to manhandle the guns into place. The battle was called off in November. Just a few kilometres of mud had been captured, with huge casualties.

A few months later, what had been captured had to be abandoned when the Germans, having defeated Russia, launched their last, desperate offensive. But by then they were exhausted and heavily outnumbered. By the summer the German army was withdrawing all along the front, and by the autumn, with revolution breaking out at home, the government sued for peace.

By the ceasefire, at the eleventh hour of the eleventh day of the eleventh month of 1918, Hugh's unit was well into Belgium, close to Mons, where Sergeant Major Lantlin had fought in one of the very first battles. Firing continued from the German lines and was returned until the very last minutes of the war.

When every gun fell suddenly silent, it seemed unbelievable. Hugh was standing with the lead horse of the team that had brought up their twenty-five-pounder field gun. As all went silent, the horse, unaccustomed to such conditions, neighed loudly. Almost instantly, there was an answering call from a horse in the German lines.

On both sides, tired, mud-spattered and dishevelled men emerged from cover. There was little more than a couple of hundred metres between them. They stood silently staring at each other. There were those on both sides who wondered if there was something symbolic in animals calling to each other while human beings just glowered in sullen silence.

Major Verrey-ffaire and Captain Hatherly stood looking across the now silent and safe no-man's-land. Immediately opposite them, a German officer stepped forward and examined them through field glasses. The captain raised his own field glasses to look at the German. He could see from his insignia that he was a major. The German lowered his field glasses and Hatherly suppressed a laugh when he saw that, like Verrey-ffaire, he had a monocle firmly fixed in his right eye.

The thought raced through the captain's head, I wonder if he has a defective right eye or if he's another vainglorious clown who thinks that thing adds to his dignity? They must have them in their army, just as we have. Aloud, he said, 'He's the same rank as you, sir. Should we do anything?'

'Like what?'

'Oh – er – well, acknowledge him in some way?'

Vague notions had been gathering in the captain's mind about the so-called chivalry of war, whereby opposing armies, dedicated to killing and maiming as many of each other as possible, supposedly did so only from the highest motives and with the most honourable intentions.

'Acknowledge him? Most certainly not. He is a defeated enemy. These people are not fit to be acknowledged.'

The German suddenly stiffened to attention and saluted. It could only be a matter for surmise as to whether he did so through chivalry or in recognition of a monocled equal in rank and possibly in personality.

'We ought to return that, sir.'

'Yes, I suppose we should.'

The major and the captain came simultaneously to attention and returned the salute. The German bowed, turned about smartly and disappeared among the ranks of his men. Truly, the war was over and, as Hugh had promised his mother, they had won in the end.

Chapter 11

Apart from the cough given to him by the combination of poison gas and the cigarettes to which he was now addicted, Hugh returned fit physically and alert mentally. But the war did not leave him unscathed; it would be years before he ceased to be plagued by nightmares caused by the horrors he had lived through. Following demobilisation, he returned to his parents' home just in time for Christmas.

Only one thing marred the general happiness of his arrival. That was the death, two days after Christmas, of the mother of his brother-in-law and oldest friend, Robert Snape. Worn out and weakened through long years of skivvying, she was a victim of the great post-war influenza epidemic. She was not yet fifty, but she had counted herself lucky to have lived as long as she had and to have achieved her one and only ambition to see her children grow to become self-supporting and out of danger of the workhouse.

She had lived long enough to see all three children grown up and settled, even to cradle her grandchildren, Robert's two young sons, in her thin, worn-out arms. Her later years had been a little easier and, throughout, she had been helped by friends like Hugh's parents. There were those for whom she was an insignificant little woman of no importance with a derisory ambition but, for scores more who knew better, her fortitude in the face of her cruel husband's beatings and then abandonment had won respect and admiration. Robert and his sisters were astonished and deeply moved at the large numbers who attended her funeral.

For all the sadness of Mrs Snape's death, Hugh's homecoming was a joyful reunion, with a great welcome that went on for days for the soldier hero, as the family, friends and neighbours saw him. He knew, though, that he must shortly move on. His parents were now in their sixties and his father was already talking about retiring from the dockyard and moving to a smaller house. He had even picked out where he wanted to go, a small, single-storey house on the bank of the wide Pembroke River. There was a large garden and the place would be ideal for him and Leah to live out what he was now calling 'the evening of their lives'.

All Hugh's brothers and sisters had long left the parental home. Albert, the sickly one, was still living with Matthew at Old Oak Farm, 'the farm', as everyone in the family always referred to it.

With the exception of Albert, all the brothers and sisters were married and had their own homes and children. Hugh reflected, not without bitterness, that if he had not had nearly four and a half years taken out of his life, he, too, might well have met the 'nice young lady' his sister May had talked about before the war and might by now have a home and children.

The first thing he had to do was to find a job. May had written to say that men were wanted in the pit at Penduffryn and that he would be very welcome back there. But he had turned against the place. He had too many memories of how dissatisfied he had become in his later years there – which had resulted directly in his joining up at the outbreak of war and in effect losing those vital years of his life, with the possibility of losing it altogether. The more he thought about it, the more he concluded that he no more wanted to return to Penduffryn than to Passchendaele.

On the spur of the moment, he wrote to his brother John, the one whose enforced marriage had exiled him to east Wales, where he, too, was a miner. John wrote back at once, to tell him that there was plenty of work in the pits, that he would be particularly welcomed as an experienced miner who was also an ex-serviceman and that he, John, could arrange lodgings for him. So, in early 1919, carrying his few belongings, he travelled to Pontcaer, where John lived.

He had not seen John for many years and had never met his wife Sarah, who was called Sally by everybody, although her parents who had always insisted on the biblical Sarah with which they had christened her. John had long since become reconciled with his parents but neither he nor Sally ever saw her parents after they disowned her because of her pregnancy 'without the Lord's command'. Her father had died suddenly in 1916. Neither Sally nor John had attended the funeral, because they knew they would not be welcomed either by her mother or by other members of the chapel whose puritanical doctrines had so spectacularly failed to influence her conduct.

Her father had died from some sort of apoplectic stroke at a relatively young age. A joke enjoyed within the Hughes family was that he had either been called early to heaven because of his piety or to hell because of his treatment of his daughter. It was originated by Robert Snape and laughed at by everyone except Matthew, who had by then outgrown any sense of humour with which he had been born.

John met Hugh at Pontcaer station. 'I'll take you to our place for a meal and to meet Sally and the family,' he said. 'Then I'll take you to the lodgings I've arranged. That's close by where we live. And there's a job waiting for you at the pit: they want drivers for the ponies.'

Hugh's heart sank slightly. He could not help wondering if he would ever get away from looking after horses.

'I've arranged for you to lodge with Dai and Jill Manners,' John went on. 'Dai is a miner also just back from the war, old mate of mine, just got married. He went all through the war like you, wounded twice. They've got a spare room and are looking for a lodger.'

'There's a lot of pits here Hugh said. 'Which one will I be going to?'

'The Robson pit, where I work.'

'The Robson pit? That sounds familiar.'

'Yes. It's called that because of the owners, the same company as owns the pit at Penduffryn – and five or six others in these parts, as well as others in the north of England.'

'You mean Sir George Robson's company?'

'Yes, it's called RMF now. He amalgamated during the war with his relation by marriage, a man called Mulholland-Flowers, grandson of old Colonel Mulholland. Remember Bellwood, that big house and estate of his near Pembroke?'

'Yes, I do. Didn't Dad used to say that there was some sort of scandal and that he got sacked for talking about it when he was working as a delivery man?'

'That's right. Flowers' father was the colonel's son and his mother was one of the maids. Jammy bugger, turned out dead lucky, got left a fortune in steel making and engineering and then married Robson's wife's niece. During the war, they amalgamated the two companies. Must be worth a million and with still more to come when the colonel dies, which can't be far off now. Oh, and he's an MP, for somewhere in the Midlands.'

'Sounds like he did a bloody sight better out of the war than you or I did.'

'That's right, boy, like all the bloody mine owners. You know how it is, "unto everyone that hath shall be given".'

'And from him that hath not shall be taken even what little he seemeth to have,' Hugh said, completing the biblical allusion.

'Too true, boy. Talking about the Bible, there's another link with Penduffryn. Our MP, Gwynfor Morgan, comes from there.'

'You mean Gwynfor Morgan who was a Methodist minister in Penduffryn?'

'That's right, he won this seat at the election. Nominated by us miners. Good man, fine speaker.'

'I voted for Willie Jenkins, the Labour man in Pembrokeshire,' Hugh said, 'but he didn't get anywhere.' He laughed. 'Dad didn't like it very much.'

Having fought for his country, he had for the first time been allowed to vote for its governance, at the 'khaki' election that had been called within days of the signing of the armistice. The franchise had been extended to all men over the age of twenty-one and, for the first time, to women, although they had to be over thirty. He had shocked his father by voting Labour. Joseph had voted Liberal at every election since he, too, had first been allowed to vote. He had. remonstrated with Hugh.

'But look, boy. Mr Lloyd George won the war for us.'

That had angered Hugh, recalling his own bitter wartime experiences. 'He did have a certain amount of help,' he had retorted in a rare outburst of sarcasm.

Now, Hugh recalled Gwynfor Morgan's brilliant sermon on the occasion of Sir George Robson's visit to Penduffryn, his silent protest at the actual visit and, no less vividly, his stormy marriage to William Yewsley's daughter.

'What's happened to Yewsley, the pit manager at Penduffryn?' he asked. 'Robson appointed him area manager in Cardiff. Gwynfor Morgan married his daughter. Terrible row about that at the time.'

'Oh, Yewsley's retired now, lives in Porthcawl. They say he has never spoken to his daughter since she married. Refused to give her away at her wedding.' John laughed wryly. 'Bit like Sally's father over our marriage.'

John, Sally and family lived in an uninspiring house in an uninspiring street all too reminiscent of Penduffryn. Sally, now a mature woman and mother, still showed all the signs of the youthful beauty that had so captivated John. They had three children, Imogen, Charlotte and Joseph. Imogen, the cause of the hasty marriage, had become an extremely pretty fifteen-year-old. She had inherited both the beauty and the vivacious personality of her mother, a combination which was a source of anxiety for her parents, both nervously concerned lest history repeat itself.

'I've got so many nephews and nieces,' Hugh said, 'that I get confused about them, and now there are three more that I've never met before.'

'We Hughes do seem to be pretty prolific,' John said. 'I suppose you'll be wanting to do something about it now the war's over.'

'Yes, but not too hastily like...' He corrected himself hurriedly, embarrassed. 'That's to say, not until I've had time to settle down.

John roared with laughter. 'You were going to say not like me,' he said. 'Don't worry, boy. Neither Sally nor I have any regrets.' John had a sharp wit, probably the sharpest of all the eleven brothers and sisters, and a ready laugh. His good-natured response to Hugh's gaffe re-established a rapport between the two brothers who had not seen each other for so long.

Hugh soon settled in. Dai and Jill Manners proved to be good friends and he soon made others.

Pontcaer was in the Rhymney Valley, where the river formed the boundary between Glamorganshire and Monmouthshire, at that time also the boundary between England and Wales. There was constant argument as to whether Monmouthshire was Welsh or English. Hardly anyone there spoke Welsh, but everyone had a Welsh accent and felt indisputably that they were Welsh, not English. There was a delightful mixture of English and Welsh place names and Hugh, from the 'little England beyond Wales', felt entirely at home. He would live to see the day when Monmouthshire, renamed Gwent, would become indisputably, officially and, as he thought, very properly a part of Wales.

Joseph Hughes' sudden death in the late summer of 1920 came as a great shock. He collapsed from a heart attack on his way to work and died within hours, his dream of retiring to his small house with the big garden gone with him. The family were devastated, and worried over what the effect would be on their mother. She, in fact, was the calmest and most self-controlled of them all.

Publicly, she was strong, dignified and firmly in control of her emotions although, away from the family, she could not keep back the stinging tears as she recalled forty-five years of marriage to the man she had genuinely loved and who, although undemonstrative, had genuinely loved her. She comforted herself with the knowledge that her loneliness in old age would be relieved by the large family he had given her and which she had been proud to bear – and by her ever-growing family of grandchildren. She never doubted that, in the fullness of time, she would be reunited with Joe in heaven.

'You won't be staying on in this house, Mam?' Hugh asked her after the funeral. 'It's too big for one person.'

No, son,' she replied, 'I think you know that Dad had planned to retire to a smaller house. I've been thinking about it and, now that he's gone, I'll be moving straight away.'

'You mean to live on your own?'

'Yes I do. I'm fit and not helpless, you know. I did bring all you lot up.'

Hugh felt rebuffed. He realised that he had underestimated his mother as, for that matter, they all had. When she had moved and everything had been settled, the family fondly believed that it was they who had arranged everything, and Leah did not disillusion them.

There was no room in the new cottage for most of the furniture. Unsentimentally, she disposed of everything she did not want by distributing it among the family. Not everyone got what they wanted, but nobody dared to show any displeasure in front of their mother. Neither Hugh nor John had any wish to take anything and they returned to Pontcaer the day after the funeral.

By then, Hugh had made numerous new friends and not least among them was Charlie Newforth. Charlie, who was from Bristol, was younger than Hugh and had not served in the war. With the post-war demand for labour, he had joined the fair number of non-Welsh workers in the pits.

Hugh had met Bristolians in the army and he was fascinated by their distinctive accent. They had an unusual, guttural sort of intonation, said 'Wells' instead of Wales and had a strange habit of adding a superfluous letter 'l' to the end of certain words. When he returned from his father's funeral, Charlie sympathetically suggested that it would be a good 'ideal' for Hugh to accompany him on a weekend visit to his parents in Bristol. His parents would be happy to put Hugh up over the Saturday night.

It was a regular practice for Hugh, Charlie and others to go to nearby Cardiff on Saturdays, especially if there was a major rugby match to attend. They would return in the early hours of Sunday, not infrequently the worse for wear after visiting more pubs than was wise. Another objective of the trips was to seek out girls, and that was something at which Charlie excelled – not that he was short of girl friends in and around Pontcaer. Hugh was not a little jealous of the ease with which his friend was able to attract women.

He accepted the offer to go to Bristol. The city, just the other side of the channel to which it gave its name and a short train journey through the Severn Tunnel, was much larger than Cardiff and reputed to be much wealthier. On arrival, they were met at the station by two young women. Charlie at once embraced and lingeringly kissed the first. When the two had disentangled themselves, Charlie introduced the girl as his fiancée, Greta, whose name he pronounced 'Gretal'. Hugh felt somewhat shocked that Charlie, given his numerous girlfriends on the other side of the Severn, should be engaged to be married.

Charlie was unabashed at Hugh's obvious surprise. Without turning a hair, he introduced the second young woman as his sister Vicky. Hugh had been embarrassed standing there through Charlie and Greta's prolonged display of affection, and felt awkward and hesitant about introducing himself. He sensed that Vicky felt the same way. She was older than her brother but of an altogether quieter and shyer personality.

They walked from the station to Charlie and Vicky's parents' home, quite a long walk, to a district which Charlie told him was called Southville, which, he assured Hugh, was much superior to the adjoining district, called Bedminster, which he pronounced 'Bemster'. Towards the end of the walk, they passed some largish houses set back from the road behind long gardens and overlooking a wide canal which Charlie said was called The Cut and which diverted the River Avon to make the docks non-tidal. Charlie pointed out one of the houses as being the home of the world-famous singer Clara Butt, who had just been made Dame Clara. They turned into a side road and arrived at the Newforth household.

Although only just behind the grand houses with their open view across The Cut towards the city centre, this was a modest, terraced house whose view from the front was the houses on the opposite side of the street and, from the back, the backs of similar houses in another street.

'We were so sorry, Mr Hughes, to hear from Charlie about your dad's sudden passing,' Mrs Newforth said.

'Thank you, Mrs Newforth. That's most kind and it's very kind of you to invite me here.'

'Ooh!' said Greta. 'I do love to hear that lovely Welsh accent. I've been enjoying it all the way from the station. I bet the Welsh girls sound lovely, too. I hope they're not trying to get at my Charlie.'

Hugh was aware that Charlie was suddenly giving him a very warning look, which all too clearly meant 'Keep your mouth shut.' Loyalty triumphed over truth. 'Oh no,' he said, 'not at all.'

'When Charlie gets married,' Mr Newforth said, 'he will have to come back to Bristol. There'll be a job for him in Wills's.' A discerning listener might have heard a note in his voice indicating that he knew his son better than the son appreciated, was not unaware of his fondness for multiple female company and believed that Charlie married might require a parental as well as a wifely eye on him. He turned to Hugh. 'I'm glad to see that you're a smoker.'

'I believe that you work in the cigarette factory, Mr Newforth,' Hugh said, anxious to make conversation and to steer away from the subject of Charlie.

'Yes, I've been there for a few years now and my little girl Vicky works there too. Nice girl, Vicky, make a good wife for some man.' This time, there was no mistaking a meaningful note in his voice.

Vicky blushed. 'Dad!' she said.

Hugh had tried to make conversation with Vicky on the way to the house. It was not easy because of her shyness, but he had already ascertained that she worked in the cigarette factory, as also did Greta, who was her friend. He thought, suddenly, how pretty she looked when she blushed.

The short weekend passed all too quickly. Charlie took him and the two girls into the city centre in the evening, with strict instructions from his father that they must be back by ten o'clock, so that Charlie could take Greta, who lived nearby, home by ten-thirty. The following morning, the four of them went on something of a sight-seeing tour, Charlie being particularly anxious to point out the

Clifton Suspension Bridge over the Avon Gorge and the docks, which extended right into the city centre. The docks, crowded with moored vessels, fascinated Hugh. He learned that Charlie's uncle Harold, his father's brother, was the captain of a small steamer trading, mostly in coal, between Bristol and Cardiff.

He was increasingly attracted to Vicky. Her shy, gentle manner appealed to him. When he and Charlie returned on an evening train, they were seen off by the two girls. In the last minutes before the train left, Charlie and Greta were embracing, oblivious of everything save each other. On an impulse, Hugh leaned forward and kissed Vicky on the cheek. She seemed pleased, so he kissed her on the mouth. They did not embrace and their lips touched only briefly. She did not object, as he feared she might.

'I hope you don't mind,' he said. 'I'd like to see you again. Can I write to you?'

'Yes,' she said. 'I'm not too good at writing, but I'll write back.'

'You haven't got a boyfriend, have you?' he asked, suddenly apprehensive.

'No,' she said.

'Well you have now.' He was startled at his own boldness and thought, as he had when her father had embarrassed her, how pretty she looked when she blushed.

He and Charlie boarded the train. 'Glad to see you got on well with my sister,' Charlie said as they gathered speed.

'She's a nice girl,' Hugh said. 'I must say, though, that I'm surprised that you're engaged. I wouldn't have thought it.'

Charlie laughed. 'Oh don't worry about the girls I see. They don't mean anything.'

However, Hugh could not find it in himself to dislike his friend. Indeed, he suddenly felt rather superior. Bet he's never been in a brothel, like I have, he thought. Then he froze; that was something about which neither Charlie nor Vicky, nor anybody else must ever know.

He wrote to Vicky within days and she replied promptly. They exchanged letters on a weekly basis, although the tone of their letters, which were essentially limited to brief exchanges of local news and good wishes, could hardly be called romantic. The chance to see her again arose shortly afterwards when the miners struck for better wages. The strike lasted a little over two weeks and Charlie suggested that they should go to his parents for a week. Hugh's feelings were mixed. The prospect of a whole week in Vicky's company delighted him but he felt that he could not stay that long without paying her parents for his keep, which would not be easy with no money coming in. Charlie, however, prevailed on him to go, on the understanding that he should make just a nominal payment.

The visit cemented Hugh and Vicky's mutual attraction. They walked out every evening when she came home from work, sometimes with Charlie and Greta, sometimes without them. Vicky went out of her way to show that she did not expect him to spend money. She was sympathetic to the miners, but her father was much less so and several arguments developed between him and Charlie. Hugh, often biting his tongue, took care to stay out of the exchanges.

Edward Newforth had grown up in the country, just outside Bristol. One of ten children, he had been brought up to be of humble station in a society controlled by the squire and the vicar. The poverty of that bleak society had driven him and several other members of the family to the city to seek work, but he had never outgrown the indoctrination of his early years.

He believed implicitly in the superiority of 'the big house' and its inhabitants and that 'the poor people' should know their place. If anyone questioned that order of society, he would defend it by extolling the munificence of the big house at Christmas in sending down logs for the poor people's fireplaces, even perhaps a few mince pies.

Mary, his wife, had grown up in the same village, also one of a large family, but she was less deferential. 'Crumbs from the rich man's table' she was liable to retort. She was also wont to recount, with a certain air of martyred pride, how, as a little girl in the Victorian age, she had once been put to bed early by her mother because she refused to curtsy to the vicar.

Edward found these occasionally revealed signs of rebelliousness quite disturbing. Such things, in his view, should not even be thought, leave alone discussed. He was proud that he knew his place and he was eternally grateful to the multi-millionaires Messrs W.D. & H.O. Wills for their generosity in giving him an appropriately lowly job in their cigarette factory. He did worry, though, about his two offspring.

It had shocked him when Charlie had left the low-paid but safe job that he himself had obtained for him in the cigarette factory. Even more worrying was the way Charlie had come back from Wales filled with ideas of trade unionism and hostility towards his employers. He was also worried by gossip on the factory floor that Charlie, from an early age, 'had a way with the girls'. At least, the boy was now engaged to be married, but he had an uneasy feeling that married life might not necessarily cure his wandering eye.

Vicky gave him worries of a different sort. She was the elder of the two and it was high time she was married. There had been a couple of young men in the factory who had shown some interest in her, but she was a shy girl and had not responded to them. Now, at last, she seemed to have a distinct inclination towards a young man, but there were some things about that young man that disturbed him.

He came from what Edward regarded as virtually a foreign country and he had that funny Welsh way of having a Christian name the same or nearly the same as his family name. Edward was suspicious of all Welshmen. True, the young fellow had met Vicky in the most respectable way possible, through her brother, but, like Charlie, he was a miner, with the same sort of subversive views that Charlie had developed.

At least, though, the boy had fought for King and country and he had to admire him for insisting on making a token payment for his keep when, temporarily at least, he had no wages coming in.

Hugh and Vicky's mutual attraction developed rapidly. He had written to May and to Myfanwy, the two sisters with whom he felt the strongest affinity, and also to his mother, to tell them of the nice young lady he had met. His mother, pleased by the news, had written back to invite him and Vicky to visit her for Christmas. Vicky's parents agreed and Vicky was delighted. Everyone knew that she was being propelled towards marriage, and even her father, despite his mixed feelings, was not unhappy at the prospect.

The two met at Cardiff station and completed the journey together. Robert and Myfanwy, both consumed with curiosity, met them at Pembroke Dock station and walked with them to Leah's house. The family gathered in strength to meet this girl with the strange accent from foreign parts who seemed likely to be the next addition to the family.

His mother spoke to him in private, the day before the two left.

'She's a nice girl, Hughie,' she said. 'It's time you settled down.'

Hugh thought that it sounded rather as if she was calling on him to end a misspent youth.

'Yes Mam,' he agreed, 'that's what I'm thinking. I haven't asked Vicky, but I'm sure she'll accept me.'

'No time like the present,' Leah said briskly. 'Best to strike while the iron's hot.' It was in her mind that all her other children had been younger when they married, with the exception of dear Joe, who had been deprived of the chance through his cruel, premature death in the war and Albert, whom she knew would never marry. Hugh knew that her advice, clichéd as it sounded, was good.

His style of proposing was not romantic. On the return journey, they both had to change trains at Cardiff, he for the valleys, she for Bristol. Throughout the journey, he had been preoccupied with his mother's advice but horribly nervous about actually proposing. It would have surprised him to know how accurately Vicky was reading his thoughts. Even when she put an encouraging hand into his, he did not really appreciate the significance of the gesture. But as they alighted from the London-bound express, he could contain himself no longer.

'Will you marry me?' he burst out.

'Yes,' she said, 'of course.'

'I shall have to come to see your father,' he said, 'to ask his approval.'

'I'm sure he'll approve,' she said, 'but whether he does or not, it won't make any difference.'

It was the most spirited and reassuring thing he had ever heard her say. Instantly, they were in each other's arms, long and lingeringly, just like Charlie and Greta had been when he and Vicky had first met on the station at Bristol.

A couple of weeks later, he went with Charlie to Bristol and formally declared his and Vicky's intentions to her parents. They, of course, were already aware of those intentions. Her father, notwithstanding his lingering reservations, was relieved that his shy daughter had at last, as he saw it, done the right thing and got herself engaged. Plans for the wedding were discussed, with talk about possibly even having a double wedding with Charlie and Greta in the summer. But an unforeseen development, beyond the control of any of them, abruptly ended any such plans.

Throughout the war, coal mining had been regulated by the government because of its likely failure, otherwise, to meet the requirements of the nation. That had led to demands for the outright nationalisation of the industry, which had infuriated the owners, not least Sir George Robson, the now elderly chairman of RMF Mining & Manufacturing Ltd, and his relation by marriage, managing director of the company, Richard Albert Mulholland-Flowers MP.

'How dare they!' Sir George snarled over brandy and cigars in his London club. 'Trying to confiscate our property and take the bread and butter out of our mouths.'

'The first thing we've got to do is to end those controls,' Richard replied. 'I've said so in the House.' Thoughtfully, he blew a smoke ring, something he was rather proud of being able to do. 'Then we've got to smash those unions.'

'And smash that Labour Party,' Sir George said. 'They're already in control of the county councils in Durham, Glamorgan and Monmouthshire, where all our pits are situated. Bloody load of bolsheviks.'

'And the time is coming,' Richard added, 'when we shall have to get rid of Lloyd George. He's only kept in power through the support of us Conservatives.'

'Where does he stand over ending these controls over mining?'

'Our people have really put the pressure on in the Cabinet. There'll be an announcement within the week.'

'Good. I trust your wife and those two young boys of yours are well.'

'They're all fine. I've got the boys' names down for Eton.'

Sir George winked. 'And how's Millie? God, wish I was twenty years younger.' He said it with real feeling.

'She's fine.' Richard's tone was curt, indicating that he did not welcome the inquiry.

Millicent Partridge-Dove was a lady who occupied a flat in Westminster and was visited by Richard at times when his wife thought he was either at his club or detained late at the House of Commons. She provided sex that was far more varied and pleasurable than any he had ever enjoyed with his wife. Not that any sex with his wife ever had been noticeably enjoyable. As well as being plain in appearance, she had been cold towards him from the start of their dynastically arranged marriage, and having, as she saw it, performed her marital duty in bearing two sons, she had become colder than ever.

'I gather from my brother-in-law in Pembrokeshire that your grandfather is not too well.'

'Not too well at all,' Richard said. 'But he is eighty-eight. I doubt if he'll see his eighty-ninth birthday.'

'You are his sole heir?'

'Yes, apart from some minor bequests.'

'What will you do with the estate at Bellwood.'

'I'm not sure. As you know, it's one of the largest estates in the county. Bellwood is not self-supporting but, on the other hand, I've checked things out and my grandfather has a large investment portfolio, bringing in something like a hundred thousand a year. Even with Lloyd George's death duties, which look like being a permanent thing, I'll get by.'

'Get by!' Sir George said. 'You're already a millionaire. You'll be one twice over – at least.'

'I have had a fortunate combination of luck and judgement, and the amalgamation of our mutual interests and then the war have all served me – and, indeed, both of us – very well. But by God, we've got to fight to hang on to the coal mines.'

On the day the government control was ended, the coal owners ended all terms of employment and announced that new terms would be imposed and no negotiations would be entertained. The same day, the government proclaimed a state of national emergency and troops were moved into the coalfields.

The new terms to be imposed on the miners involved huge reductions in wages. Hugh, who was a skilled man, found that his wages were to be reduced from nearly six pounds a week to well under three. The miners were totally united in refusing to accept such terms and were promptly locked out. Hugh was doubly angry, he knew at once that his wedding would have to be postponed.

Orders were given that the pit ponies were to be brought to the surface, a sure sign that the owners expected a lengthy dispute. Hugh was told that he would be expected to work on the surface through the lockout, on the new terms, to tend to the animals. He refused angrily. He guessed that his refusal would not be forgotten.

Numerous rallies and demonstrations were held throughout the coalfield and, accompanied by his brother John, Charlie Newforth and Dai Manners, with whom he lodged, he attended a large open-air rally held close to the Robson pit. There was a strong presence of troops and police. Like all those miners who were ex-servicemen, Hugh and Dai made a point of wearing their campaign medals from the war. There were ugly scenes when some inexperienced and over-zealous young troopers attempted to block their way as they joined the demonstration.

'Get out of my way,' Hugh said angrily.

'Who the fuck do you think you are to tell a soldier wearing His Majesty's uniform to get out of your way?' demanded a fresh-faced young trooper.

Hugh looked at the soldier's tunic, unadorned with any medals. He was suddenly shaking with rage. Looking back on the incident later, he would be hard put to recall anything that had made him more furious.

'I'm telling you,' he shouted at the top of his voice. 'I, who was wearing that uniform when you were in short trousers.' He pointed to his medals. 'And I was wearing it in the hell of the western front with other British soldiers to fight Germans, not to fight British workers trying to earn a decent living.'

By that time, Dai and several other war veterans, all wearing medals, had gathered round him, while a group of soldiers had likewise gathered round their comrade. Rifles were being raised as if to use the butts to strike the miners. There was every sign of an ugly and likely bloody confrontation. It was stopped by a sudden, stentorian roar.

'What's going on here? Stop it, whatever it is.'

Hugh recognised the voice instantly. It was Sergeant Major Lantlin, who suddenly emerged from among the soldiers, decorated with the Military Medal and campaign medals from both the Great War and the Boer War. Hugh recalled his intervention in support of the soldiers at Etaples against the silly Major Verrey-ffaire.

'These men are trying to stop us getting to the rally, Sar'nt Major Lantlin,' he said.

The sergeant major looked surprised. 'How do you know my name?' he asked.

'I was with you in the artillery on the Somme and at Passchendaele,' Hugh said.

'I see.' He looked at the now numerous nearby miners wearing medals and then turned to the raw young soldiers. 'These men have fought for their country in conditions that I hope none of you will ever have to see,' he barked. 'Stand aside and let them through.'

The soldiers obeyed sheepishly. The miners applauded and joined the throng waiting for the rally to start. A number of them patted Hugh on the back.

To a storm of applause, Gwynfor Morgan MP, accompanied by union officials, climbed onto the lorry which served as a platform. Now middle-aged and plumper than when Hugh had last seen him, he was wearing the dark coat and homburg hat that were the virtual uniform of those in his position. He had lost none of his brilliance in oratory.

'I have had some experience, myself, of Sir George Robson, who is the chairman of the company that owns this pit,' he declaimed, 'dating back to the days when I was, myself, a pit boy at Penduffryn. And now, he has amalgamated with his relation by marriage, who rejoices in the name of Richard Mulholland-Flowers MP. I sit opposite that man in the House of Commons, who is just one among many in serried ranks of hard-faced men who have done well out of the war.

'I look around me now and I see many locked-out miners wearing their medals from the war. Is this what you fought for? Is this what so many of your comrades and brethren died for? To see your wives and families starved into submission for the profits of men like Robson and Mulholland-Flowers?

'Mr Lloyd George,' he went on, 'announced at the end of the war that he wanted to create a land fit for heroes. Heroes! You have to be a hero to live in it.'

Gwynfor's speech was interrupted constantly with applause and at the end they sang 'For He's a Jolly Good Fellow'. But it made little ultimate difference. For week after week, the miners held out, facing intimidation, arrest, brutality. Hugh saw his brother's three children and many others becoming increasingly underweight. He, John and Sally all went without to provide food for the children. He drew on his savings, such as they were, in order to help others who were in greater need. Several times, postal orders arrived from Vicky to help out. He wondered if her father knew that she had sent them; he surmised not. Men, women and children alike stood together but, eventually, with all the power of capital and the state against them, the men were starved back to work on the coal owners' terms.

Shortly after the lockout ended, Richard Mulholland-Flowers and his wife dined with Sir George and Lady Robson, his wife's aunt. Champagne flowed freely, for it was a double celebration. Just a week before the lockout ended, Colonel Mulholland had died and Richard had inherited the great bulk of his very considerable fortune. His grandfather's last words to him had been 'Beat those damn bolsheviks, whatever you do.'

'Have you made up your mind now about what you'll be doing with the estate at Bellwood?' Sir George asked.

'Not yet. For the time being, I shall keep it going. It is, after all, my ancestral home – in a manner of speaking.' He chuckled ironically.

Sir George chuckled in unison, although the two women remained demurely silent. There was an affinity between the two men that stretched beyond their business association. Both, although in different ways, had started life in humble circumstances. Both had come to the top of the ladder. Both were aware that they were objects of dislike and distrust, even frustrated scorn because, although very wealthy, they were not 'gentlemen'. Both held their detractors in contempt.

'You could get yourself a knighthood,' Sir George said. 'All you have to do is make an appropriate donation in the right quarter. Lloyd George will do the rest.'

'Not for me,' Richard said. 'Do you know there's a subversive song going round. It goes to the tune of "Onward Christian Soldiers" and simply consists of singing over and over again, "Lloyd George knew my father! My father knew Lloyd George".'

In the coalfields, there was no jollity, only a legacy of hatred that would never die. For Hugh, things proved even worse than for others. On reporting back for work, he was told that there was no job for him. Charlie Newforth and Dai Manners were told the same. They had been too active in the lockout. Of their little group, only his brother John had a job to go back to.

Chapter 12

'The best thing we can do is to go to Bristol,' Charlie said to Hugh. 'There's no chance of a job here, and since you're marrying Vicky, it seems as good a choice for you as for me.'

'I don't know,' Hugh said warily. 'What job would I get there? I don't really know anything except pit work.'

'There are pits around Bristol,' Charlie said, 'but I'm buggered if I'm going to work in one, they're even worse than these ones here. They say, too, that they're getting worked out and won't last much longer anyway.'

Hugh turned to Dai. 'What are you going to do?' he asked.

'I don't know,' Dai said. 'Like you two, I'm blacklisted in the pits, but there's no way, anyway, that I intend to work any more for those bastards.' He paused. 'You know that chap Tommy Thomas who has started a garage down the valley – petrol pumps and repairs. He says that the motor transport is going to get big. He did speak to me some time ago about joining him. I might take him up on that. Be tough at first, I'm sure, but so is everything else.'

Hugh and Charlie duly went to Bristol. Charlie's father, now a chargehand, recommended him to his superiors at the cigarette factory and Charlie returned to working there. He and Greta were married a few months later and took up residence in rented rooms.

Edward suggested to Hugh that he could 'speak' for him, too, for a job in the factory, but the idea did not appeal to Hugh. Charlie's father was bewildered that anyone, especially someone out of work, should not want to work for Messrs W.D. & H.O. Wills. He was an avid reader of right-wing newspapers and believed implicitly in the fantasies they purveyed. He hoped that his prospective son-in-law was not one of those thousands they depicted as idlers living on the dole because they were too lazy to work.

Reluctantly, Hugh and Vicky agreed that their wedding would have to be put back until he found work. He moved into temporary lodgings and signed on at the local labour exchange. It was the first time he had been out of work. He felt humiliated and disgusted at having to line up to draw the meagre 'dole'.

Fortunately, that did not last too long. There was a coal mine on the outskirts of the city, so he walked out to it and was taken on. It was a much smaller pit than those to which he had been accustomed. As there was no work for a pony driver, he became instead a coal-face worker, hewing out the coal with pickaxe and shovel, dirty, dangerous work that paid much less than his previous job, but he felt that at least he had regained his self-respect by being again able to earn his living, however restricted a living it might be.

He had been dreading the long walk between the pit and his lodgings, especially after coming off shift, in his filthy working clothes and grimy from head to foot. For this was a city where mining was not a major industry, where such sights in the streets were uncommon and even likely to arouse hostility. He knew, too, that his landlady was unenthusiastic at the thought of a grimy miner coming into her nice house close to the cigarette factory, where the workers were clean and respectably dressed. She could not bring herself to believe that dirty miners, who were always going on strike, did not go home to dirty homes, that miners' houses could be as spotlessly clean as her own and their wives as house-proud as she was.

The pit was in open country, in sight of but clear of the built-up outskirts of the city. There was a row of cottages which, although clearly for miners, were more attractive than any such that Hugh had ever seen before, with gardens back and front. With their open location, they were arguably superior to the houses crammed into the city streets. On being taken on, he enquired as to whether any lodgings might be available and was directed to a particular house. There he was greeted by a homely miner's wife, agreed terms then and there, moved in the next day and started work the day after that.

He and Vicky were to be married shortly before Christmas. They seemed to be bogged down in endless preparations for months in advance. Hugh worried himself to a state of near distraction over who should be the best man. Should it be Charlie, through whom he had first met Vicky and who was to become his brother-in-law, or should it be Robert Snape, his friend from school days who had been his brother-in-law for years? He was quite unable to make up his mind.

Vicky, by contrast, had no problems choosing bridesmaids. They would be the two young daughters of her father's younger brother Harold, the one who was skipper of the small coaster trading in the Bristol Channel, while her best friend Greta, now Charlie's wife, would be matron of honour. In the event, exasperated at Hugh's indecision, she more or less bullied him into coming to a decision and they settled the matter in a single conversation with her brother, which rather left them both wondering why so much time had been spent worrying about it.

'If you want me, of course I'll be your best man,' Charlie said, 'but I understand if you want your oldest friend to stand for you.' Secretly, he was relieved.

Robert, much less inhibited, accepted with alacrity, performed the duties admirably and made a witty and well-received speech at the reception. Hugh was much less at ease at being called to speak before so many people, so he simply thanked them for being there and for their many presents.

He was genuinely pleased that so many of his family and friends were there, having been worried that they would not want to make their various journeys from Wales. His mother and his sister Alice, the one between him and Myfanwy, with her husband Emrys, travelled with Robert and Myfanwy from Pembroke Dock. John and Sally came from Pontcaer and his sister May and husband John from Penduffryn. He was especially pleased that every one of his brothers and sisters who could not be there sent telegrams of good wishes. There was also one from Dai Manners, now a struggling but hopeful partner in the garage he had talked about.

There were two unexpected guests, Mr and Mrs David Jones, better remembered as Dai horses and Blodwen post. Hugh had not seen them since leaving to join up in 1914, but Dai was a well-remembered and respected mentor of his formative years and Blodwen, whom he knew less well, he still remembered as the first person he had met in Penduffryn on that day when he ran away from Round Pond Farm.

'Do you still oversee the pit ponies?' he asked Dai.

'No,' Dai replied, 'I've left the pit, thank God. My brother Ioan died a couple of years ago. He never married and as I was his only close relative, he left the farm to me. Having grown up there when my dad worked it, I do know something about how to run the place and, of course, I have taken over the contract to supply the ponies. We live on the farm but Blodwen is still the postmistress.'

Hugh was curious. 'With so many out of work, do people complain about Blodwen being a married woman and still working?'

Dai laughed. 'Some do. You know what people are, but most of them accept it. There's nobody else qualified to run the post office.' He squeezed his wife's hand. 'Besides, she's been there so long that she's a village institution. After the strike, I took on a couple of the blacklisted miners and that has made a very good impression.'

'Not with the mine owners, I should think.'

'Bugger those bastards,' Dai said with conviction. Hugh recalled that he had never been the man to miss out on appropriate expletives. Blodwen was not entirely tactful in her greeting.

'Why Hughie, what a lot has happened since that day you arrived in Penduffryn, a little boy complete with bicycle and wellington boots. And now here we are for your wedding.'

'I heard how you and Dai got married, just after the war started,' Hugh said. He was a little irritated by her manner.

Dai was well aware that his wife's words were not always as well chosen as they were well meant. He guessed too that Hugh, his nerves already a little on edge, might take offence where none was intended. It was an anxious moment.

'Getting married was the best thing I ever did,' he said hastily. 'I hope you and Vicky will be as happy as we are.'

'And that goes for both of us,' Blodwen said. She handed him a gift-wrapped parcel. 'A wedding present,' she said.

'Thank you so much,' he said. Tension was released, although he could not prevent himself from thinking a little maliciously that Vicky and he had made up their minds to get married a damn sight more quickly than Dai and Blodwen had.

When opened, the gift proved to be a cut-glass butter dish in a presentation box, with a silver-plated cover and salver. It was one of the most expensive wedding presents they received.

Hugh still felt that Blodwen was a slightly jokey name and he thought that she looked more of a Blodwen than ever. She still wore pince-nez glasses, which he thought couldn't be very comfortable, and she seemed even more well-bosomed than he remembered. She reminded him of a comic postcard he had seen, with a big-breasted pub landlady leaning over the bar, pointing to a photograph on the wall behind her of a man in a swimming costume. She was saying to a customer, 'That was me 'usband. Champion breast stroker of the navy 'e was'. He wondered facetiously if Dai now qualified to be called the champion breast stroker of Penduffryn.

He was grateful that so many family and friends had travelled to be at the wedding and pleased above all at his mother's presence.

For Leah, it was an occasion to which she had looked forward with mixed feelings. She had never before travelled outside Wales and she, who was so capable and self-assured in her own environment, was nervous at the prospect, reassured only by the company of her family. The lengthy journey, with two changes of train and terminating in the big, noisy station, had not helped.

She had never before been in a big city and the bustling, crowded scene bewildered her. Then there were all these people with their strange accents who were to be her new relatives. But these natives proved to be friendly. As curious to meet her and the bridegroom's family as she was to meet them, they made her welcome and she liked them, although sorting out who was who among the profusion of Vicky's aunts, uncles and cousins was a little overwhelming. One of the most successful acquaintanceships proved to be with Vicky's parents, with whom she stayed. On their best behaviour, they made her particularly welcome and there proved to be warm rapport between her and Vicky's mother, not least perhaps because they had both been country girls, with more in common than geography and accent might have suggested.

The wedding was celebrated in the local Anglican parish church, not from any religious convictions on anybody's part but simply because it was the conventional thing to do. Edward and Mary hired the church hall for the reception, which was an entirely do-it-yourself affair, with all the catering, including the wedding cake, provided by Mary, with the help of Vicky's aunts and cousins. Photographs were taken by a local professional – only a few because that was all they could afford.

Vicky, clutching her bouquet, was splendid in her wedding dress, which was shortish and above the ankle in the new post-war fashion, showing off her white wedding shoes. Some of the less sophisticated of her extended family, as well as some of Hugh's, including his mother, were mildly concerned at the shortness of the dress. Hugh wore the newly-bought serge suit that would last as his best suit for many years and he carried the new trilby hat which would serve similarly. He was not very comfortable with his stiff white collar or with the new black shoes that he had polished to perfection.

They were seen off on their honeymoon by a large, cheerful, confetti-throwing throng. The honeymoon consisted of a few days at nearby Weston-super-Mare, where they stayed at the home of a couple known to Edward and Mary. With little experience of sex on Hugh's part and none on Vicky's, they faced the prospect of the wedding night with trepidation.

The vicar who had married them had talked to them before the wedding; talked down to them would be a more accurate description. He had talked about their sacred duty to forsake all others and to procreate children, but he had told them nothing about the actual facts of how to do the latter and was as embarrassed as they were.

Hugh's new-found workmates among the Bristol miners had told him that 'not to fuck her on the first night' was the biggest insult he could give her and a sure recipe for a disastrous marriage. Vicky's friends at the factory had told her that she must 'lie back and let him have his way'. It was a fair demonstration of the massive ignorance about such matters among their generation.

As they had come away from the pre-marital talk with the vicar, she had squeezed his hand.

'I'm sure we'll be all right, love,' she had said.

'I'm sure we will,' he had replied.

Like their parents, they had been brought up in the belief that sex was basically sinful and 'dirty', something to be neither discussed nor enquired into, something which was, somehow, to be revealed as if by magic through the process of marriage.

The actual process of 'revelation' was not made any easier by their icy-cold bedroom and the heavy blankets under which they slept. In the event, the marriage was consummated on their third night together, after a series of tentative experiments which, notwithstanding the cold and the blankets, they found increasingly, if at first embarrassingly, pleasurable, exciting and not guilt-making.

From the day he started at the pit, Hugh knew that his days there would be numbered, since the reserves were being exhausted and closure was approaching. He did not find the prospect wholly depressing. He felt confident that, given the variety of jobs available in Bristol, he would be able to put mining behind him for ever.

He and Vicky were lucky in obtaining one of the miners' cottages for their home. Shortly before their wedding, a cottage fell vacant and he seized the opportunity to rent it. So they avoided the lot of most of their contemporaries, who had to live with in-laws or rent rooms in someone else's house.

Like all the miners' houses, the cottage was the property of the colliery company. When they decided to close the mine, they were anxious to dispose of the houses, so they offered them to the occupants. Since the company was looking for quick disposals, the terms were not unfavourable. It was made clear though that any who did not take up the offer would be evicted on the closure of the pit and their homes put on the market. Some were in no position to buy and were left without homes or jobs. Some ended up, inevitably, in the workhouse, where, as the 'undeserving' poor, husbands were separated from wives while children, separated from their parents, were given the minimum of schooling and subsequently put to 'useful' work.

Where possible, the miners' union helped their members. Through their good offices, a long-term mortgage could be arranged for the purchase of the cottages, with a low repayment rate. The snag was that a deposit had to be found. There was no way that Hugh could afford the deposit. He was at his wits' end, seeing his marriage wrecked even before it had properly started. Unexpectedly, and generously, Vicky's father, no less alarmed for his daughter's future, came to the rescue.

'I've got over a hundred pounds in the Post Office Savings Bank,' he said. 'I'll draw some of that out and give it to you as a wedding present.'

'That is most generous, Dad,' Hugh responded, already getting accustomed to addressing him in that manner.

'Glad to help,' Edward said. 'Nothing like owning your own home. An Englishman's home is his castle.'

'As long as it is a castle,' Hugh said.

Edward did not reply. It was a thought that had neither been put to him before nor had ever occurred to him.

Within a year, Vicky was pregnant and their firstborn, a boy, came into the world in the summer of 1923. The birth was difficult and Vicky's mother, really worried, moved temporarily into the house to provide the constant and devoted care without which the little boy might not have survived. The first two weeks of his life were a time of immense worry and seemed to go on for ever but, when it at last became clear that he would live, Hugh was seized with an immense sense of pride as he cradled him in his arms. For the first time since he was a small boy himself, there were tears in his eyes.

Naturally, he knew nothing of the supercilious Dr Jones who had attended his mother for his own birth and whose perfunctory ministrations, had they now been applied, might well have resulted in the loss of both mother and child. The doctor who attended Vicky could not have been more different.

Dr Andrew MacBrayne was a well-known local practitioner. He was retained by the miners' union, which was how Hugh had first come across him and, in those days long before the National Health Service, he had registered on the doctor's panel. Dr MacBrayne was a fiery Scot who made no secret of his strong Socialist views, which had been formed from his experience of the lives of his working-class patients on his native Clydeside and by wartime experience in the Royal Army Medical Corps. There, he had been repelled as much by the attitude of upper-class colleagues (like Captain Carmichael, who had treated Hugh when he had been wounded) as by the criminal slaughter of the battlefields. He was blunt with Hugh.

'You are a very lucky man,' he said. 'Your wife has had a difficult and painful time. You need to consider very carefully about having any more children.'

The difficult birth had severely shocked and worried Hugh. The doctor had told him in advance that there could be problems, but neither he nor Vicky had properly absorbed the warning. They were dangerously naive; their knowledge about such matters was based almost exclusively in the experience of their own families, among whom most mothers had healthily borne healthy children, often against the odds, given the way social conditions were loaded against them. Where there had been difficulties, even the occasional lost baby, there had invariably developed a wall of family silence. So, with their limited knowledge, they had treated the doctor's warning far too lightly and they had simply not expected problems.

Now, Hugh was taken aback by the doctor's bluntness. 'Why must we consider not having any more children?' he asked. 'I want my son to have at least a brother or sister.'

'The fact is that your wife could lose her life in childbirth and the baby could be lost as well.' The doctor's tone remained blunt but, inwardly, he felt sympathetic.

'Do you mean that we should stop – er – I mean…' Hugh's voice stumbled and trailed off in embarrassment.

'You mean should you stop having sexual intercourse with your wife? No, not necessarily. I will let you have some information about birth control.'

No one had ever spoken to Hugh before in such clear language and with such obvious authority. Knowledge about family planning was in its infancy, hardly even born and it was as taboo a subject as masturbation. In respectable company, where prudery reigned supreme, you never talked about such things.

But talk of contraception had come up among workmates and he recalled the furious reaction of one who was a devout Roman Catholic. The man in question, being blessed with both a strong sexual appetite and a fecund wife, was already the father of five children and living, as a consequence, well below what would later come to be called the poverty line.

They named the baby Kenneth, a departure from both Hugh's and Vicky's family tradition. There had never before been a Kenneth in either family. There was no reaction from any of the Hughes but Edward Newforth was not happy.

'Every baby born into my family has been named after a King or Queen of England,' he said. 'Why don't you call him George after His Majesty?'

'Because neither Vicky nor I like the name George,' Hugh replied.

'Well I don't like this. I know you don't like the royal family but couldn't you call him Edward, after me?'

'We are calling him Kenneth Edward Joseph, that's after you and also after my father.'

'I shall call him Edward.'

'That's entirely up to you, but his first name is Kenneth, and Kenneth or Ken is what we shall call him.'

Eventually, common sense got the better of prejudice and Edward compromised by addressing his grandson as 'Kenneth Edward'.

Just over two years after Kenneth, their second son was born, not least because neither parent was inclined to follow the doctor's advice about birth control. They neither properly understood the advice nor the consequences of not putting it into practice. Above all, though, they longed for a second child. They had hoped for a girl but did not complain. The birth was again very difficult.

Dr MacBrayne did not mince his words. 'Your wife, Mr Hughes, will never be able to have any more children.'

'You mean, doctor, that we must not try for any more?'

'Whether you "try" or not, your wife cannot have any more children. The birth, as you know, has been even more difficult than that of your first child. Fortunately, this baby, like his brother, is healthy, but the birth has done certain damage to your wife, making it impossible for her to conceive again. You declined to act on my earlier advice but you have been very lucky. It's a matter of luck and the workings of nature that I don't need to advise you this time.'

'But is my wife going to be all right?' He was really worried.

'Yes, fortunately, she is. You may well live, both of you, to a good age.'

They took the mixture of good and bad news stoically. They had settled into a happy companionship and the second difficult birth served to bring them closer together. They were proud to have two healthy children, and although they would have liked to have a daughter, they were resigned to the fact that it would never be possible.

They rather liked the idea of giving the new baby a Welsh name, but they wanted a name that would be acceptable to his English relatives and also his Welsh ones, none of whom, apart from Myfanwy, had ever been given specifically Welsh names. They discussed calling him after his father, although spelling it Huw, but, eventually, they settled on Owen, with William as his second name. The choice pleased his grandfather, who thought that Owen was rather distinctive and felt that William retained his own family tradition of names taken from Kings of England. Who knew, the boy might prove to be a conqueror! As with his other grandson, he always called the boy by both his first names. For him, to his dying day, they were Kenneth Edward and Owen William.

Hugh was aware that he had reached a turning point. He was the father of two children, responsible for seeing that they and his wife were fed, clothed and housed. He was a householder, a comparative rarity in his social stratum. For perhaps the first time in his life, he took himself to be a person of some standing.

Shortly before his first son was born, he had changed his job, putting mining behind him for ever, with a feeling of vast relief. There was not really any choice. The closure of the pit was expected to be announced any day, whilst, with the purchase of the house safely completed, he would have the mortgage repayments, relatively modest though they were, as an additional burden. He looked around and was fortunate to obtain a job with a local builder.

Financially, things remained difficult. He started as a labourer, carrying bricks in a hod, but came gradually to acquire skills like house-painting, wallpapering and bricklaying, which proved immensely useful and money-saving at home. By the time Owen was born, he had started on a well-constructed extension to the house, effectively adding another room. By then, too, he had become an accomplished gardener, finding an inherent skill probably bequeathed to him by his father and, like his father before him, he utilised every inch of space in his garden to grow vegetables which both saved money and tasted better than those bought in shops.

Becoming accustomed, in his new job, to working out of doors in all weathers was no more easy than had been the total contrast of working underground. He reflected wryly that at least his experience in the trenches in all weathers now served him well.

He did not voice the thought. Like most of his generation, he talked little about his wartime experiences. It was as if there was a sort of self-inflicted, collective amnesia to block it all out. As for its being 'the war to end wars', one certainty was that it had done nothing to end the class war against the working people who had provided the cannon fodder. As for the 'land fit for heroes', Gwynfor Morgan's comment that you had to be a hero to live in it summed it up pretty accurately.

He had joined the newly-formed British Legion, inspired by its proclaimed objective to provide for disabled and unemployed ex-soldiers, but had become disillusioned by its patrician leadership, which sought only to achieve that objective whilst retaining the existing order of society which was responsible for the problems in the first place. For his part, he thought that what was needed in Britain was a revolution like there had been in Russia, to sweep away the rule of the aristocracy.

The *Daily Herald*, a paper originally established before the war by striking journalists, was his regular reading. The paper was an advocate of progressive causes, contributed to by some of the most brilliant writers of the day. Among things he read was that a new musical work called *A Pastoral Symphony* had appeared. It was composed by Ralph Vaughan Williams. He realised that the composer was the large ambulance orderly in the ill-fitting uniform who had helped take him from the front line to the hospital and whom he had seen writing down the notes of a bugler practising behind the line during quiet evenings. He saw that a friend of the composer had described the work as 'RVW rolling over and over in a ploughed field on a wet day'.

Hugh knew his own limitations. He knew that he would almost certainly not understand the music, even if he had the chance to hear it, and he knew there was no way he could evaluate the views of the sophisticated critics. But that did not prevent him from conjecturing, more accurately than he could possibly know, that the rolling over and over in a field was probably more related to soldiers in the muddy and blood-soaked battlefields of the Somme and Passchendaele than to any English pastoral scene.

Chapter 13

Sir George Robson was not a man to make New Year resolutions. In fact, he regarded the whole process as damn silly. His whole life had been guided by a single resolution – to make as much money as possible and to use it to enter the 'society' from which his origins otherwise excluded him. He saw no reason to renew that resolution on a merely annual basis.

However, as the year 1925 wore on, he came to the conclusion that the New Year would be an appropriate time to retire. It was a difficult year, especially in coal mining, which had been the foundation of his fortune and he could see greater difficulties ahead. He was forced to admit to himself, although he would never do so to any other person, not even the wife to whom he had been satisfactorily married for so long, that he was growing old and becoming increasingly weary of the constant battles and decision-making that he had formerly enjoyed.

After all, he reasoned, he had done his share over a long time. The crown of his achievements had been in creating, in partnership with Richard Mulholland-Flowers MP, the company RMF Ltd, with its extensive operations in mining, steel making and engineering. He reflected that he had achieved pretty well all his ambitions. He was wealthy, he was a knight of the realm, his daughter had married into the aristocracy and his granddaughter had been presented at court and seemed to have good marriage prospects.

His greatest disappointment was in his son, who, he had long realised, was not up to following him into the chairmanship of the company. Nor was the son up to achieving his father's ambition that he should follow him into Parliament, a position which Sir George thought required much less ability. For all his father's influence or, as some of the more snobbish members of their party thought, because of it, it had been impossible to find a constituency prepared to accept the son as its candidate.

Nor was he happy about his son's marriage. True, the boy, like his sister, had made what was called a 'good' marriage into a wealthy family of impeccable lineage. If you traced the lineage back far enough, you came to nothing less than one of the numerous illegitimate offspring of King Charles II. But Sir George did not like his daughter-in-law. She had a haughty, condescending manner and when she laughed, it reminded him of the neighing of a horse. There was the added disappointment of the couple's failure to produce children, so that there was unlikely to be any continuation of the family name.

With all these things in mind, he suggested to Richard that they meet for dinner at their London club. That was always their practice when business decisions of major importance had to be taken. They duly wined and dined during the first week of the new year of 1926 and, following what had become a regular ritual, after eating, they retired to another room for coffee, port and cigars. Only then would they come to the real business of the evening: their joint money-making.

'I don't like this gold standard nonsense,' Sir George declared. 'When the government put the pound back to its pre-war level, they should have known that they would be pricing our coal out of all our overseas markets.'

'I agree,' Richard replied. 'The same applies to our engineering exports.'

'Don't they know that we are a country dependent on exports?' Sir George demanded sarcastically. 'What are they playing at?'

'It's a decision taken to appease bankers,' Richard said. 'Business doesn't want it and I spoke against it in the House. Among the problems is that fellow Churchill, the Chancellor of the Exchequer. He still thinks we're in the pre-war days of the British Empire, when the City of London more or less controlled the world money markets. He and, I am afraid, all too many others, don't seem to realise that the pre-war world is gone for ever.'

'It was inevitable that wages would have to come down to realistic levels and hours of work be extended,' Sir George said. 'It is disgraceful that when those bolshevik trade union bosses threatened to bring the pits, the railways and the docks to a standstill, the government capitulated and introduced a coal subsidy, to keep miners' wages artificially high with taxpayers' money.'

'That can't and won't go on – and the government knows it,'

Richard assured him. 'You will have seen the announcement of the Organisation for the Maintenance of Supplies, to recruit volunteers and that preparations are in hand for a state of emergency. I am afraid that we are heading for bigger trouble than we've ever seen before; much greater than in 1921.'

'That's what I want to talk to you about,' Sir George said. 'With all this looming up before us, it's time for me to hand over to someone younger. I propose to retire from the chairmanship of the company – subject, of course, to your agreement on mutually acceptable terms.'

Richard successfully prevented the jubilation in his heart from showing in his face. As shrewd a calculator as Sir George, he had expected that this was to be the purpose of their dinner. His response was already decided.

'I'm genuinely sorry to hear that,' he said smoothly and hypocritically. 'I've no doubt, though, that we can come to a mutually acceptable agreement. Perhaps I might combine the chairmanship and the managing directorship as executive chairman.'

'I thought you might have something like that in mind.' Inwardly, Sir George thought: You're a hypocritical bastard, Richard, as well as a clever one. You've been waiting for this for ages. Aloud, he said, 'As you know, I had at one time hoped that Gordon, my son, might succeed me.' He paused and looked Richard straight in the eye. 'But you're a clever man, Richard, and an observant one, and you know as well as I do that Gordon isn't up to it.'

'I wouldn't underestimate Gordon,' Richard said, smoother than ever.

Sir George replied in a voice lacking any trace of parental sentiment. 'Neither would I. We both estimate him at his real value, neither under nor over. I shall, of course, want him to remain a none-executive director of the company and to continue to draw the fees he receives.'

'I'm sure that presents no problem,' Richard said. Inwardly, he was already thinking about how long it might take for an opportunity to arise to get the useless idiot off the board.

'As to my own position,' Sir George said, 'I shall retire from the board but I shall, of course, retain all my shares and, subject to your approval, I will translate my salary as chairman into a lifelong pension, to be transferred to my wife for her lifetime if I predecease her.'

'We can agree that,' Richard said.

Both men knew exactly how things stood. Sir George knew he had the whip hand, Richard knew there was no choice. He and Sir George held the bulk of the shares but neither had a controlling interest. The only other directors and shareholders were Sir George's wife, his son and Richard's wife, who was Lady Robson's niece. If it came to a showdown, Sir George controlled three of the five votes and possibly even that of Richard's wife, to make four of the five. Richard knew that he could not necessarily count on his wife's support and, even if he could, he could still not win.

'So that's settled,' Sir George said. 'We'll call a board meeting next week and finalise it.'

That was the usual way the company's policy was decided. The two would meet at the club, decide the policy and then put it to the board, who rubber-stamped it. Board meetings were only held irregularly, no more than was necessary to meet legal requirements and to endorse decisions taken by Richard and Sir George.

'How's Alice?' Sir George asked.

'She's fine.' The response was curt, clearly indicating that the subject of his wife was not to be pursued. Sir George took the point, he knew as well as Richard that it was now a marriage in name only. He had long stopped enquiring about Millicent Partridge-Dove, who provided Richard with so much that his wife denied him. 'I wonder what the outcome of that will be?' he mused.

As Richard's chauffeur drove him home to his cold wife, he reflected that his career was now at its zenith. He was very wealthy, about to become head of a powerful industrial conglomerate and he was a Member of Parliament in a comfortably safe seat. He had no further political ambitions; he had entered politics to advance business contacts rather than seek ministerial status. His constituents were quite happy with the three or four visits a year he paid them between elections.

Not bad, he thought. Yet, never absent from the back of his mind was the knowledge that luck had played a remarkable part in his life.

His mother and her husband had been lucky to obtain employment with the wealthy Mr Black after the Colonel threw them out. In turn, he himself, had been extraordinarily lucky in that the childless Mr Black had paid to give him an elitist education and then made him his heir. Then, when the father he had never known had been killed in the Boer War, it was Henry Black who had done so much to ensure his recognition by his grandfather, who had eventually also made him his heir.

He knew that there were few indeed who could look to such a sequence of events in their lives. The only real downside had been in his unhappy arranged marriage but, at least, that had provided two sons, of whom he was proud. They believed that, like their hero grandad who had been killed in battle, their paternal grandma was dead. They knew nothing of the Georgian house in Tenby where, thanks to Henry Black's munificence, she still lived in some style with her husband, stoically accepting estrangement from her grandsons.

Richard acknowledged that, sooner or later, he would have to reveal their true antecedents to the boys, not least because of a late, quirky codicil to Henry Black's will that the house in Tenby would eventually go to the first of any progeny of Richard's. It might prove difficult, but he was confident that he could deal with it when the time came.

More immediately important was that there was an immense industrial dispute arising and nobody could be sure what the ultimate outcome might be. He knew that living costs had risen since the war and that the miners needed a rise rather than a cut in wages, simply to retain their already inadequate living standards. They, too, had wives and families. But he was situated irrevocably on the other side of the class war and would see to it that all the power of capital and the state was brought to bear to keep them down.

Yet, try as he might, he could not banish the thought that, had it not been for the series of lucky events that had played such a part in shaping his life, he could have been one of those miners rather than the very wealthy industrialist, landowner and member of the ruling class that he now was.

Although Hugh was immensely relieved to have put mining behind him for ever, he could not lose interest in the industry and he had followed the developing conflict closely and with growing anger. His was a letter-writing family, and apart from what he read in the newspapers, he could see from letters from his brother in Pontcaer and his sister in Penduffryn that a huge struggle was building up.

His post-war experience had turned him wholly against the established order. He read that a Labour MP called Clement Attlee had said that every ideal he had fought for in four years of active service had been betrayed. That was exactly how he felt and that was how many others felt. 'We could do with that chap as Prime Minister,' he said to Charlie, his brother-in-law.

More immediately, he was preoccupied with his new-born son Owen, who cried constantly and was said by everyone to resemble his father, as compared with Kenneth, now a toddler who always needed watching and was said to take after his mother. When Kenneth was six months old, Hugh and Vicky had managed to scrape the money together to make a short visit to Pembroke Dock to introduce Leah to her latest grandson. They thought that they might go there again in the spring, to show Owen to his grandmother and his numerous aunts, uncles and cousins.

Meanwhile, there was good news for Charlie and his wife Greta. They had been married four years and had begun to think, as Greta put it, that they 'were not going to be blessed with children' but suddenly and joyfully, she was pregnant. It was a happy family group, Charlie and Greta, Edward and Mary, who assembled at Hugh and Vicky's a month before Christmas for a Sunday afternoon tea party, a regular family ritual that rotated between their various homes.

The children had been put to bed, the women had washed up and they were all sitting round the fire in the one heated room in the house.

'There's going to be big trouble in the pits,' Charlie said.

'Yes,' Hugh agreed. 'The owners, as usual, want lower wages and longer hours.'

'And the government's spoiling for a fight as much as the owners are,' Charlie said.

'If it comes to a showdown,' Hugh said, 'I reckon the railwaymen and the dockers will come out as well.'

'They can't do that,' his father-in-law argued. 'That would be challenging the elected government.' As always, he based his views on what he read in right-wing newspapers.

'About time that lot *were* challenged,' Charlie said.

'It's getting late,' his mother put in hastily, only too aware that an unpleasant argument could be developing.

'I suppose we should,' Edward said. There was by then a tacit agreement that arguments about politics within the family were to be avoided, since they invariably became heated and there was no hope of reconciliation between implacably opposed views.

Early in the New Year, Hugh and Vicky took the boys to Pembroke Dock for a short stay with their grandmother. On the long walk from the station to Leah's house, no easy task with two small boys squashed into a perambulator, they stopped, as always, at Robert and Myfanwy's house, which made a convenient resting point. A shock awaited them there.

'The government is going to close down the dockyard,' Robert told them.

Hugh was aghast. 'But they can't,' he said. 'It'll finish the whole town. The dockyard was the only reason the town was built in the first place.'

'They couldn't care less about that,' Robert said. 'Look at what they're doing to the miners.'

'What'll you do?' Hugh asked anxiously. 'You've been there since a boy, time-served fitter and now a foreman.'

'There's talk that some of us may be offered places in the government dockyards at Plymouth or Portsmouth,' Robert said. 'But that will only be for a lucky few. God knows what will happen to the rest and, as you say, the town will be finished.'

So they returned home in gloomy mood. Pembroke Dock, the town he knew so well, was facing catastrophe. In coal mining, which he also knew so well, a huge dispute was threatening, which the coal owners, allied as usual with the government, would try to end by starving the miners into submission. He could see that it was going to go farther even than that. Millions of families would be affected, including his own.

Was this the 'land fit for heroes' that he and millions of others had fought for in conditions of sheer hell and from which so many had gone to premature deaths or been left shattered, disabled and abandoned?

Events moved, with a momentum of their own which no one seemed able to stop, to the calling of the general strike. A state of emergency was declared and the government did its best to try to mobilise the organisation it had created to provide blacklegs. Hugh and his fellow workers were not called out, building workers being exempt, a situation about which he felt angry and frustrated, even more so when the strike was called off after nine days, in what he felt was a betrayal of the miners.

There were heated arguments among his workmates. He and some of the others were for downing tools. They were dissuaded from doing so by Jim Wall, their foreman. Jim, older than most of them, although foreman, was no bosses' lickspittle. He was a fair man who knew his job and the men respected him. He somewhat reminded Hugh of his old friend and mentor of his youth, Dai horses.

'Look boys,' Jim said, 'in the first place, house builders, which is what we are, are not called out. In the second place, the boss has already told me that anybody who does come out will be sacked – and I won't be able to do a thing about it.'

He looked straight at Hugh. 'I know you used to be a miner, Taff, and I know you have family in the pits in Wales, but you also have a wife and two small boys. What chance will they have if you're sacked and probably blacklisted into the bargain?'

Hugh knew that what Jim said was true. Like all of them, he was trapped in a system designed for their exploitation. Something came into his mind that he had heard the Reverend Gwynfor Morgan quote from the Bible in a not dissimilar situation many years before: 'It is hard for thee to kick against the pricks'. He also recalled an obscene version thought up by miners at that time in relation to the coal owners: 'Those pricks want kicking in the bollocks.'

Jim Wall was speaking again. 'I'm going to organise a collection, which I will send to the proper place, to help relieve hardship.'

The collection was made on each weekly pay day, secretively, in case the boss found out, which might have put Jim's own job in jeopardy. The miners stood out for another six months after the general strike was called off, until they were finally forced to accept the coal owners' terms. A Miners' Distress Fund was instituted and the men voluntarily levied themselves each week to contribute to it.

Shortly after it was all over, Hugh, accompanied by Charlie, now the proud father of a baby daughter, made a brief visit to Pontcaer, carrying parcels of food. They were appalled at what they found. There was poverty and degradation everywhere. Hugh's brother John was thin and emaciated and his wife Sally looked drawn and older than her years – the youthful beauty she had carried into middle age was gone. The three children looked gaunt. Imogen, the oldest, was now a young woman of striking beauty, as her mother had been before her, but clearly undernourished.

'My God!' Hugh said. 'They'll pay for this one day.'

'One day perhaps,' John said. 'But they've got the whip hand now, and they mean to use it.'

They both knew from letters from their sister May Burrows at

Penduffryn that the situation there was identical, as it was in every Welsh mining valley and in every coalfield throughout Britain. Hugh and Charlie returned to Bristol for a Christmas that would be overshadowed by what they had seen.

However, Hugh gained some satisfaction from a letter from May that came with her Christmas card. She wrote that Richard Mulholland-Flowers had come to Penduffryn shortly after the lockout had ended. The police had advised him against going to the pit, but he had insisted. May described how his car had been surrounded by an angry mob and only the heavy police escort had prevented his being dragged out of the vehicle. The car had been pelted with stones and the windscreen had been smashed with, appropriately, a missile taken from the slag heap. The crowd had immediately closed ranks and the police had not been able to arrest anybody, not that they had shown any great zeal about doing so.

'There's a job come up to renovate a cottage on the Ashton Court Estate,' Jim Wall announced. 'At least, they say it's a cottage but it's several weeks' work, so it must be more of a house than a cottage. We start on it next Monday.'

The job proved to be memorable. Ashton Court was a large country estate on the outskirts of Bristol. It was situated on the opposite side of the pleasant, shallow valley in which Hugh's house was situated. From nearby rising ground, you could see the large mansion from which the estate took its name. Only a mile or so separated it from his own modest home, but they were in different worlds. His house was in a terrace, close to the defunct colliery and its slag heap. The mansion stood in well-wooded grounds that extended over the low hills behind it. Its owners could command views over miles of land which they owned, both in the country and in the southern part of the city.

Over many generations, they had never doubted that, since they owned the land, they had a God-given right to govern it. They also owned the company that owned the colliery. The company had been set up by minions, well back in the nineteenth century, when it became known that there was coal beneath the family's land, and throughout its existence, minions had run it, ensuring that its profits were duly paid into the family coffers. No one in the family had ever really known the value of the company or how much money it had brought them. They never discussed such things, which, being trade, they believed to be wholly unfit for polite conversation.

Another colliery in the same ownership had once stood in the built-up outskirts of the city, not far from the street where Vicky's parents lived. It had been closed and the site turned into a children's playground, an unattractive, paved area with a few struggling trees and a bandstand whose only regular users were the local Salvation Army. The place was called the Dame Emily Playground. Further out, on the edge of the city, was a large and more pleasant public park called Greville Smyth Park.

Greville Smyth was the name of the land-owning family at Ashton Court. Dame Emily, the last of the line, was regarded as a public benefactor because of her generosity in handing over the two small portions of her large estates for the enjoyment of the citizens of Bristol. She was a mysterious, reclusive lady who was never seen in public.

When the builders went to work on the cottage which stood in her grounds, they had to enter through a lodge, one of several in the wall which kept the estate secluded from the outside world and which was said to be seven miles long. They travelled each day in the lorry which also carried equipment and materials for the work and for which the lodge gates were only opened on production of a letter of authorisation from the building contractor.

'I've got to count you,' the lodge keeper said, 'and count you out again when you leave, to make sure that nobody stays inside without authority from Mr Smallwood.'

'Who's Mr Smallwood?' asked Jim Wall.

'He's the estate manager who's authorised the work. I dare say he'll be looking in regularly to keep an eye on things. Mr Retchins will meet you at the cottage. He's the butler and his wife's the housekeeper.'

'Must be a pretty big cottage to have a butler and a housekeeper, as well as the family living there.'

'Oh, it's not a family, just a single gentleman.'

'Lucky man to have two people to look after him. Is he a relation of the Greville Smyths?'

'You might say that,' the lodge keeper said. He smirked, then winked. 'Decent chap. Bit of a card. You wait till you see him.'

The cottage stood at some distance from the mansion and indeed proved to be larger than any cottage any of them had ever seen.

'Bit different from my miner's cottage,' Hugh remarked. 'Looks like we're going to see how the other half lives.'

'More like the other twentieth,' said Bill Weldon, one of the workmen, a ginger-haired, freckle-faced twenty-year-old who was noted for his cheekiness and who, with Hugh, had been one of those wanting to down tools the previous year in the general strike.

They were greeted, as promised, by Mr Retchins, the butler. He had the appearance and bearing of an ex-army senior non-commissioned officer. He also had rather a red nose, suggesting that he could be an experienced connoisseur of his master's wine cellar. The manner of his greeting indicated that he still thought of himself as obligated to keep the lower ranks in order. He spoke with a London accent, which he tried, wholly without success, to hide. Hugh thought immediately of his old teacher, Mr Kendle, who had tried to disguise his Welsh accent. But whereas Mr Kendle had commanded respect despite that little foible, this man merely sounded affected and ridiculous, with a tendency to drop aitches where they were needed and to pronounce them where they were not.

'You will stay in the 'ouse or close by at hall times,' he said. 'You will not go anywhere else within the estate unless hescorted by a hauthorised person.'

'Afraid we might steal a few blades of grass?' asked Bill Weldon. A withering glare was his only acknowledgement, delivered as from a great height to a cheeky schoolboy. Retchins was not good at repartee.

'I hope we shan't inconvenience the household too much,' Jim Wall said. 'As well as the outside work, we've got to work in turn in every room.'

'My wife and I have the full use of the 'ouse and we shall be able to move out of our own accommodation and use the master's rooms as and when required,' the butler said. 'While the work is being carried out, the master is residing temporarily at the big 'ouse.' He had some difficulty in getting out the word temporarily.

They set to work wondering if they ever would see the mysterious master of the house. Mr Smallwood, the estate manager, visited them every day. He was a taciturn man with an authoritative, not to say authoritarian manner, but it soon became clear that he was well able to assess the quality and progress of the work. Jim Wall ventured to ask him about the master of the house.

'I understand he is staying at the big house. Is he a relative of the Greville Smyths? We don't even know his name.'

'I cannot comment on family matters that are none of your business,' Smallwood said curtly. 'All you have to do is get on with the work.'

They had been working for nearly three weeks when the mysterious master suddenly appeared, unannounced. By then, the outside work had been completed and they were working in the parlour. Through a window, Hugh caught sight of the back of a well-dressed man on horseback. Retchins hurried out to meet him.

'What ho, Retchins!' the man said. 'Thought I'd ride over to see how it's going.'

'Thank you sir, hit is going quite well.'

'I ham glad to 'ear it.'

It was obvious that he was mimicking the butler's absurd way of talking, although Retchins seemed entirely unaware of it. The mimicry seemed to confirm the lodge keeper's description of the master of the house as 'a bit of a card'. He dismounted and, on turning to face the house, he gave Hugh something of a shock. He was middle-aged, of average stature, with a beard, moustache and features which appeared startlingly recognisable.

'But it can't be,' Hugh said aloud. He turned to the others. 'Come here boys, you'll never believe who the bloke outside looks like.' They crowded to the window.

'Well, I'll be buggered,' Jim Wall exclaimed.

'Not by any of us, you won't,' Bill Weldon said, as cheeky as ever.

'You watch it, young Weldon' Jim warned.

They heard the man say to Retchins, 'I'll go inside and have a word with the chaps.'

'I wouldn't advise it, sir. They are only common workmen.'

'Don't be such a snob, Retchins. Here, take my hat.'

'With respect sir, it's nothin' to do with snobbery, I'm only tryin' to protect you.'

'Well you're not bloody well goin' to.'

He strode into the house and into the room where the men were working. They hastily scrambled away from the window to give a show of working but could not resist stopping to stare when he came in. Close up, it was startling. He was the spitting image of King George V.

'Hello lads,' he said. 'Everything going OK? Hope this bugger

Retchins ain't givin' you any trouble.' He laughed loudly.

Jim Wall found his voice after a brief struggle for words. 'It's going well, thank you, your – er – that is, sir.' He inclined his head, the inculcated deference of a lifetime getting the better of him.

'No need to bow to me,' the man said, 'although I know why you're doing it.' He paused and leaned forward, eyes twinkling.

'It ain't everybody can say he's a king's bastard,' he added, stroking his beard. 'Right lads, I'll leave you to get on with it.' He swept out of the room. They heard him shout, 'How are you, Mrs Retchins me old dear?'

Retchins hung back briefly before leaving the room.

'You lot be damn careful not to say anything to anybody about this,' he said threateningly.

It was a predictably useless instruction. They quickly determined that, since the lodge keeper seemed likely to be more forthcoming, they would tackle him on leaving the estate.

'So he's visited you,' the keeper said. 'I guessed he would sooner or later. Remember, I told you to wait till you saw him.'

'Is he really, as he says, a king's bastard?' Hugh asked.

'What do you think, looking at him? What I can tell you is that he deliberately grew his beard and moustache to make him look as much like the King as possible.'

'Is he some brother of the King who has been disowned or something?' Jim asked.

The lodge keeper laughed. 'You might say that. More like a half-brother they don't want to know about. The old King, Teddy, when he was Prince of Wales, used to be a regular visitor to this place.'

'Is Dame Emily his mother?' Jim asked.

'Well, I can't say about that. Officially, she was made a Dame because of public services to the local people and to the city of Bristol.' He tapped the side of his nose before continuing. 'There's those as says though, that it was more to do with private services to 'is late Majesty.'

'Who knows about this?' Hugh asked.

'Not many,' said the lodge keeper. 'He hardly ever goes outside the estate, but he's well looked after. Gets a regular monthly income, so I'm told, but nobody knows where it comes from and nobody really knows exactly who he is – at least, nobody who does ever lets on. He knows, though, and don't mind anybody else knowing.'

Hugh couldn't wait to get home to tell Vicky about the remarkable encounter.

'Better not say anything to my dad,' she said. 'He wouldn't believe you. You know how respectful he is to the royal family and to the gentry.'

The men saw the bearded stranger once more, on their last day at the house, when the work was completed and they were preparing to leave. He arrived in a motor car, driven by Mr Smallwood, the taciturn estate manager. Smallwood and Retchins unloaded a crate of bottles of beer from the car and carried it into the newly decorated and refurbished parlour. The man who looked so much like the King of England ordered Retchins to bring glasses and open the bottles. Then he ordered the butler and the manager, both of whom clearly disapproved, to leave the room.

He poured himself a glass of beer and invited them to do the same.

'Thank you gentlemen,' he said. 'You've done a good job. Your health!'

'Your health sir!' they chorused.

'No one will ever believe us,' Jim said as the lorry took them back through the lodge gates.

'No, too many damn royalists about,' Hugh said, thinking of his father-in-law.

It was Bill Weldon who had the last word, putting his own seal of authenticity on the episode.

'You notice,' he said, 'that he had glasses brought. You wouldn't expect him to drink out of the bottle and he didn't expect us to. Real gentleman!'

Chapter 14

Further speculation about the occupant of the house was put out of Hugh's mind by a telegram from his brother Matthew, to inform him that their brother Albert was dead and that the funeral would be in a few days' time from their mother's house.

Albert had never enjoyed good health. Arguably, it was surprising that he had lived as long as he had. He had only ever had heavy labouring jobs, none of which had done anything other than harm his fragile constitution. In latter years he had lived and worked with Matthew at Old Oak Farm. Although Matthew had grandly proclaimed that he was taking him in because the fresh country air would be helpful to him, in fact Albert had never been away from the healthy air of Pembrokeshire and had never lived or worked in any polluted atmosphere. Matthew had further demonstrated his generosity by paying his brother little more than pocket money. To his thinking, such low pay was entirely justified because he provided Albert with board and lodging. The long hours and the nature of the work were no less arduous than in any of Albert's previous jobs.

For by no means the first time, Hugh thought of how different Matthew had become since the days, which now seemed so long ago, when he had championed his own interests against the mean and surly Kramers, from whom he had run away in his boyhood. He thought philosophically that, no doubt, everybody changed as they grew older, some for the better, some for the worse. Now, only two of his four brothers were alive. Joe, who had been his favourite, had been blown to pieces in the war. Now Albert was dead prematurely from chronic ill health and excessive hard work.

John and Matthew were left. John was living with his family on the poverty line in the valleys, too poor to attend his brother's funeral. In contrast, Matthew was now running three farms, exploiting his own children and as few, part-time, hired hands as possible, mostly desperate boys who had no choice except to work at the low wages which were all he was prepared to pay. His claim that he could not afford to pay more was not entirely unjustified, given the desperate straits to which farming had returned after the brief prosperity of the war. Matthew also worked long and hard himself and showed no signs of affluence.

Hugh travelled overnight to attend the funeral, arriving at Pembroke Dock on the first train, to find a town devastated and demoralised in the aftermath of the closure of the dockyard. Emerging from the station and looking towards what had once been the busy shopping streets in the most prosperous town in the west of Wales, he could see a number of once busy shops now closed and boarded up. Early as it was, a few ill-dressed, unemployed men with nothing else to do were already to be seen chatting idly.

His two closest relatives who had worked at the dockyard had moved away; they were comparatively lucky because their skill and experience were still required elsewhere. His sister Lizzie's husband, Ray Jones, a senior foreman, had been transferred to the government dockyard at Portsmouth. Robert Snape, also a foreman, had been transferred to the government dockyard at Plymouth.

Shortly after the shutdown at Pembroke, Hugh had read an article in the *Daily Herald*, written by Robert, a vivid account of the effect of the closure. Since the bitter reactions to his wartime articles in the local press in Pembrokeshire, his old schoolfriend had not written anything that had been published. Now, with events stirring his innate need to express himself and with a publication prepared to help him do so, he took again to his aging typewriter. Other occasional articles on current affairs had followed.

With the assembled family gathered round, Albert's coffin was lowered into the grave. All his short, disadvantaged life, he had worked hard for the profit of others, often in pain, but he had never complained. Outside his family, and by some within it, he would quickly be forgotten. After the funeral, the mourners returned to Leah's little house. Matthew took charge.

'Albert did not make a will,' he said, 'but he had nothing to leave anyway.' He drew attention to a small, cheap suitcase that he had packed and brought there. 'All his possessions are in this case, just some clothes and a few papers. If anybody wants anything, they can take it. If not, Mam should have it all.'

Nobody spoke and so the few pitiful belongings of Leah's sixth-born went to her. She, still as practical and unsentimental as when

Joe, her beloved husband, had died, found them to be of no use and quickly disposed of them. The well-worn items of clothing that constituted virtually Albert's entire estate were passed on to impoverished neighbours.

'So you now have three farms,' Hugh said to Matthew.

'Yes, when Squire Hatherly died, his son Edgar inherited the estate. He sold off practically all the land and I picked up Trevill Hill quite reasonably. Joe is living there and running it. Got the makings of a good farmer. Takes after his dad.'

God help him, Hugh thought, adding aloud, 'Edgar Hatherly isn't married, is he?'

'That's right and not really got much idea of how to run things.'

'What will happen after him?'

'I believe the next in line is the younger brother. He's in the army, quite high rank – colonel, I think.'

'Oh that'll be Jeremy,' Hugh said.

'You speak as if you know him.'

'Well yes, in a way I do. I met him at Round Pond Farm. It was the day before I left there. Then I met him again in the army, on the western front. Decent bloke, damn sight better than most officers. About my age. I don't suppose I shall ever see him again.'

Leah broke into their conversation. 'I've had hardly any chance to speak to you, Hughie. It was good of you to come for Albert's funeral, especially travelling overnight and then that long walk from the station. You'll stay here tonight, of course. Although it's a sad time, it's so good to see you. So many of the family now seem to be scattered round the country.'

'It's always good to see you, Mam. Vicky sends her love and, of course, so do the boys.'

'How's Vicky?'

'She's fine, and the boys, although they are a bit of a handful.'

'I can well believe it. After all, I brought up eleven of you.'

When he left, the following day, his mother pressed two shilling pieces into his hand.

'These are for the boys,' she said.

'Mam, you don't have to.' He knew that she was not really in a position to make the gesture.

'Oh yes I do,' she said. 'My two youngest grandsons mean a great deal to me.'

The renovation job in the Ashton Court estate had provided weeks of employment, but the work situation was deteriorating all the time. Their employer was finding it increasingly difficult to obtain contracts and the men were more and more on short time. Unemployment was rising continuously. The day they had been dreading came inevitably. Jim Wall broke the news on a Friday pay day.

'I'm sorry boys,' he said, 'but I'm under orders to pay off the entire gang. You've seen for yourselves how little work there is. I'm afraid there's simply nothing for you.'

So Hugh found himself on the dole again, realising, sick at heart, that unless he could get another building job, which seemed very unlikely, he had no skill or experience to offer other than as a labourer. And now he had a wife and two small sons to look after. At least, though, the mortgage on the house was largely paid off. He and Vicky had both been brought up to believe that it was practically sinful to be in debt. They regarded the mortgage as a form of debt and it was always in their minds. Consequently, whenever there was any cash to spare, it had been used to reduce what was still owing, and thus the monthly payments. They calculated that, so long as they did not fall too heavily into arrears, they could scrape by. Horrific though the thought was, they even discussed what items might be pawned if that became necessary.

It was said that there was work at the docks, so Hugh went there. The system was casual labour, the industrial equivalent of the agricultural hiring and firing from which his father had tried to save him as a boy. Nearly three decades and a world war later, with a wife and two children, he found himself in the situation his father had tried to avoid.

At the docks, the system was known as 'the pen'. Early in the morning, the men turned up and the stevedores selected those they required for the day. Hugh turned up day after day without being selected, but he persisted. Each stevedore tended to choose men who had previously worked for him and whom he knew. The technique, it was thought, was to attend regularly so as to be recognised as someone desperately seeking work then, hopefully, be selected and established in regular work.

It was weeks before one of the stevedores, with an unusually large demand for labour, picked him. It gave him three days of hard, unrelenting toil, working in the hold of a ship to move crates into position to be picked up by the dockside cranes. Alternatively, he would be on the dockside, manhandling unloaded cargo into railway trucks for onward transportation. There would be days without work and days of back-breaking labour which sent him home as dirty as when he had been a miner, after working in the hold of a ship, shovelling coal into buckets for lifting by the cranes to supply the dockside gas works.

As the effects of the faraway Wall Street crash spread worldwide, even such menial work dried up and he found himself full-time unemployed again and subjected to another humiliation, the means test. He was appalled when the minority Labour government he had voted for in 1929 was betrayed by its own Prime Minister, Ramsay MacDonald. Faced with an economic crisis which neither he nor anybody else, either in the government or the opposition, knew how to handle, MacDonald had betrayed his own government and party to form a Tory–Liberal dominated 'national' government. The Labour Party, which Hugh had always supported, had come near to being wiped out in the general election then called by MacDonald, and one of the first actions of the new government had been to institute the means test to assess those seeking government help.

An official from the labour exchange called at the house. One of the pieces of furniture was an upright piano which Vicky's father had bought for her in earlier days, although she had never become proficient at playing. The official looked at it.

'You can sell that to start with,' he said. 'What about this house? How much is your rent?'

'I don't pay rent,' Hugh said. 'I'm buying the house. I have a mortgage.'

'A mortgage!' The man was aghast. 'You're actually claiming the dole when you own your house! You can sell the house, then you would have enough to live on for years without claiming on the state.'

'And where the hell are we supposed to live?'

'If the worst comes to the worst, you and your family can be looked after in the workhouse.'

Hugh nearly exploded with rage. 'Get out of here,' he shouted. 'Is that what I fought for in four years on the western front?'

'I fought for King and country myself,' the official said.

'Never mind King and country. I fought to get a decent life for my wife and children. And ever since the war, I've had to fight King and country for the same thing.'

'You do realise,' the official said, 'that if you reject my advice, you will disqualify yourself from receiving unemployment pay.'

'Well we'll bloody well do without it. I can't see that we'd be any better off with it than without it. Get out of my house.'

'Very well. I suggest that you find work pretty quickly. Your dole money will be stopped forthwith.' He picked up his documents case, put on his bowler hat and left.

Vicky and the two boys, who were just home from school, had been witnesses of this angry scene.

'Oh Hugh,' Vicky said, 'what have you done? What shall we do?' She supported him completely, but there were times when she felt that what she termed 'his hot Welsh blood' caused him to respond unwisely to provocation.

'We'll manage somehow. How dare the likes of him talk to me like that in my own house.'

'Good old dad,' Kenneth said. 'You put that bastard in his place.'

His father and mother were startled. Hugh rounded on him almost as fiercely as he had on the official. 'Don't you ever let me hear you use that sort of language in this house again,' he said. 'Whatever happens, I'll not have you talk like that in the house and in front of your mother.'

'But you told him you could bloody well do without his money.'

'Yes, I did, but that was because he made me lose my temper, for which I am sorry. Have you ever heard me swear in the house before?'

'No Dad, sorry.' Kenneth was chastened. He had learned a valuable lesson. Whatever language you heard and used among school mates, among whom obscenity was the norm and where there was peer pressure to use it, you never used it at home.

A few days later, Hugh attended a meeting of his branch of the British Legion, still seething inwardly. There were others there who had been treated as badly as he and there was an angry discussion.

As in his younger days at union meetings, he was not given to intervening greatly in discussions, and was irritated by some of the more loquacious, who seemed regularly to be able to go on at length without ever really saying anything useful. This time, though, the government official had, as he was wont to say 'put the devil in him' and he was determined to speak out.

'We ought to do something public to show our disgust,' he said. He had brought his wartime campaign medals and ribbons in his pocket. He produced them. 'Why don't we go to Bristol Bridge and throw this lot into the river to show what we think?'

The chairman, who was not radically minded, was horrified. 'We can't do that. That would be a deliberate insult to King and country who awarded us the medals.'

The secretary was much less establishment. 'Bollocks to King and country,' he said. 'We put ourselves on the line for them. A million never came back and, every day, you can see men permanently disabled in the war, begging in the streets. What the hell have King and country done for us in return for what we did for them? I propose we do as Hugh says. We'll set a date for those who are willing and I'll write to the local papers to let them know, so that we can get it reported. I put that as a formal proposal.'

Applause greeted his statement. The chairman insisted that they should not act 'precipitately' as he put it, but the motion was carried overwhelmingly on a show of hands.

Emboldened by the success of his suggestion, Hugh spoke again. 'It'll soon be November 11th, Armistice Day. Why don't we do it then, at the end of the two minutes' silence? That ought to help get it reported.'

'I really don't think that's a good idea,' the chairman said.

'Well I do,' said the secretary, and again it was clear that the meeting was strongly in favour.

When the time came, a number backed out but about a dozen assembled on the bridge shortly before eleven o'clock on November 11th. All were wearing their medals and British Legion poppies. Hugh took the two boys, also wearing poppies; he wanted them to witness what was happening and to understand why. Several others also brought their children. A few of the men were also wearing the recently introduced white peace poppies, made by the Women's Co-operative Guild.

In accordance with the custom of the time, as eleven struck, everything came to a halt in respect for the fallen. All vehicles came to a standstill. Pedestrians stopped, men removed their hats and most stood for two minutes with bowed heads.

As the silence ended, the Legion's branch secretary, whom they had appointed because he was the most articulate, stated briefly what they were doing and why. Then they all removed their medals and threw them into the river. A few curious passers-by watched and then went on their way. The press ignored the invitation to attend and the demonstration went unreported.

Unexpected help came suddenly. Hugh's father-in-law's brother, Harold Newforth, the one who was captain of a steam barge trading out of Bristol docks, called at the house. He was always welcome. He had always struck Hugh as a sympathetic character, and the boys adored him.

'I've got a vacancy for a seaman,' he said. 'If I recommend you, the boss will take you on. There'll be four on board: me, the mate, the engineer and you.'

Hugh was slightly at a loss. 'But I don't know anything about the sea,' he said doubtfully.

'You'll soon learn, I'll see to that, and I want someone right away.'

'For God's sake, Hugh,' Vicky said, 'you know you can't afford not to accept. We're desperate.'

'That settled it; not for the first time, his quiet, reserved wife had made up his mind for him when it came to the crunch.

'Thank you, Uncle Harold. Of course I'll take it on.'

'Fine! I'll meet you at the firm's office tomorrow morning at nine and get the boss to sign you on. We mostly only go to Cardiff to load coal for one of the power stations here, or, sometimes, up the Severn to Sharpness.' He smiled. 'After all, you've had plenty of experience with coal, if not with the sea, and if you get sea-sick, you'll recover after a few trips. Oh, and by the way, the coal is pulverised and washed for the boilers which are fired by machine. Not too much dust.'

So, in the midst of the great depression, Hugh entered into an entirely new type of work and a new way of life. His job was arduous, potentially dangerous and meant days and nights away from home, dependent on the tides, which, as he soon came to learn, in the Severn estuary had the second highest rise and fall in the world. By a fortunate accident of nature, he was not subject to sea-sickness. To the amusement of his shipmates, he did initially have a problem finding his sea legs. That was to say, when he came ashore he still felt the movement of the vessel and was unable to walk steadily.

The little ship, named *Emerald*, had originated on Clydeside. She was, as Harold said, 'a good little seaboat' that handled well in the stormiest conditions. He had been her captain for years and loved her. Hugh started to succumb. He found the job more congenial than any he had done previously. He enjoyed the sea, the marvellous sea air and the motion of the vessel during the short voyages, even in rough seas when she rolled and pitched under the assault of heavy waves but always righted herself under Harold's skilful seamanship, when, oilskin clad against the cold, lashing spray, he would join the skipper and the mate to control the steering wheel. He was soon learning sea-going jargon. What more poetically minded people called the romance of the sea, which had meant so much to his lost brother Joe, entered into his own life.

The power station to which they carried the coal was some way up the docks. The mast and funnel had to be lowered to pass under bridges and one of Hugh's duties was to lower them to pass under Bristol Bridge and over his war medals, sunk there in the mud of the harbour bed.

After a couple of years, by which time he was every inch a seaman, he was moved to one of the company's larger vessels. This supplied the power station at Portishead, situated on the Severn estuary just below the mouth of the River Avon. Sometimes, for this larger coaster, there would be longer voyages, carrying coal from Cardiff to Cornwall and, occasionally, to Belfast, when the sea would often be particularly rough as they rounded the coast of his native Pembrokeshire. Then, to his pleasure, he was promoted to mate, second to the captain among the small crew. None of the company's captains held master's certificates and none of the mates had paper qualifications, but they all had sufficient experience and knowledge to cope with all the conditions likely to be met in the waters where they worked.

For the first time in his life, he found himself reasonably paid, able to provide for Vicky and the boys as adequately as he would wish. Each summer, he was able to take them on a week–long holiday. They always went to stay with his mother and from outside her house he found it salutary to look down the Pembroke River to where a long line of ocean-going ships were anchored side by side in Milford Haven because there was no work for them. He insisted on recompensing his mother for their board and lodging.

Leah fitted them expertly into the little house and took huge pleasure in their visits, especially in the all too rare contacts with her two youngest grandsons. They, in turn, loved meeting their 'gran

Hughes' as they called her but they were bemused by their large number of cousins, some of whom were adults with small children of their own. The cousins, for their part, were intrigued by the boys' distinctive Bristol accents. Vicky remarked that every time they went there, she met some new relative she did not know existed.

The visits came to an end with Leah's death. She was eighty, considered a great age in those days. She had become increasingly frail and her hair had long turned white but, to the end, she remained active, alert and unperturbed by approaching death. She had never been well off and most of her life had been a struggle but she had lived it magnificently. 'She just wore out,' Hugh said.

After the funeral, the family divided her possessions among themselves. Fortunately, there was no dissent as to who should have what. Hugh's attention was drawn to a shoe box filled with letters, which he took. There were two correspondents, both elderly ladies, one in the Canadian prairie, the other in Pennsylvania in the USA. They were his aunts, his father's sisters who had emigrated before he was born. They had regularly exchanged letters with his father and, after his death, his mother had kept up the correspondence.

Both the aunts' families had suffered the effects of the Wall Street crash. Beatrice, the younger, had moved with her daughter and her family to Pennsylvania and they had become American citizens. Both sisters had large families who, in turn, had also been prolific. For the first time, Hugh realised that he had at least as many cousins in North America as he had relatives in England and Wales. He wrote to his two aunts to tell them of his mother's death and received grateful and sympathetic letters in reply. An irregular correspondence ensued. Within a short time, both aunts died but the correspondence was carried on in each case by one of their daughters.

Meanwhile, he and Vicky were absorbed and fascinated with the development of their two sons. Kenneth was a lively, extrovert, cheeky youngster who sometimes sorely tried their patience. Owen was altogether quieter and more reserved. Kenneth was inclined to dominate his 'kid' brother, which Owen resented, and there was something of a love-hate relationship between them. But one thing that was clear was that both boys were bright.

As Kenneth approached eleven and the examination they called 'the scholarship', later to become the eleven-plus, there was much speculation as to how he would do. Parents and grandparents desperately wanted both boys to do well.

In a parsimonious society that rationed education, children who did not do well went on to what was called elementary school, which finished at age fourteen. Those who did better went on to secondary school, where they were encouraged to stay to age sixteen and take the examination called the school certificate. There were also grammar schools, which were semi-independent of the state system, where those who did best in the scholarship could obtain places and be educated among the children of well-heeled, fee-paying parents. For working-class children, grammar schools were the only gateway to university education. Secondary schools also took fee-paying pupils from ambitious parents who were less well heeled than those able to pay for grammar schools. Ninety per cent of pupils failed to pass the scholarship. University education only reached five per cent of the nation and the overwhelming majority of those were from the privileged background of the ruling oligarchy.

'Do you think he will pass?' Vicky asked Hugh on the fateful day of the examination.

'I don't know. He can only do his best. We've done everything we can to encourage him.'

'Miss Poulton says he's one of the brightest boys in the class.'

Miss Poulton was Kenneth's class teacher, dedicated to her job and only too conscious that many of her pupils who deserved better would not pass the scholarship and would be branded as failures for life. She looked upon the scholarship as more of a lottery than a measure of potential, but she was determined to do all she could to get as many through it as she could.

'I hope he does pass,' Vicky said. 'He'll be terribly disappointed if he doesn't but, if he does, I don't want him to get potty.'

By 'potty' she meant snobbish, only too aware that some youngsters, mixing with fellow students from fee-paying middle-class backgrounds, became ashamed of their own background and contemptuous of their parents. Although she did not realise it, she was expressing the major criticism of the scholarship system: that it was a piece of social engineering which not only denied a great reservoir of talent to the nation but was designed to separate those likely to become working-class leaders, and turn them into enemies of their own class, so preserving the class-based social system.

The names of those who were successful in the scholarship were published in the local press in the order they had come in the examination. The family almost dreaded to look at the list, but there it was, Kenneth Edward Joseph Hughes; not high enough to go to a grammar school but well up in the range of those destined for secondary school. The following day, they received an official letter of confirmation. Vicky was secretly relieved that he had not come high enough for grammar school. She thought that at secondary school there would be less chance of his becoming 'potty'. They had to buy school uniform, books and sports kit. It was expensive but they spent the money gladly, determined that their boy would keep up with the best.

Three years later, Owen was also successful and went to the same school as his brother. In the way that grammar schools were run as imitations of the so-called 'public' schools, the secondary schools were run as imitations of the grammar schools, so the two boys inevitably became Hughes major and Hughes minor. Kenneth had quickly established himself as a good scholar. Physical education, then known as physical training or simply as PT, was an important part of the curriculum, and he also became a mainstay of his form, house and school football and cricket teams. His achievements, both academic and sporting, were a source of pride to his father, who, when work permitted, never lost the opportunity to turn up on Saturday mornings in the season to watch him play in inter-school football matches. But he regretted that rugby was not played at the school.

Owen maintained an academic placing in the middle of his form and was not sufficiently interested in cricket or football to become proficient at either. He did, however, take to the swimming classes and acquired certificates for life-saving. For his father, it brought memories tinged with sadness of Joe and his epic swim from Pembroke Dock to Milford Haven, so many years earlier.

In the public baths, where the boys had been taught, there was strict segregation between males and females, who were not allowed to bathe together. When what was called mixed bathing was introduced, there were protests in some quarters and there was concern about what were felt to be immodest costumes. Most men still swam in torso-length costumes, but trunks, known as 'shorts', were becoming popular, the trend set inevitably by famous film stars who had the physique to show off.

All the schoolboys wore the older, body-length costumes for their classes but it became the fashion among them that, once you learned to swim, you changed over to trunks. Kenneth, as the elder, was the first to ask for the money to buy a pair. Vicky was doubtful. She was nervous about any expanse of water larger than a domestic bath tub and had never donned a bathing costume in her life. Prone to working-class prudery, she was alarmed at the thought of the boys appearing 'practically naked' in public. But she had to bow to the inevitable.

As the nineteen-thirties advanced, it was becoming clear that another great war was looming. Hugh saw the 'drilling, trampling foolery in the heart of Europe' that he had gone so gaily to fight against in 1914 had now, under the Nazis, become a drilling, trampling criminality. With two sons who would both be of military age if war did come, he hoped fervently that it would not.

Financially, he was better off than he had ever been and, for all the unemployment and poverty in the country at large, there was no shortage of others who were becoming better off and ambitious, among other things, to have better homes. There was a large building programme of modest houses for sale and, whereas their row of one-time miners' cottages had been surrounded by fields, new houses were spreading out from the city to reach them. He and Vicky began seriously to consider selling their home and taking out a new mortgage to buy one of the newly built houses.

A decision taken by Vicky's father helped to make up their minds. Edward, ever faithful to his cigarette-manufacturing employers, had been promoted to a slightly higher level of foremanship, as a reward for length of service rather than for qualities of leadership. The promotion had been conditional on his moving to another factory at some little distance away. Being accustomed to only a few minutes' walk to work, he had decided to move home, and had bought a house in the appropriately named Raleigh Road, where the factory stood.

He had conceived what he felt to be a bold plan: to sell his previous house cheaply to his son Charlie, who lived in rented accommodation. This led Hugh and Vicky to decide that it was time to keep up with the Newforths. Hugh put his house on the market, sold it successfully and prepared to move the short distance to one of the newly-built houses, semi-detached and with all the 'mod cons' of the late nineteen-thirties. The house cost £525.

Edward had a vague and confused idea that his plan would help Charlie and Greta, whose marriage had run into difficulties, although neither he nor anybody else was clear as to how a change of residence would help. But with three families caught in a surge towards new homes, rational thinking no more prevailed than in the Fascist states' rush to war.

Hugh was saddened but not surprised by what had happened between Charlie and Greta. He recalled how, when they were working together in the Welsh pits, Charlie had always had a variety of girlfriends and had been adept at picking up new ones on weekend trips to Cardiff, although, unbeknown to Hugh, all the time he had been engaged to Greta.

In the early years of Charlie's marriage, there had never been any evidence of his roving eye. The truth was that his relations with his large number of girlfriends had been innocent. Charlie was certainly what they called a ladies' man; he enjoyed the company of women and sparkled in their presence but, despite the impression given to and eagerly received by his male friends, none of his relationships had gone beyond elementary kissing and cuddling.

Hugh thought that, with Charlie working among large numbers of young women in the cigarette factory, there must be no shortage of temptation in his way. He had been relieved that Charlie did not seem to be succumbing to such temptation and that he and Greta were obviously devoted to each other. They had been disappointed that several years of marriage had produced no children and were palpably delighted when Greta became pregnant and gave birth to a bonny little daughter.

They had named the little girl Elizabeth, to the unalloyed pleasure of Charlie's father as the name met his strange predilection that children ought to be called after kings and queens of England. In practice, everyone called her Liz. Some were inclined to call her 'Lizzie' but, out of deference to her grandfather, who seriously disapproved of such practice, that custom was soon dropped in favour of what he considered to be the still regrettable but less inappropriate 'Liz'.

Hugh felt that all his fears about Charlie philandering would vanish with Liz's birth. Unfortunately, the opposite proved to be the case. Greta gave so much care and devotion to her firstborn and seemed so convinced that her husband was not capable of attending to his daughter that a gap was created between husband and wife. Charlie was, in fact, utterly devoted to his little daughter and hugely proud of her. Inevitably, he came to resent being, as he saw it, frozen out of Liz's care by the over-possessive attention of her mother. He became more and more frustrated and relations soured between him and Greta.

Within a year of Liz's birth, there was open gossip that Charlie was 'carrying on' with one of the factory girls. The talk inevitably reached his father and it led to a furious row between the two. For Edward, it was appalling and intolerable that his married son should have any sort of relationship with another woman. Quite apart from the shame it brought on the family, it was undermining the very foundations of the British Empire! His clumsy handling of the situation brought the matter to the notice of a tearful Greta, but she had neither the grace nor the sense to recognise that she had some responsibility for the situation. She did, however, try genuinely to change her attitude to her baby and her husband. Charlie, guilt-ridden, ended his brief affair and they settled back into a loving, caring marriage, both of them devoted to their daughter.

Sadly though, the advent within a couple of years of a second daughter, whom they named Charlotte but who became universally known as 'Lottie', re-awakened Greta's over-possessiveness towards her children at the expense of her husband. Charlie, angry and frustrated, drifted into another dalliance. There was another furious row and the dalliance was ended. But, this time, there was no reconciliation between husband and wife.

Had they been adults of their daughters' generation or a later one, or in a different social class, they would have divorced. But for them, with their strict, early twentieth-century working-class backgrounds, such a thing was inconceivable. Apart from the fact that for them divorce proceedings were impracticable, it was something with a terrible stigma that was only for toffs. As they saw it, they had made their bed and they had to lie in it. So they drifted into a cold, angry relationship that tried to keep up appearances but blighted not only their own lives but also those of their two daughters.

Chapter 15

In the ruling class, the troubled marriage of Richard Mulholland-Flowers MP fell apart with spectacular and damaging publicity. At around the same time, he was beset with problems as a coal owner and industrialist. It was as if the extraordinary good luck that had favoured him practically from the time of his contentious birth might be running out.

After his experience when visiting the colliery at Penduffryn in the aftermath of the 1926 lockout, when only a police escort had prevented his being pulled from his chauffeur-driven car and seriously assaulted, he had never again visited any of the company's pits, either in Wales or in the north east of England. When company business required his presence in the coalfields, he never went beyond the regional offices in Cardiff and Newcastle upon Tyne. Even in those places, there had been demonstrations outside the offices on several occasions when advance news of his visits had reached the pits, making him acutely aware of the sheer hatred in the coalfields against the coal owners and against the 'National' government in whose support he sat in the House of Commons.

As the depression deepened, causing contraction in the company's steel-making and engineering activities as well as in mining, he started looking to diversify. He noted that, even in those difficult times, there was growing development of the radio and gramophone. So he set up a new company on borrowed capital, to manufacture radios and gramophones. He was not initially successful and loan repayments were crippling but by the mid-nineteen-thirties, the venture was starting to pay off.

However, just when he felt that the most difficult period he had ever known was beginning to get better, his family troubles built up to a crisis.

Events were triggered by the death of Albert Flowers, his mother's husband, whom he still looked upon as his stepfather. Richard went to Tenby for the funeral, to find that his mother's health was also deteriorating. Her days were numbered and she knew it. She insisted that before she died, she must see her two grandsons.

A problem that had been looming for years was now urgent; he could not deny his mother's wish. In any case, when she died, the boys would learn of her existence because of the codicil in the will of Henry Black, whereby her house in Tenby would be inherited by his elder son. Richard junior, now twenty, was studying at Cambridge University and contemplating a career as a barrister, to the entire approval of Richard senior, who could see future advantages in having a qualified lawyer, particularly if he specialised in the lucrative field of company law, as a director of one or more of his companies and eventually as his successor at the top. His sixteen-year-old younger son, Edgar, was at Eton College.

Marital relations between Richard and his wife Alice had long since broken down. Publicly, they kept up a pretence of normal marriage but in private, they sometimes went for long periods without speaking and they slept in separate rooms. Not infrequently, Richard did not return home at night, staying instead with his long-standing mistress, Millicent Partridge-Dove. Sexual ardour between those two had ceased to be the central feature of their relationship, but a lasting bond had developed between them that was far more akin to a successful marriage than the disastrous union he had been manoeuvred into in his youth.

On returning from the funeral in Tenby, he confronted his wife. 'My mother has not long to live and she is insistent that she must meet her grandsons before she dies.'

'Really!' Alice said. 'Why should we accede to such a request? She has never met them and they believe she is dead.'

'The facts will have to come out anyway when she dies,' he reminded her.

'And what is all this going to do to the boys, their grandmother a servant and a whore and their father a bastard?'

'You may say what you wish about me, but how dare you speak of my mother as a whore.'

'Well, wasn't she?'

'No, she was not. She was the victim of "the young master", as they say, who was my father.'

'I gather that she was not the unwilling victim nor was he the only one whose attentions she was receiving. Had it not been for an accident of nature, Albert Flowers, another servant, could have been your father, in which case you and I would never have met.'

'Well, he was not my father and we did meet and it was only at the insistence of my grandfather and with the connivance of your father that we were married. You were otherwise unmarriageable, and both you and your father had your eyes on my money.'

'Which you only had because it was left to you by Henry Black, whose paramour your mother was also.'

'What a nasty bitch you are to say things like that about an old lady who has little enough time to live.' His voice rose in uncontrollable anger. 'And don't you forget that your family estate in Pembrokeshire has only been kept going for decades because of the generosity of your aunt, Lady Robson, not to mention help that I have given.'

'At least my father was a gentleman.'

'So was mine, by birth if not by conduct. He was also heir to a damn sight more money than there ever was in your lot.'

'Oh, of course you would bring that up. The Mulhollands always considered themselves a cut above the rest of the county, but at least my family has no history of fathering bastards by servants.'

Furious as he was, Richard knew that he had to try to bring some semblance of sense into these disastrous exchanges. He made a desperate attempt. 'None of this alters the fact that we both have responsibility towards the boys. Their grandmother's origins and mine are bound to become known to them after her death. But I am determined to grant an old lady's wish to see her grandsons before she dies.'

'Well, I'm having nothing to do with it. If you want to tell the boys, you'll have to do it yourself.'

'They're your sons as well as mine. It was more your decision than mine all along to keep them ignorant about their grandmother.'

'Given what she is, I have no regrets about that.'

Richard finally lost control. 'Go to hell then,' he shouted. 'We'll see what regrets you have about the outcome of all this. I'm not staying here to listen to any more.'

'That's right,' she shouted back. 'Go to your whore. Like father, like son!'

They were both too angry to have any thought for the consequences of what they were saying, but both knew in their hearts that this was the moment of truth they had been building up to for years, the moment when they finally realised that even the pretence of their marriage was over.

He went straight to Millicent Partridge-Dove, telling his chauffeur that he would not need him until the following morning, at her address. The chauffeur was not surprised. The servants were well aware of the situation between husband and wife and of the master's extramarital relationship.

Arrived at Millicent's flat, Richard poured out to her what had happened and the stark task now facing him – that he must tell his sons that they had been lied to all their lives about their antecedents.

'Oh my dear Richie,' she said. She was the only person in his close circle who ever called him anything other than Richard. 'What a terrible mess, but you will have to tell the boys as soon as possible. You can't deny your mother what is really a dying wish to see her grandsons. And if you don't tell them, you can be sure Alice will, and you can guess how she will use it to poison them against you.'

'But how can I go about it?' There was a note of something like desperation in his voice, something she had never heard before.

'Why not write that you have something very serious to tell them urgently and arrange to meet them together, maybe at your club in a private room.'

'They'll probably think that it's to tell them that I and their mother are parting company. They both know as well as you and I do how things are between Alice and me, but this is going to be far worse for them.'

'Yes, the young are so puritanical about their elders. But never underestimate their resilience. They are probably far more worldly wise than you think.'

'You are so sensible. If only I could have met you before I was married. You could have been the mother of my sons. I'd marry you tomorrow if that was possible.'

'I know you would, but it's not possible.' There was a sudden spark of humour in her eyes. 'But it requires the most careful thought before a man leaves his wife and marries his long-term mistress. How much do the boys know about me?'

'They are aware that there is another woman in my life besides their mother, but they don't know any more than that – at least, not to my knowledge.'

Within a week he arranged to have Richard and Edgar meet him at the club. It was the first time either of them had been there, although he already had it in mind to propose Richard for membership.

'Well father,' Edgar piped up. 'I suppose it's something pretty serious. Are you and mother breaking up?'

His father could not but marvel at his perspicacity, to say nothing of his unabashed directness.

'No,' he said, 'but I have something to tell you that you may find more shocking and which I deeply regret that you have not been told before.'

'Spit it out then, pater,' Richard junior said. It occurred to him that for the first time, his father was going to talk to him as man to man rather than as man to boy. But he was not easy about it.

'Very well.' The father realised how right Millie had been in forecasting that the boys would be more worldly wise than he expected. The scene suddenly flashed across his mind of his first meeting with his grandfather, when he had been taken to Bellwood House at the age of sixteen to stake a claim to his inheritance. He could recall it as clearly as if it had been yesterday. God, he thought, they say a drowning man's life flashes before him ... but for Christ's sake, I'm not drowning. He took a deep breath, as much to steady himself as to launch into speech again.

'You have always believed and, I am afraid, have been deliberately led to believe, that your grandmother, my mother, has been dead since before you were born. The truth is that she is alive, she is now an old lady and has not long to live and she wants to see the two of you before she dies.'

The effect was as he had expected. They were stunned. He found himself thinking, Dear God, please don't let them turn against me.

It was the elder son who broke the silence. His voice was cold, giving an early indication that his father's prayer was unlikely to be answered. 'Why have we been deceived all these years?'

'It's a long and complicated story.'

'Well, we'd better hear it.' His legal aptitudes were already giving him the manner of a cross-examining lawyer.

'I'll start at the beginning. I never knew my father, your grandfather. It's true that he was killed in the Boer War. The fact is that my mother was a servant in your great-grandfather's house whom he made pregnant. My father denied his responsibility and another servant, a footman, was given the blame. They were both dismissed; they married and he gave me the protection of his name. He has just died. I was the same age as you, Edgar, when the father I never knew was killed. I was then taken to meet your great-grandfather and, eventually, he accepted me and made me his heir.'

Richard junior was hostile and lawyer-like. 'So you are illegitimate and our grandmother is a servant. Where does she live?'

'She lives in Tenby. I want to take both of you down there to meet her.'

'Why should we bother?' Richard snapped.

'Because, one, she is your grandmother and wants to see you and, two, because you, Richard, will inherit the not inconsiderable house in which she lives as well as the income she has to maintain it.'

'How does that come about?' He was angry as well as confused.

'She and her husband were taken in as butler and housekeeper by a wealthy retired industrialist called Henry Black. He was a widower who had no children. He paid for my education and made me his heir. All the wealth and privilege that you enjoy stems originally from his generosity to my mother, her husband and, above all, to me. The one clause in his will which has not been fulfilled is that the house in Tenby and the money which maintains it should go to the first of any children that I might have. That, of course, is you, Richard.'

'Do I get anything?' Edgar demanded.

'Not to my knowledge, but you're not exactly on the bread line, are you?'

'As a matter of interest, what is our grandmother's name?' asked Richard.

'She is Mrs Albert Flowers. I was originally christened Albert Mulholland Flowers.'

'So that's why we're Mulholland-Flowers,' Edgar said.

'Correct. Your great-grandfather insisted that I take the family name Mulholland but, as I owed so much to my stepfather and to my mother, I insisted in turn on combining the two names. Your great-grandfather also insisted on my arranged marriage with your mother.'

'And that hasn't exactly worked out very well,' Richard junior said.

'But you've got a fancy woman, haven't you,' Edgar said.

'That's none of your business,' his father said sharply. He was taken aback by the boy's tone and worldly-wise bluntness.

'But it is. Will you be divorcing mother and marrying again?'

'I have no grounds to divorce your mother.'

'But she has plenty to divorce you,' said the up and coming lawyer Richard.

'Be that as it may, but she would never agree to a divorce.' He hastened to change the subject. 'I intend to take you both down to Pembroke to meet your grandmother,' he said. 'We will stay at Bellwood and drive over to Tenby. It isn't very far.'

He had maintained Bellwood House since inheriting it and they usually spent the summer holidays there. So, not long afterwards, in August, the family went there in the usual way, although with an uneasy and, to a degree, sullen air hanging over all of them. At an early stage in the extended visit, Richard took his sons to meet their grandmother.

Predictably, the meeting was not easy. Richard, although outwardly calm, was nervous; his sons were cold and unsure of themselves. Molly, not in good health and knowing her grandsons only from photographs, was very anxious as to how these grand, upper-class young men would greet her, notwithstanding that they were her own flesh and blood. She went to great lengths to clean the house and to provide tea and excellent home-made cakes. In the event, the boys, for all their preconceived reservations, were not unimpressed. Their father invited her to visit Bellwood and to stay for some time, so that they might all get better acquainted. She accepted; it was the first time she had been there since Richard and Alice's wedding.

Alice refused absolutely to meet her and returned to London the day before her visit, but Molly was relieved rather than snubbed. The two young Mulholland-Flowers came to accept her to a degree, but it was not a warm acceptance. In fairness, they behaved well towards her and even got round to calling her grandma, but they were embarrassed and inwardly repelled by thoughts of their own humble, not to say complicated, background.

Shortly after the end of the extended vacation, Richard's full attention had to be diverted, with the calling of a general election. Relations with Alice had settled into what might have been described in a later era as a state of cold war but she dutifully appeared with him in his constituency during the campaign. He retained his seat comfortably and the 'National' government was returned with another large majority.

When he returned in triumph to his campaign headquarters after the counting of the votes on the day after polling, there was a telegram from a solicitor in Tenby to tell him that his mother had died that day. Nothing of her existence was known in the constituency and, fortunately for him, no one had opened the telegram. He left at once for the funeral, hurriedly explaining that something urgent, which he did not specify, had arisen and that his wife would stay to represent him at the planned victory celebrations. There were a few raised eyebrows but no one seriously questioned his hurried departure; they were too deferential to do such a thing.

The house at Tenby duly passed to Richard junior, together with the capital and the interest derived from it that Henry Black had left to maintain Albert and Molly. Edgar also came into an unexpected legacy. Henry Black had left sufficient for Albert and Molly to employ servants, it being beyond his comprehension that the house could be maintained without them. But, with their long experience and practical ability at housekeeping, they had not engaged any help. Consequently, they had been able to put by a fair amount of savings, and Molly, anxious that her younger grandson should not be disadvantaged in comparison with his brother, had made a will leaving the money to him. Built up over more than twenty years, the amount was substantial.

Since Richard junior had no use for the house in Tenby, he sold it on the advice of his father, whom Molly had made her executor. Richard senior reflected sardonically that both his sons, neither of them yet earning, now had independent means, even if modest by the standards to which they were accustomed and took for granted.

After probate had been obtained, a brief report of Molly's will appeared in a local newspaper. There was an oblique reference to an 'unexpected' inheritance received by two young men, the sons of a Member of Parliament who, although not well known in the county, was head of a long-established local land-owning family. Richard had been contacted by the paper but he had declined to comment. The paper had deferentially accepted his refusal, but the enquiry made him uneasy. His uneasiness proved to be justified.

He received a message at his club, asking him to telephone a Mr Lighteller. With no idea who the man was, he called the number.

'*The Sunday Shaft,*' announced a pert and young-sounding

woman. She added mechanically, 'The paper that shines shafts of light into dark places.'

Richard was on guard instantly. *The Sunday Shaft* was a well-known scandal sheet. He was tempted to put the phone down but decided that it was probably wiser at least to see what they wanted.

'I have a message to ring a Mr Lighteller,' he said.

'Is that Mr Mulholland-Flowers?' she asked. 'I'll put you through.'

'Len Lighteller here,' said a smooth voice. 'Thank you for ringing, Mr Mulholland-Flowers. I wonder if I could ask you a few questions?'

'About what?'

'I understand that your two sons have recently inherited from a lady who died last year in Tenby, Pembrokeshire. I understand she may have been your mother, of whose existence nobody knew anything until she died. Would you like to comment?'

'No I would not. My family's private affairs are none of your business.'

'But you are a Member of Parliament, Mr Mulholland-Flowers, and also a coal owner and businessman. The public have a right to know about these things.'

'The public have every right to know about my public life and they know enough about it to have re-elected me last year with a resounding majority. My family's private business is neither their concern nor yours. I have no other comment to make to you.'

'You do realise, Mr Mulholland-Flowers, that we reserve the right to make further enquiries?'

'In order to put the worst possible slant you can get away with, I suppose.'

Lighteller's voice became even smoother. 'We aim only to report events. We are just the messenger. Don't shoot the messenger.'

'Messenger be damned! You are a powerful vested interest with your own agenda and a complete lack of scruple in pursuing it. I have nothing further to say to the likes of you.' He slammed the phone down angrily, but he knew he was not on strong ground. His worst fears were realised the following Sunday.

The intent of the front-page headline was unmistakeable. 'Mystery Over Multi-Millionaire MP's Origins', it screamed. The text opened with 'How did the poor boy christened Albert Flowers suddenly become Richard Mulholland-Flowers and why is he the first of the long-established Mulhollands to be Mulholland-Flowers?'

Clearly, the unctuous Len Lighteller had been digging for dirt. On an inside page, two old photographs were reproduced from local papers, one of his father when his death in battle in 1900 had been reported, the other taken from a report of Richard's wedding. Attention was pointedly drawn to the striking family resemblance between father and son. 'But his father never married', the paper trumpeted. 'Who is the mysterious Mrs Flowers who has left money to his two sons? Is Richard Mulholland-Flowers the illegitimate son of a servant?'

Within days, there was scarcely a newspaper in the country that had not picked up the story. Richard, badgered incessantly by journalists, refused to comment to any of them, which did nothing to prevent each paper adding its own fanciful elaborations to the story. The following Sunday, the *Shaft* dealt another blow. 'Discredited MP's Love Nest Discovered', it thundered over an article giving Millicent Partridge-Dove's address.

At home, Alice tried to lock him out but he frustrated her by obtaining an injunction, on the grounds that she had no right to do so, since he was the owner of the house. So she left the house and, without disclosing her destination, went to stay with her uncle and aunt, Sir George and Lady Robson. Developments were avidly observed and reported in the papers.

He dared not go to Millicent's, where a posse of photographers was camped out, waiting to snatch a picture to feed the stories about him. He stayed at his club, but there, too, he could not escape a gauntlet of reporters. There was a move to expel him although it was not followed up, largely due to pleading by Sir George, who had originally proposed him for membership and who was by then the most long-standing member. There were also committee members who were dubious about expulsion because they feared he might release information about their own private lives that he had learned from years of club gossip. At the House of Commons, he was painfully conscious of being an object of sniggering contempt, not made any the less painful by the knowledge that he was by no means the only one there with entanglements best kept from public gaze.

'Always thought there was something fishy about the fellow,' one fellow Tory MP said. The remark was not true: he had never previously thought anything about Richard or, for that matter, about much else. A Labour MP from the coalfields remarked, 'Bastard literally as well as metaphorically.'

To embellish his story, Len Lighteller approached Gwynfor Morgan, as he was an MP representing a constituency containing a Mulholland-Flowers coal mine and had started his working life as a pit boy in another of the company's mines. Gwynfor had refused to comment and had indicated his disapproval of Lighteller's dirt digging. Lighteller, frustrated, responded with an article calling him a hypocritical Methodist preacher who had once called Mulholland-Flowers a hard-faced man who had done well out of the war but was now refusing to condemn his immoral conduct. He wrote as if there was some sort of political collusion between the two. 'Shades of Ramsay MacDonald?' was the headline. Gwynfor found himself having to argue against ill-judged, knee-jerk press comments dragged out of one or two of his more gullible Labour colleagues.

There had never been any personal contact between him and Richard. They only knew each other as opponents to be regarded with hostility but Richard was moved to write Gwynfor a note 'as from one Member under criticism within his own party to another,' suggesting that they might meet. Gwynfor agreed, and they met in the smoking room, where conversations between Members were regarded as absolutely sacrosanct. Richard, Savile Row-suited and expensively shod, Gwynfor appropriately but much less expensively suited and shod, seated themselves in the leather armchairs, attracting curious, in some cases meaningful glances from other, mostly Tory, MPs. The barman approached them.

'Can I buy you a drink?' Richard asked.

'No thank you, I don't take alcohol.'

'Something non-alcoholic?'

'Very well, so as not to appear unsociable.'

'We have never spoken before,' Richard said, 'but I thank you for your remarks about the campaign against me.'

'Gutter journalism disgusts me,' Gwynfor explained. 'My party suffers more from it than yours but, having been dragged into this, I felt I had to speak out, notwithstanding that I detest your politics as much as you detest mine.'

'I understand that, apart from having one of our pits in your constituency, you have a much older background with our company,' Richard said.

'That's right. I started as a pit boy in Penduffryn. Then I was sacked in the 1893 lockout and blacklisted throughout the coalfield.

I returned there in the early 1900s as the Methodist minister and in due course married the daughter of the man who had sacked me and got me blacklisted.'

'I didn't know that,' Richard said. 'That must have been William Yewsley. And you married his daughter?'

'I did,' Gwynfor said. 'He's dead now, of course, but he refused to give Margaret away and he never spoke to either of us again.'

'Your marriage has gone well?'

'Very well and, like you, I have two children – a little older than yours, I think – a son and a daughter, fine young people, now making their own way in the world. I've had some difficulty in persuading my son against giving up his job as a teacher to go and fight in this Spanish civil war. I have, though, sympathy with his desire to go to Spain. We all share the same politics in our family.'

'So do we in mine, but that's about all we do share, apart from my money, which you don't approve of.'

'I have no wish to discuss your private problems,' Gwynfor said, 'but I will stand by my criticism of the disgraceful press treatment you have been subjected to.'

'Thank you,' Richard said. 'I greatly appreciate your concern, and I am sorry that you have been subjected to similar treatment for standing up to your principles.'

The Chief Whip called him into his office. 'You do realise, Mulholland-Flowers,' he said, 'that you are bringing discredit to the party. What do you intend to do?'

'Nothing, I will not even acknowledge the scurrility of the gutter press.'

'It's not just the gutter press, there is a report in today's *Times*.' He was clearly more horrified by a couple of paragraphs in the authentic voice of the establishment than page after page in the more widely read papers.

'I would have thought they had better things to write about, with war on the horizon, to say nothing of the King's entanglement with that divorced American woman.'

The Chief Whip was shaken. 'What do you know about that?' he demanded. 'There's been nothing made public about that at all.'

'Not here, but newspapers in every other country are reporting it. I've recently been in France on business and since I am fluent in French, I've read all about it there.'

'Well, you be damn sure not to say anything public here, and it doesn't alter the fact that all the publicity about you has brought discredit on the party.'

'Are you asking me to resign? If you are, forget it. You'd better think about the outcome of a by-election.' That ended the interview.

A letter arrived inviting him to meet the chairman of his constituency association. The chairman was Sir Gerald Verrey-ffaire, who had served in the war with Richard's brother-in-law, Jeremy Hatherly. Verrey-ffaire had left the army after the war and returned to manage the family estates. When his father died, he inherited the baronetcy. Jeremy had stayed in the army to pursue what proved to be a successful military career. He had kept in touch with his old comrade in arms but, in private conversations with Richard, he was not averse to referring to him as 'Colonel Blimp'.

Richard met the chairman in his Queen Anne house, situated in his ten thousand-acre estate in the rolling rural part of the south Midlands constituency. Sir Gerald was tweed-suited with, as ever, his rimless, cordless monocle so firmly fixed as to appear virtually a natural part of his features.

'I must say, Mulholland-Flowers, that I and other leading members of the association are seriously concerned over the very adverse publicity you are currently receiving. Furthermore, I begin to wonder if, in view of what has come out, you should now be known as Flowers, rather than Mulholland-Flowers.' He was deliberately offensive; quite apart from all this scandal, the fellow was in trade and he had always regarded him as a social inferior.

'My name is legally Mulholland-Flowers and I expect to be known by it,' Richard said icily. He was contemptuous of what he saw as a stupid, aristocratic buffoon.

Verrey-ffaire continued as if without interruption. 'You do know, I think, that I served in the war with your brother-in-law, Jeremy Hatherly. What does he think about all this?'

'The circumstances of my birth, they are no secret to him, he has known them all along.'

'Really! He's been quite successful, I believe, high rank now. Must say I'm surprised. He was always questioning orders as a junior officer.'

'I believe,' Richard said, 'that he has a questioning and independent mind which the War Office has had the good sense to see as a valuable asset.'

That did not register with Verrey-ffaire, who again carried on as if Richard had not spoken. 'And what about this woman Partridge-Dove?' he demanded. 'What does Hatherly think about that and the way you've treated his sister?'

'My relationship with Millicent arises because of the way his sister has treated me, but I will no more discuss that with you than with the press.'

'I see. I think you should consider your position.'

I have already discussed that in the whips' office. I have absolutely no intention of resigning my seat and there is absolutely nothing you can do to make me.'

'I know that, but you must realise that it is very unlikely that the association will re-adopt you as candidate at the next election.'

'We'll see about that when the time comes. The way things are going, it looks likely that there will be another war before the next election is due.'

'Well, you know where we stand. I see no point in continuing this conversation.'

'Frankly, neither do I,' Richard said. 'I will find my own way out.'

The press coverage was brought to an end and quickly faded from most of the public memory with the bringing into the open of a far more sensational tangle of private relationships and public responsibilities. On December 10th of that year, Edward VIII abdicated, in order to marry the twice-divorced American Mrs Simpson.

Among Richard's acquaintances, one of the few who had stood by him was his old business partner, Sir George Robson. But Sir George's health was deteriorating into terminal illness.

'You know, Richard,' he said, 'I was in the House when that fellow Keir Hardie said, at the time of the King's birth, that he would make a morganatic alliance and that it would all end with the country paying the bill. We made a hell of a row about it, but I have actually lived to see it come true.'

In the last weeks of his life, Sir George made some important changes to his will. Previously, he had left the bulk of his shares in RMF Ltd to his son Gordon, with a lesser number going to his wife, but he had become disillusioned with Gordon's ability to play any major role in the business, leave alone to control it. So, at the end, while leaving both his wife and his son as substantial shareholders, he left sufficient shares to Richard to ensure that he would hold a controlling interest.

Gordon and Lady Robson reacted with fury and there was talk of contesting the will on the grounds that Sir George had been of unsound mind when making it. But medical evidence, together with that of Sir George's solicitor who had drawn up the will, disproved the claim. Lady Robson and Gordon were in any event well provided for and the idea of contesting the will was eventually dropped, much to Richard's relief, but it left a schism between Robsons and Mulholland-Flowers that would never be healed.

Richard was richer than ever but his marriage, never happy, was finally, publicly and humiliatingly finished. He found it particularly hurtful that his sons sided with their mother and became cold and distant towards him. They had both, the one at school and the other at university, suffered cruel and humiliating taunts for which they blamed him and could not forgive him. He was in full control of RMF Ltd but he was faced with a hostile board, and he had lost a lot of political credibility. It would never again be glad, confident morn.

Chapter 16

Brigadier Jeremy Hatherly DSO stood at a window of the War Office, listening to the radio and looking down Whitehall towards the Cenotaph and Downing Street, from where the Prime Minister, Neville Chamberlain, was broadcasting to announce that the country was at war with Germany. Within minutes, air raid sirens sounded. It was a false although probably deliberate alarm, a chilling reminder of expected horrors to come…

After the Great War, Jeremy had been posted to India where, almost immediately, he met and married a noted beauty. She was the daughter of a high-ranking civil servant of the Raj and as much sought after for her looks as for her wealth. The marriage was a genuine love match, with the added advantage of very substantially increasing Jeremy's private income – no small consideration as he climbed the inter-war military ladder – and it quickly produced twin daughters and then a son.

For both parents, the children's education became a matter of high priority. Anything other than private education in England was unthinkable, so the girls' names were soon put down for a top school and the boy's name for his father's old school, Rugby. As neither parent wanted to be thousands of miles away from their children, appropriately timed and influential representations at the War Office secured Jeremy's posting back to the United Kingdom. His marriage-enhanced income enabled him to purchase a house in a fashionable square in the Westminster area, and to pay the school fees in domestic as well as financial comfort.

Jeremy and Gerald Verrey-ffaire frequently irritated each other but between them there was something of the attraction of opposites, cemented in a shared belief that their mutual survival through four years on the western front without even minor wounds was something near miraculous. Often, they would recall the names of the large numbers of young subalterns whose lives had been thrown away as senselessly as those of the men they had led in futile charges from the trenches.

That Jeremy's sister was married to Richard Mulholland-Flowers MP provided further cement for the relationship. Jeremy and Gerald did not meet frequently, which helped to make their friendship enduring. When they did meet, military matters always featured in their conversations, with Gerald mostly looking back while Jeremy was more concerned with the present and the future.

'The next war will be very different from the last,' he had said as he saw that another war was becoming only too likely.

'In what way?'

'To start with, it will be fought largely in the air, while the country will never stand for the senseless throwing away of life like we saw last time. Do you remember that terrible first day on the Somme? Nearly sixty thousand casualties, twenty thousand in the first two hours.'

Gerald became again the not very bright major he had been on that terrible day, monocle glinting, moustache bristling. 'I still recall,' he said coldly, 'that you wanted to send back to HQ to tell them to stop it.'

'Yes I did, and I tell you here and now that such stupidity at the top must never be repeated.'

'I do not, of course, accept your allegation of what you call stupidity. But how do you suggest that it should be done?'

'To start with, the days of cavalry charges, infantry on foot and horse-drawn artillery are over. We need a mechanised army with fast-moving tanks, mechanised artillery, troop-carrying vehicles to move the infantry forward at speed and front-line air support. And while we are still dithering about it, Hitler is building up a new German army on precisely those lines.'

'Do you think that nasty little ex-corporal is actually preparing for war, not just blustering?'

'Yes I do and I am appalled at how little we are doing to stop him and at the sheer complacency and refusal to face the facts among so many in high places. I've even started to think about leaving the service.'

'You can't do that. You're a full colonel now, and if you are right, you're exactly the sort of senior officer the army needs.' Gerald had been shocked into the only sensible military opinion he had ever expressed.

Jeremy had, in fact, already talked over the possibility of handing in his commission with Marion, his wife. She, who understood him so well, assured him that whatever he decided to do, she would of course support him. She knew as well as he that the other great love of his life outside his family was the army and that he despaired at the way he saw it going, to say nothing of his depression over the national failure to recognise or challenge the Nazi menace. As for herself, for all the patrician background she came from, it would not worry her to be no longer 'the colonel's lady'.

Unusually for Jeremy, he could not make up his mind. He 'felt as useless as the top brass', as he put it to Marion. Then, as he agonised, came an event to jolt him towards a decision. His elder brother, Edgar, died unexpectedly and he inherited the family home, Larkfield Lodge, with the responsibility of maintaining it. The idea came to him that he could retire to live partly in London, partly in Pembrokeshire to carry out these newly inherited responsibilities and, freed from military discipline, write questioning critiques and deliver lectures on military matters. After further agonising and further discussion with Marion, he finally put in an application to retire. Even so, his feelings were still very mixed.

He was called to the War Office, where he was surprised to be confronted by no less than a full general, who pressured him to stay. The general opened the interview by pointing out that some preparations at least were at last being made along the very lines he had advocated.

'I know,' he said, 'that it can be called the usual story of too little, too late, but there has never been a greater need for chaps like you in the army to push reform and rearmament along and see it through.'

'I presume that if I do stay, there will be some promotion in view,' Jeremy said cautiously. 'Not that I am agreeing to stay.' He was not the man to overlook a tactical point.

The general smiled without humour. 'I was wondering when we would get round to that. You must excuse me for a while, I must take some advice. I'll have some tea sent in.'

He was away for what seemed an interminable half-hour.

'I'm sorry to keep you waiting, Colonel,' he said on his return. 'I have been directly in touch with the minister's office. Your promotion to brigadier is authorised, with a staff posting. Such a posting will give you influence.'

'You're really anxious for me to stay, sir,' Jeremy said.

'And not only me,' the general replied. 'You understand better than most of us about the state we're in and you know what's got to be done. We need you, Hatherly. Don't let us down.'

Jeremy made mental note of being addressed for the first time by his name instead of by his rank. He'll be calling me Jeremy next, he thought. Aloud, he said, 'I would like to talk it over with my wife.'

'No, Jeremy,' the general said in an instant fulfilment of Jeremy's prophetic thought. 'You must decide here and now.' As if it was an afterthought, which of course it was not, he added, 'There could be promotion to general rank in a couple of years. Oh, and by the way, I think a decoration to mark your already distinguished service would not be out of place. I note that during the war you were twice mentioned in dispatches but not decorated.'

'Very well sir, I will stay,' Jeremy said. His tone was not without a certain dryness as he realised that the army had made up his mind for him.

'Good man,' said the general. 'How are your wife and children?'

'They are all very well, thank you.'

'And your wife's father, Sir Henry? Do give him my kind regards when you are next in touch.'

'With pleasure. Do you know him?'

'Oh yes, we are distant cousins.'

Jeremy had not known that but it did not surprise him. As he was escorted through the War Office corridors to the main entrance, he found himself wondering what part the family relationship had played in having that particular general deputed to meet him. He mused on how so many of the tiny proportion of the population who ruled the country and the empire were all related to each other. He, a senior officer, was married to the daughter of an empire builder who was a cousin of the general he had just met. His own cousins had married into the aristocracy, and his brother-in-law was a Member of Parliament and a major industrialist. Upon the decisions of this tight oligarchy, who enjoyed all the advantages of life and for which his own children were being exclusively educated to form the next generation, depended the future of the country and the fate of millions who enjoyed few advantages.

'We haven't made a particularly good job of it.' Unconsciously, he said it aloud.

'Beg pardon sir.'

He was on the pavement outside the main entrance and being addressed by the driver of the staff car that had been sent to take him to and from the War Office. The young soldier was standing rigidly to attention and saluting. Jeremy smartly returned the salute.

'It is I who should beg your pardon, Corporal,' he said. 'Senior officers are not supposed to daydream.'

The driver, unaccustomed to receiving apologies from officers, was struck dumb and did not speak again.

Sitting in the back of the car, Jeremy found himself wondering what would happen to that young soldier, who might well be in the front line in the coming war, under fire and driving one of the vehicles that he was advocating as essential, while he himself would likely be in the comparative safety of headquarters behind the front. He had a sudden recollection of how, as a schoolboy on holiday in Pembrokeshire, he had gone with his father and his father's estate manager to visit a farm, where he had met a farm boy, a few years younger than himself. Years later, he had met the same young man on the western front. He could recall his name, Hugh Hughes, a very Welsh name, notwithstanding his origins in the little England beyond Wales. Hughes had received the news, in the front line, that his brother had been killed in the navy. He knew that Hughes had survived the war. What, he wondered, had happened to him and to any children he might have fathered, to any other brothers, sisters, cousins? What a different life they must have lived compared with that of his own family.

His promotion and staff posting came through quickly. In the following Birthday Honours List he received the Distinguished Service Order.

From the time of their return from India, he and Marion had been occasional weekend guests of Sir Gerald and Lady Verreyffaire. Formerly, Richard Mulholland-Flowers and his wife had sometimes been guests, but after Richard's fall from grace, he was not welcome. On acquiring his own country house after his brother's death, Jeremy had invited Gerald and his wife there but Gerald had not taken up the invitation.

Absolutely firm in the belief that he was a true born and bred English gentleman, he regarded everything beyond the Welsh border with distaste. Secretly, he regretted that his old friend was Welsh but it did not surprise him that Mulholland-Flowers was.

Jeremy and Marion were Gerald's weekend guests shortly after

Neville Chamberlain returned from meeting Adolf Hitler at Munich, announcing that he had brought 'peace in our time'. Gerald fully supported the Prime Minister. Throughout the country, though, there was intense and angry argument.

'I see that fellow Churchill is, as usual, attacking the government,' Gerald said. 'Turncoat! First a Conservative, then a Liberal, then a Conservative again and now making warmongering speeches attacking the government all the time.'

'He has been wrong on numerous occasions in the past and may well be so again in the future, but he has seen more clearly than most how things have been moving,' Jeremy said, adding, 'As a matter of fact, I have met him.'

'What!'

'Knowing my views on the need for rearmament, he contacted me privately to give him a briefing. Oh, and I have also done the same for Attlee.'

'The Leader of the Opposition! That Socialist! He's a pacifist, isn't he?'

'No, don't forget that he is Major Attlee and went all through the war like you and me, South Lancs Regiment and Tank Corps. He has a more incisive mind than Churchill. His problem is that he has a large pacifist wing in his party.'

'Well, I can't stand these constant criticisms of Chamberlain. What man has done more for England?'

'Or less for Czechoslovakia,' Jeremy said.

Less than eleven months later, he was standing at the War Office window, listening to the broadcast declaration of war.

As war loomed, Hugh and Vicky in Bristol were preoccupied with moving house. It was only half a mile to their new home on the speculatively built new estate that surrounded their old house. The once isolated row of miners' cottages now constituted one side of a road with new, terraced houses on the other side.

The walls of all the new houses were covered with pebble-dash, about which Hugh, with his building experience, had reservations, considering it to be a cover for shoddily built walls. Nevertheless, he had succumbed to the lure of a new, modern house with a reasonable garden back and front.

Roads had been laid out for a still larger extension of house building but the threat of war had stopped that, so there were still fields, complete with grazing cows who sometimes came to look morosely over the fence at the end of the new back garden. The sale of the old house had made possible a substantial deposit on the larger new one, thereby satisfactorily cutting the monthly mortgage payments and making Hugh feel sufficiently secure to be able to take the family for a seaside holiday.

The holiday fell in the week before the war started. They went to Weymouth, a favourite resort among those Bristolians who could afford holidays. Fine weather lasted all the week and they visited the crowded beach every day, where the boys, keen swimmers both and especially Owen, were in the sea as much as they were out of it.

Vicky overcame her reservations about what she had originally seen as the boys' inadequate bathing dress, which was just as well, since practically every other male bather was similarly attired or, according to how you saw it, disattired, and it was those who stuck to the older-style costumes who were objects of curiosity. The boys tried to persuade their parents to buy costumes and join them in the sea but both declined firmly.

If moving house was preoccupying Hugh and Vicky, they were no less preoccupied with the knowledge that the boys were growing up and maturing. No longer were they lovable little boys given to occasional naughtiness and tantrums which could nevertheless be contained, they were becoming independent and sometimes aggressive personalities, very much with minds of their own. It had not escaped the parents' notice that sixteen-year-old Kenneth, in particular, had very appreciative eyes for pretty girls in bathing dresses, whilst both boys were prone to exchanging giggling remarks out of earshot that were clearly not for their parents' ears.

It was on the last afternoon of the holiday that a suddenly embarrassed Kenneth, standing up and eating a sandwich, hurriedly gulped it down, hastily spread his beach towel and then quickly spread himself on it, face down. The cause of his red-faced embarrassment was an all too obvious erection under his bathing trunks.

Owen, usually the underdog, was enjoying his brother's discomfort. 'Another sandwich?' he asked teasingly, kneeling close beside him.

'No, I'm not hungry.'

'How about a swim then?' Suppressing a giggle, he added in a low voice, 'That'll cool you down.'

'How can I walk down the beach like this?' Kenneth hissed, frantically wishing that the unwelcome tumescence would subside. It seemed agonising ages before it did and he felt able to get up and go with Owen to the water, He hoped desperately that his parents had not seen the cause of his embarrassment.

Both parents were in fact aware of what had happened and they, too, were embarrassed. They did not speak because they could no more discuss such things with each other than with their offspring. In line with the mores of the times, they were bringing up their sons as untutored in sexual matters as they had been themselves. They had vague hopes that, in due course, both boys would meet and marry 'nice girls' and that there would be grandchildren, but it was beyond them to bring themselves to explain to the boys anything of the physical processes of achieving such a desirable outcome. They would have been shocked to hear the boys' talk as they made their way to the sea.

'You horny bastard,' Owen said. 'Was it that little filly in the green swimsuit?' In their jargon, all attractive girls were little fillies, less attractive ones were tarts.

'Yes it was. Did you see how her tits were showing through her wet swimsuit when she walked past us? I couldn't keep my prick down. I reckon I shan't be able to get to sleep tonight unless I have a wank.'

'Wanking is supposed to be bad for you.'

'I know that's what they say, but I reckon everybody does it, girls too.'

At the lodgings, they were sharing a bedroom. Owen had a sudden idea. 'Tell you what,' he said, 'I'll do the same and we'll see who can come first.'

'Don't be daft,' Kenneth retorted, crushingly re-asserting his older-brother status. 'The proper way is to delay coming as long as you can. It's much better that way, and when you get to fuck properly with a girl, that's the way to make it best for both of you.'

In the event, tired out by their long and active day, they both fell asleep as soon as they were in their beds.

The morning after they returned home, Hugh listened with the boys to the Prime Minister's broadcast. Vicky was hanging out washing in the garden. She knew that not all the neighbours approved of washing clothes on a Sunday but she had set about washing the used holiday garments first thing, more concerned with cleanliness than with prying disapproval. Hugh, in the kitchen, was peeling potatoes for the Sunday lunch. He stopped to join the boys by the wireless in the living room.

They listened in silence; it was what everyone had been expecting. Owen was the first to speak.

'I must go and tell mam,' he said. At the back door, he was unable to contain his excitement. 'Mam, we're at war with Germany,' he shouted.

Vicky came into the house. 'How long will it go on?' she asked Hugh.

'At least as long as the last one, I should think.'

'The boys!' she said. 'If it does, they'll both be old enough to have to go.'

Conscription had already been introduced and, seeing soldiers marching on the promenade at Weymouth, they had speculated as to whether or not they might be 'militiamen', as the conscripts were called.

'Yes, I'm afraid they will. So much for the "war to end wars" that I went to last time. Remember how Chamberlain came back from Munich last year, saying he had brought peace in our time.' He despised Neville Chamberlain and he added bitterly, 'Knew he had one foot in the grave and the other no business out of it.' Uppermost in his mind was the prospect of his sons having to go through and possibly not survive the horrors that he had experienced in his own younger days.

For Kenneth, school days were over. He had taken the culminating school certificate examination, and the results came through shortly after the holiday. They were good, enabling him, notwithstanding that there were still nearly two million unemployed, to get a job with prospects, as a junior clerk in a local bank.

His parents were delighted. Hugh could not conceal his pride as he contrasted Kenneth's school-leaving with his own. His boy would work sensible hours – and in a bank, no less – go to work in a suit and tie and have prospects of promotion. The authorities were warning that the war must be expected to last three years, which would mean that Kenneth would become of military age. Owen would also become liable for service if it went on longer. Recalling the August 1914 talk of it 'being all over by Christmas', Hugh thought it only too likely that it would go on longer than that official forecast.

It was the winter of what came to be called the phoney war because, after the German conquest of Poland which had started hostilities, it settled into a stalemate with little fighting. It was a cold and especially miserable winter, made more so by the panic shutting-down of cinemas and other places of entertainment in expectation of air raids. Blackout was imposed and strictly enforced. A chink of light from a window in the new house brought a raucous shout of 'Put that light out', which was to become a new street cry. The shout was followed by a hammering on the front door and a telling-off from a self-important and officious air raid warden.

'Bloody little Hitler,' Hugh called him after he had left, using what was destined to become another much repeated saying on the home front.

Everyone was issued with a gas mask, contained in a cardboard box with a shoulder-length string so that it could be carried at all times. From London and other cities thought to be targets for air raids, tens of thousands of children were evacuated to the country, but Bristol was considered unlikely to be bombed and there was no evacuation.

In one of the worst-kept secrets of the war, the headquarters of the BBC were moved from London to Bristol. Bristolians uniquely referred to air raid sirens as 'sireens'. Posters with the message 'Careless Talk Costs Lives' were appearing but at least one broadcaster, coyly referring to the new 'secret' location as if he was exiled from London to some remote, yokelish spot in the sticks, drew attention to that unique pronunciation, instantly revealing the location to any locally posted German spy who might not already know it.

Plans had been drawn up for ocean-going ships to sail in convoys protected by warships, as in the previous war, but for small vessels such as Hugh and Harold Newforth worked on, making short voyages in coastal waters, convoys were impracticable. The chairman and managing director of their company, Geoffrey Jewell, had been visited by naval officers and told that little could be done.

Geoffrey Jewell was the third generation of the owners, grandson of the founder of the company, John Jewell, who had started in late Victorian times by purchasing two small, somewhat decrepit coasters. He had grandiosely registered the company as The Jewell Line and decreed that all its ships would be named after precious stones, hence the *Emerald* on which Hugh had started and the *Ruby* on which he was now the mate. However, John Jewell's dream of a fleet of ocean-going ships had never materialised.

The company had passed through difficult times but by the late 1930s, it was recovering from the depression years, especially through an increased demand for coal for the power stations it was contracted to supply. Two brand-new diesel-engined colliers were commissioned to be built in the shipyard at Bristol, with a view to replacing some of the older vessels. It was the first time the company had commissioned the building of new ships instead of buying second-hand ones.

The first was named *Pearl*, after Geoffrey Jewell's wife. The second was named *Jade*, after his daughter. There had been some debate as to whether jade really qualified as a precious stone but Geoffrey was insistent. and that was that.

Harold Newforth was promoted to be captain of the *Pearl*. He was not keen; he loved the smaller *Emerald*, 'the good little seaboat' that he had skippered for years, and he was reluctant to leave her.

'I don't know anything about diesel-engine ships,' he said to Geoffrey.

'Handling the engines is the engineer's job,' Geoffrey replied. 'Your job is to handle the ship.'

'But I have no experience of handling such a large vessel, sir.' He would never have dreamed of calling the boss anything other than 'sir' or 'Mr Jewell'.

'Nonsense Captain. You are the company's most senior and experienced captain, you should have gone on to one of the larger vessels years ago. Nobody knows the Bristol Channel better than you. It is only proper that, as the company's commodore, you should command its flagship.' His talk of 'commodore' and 'flagship' in a company owning eight small coasters showed some of the inherited grandiosity of his grandfather.

'I have every confidence in you, Captain. As is appropriate to your position, you will receive a substantial increase in wages. You will be due to retire in a few years' time and it is only right that you should finish your job in this position.'

For all the use of otherwise grandiose terms, he would no more have used the words 'salary' or 'career' instead of 'wages' or 'job' than Harold would have addressed him other than as 'sir' or 'Mr Jewell'. The class system prevailed effortlessly.

They had all assumed that the Bristol Channel in wartime would be relatively safe, at least in its upper reaches. The various shallows and sandbanks would preclude submarines, whilst the German air bases would be too far away for their aircraft to reach the area.

That assumption was shattered by the German conquest of western Europe in the spring of 1940. The British army was evacuated from Dunkirk, with the loss of all its equipment, in a heroic fleet of small, largely civilian boats. The expression 'The Dunkirk Spirit' entered the language and a huge military defeat was mythologised for ever as a great victory. The Germans now had seaports and airfields in France that brought the entire British Isles within easy reach. Invasion seemed imminent.

Hugh, smoking a cigarette, discussed the situation with George Fenn, the captain of the *Ruby*. They had loaded at a coal staith in Cardiff and were waiting to sail on the night tide.

'If the Jerries do land on the south coast, I reckon they'll be in Bristol in a fortnight at the most. We've got nothing to stop them,' he said.

'Yes, I reckon you're dead right,' George agreed.

'You know those Local Defence Volunteers that have been formed, the Home Guard as they've renamed it. My older boy, Kenneth, the one who works at the bank, went down to the police station to try to join it.' Whenever he spoke of Kenneth, he could not conceal his pride over Kenneth's job.

'How did he get on?'

'Turned away, told there were no weapons and no uniforms and that he was too young anyway.'

'Did you see that some idiot in the House of Lords said that as there are no rifles, the Home Guard could be armed with pikes?' George said. 'Pikes against tanks, for Christ's sake.'

Hugh threw the stub of his cigarette over the side. He had a bout of coughing, not unusual when he smoked.

'These fags aren't doing you any good,' George said. 'You ought to give them up.'

'I know, that's what the doctor says. But it's not the fags, it's the gas I got in the last war.' He had been to see the doctor about his persistent cough, now of many years' standing. Dr MacBrayne had examined him and told him, in his usual blunt manner, 'Give up smoking and I can cure you of that cough, but if you keep up that dirty habit, I can't.'

Shortly after eleven o'clock, the tide was high enough for them to sail. With a rising tide, the Bristol Channel was busy with both deep-sea and coastal vessels. All were blacked out, with only their navigation lights showing, but between occasional clouds, the flat sea reflected a brilliant moon and showed up the shipping only too well. They were well on their way when they heard the drone of an approaching aircraft.

'That's not one of ours,' George said.

'If he's going to bomb anything, I should think he'll go for one of those big fellows,' Hugh said. Suddenly, there was the whine of falling bombs.

'Jesus Christ!' George shouted. 'He's aiming at us.' Before the words were out of his mouth, there were two huge explosions, throwing up great columns of water, one on either side of them. The plane had dropped a stick of bombs. Fortunately for the *Ruby* and her crew, they had all missed their target and fallen into the sea, although the blast and the waves caused the ship to roll alarmingly. The single bomber droned away back to its French base.

'I'll check to see that there's no damage and that everything's OK in the engine room,' Hugh said. He left the bridge for an urgent tour of inspection. He found the two deck hands, who had been brewing tea in the galley, visibly shaken but unhurt, whilst all was well in the engine room. Bill Horden, the engineer, the oldest of the crew, was unperturbed.

'No damage,' he said over the reassuringly continuous pounding of the engine, 'but I bet that bastard will go back to his base and report that he sank a big ship. Mike's a bit shaken, but he's OK.' Mike was the fireman, at seventeen the youngest of the crew.

Hugh returned to the bridge to take the wheel while the captain recorded the attack in the log, with the laconic comment *No damage done.*

They reached their destination without further incident. When he got home in the morning, Vicky told him that the air raid sirens had sounded the previous evening but there had been no raid. He did not tell her about the bombing of the ship, judging that she was already too worried by the state of things in general to be further upset. She had been really alarmed when Kenneth came home disappointed at his unsuccessful attempt to join the Home Guard; he had told his parents nothing in advance.

'What is this Home Guard supposed to do?' she asked Hugh.

'The idea is that if there is an invasion they, with their local knowledge, will be a valuable force in fighting the Germans.'

The thought horrified Vicky. 'Dear God, if they caught him, he could be put against a wall and shot.'

'Oh don't be silly. You can understand any young fellow his age wanting to do something.' He was unusually brusque and he regretted it at once, realising that it arose from a delayed reaction to the experience of the previous night. He took her in his arms. They were happy together but it was a rare demonstration of affection, its own measure of the tension under which they were living.

Neither of them believed the endless propaganda about how high their morale was. They knew that the national mood was more one of helpless doggedness in a seemingly hopeless situation. They were not alone in believing that if the country was invaded, it would be overrun in a matter of weeks, that the government and the royal family would be evacuated to Canada and the people left to their fate. There would be no shortage of those in the ruling class prepared to set up a puppet government to collaborate with the Nazis.

Yet, for all his experience of the way working people had been downtrodden before the first war, cannon fodder during it and branded enemies of the state they had fought for whenever they stood up for their rights after it, he still retained a gut feeling that, whatever happened, the Germans had to be fought, if necessary to the last ditch.

He was as proud to be a seaman as he had once been proud to be a miner, doing a dangerous and essential job. The merchant fleet had been designated the Merchant Navy and recognised as ranking with the Royal Navy, the army and the RAF as an equal partner in the defence of the country. He had no regrets about having ceremoniously thrown away his medals from the first war, but he wore the silver-gilt badge with the letters MN for Merchant Navy with pride.

Although the main fighting in the aerial Battle of Britain was over the English Channel and the south east of England, there were spasmodic daylight raids in the Bristol Channel area. They included a devastating attack on the Admiralty oil tanks at Pembroke Dock that set them blazing for nearly three weeks. Hugh was mightily relieved to receive a letter from his sister Alice, the tenth of the family, born between himself and Myfanwy, to reassure him that all the family were safe.

But family tragedy struck on a bright September afternoon. The

Ruby was following the *Pearl* up the Channel and, as usual, Hugh was on the bridge with the captain.

'Harold is due to retire next year,' George said, referring to his fellow captain on the ship ahead, 'but I should think he'll want to carry on as long as the war lasts.'

'I don't know if they'll allow him to go on into his late sixties,' Hugh said. 'But then, with the war, every possible seaman is needed. And you can't keep an old sea dog down.'

Just a few minutes later, all such speculation was ended. The *Pearl* was engulfed in an almighty explosion. When the column of water subsided, her remains, her back broken, disappeared beneath the surface in seconds, all her crew, or what might have been left of them, going with her.

'Jesus Christ!' George shouted. 'What the hell happened? The poor buggers never had a chance.'

They were all numb with shock, their thoughts above all with the crew whom they had seen destroyed. For Hugh, it felt especially horrifying that the captain, Vicky's uncle Harold, had gone so suddenly and horribly. He had a great regard for Harold and felt that he owed so much to him. Harold, who had got him a job when he was desperately in need of one at the height of the depression and who had tutored him so well in the ways of seamen. Harold, who had been modestly reluctant to take the captaincy of the flagship with which he had now gone down in appalling circumstances. Harold, who was one of the most respected skippers among Bristol Channel seafarers.

The *Ruby* was close behind the *Pearl* so it was necessary to put her full astern to stop at the spot where the *Pearl* had gone down. They hoped against hope that there might be survivors, but all that remained was some floating wreckage that was already drifting away on the flowing tide. Within minutes, a fast-moving naval minesweeper had come up and taken charge. A line of ships making up channel had all come to a stop; there was no small danger of collisions. The minesweeper came close and her captain shouted through a loud hailer.

'Ahoy *Ruby*. I'm sorry there's nothing can be done, skipper. Please get under way and proceed on course. We'll drop a buoy to mark the spot.'

George Fenn took the *Ruby*'s loud hailer. 'What happened?' he asked. 'There was no warning.'

'It's a new type of mine they're dropping from aircraft. It rests on the sea bed and is set off when a vessel passes over it.'

'Aye aye skipper. Proceeding on course.' With a heavy heart, he signalled slow ahead to the engine room, only increasing to full speed after they were clear of the spot. Hugh ran to the stern to lower the flag, the mercantile red ensign, 'the red duster', as it was universally known. Even the engineer and fireman briefly left the engine room as the crew lined the deck, hats off, in tribute to their lost comrades.

There had been much talk of German secret weapons. The mine that destroyed the *Pearl* was one of them. It was a magnetic mine, dropped to lie on the sea bed in shallow water, to be triggered by the magnetic field of a ship passing over it. When it exploded it caused far more devastation than the older, floating mines. Scientists worked frantically to produce means to counter it, coming up with a process known as degaussing, to neutralise ships' magnetic fields. But that was too late to save the *Pearl*.

Nothing was found of the five crew members. All that was left were some pieces of floating wreckage, some of which was washed up at various points on the coast, the rest taken out to sea.

A memorial service for the lost seamen was held at a church in Bristol, close to the city docks. It was packed to capacity, with a large turnout of seamen, dock workers and others representing practically every ship-owning and otherwise sea-connected company in Bristol. Geoffrey Jewell, clearly deeply moved, read the lesson.

For the family, there was an added poignancy in that Harold's widow, Yvonne, was supported by a young soldier, a cousin who had been rescued from Dunkirk by one of those heroic little ships.

As the service proceeded, it came to Hugh that his brother Joe had been blown to pieces at sea in the last war whilst, now, a no less loved uncle – as he always thought of Harold – had gone the same way in this one. They sang the hymn 'Eternal Father, Strong to Save'. When they came to the haunting line 'For those in peril on the sea' he was suddenly and uncontrollably too choked to continue and there were tears in his eyes – a rare occurrence.

Vicky wept openly, also a rare occurrence. He put his arm round her shoulder and they stood in silent sadness, each taking comfort from the closeness of the other. Kenneth, standing at his mother's other side, took her hand. 'Don't cry, Mam,' he said, awkward and unable to think of anything else to say or do to comfort her. For him and Owen, wearing newly acquired black ties, it was the first death-related ceremony they had attended. They were both moved, but youthful resilience, aided and abetted by what they had both been taught at school about the paramount importance of always keeping 'a stiff upper lip', enabled them to conceal their emotions more successfully than their elders. But then, whoever died and in whatever circumstances, life continued, especially for those who had all their lives before them.

Chapter 17

As the *Ruby* cleared the Welsh coast off Cardiff on the dark night of Sunday, November 24th 1940, the sky ahead was brilliantly lit from the fires of a city ablaze and there was the constant drone of waves of bombers. It was clear that Bristol was under heavy attack.

Hugh was watching from the bridge with the captain and the two able seamen deck hands, all of them powerless witnesses of an unfolding tragedy that could be killing their loved ones even as they watched, all of them filled with horrified foreboding of what they might find on getting home in the morning.

'They're doing the same to Bristol as they did to Coventry,' Hugh said despairingly.

It was just ten days since the German air force had totally destroyed the city centre at Coventry, boasting of their achievement and comparing it with what they had earlier done to Warsaw and Rotterdam.

By the time the *Ruby* reached her destination at Portishead, the raid was over. Portishead itself, eight miles or so from the city, appeared not to have been attacked. George Fenn lived close by and was able to walk home as soon as the vessel was moored for unloading, but the others, who lived in Bristol, had to wait at the dockside station for the first train, which had first to come from the bombed city. They were on the platform long before it was due and wondering if it would come at all. It was at least something of a relief when it arrived and duly departed on time for the return journey.

'Terrible damage,' the guard told them. 'Whole city centre on fire. Big fires in Clifton, Bedminster and other parts. Gas, water, electricity all off in many parts.'

The single-track line ran through the Avon Gorge, and as the train emerged from the short tunnel that took it under the Clifton Suspension Bridge that was so much the symbol of Bristol, the truth of the guard's words became clear. They now had a view across the city and it seemed as if the whole skyline was alight.

At the local station where Hugh left the train, Kenneth was waiting for him, hatless, dishevelled but smiling.

'I knew you'd be on this train, Dad,' he said. 'I knew you'd be worried, so I came to let you know that we're OK. Owen is at home with mam.'

'How is your mother?'

'She's OK, very shaken though. We sheltered under the stairs during the raid.' Very few air raid shelters had been provided, and that was where most people went for protection.

'The electricity is on but there's no gas and the water pressure's low,' Kenneth added.

Hurrying from the station, they met the air raid warden who had so annoyed Hugh in the earliest days of the war. The man was a neighbour and he had been on duty all through the raid. Still wearing his steel helmet, he was tired, haggard and dirty.

'There's no serious damage in this part,' he said, 'but there are unexploded bombs and we have had to evacuate a lot of people from their homes. There's no danger to your house.'

Vicky was distraught; she had been really frightened. All through the bombing she had attempted to hide her fear from the boys, trying not to frighten them. For her, they were still her little boys who had to be shielded at all cost. But they were no longer little boys, one already working for his living, the other moving towards the end of his school days and growing up rapidly. She was not successful in hiding her fear; in fact they were far less frightened than she and they felt even more protective towards her than she felt towards them.

'It's all right now, kid,' Hugh said. 'Kid' was a favourite expression of endearment between them.

'There's a lot of bombs haven't gone off,' she said. 'People have had to leave their houses, some of them are just in the streets. We ought at least to give as many of them as we can a cup of tea.'

Before she was able to offer such characteristically British succour, her brother Charlie arrived. He had cycled over but had been forced to wheel and even carry his bike in places through streets strewn with rubble.

'We're all right; he said. 'Got some windows blown out and several houses near us were hit. I'm afraid several people have been killed. I called on Mam and Dad on the way. They're OK and there's no damage to the house. They're a bit shaken up though.'

Charlie left, saying that he had to get back home and then off to work. Kenneth announced that it was time for him, too, to get ready for work and Owen announced, not to be outdone, that it would soon be time for him to 'go and make sure that the school was still standing'.

'Is it safe for them?' Vicky asked anxiously.

'As safe as it's likely to be,' Hugh said. 'We've got to show these damn Huns that, whatever they do, we can take it and will carry on. But you boys be sure to be careful how you go.'

Kenneth washed, shaved and changed into his suit to go to work. He had not long started shaving on a daily basis and felt that it was an essential ritual to demonstrate his manhood. Low though the water pressure was, there was sufficient for his ablutions. Looking at himself in the bathroom mirror, he engaged in silent self-congratulation, seeing himself as the man of the house who, in the absence of his father, had safely seen his mother and kid brother through the night of peril. His father's sentiment that they had to carry on, no matter what 'the Huns' threw at them, struck a very responsive chord. It was at his suggestion that, within hours, his branch of the bank was displaying a notice 'Business As Usual', words that had already become a national slogan.

The unexploded bombs were successfully defused by soldiers within a couple of days, to the immense admiration of everyone for their bravery. A couple of neighbours from their old street whom Hugh and Vicky had taken in were able to return home. Gas, water and electricity supplies were restored. Eight days later, there was another heavy air raid, and through the winter and the spring there were altogether thirty attacks of varying intensity on Bristol. During the long nights of midwinter, two of them lasted for more than twelve hours.

For Hugh and the family, the raid that would remain longest in their memories, apart from that first one, was on the night of Good Friday, April 11th 1941, an attack they would talk about for years as 'the Good Friday raid'.

Hugh was at home that night. As soon as the sirens sounded, he ushered Vicky and the boys into the cramped cupboard under the stairs, for they still had no air raid shelter. By that time, they had all acquired a certain stoicism, accepting a popular if resigned saying that 'if it's got your name on it, there's nothing you can do about it'. Both parents had made wills, each leaving everything to the other and to the boys. That the boys might be killed with them was a thought they tried resolutely to keep out of their consciousness. But it could not be kept out of the subconscious and on raid-free nights it would sometimes awaken them from nightmares.

Within minutes of the alarm, the sky was brilliantly lit by flares drifting on parachutes immediately above them and, before the bombs, the night was shattered by the deafening roar of anti-aircraft guns firing from a close-by battery.

Then came thousands of fire bombs. One landed on the house but miraculously failed to penetrate the roof. It fell blazing, half as high as the house, onto the front garden path, setting alight the wooden garden fence. Had it gone through the roof there would have been no hope of saving the house.

'Get the stirrup pump and bucket,' Hugh shouted to Kenneth.

By that time, every house had been issued with a stirrup pump, a hand-operated device to spray water from a bucket to put out fires. They kept it permanently to hand with a bucket of water.

Kenneth was out from under the stairs as quickly as his father, filling a second bucket and replenishing the first as Hugh tried to dowse the bomb. Their next-door neighbour was trying to deal with the burning fence. Incendiary bombs were on fire all round. Some distance along the road, a house was burning. There was no small added danger from shrapnel falling from the anti-aircraft shells. The bomb in the garden eventually expired, enabling them to add to their neighbour's fight to put out the burning fence.

Owen emerged from the house. 'What can I do, Dad?' he shouted.

Hugh practically screamed at him. 'Get back under the stairs with your mother. You could be killed out here.'

'We could all be killed, but I want to do something.'

Kenneth intervened. He was much less vehement than his father. 'Do as dad says. You can't do anything here that dad and I can't. Mam needs you more.' His tone was very firm but the aggression was absent that so often characterised both brothers' older–younger, love–hate exchanges. Owen returned indoors without comment.

'It's all right, Mam,' he said. 'Don't worry, dad and Ken are dealing with that bomb. We'll be all right here.' It was an important moment: youthful courage, care and common sense at its best.

After the storm of incendiary bombs came the high explosives. Several nearby houses were destroyed by direct hits and their inhabitants killed. As usual, the raid ended before dawn so that darkness covered the aircraft returning to their bases. As daylight came, the extent of the damage was only too clear. There were also unexploded bombs, with uncertainty as to whether they had failed to explode or were fitted with timing devices to explode them later.

'I'll go over to Southville to see if your mam and dad are all right,' Hugh said to Vicky, 'and see if I can find out how Charlie, Greta and the girls are.'

'Can we come, Dad?' It came spontaneously from both boys.

Hugh hesitated. 'Will you be OK if we all go?' he asked Vicky.

'Yes, I'll stay here. People are being evacuated where there are bombs that didn't go off, and we may be needed to take some of them in. Please God that everyone is all right. Get back and let me know as soon as you can.'

They made their way through the chaos of bombed streets, having to make a couple of detours so as not to obstruct firemen, ambulance crews and other rescue workers at their grim tasks. In Edward's road, not far from his house, there was a huge crater in the road. Edward's front door and windows had been blown in and many of the tiles had been blown off the roof. Many other houses had been damaged too, some of them much more seriously.

Edward and Mary, with other dazed people, were in the street. Of the two, she seemed the more composed. Her immediate action was to enquire anxiously after Vicky. Charlie was already there, with the reassuring news that Greta and the girls were unharmed. He too had been fighting fire bombs during the raid.

'The civil defence people have been here already,' Edward said. He lit a cigarette with shaking hands. 'We shall have to move out but they say the house will be made weatherproof quite quickly. There's not too much damage inside, so we shall be able to move back as soon as they're done.'

'You will come and stay with us – in your old home – until you can move back,' Charlie urged.

A policeman was standing by. 'And while you're away, Dad, one of us will be on duty all the time to make sure there's no looting,' he said.

'Surely no Englishman would loot a bombed house,' Edward said indignantly.

'You'd be surprised,' the policeman replied. 'I'm afraid there's only too many who would.'

Edward seemed almost more shocked by such knowledge than by the damage to his home. He looked along the road to the cigarette factory, from which he was soon due to retire. 'I hope they haven't hit the factory,' he said.

Kenneth could not contain himself. He burst out, 'For God's sake, Grandad! How can you stand there, bombed out of your home, and worry about that bloody factory!'

Hugh intervened quickly. 'That's enough,' he snapped.

He could see that an angry confrontation was in the making. To his relief, there came an unexpected and timely distraction. A couple of official cars with police outriders rounded the corner at the nearby end of the road and stopped at the bomb crater. The first car bore the city crest: it was the Lord Mayor's official vehicle. From it, accompanied by the Lord Mayor and to gasps of surprise from the onlookers, emerged the unmistakable, bow-tied figure of Winston Churchill. The policeman on duty snapped to attention and saluted. Edward's emotions were transformed.

'It's like a miracle,' he gasped. 'He has actually come among us in our hour of need.'

'You talk as if he was Jesus Christ,' Kenneth said.

'Who do you think you are, young Kenneth Edward, to dare to question the likes of a great gentleman like him?'

'Somebody who thinks for himself and doesn't fall for everything he reads in Tory newspapers,' Kenneth retorted.

Hugh grabbed him by the arm. 'Don't you talk to your grandfather like that,' he said. 'He has seen a lot more of life than you have.'

'Pity he hasn't learned more from it.'

'Shut up!'

He pulled Kenneth away, although in truth his own sympathies were more in tune with those of his rebellious son than with those of his father-in-law. This Prime Minister was the man who had ruthlessly put down the miners and whom he had always held personally responsible for the huge loss of life in the Gallipoli disaster in the last war.

Churchill removed the trade-mark cigar from his mouth. 'They will get this back, in time, ten times over,' they heard him say.

But Hugh's attention had been attracted to another figure, just emerged from the second car, a very senior soldier, a brigadier no less. He recognised him instantly.

'Come with me,' he said to Kenneth and Owen. There was a note of excitement in his voice that surprised them. The three of them picked their way past the other side of the bomb crater from where the Prime Minister was standing.

'Excuse me sir, Brigadier Hatherly, I believe,' Hugh said, then added, 'Hughes, I served with you on the western front in the last war.'

Jeremy was surprised and there was a slightly awkward pause. A soldier quickly stepped forward in case of trouble. Then recognition dawned.

'Hugh Hughes,' he said. 'Your brother was killed in the navy at Jutland. But we first met as boys. That must have been forty years ago.' He stepped forward and shook hands warmly.

'Yes,' Hugh said. 'We first met at Round Pond Farm in Pembrokeshire – which my eldest brother now owns.' He could not resist making the point, recalling that, at that time, the farm had formed part of the estate of Jeremy's father.

'You live here in Bristol now?'

'Yes, I go to sea myself now. I'm in the Merchant Navy. I've lived in Bristol for twenty years. These are my two sons, Kenneth and Owen.'

'Two fine–looking young men. I can see the likeness.' He shook hands with the two slightly awestruck youths, then turned again to Hugh. 'Would you like to meet the Prime Minister?'

'No.' The response was sharp. 'I have too many memories of how he treated the miners.'

Jeremy spoke slowly. 'I understand why you say that, but he foresaw this war more than anybody else and he has provided immense inspiration since he became Prime Minister. Whatever his past, he is the right man in the right place now.'

'He only became Prime Minister because the Labour Party supported him,' Kenneth said.

'A well-informed young man,' Jeremy said. He smiled slightly. 'I dare say he gets it from his father.' He added, addressing Kenneth, 'I know Mr Attlee as well, you know.'

He knew what they did not, that Churchill had had to fight a tremendous battle within his own cabinet to defeat those who wanted to sue for peace, which would have been on Hitler's terms. In strictest secrecy, he had talked about it at the time with his old friend Gerald Verrey-ffaire.

Gerald had been furious because Richard Mulholland-Flowers,

with whom he had hardly spoken since their angry exchanges before the war, had voted against Neville Chamberlain in the vote of confidence that brought about his resignation. The last straw for Gerald was when Richard had also sided with the Labour Party in their refusal to join the government except under Churchill's leadership. Gerald, a party loyalist to the core, had supported Lord Halifax, with whom he was acquainted through the Country Landowners' Association and whom he knew to be Chamberlain's choice to succeed him. Halifax had led the faction that wanted to open negotiations in the hope of avoiding an invasion.

Angry with Richard and haunted by his memories of the terrible destruction of the French countryside in the last war, Gerald was horrified at the possibility of his own estate becoming a battleground and his house being destroyed in some last-ditch stand. His conversation with Jeremy in that fateful summer of 1940 had developed into a furious row and Jeremy had tactfully avoided contact with him since.

He realised that the present conversation in this bombed Bristol suburb could also be approaching an argument into which he could not enter. The subject had to be changed.

'Have you suffered any casualties in your family or damage to your home?' he asked Hugh.

'No, I live some distance from here. We had an incendiary bomb on the roof last night but we were lucky. It fell off the roof and only burned the garden fence.'

'I'm glad to hear it was no worse.'

'My father-and mother-in-law live here and they haven't been so lucky. One of these damaged houses is theirs. As well as that, my father-in-law's brother was killed last year. He was the captain of a coaster that was sunk with all hands by a magnetic mine in the Bristol Channel.'

'I really am sorry to hear that. Please accept my sympathy and convey it to your parents-in-law. We are, I'm afraid, engaged in total war, and the front line has been brought to every home in the country.'

Kenneth was now fully recovered from any sense of awe he might have had at his father's acquaintance with this obviously very important person. 'How is it that the Prime Minister is here?' he asked.

'Later today, in his capacity as Chancellor of the university, he is going to present honorary degrees to the Australian Prime Minister and to the American Ambassador. Immediately on arriving here, he insisted on touring the city to inspect the damage.'

The driver of his car intervened. 'The Prime Minister is ready to move on, sir.'

Jeremy shook hands with Hugh, Kenneth and Owen again. 'I wish you all God speed,' he said. 'But do remember the Prime Minister's words. As he said, the time will come when they will get it back ten times over.' The official party returned to their cars and moved on.

Edward was still awestruck from being in the presence of such high and mighty people. He would talk about it for the rest of his life.

'How do you know that general?' he asked Hugh.

'He's not a general, Dad, he's a brigadier – one step below a general. How I got to know him is a long story. I'll tell you about it some other time. We must get back home.'

'How did you get to know that brasshat?' Kenneth asked, as they made their way.

He related the story to them. It was the first time he had talked to them at any length about his experiences in the last war, although they did know that they had an uncle who had been killed in the navy, whilst they had never forgotten being taken to see their father throw away his medals in disgust at the way ex-servicemen had been treated. As to his childhood, normally he only spoke about that to tell them how much better off they were than he had been at their age. The boys, often critical of their parents in the adolescent manner, were aware of seeing their father in a new light and were suitably impressed.

When work resumed after Easter, Kenneth came home with another story of the air raid. Near the bank where he worked, there was a large, well-known local pub, rather improbably called the Hen and Chicken. A nearby bomb had done damage to it and, remarkably, a parked car had been blown up onto the roof of the three-storey building. It had come to rest perfectly upright, and there it remained for the rest of the war.

News of the aerial assaults on what Hugh thought of as 'the three Ps' – Plymouth, Portsmouth and Pembroke Dock – came regularly from his sisters in those places. He and his sisters were inveterate letter writers, all employing, with only minor adaptations, the 'joined-up' writing they had been taught so many years earlier under the suzerainty of their long–dead teacher, Edward Kendle. It was hand-writing designed to be standardised, legible and as devoid as possible of any expression of individual personality.

Only Matthew, the recognised head of the family and the strongest personality among them, had broken out of the mould. With no literary interest at even the most minimal level, he had become impatient with what he saw as the laborious style of writing he had been taught. He had acquired an aversion to all writing that could be avoided and his hand had deteriorated into a scribble that was perhaps some reflection of his personality. Matthew did not correspond much with anybody. Hugh never wrote to him and only received occasional news of him from their sister Alice in Pembroke Dock.

Just a month after the Good Friday raid, a letter from Alice brought news of a severe raid on Pembroke Dock, the latest and most damaging of many, that had caused severe damage and casualties. Alice and her family had to be evacuated temporarily from their damaged home. Beyond the town, a bomb had fallen onto Matthew's land. There had been no casualties to people or animals but a growing crop of potatoes had been destroyed, causing Matthew to complain loudly about his 'crippling' loss of income.

More surprisingly, Hugh's friend from school days, Robert Snape, had also developed an aversion to letter writing. Between the wars and following his move to work at the Admiralty dockyard at Plymouth, he had again written occasionally for newspapers but, with the advent of the second war, shortage of newsprint had drastically cut the size and range of publications and he had stopped writing, whether for publication or for family. So it was Myfanwy who had kept up the correspondence with Hugh.

Plymouth was subjected to some of the heaviest bombing of any city in the country and Robert and Myfanwy had been bombed out of their home at an early stage, fortunately without personal injury. Their two sons were both in the navy and the elder had served in one of the destroyers that, under immensely heavy fire, had rescued soldiers from the beaches of Dunkirk. If Hugh had any favourites among his many nephews and nieces, it could be said to be those two, and he always awaited news of them in their mother's letters with interest, not unmixed with anxiety.

Then there were the letters from his sister Lizzie Jones, whose husband had moved to Portsmouth on the closure of Pembroke

Dock, telling him of the savage attacks on that other great naval city. Ray and Lizzie had not been bombed out, although their house had suffered damage in two separate air raids.

Hugh and Vicky would not have been as aware of the extent of the bombing without these family letters, for strict censorship in the newspapers and on the wireless gave only carefully managed reports. Where it was officially not possible to conceal news of air raids altogether, the practice was to announce, as for example in the case of Pembroke Dock, an attack on a town in the west. It was argued in defence of the censorship that it was important not to let the Germans know which places they had bombed.

The irony was not lost on Kenneth. 'Funny how they think the German pilots don't know where they are, but we are always told that our pilots know exactly where they are if we bomb anywhere in Germany,' he remarked.

But the blitz against Britain was being run down and more German bombers were being shot down by British night fighters. The development of radar was a closely guarded secret and, by way of explanation for the growing success, it was put about that night fighter pilots were fed on a special diet of carrots, which enabled them to see better in the dark.

It irritated and disappointed Edward Newforth, who complained, 'I've tried eating more carrots from the allotment but they don't seem to help me see any better in the blackout.'

'Must be your age, Grandad,' Kenneth consoled him.

Everybody listened avidly to the news on the radio. In practically every household in the country, listening to the heavily censored news was an essential family ritual, when all conversation came to a halt. A great controversy arose, and was assiduously stirred up, over the accent of a popular entertainer called Wilfred Pickles, who was given the additional task of reading the news. His voice pleasantly reflected his native Yorkshire. In houses, workplaces and pubs throughout the land, argument raged as to whether it was proper for the news to be read by anybody who did not speak in the established Oxbridge accent of the BBC.

For Hugh, who had never lost the lilt of his Welsh accent, it all seemed silly. 'It's an educated Yorkshire accent,' he said. 'Everybody can understand every word he says. Surely that's what matters.'

His father-in-law, deferential as always to all things pertaining to the established order, did not agree and said in his strong Bristol accent, 'having somebody like him to read the news is not a good ideal.'

The debate continued. In some of the darkest days of the war, a country fighting for its life was consumed with argument over a newsreader's accent.

Chapter 18

Hugh and Vicky readily recognised that their sons were more 'brainy' than they were, and it pleased them. They did speculate as to 'where they got it from' and, knowing nothing of genetics, they could only put it down to the boys having received schooling that was superior to theirs .

What they wanted above all was for the boys to have better starts in life than they had known, but Vicky worried about Kenneth. She had been brought up by her parents, her father especially, to know her place in a deferential society, and she worried that her elder son's unconcealed contempt and outspoken criticism of so much he saw around him could 'get him into trouble'.

Hugh, on the other hand, was pleased that both his sons had a keen sense of social awareness and that Kenneth, in particular, was not afraid to express it, but he did worry about Kenneth's brash criticism of his elders. He even found himself wondering occasionally as to what Kenneth might think privately about his parents. The young man's contemptuous attitude towards his grandfather on that Saturday morning after the Good Friday air raid had shocked him.

'Honour thy father and thy mother that thy days may be long in the land' was a slightly misquoted biblical text that had been drummed into him by his own father and also by his school teachers. The quote was embedded in his memory, although he could never make out how being good to your parents could be related automatically to living a long life. Nevertheless, he tried to drum it into his own sons. He had no more time for his father-in-law's servility towards his employers and towards the elite in general than Kenneth, but Kenneth's scarcely hidden contempt for his grandfather, who had been bombed out of his home only hours before on that dreadful night and could have been killed, had angered him.

If the parents were anxious about the sons, the sons had their own anxieties about the parents. These were never expressed but they sometimes amounted to a rebellious contempt that occasionally led to open quarrels, which Hugh regarded as unacceptable insubordination. Had he been more introspective, like his younger son, he might have found some parallel with his own feelings as an adolescent against his own father, after being arbitrarily put to work on a farm among people he grew to hate. But all that was a long way behind him and had slipped his memory. He was, in any case, of a generation accustomed to being much more in awe of their fathers than his own sons were of him.

Yet, for all the misgivings between the generations, there was a strong family bond, and it was strengthened by the times through which they were living. For the first time ever in British society – and probably the last – the war had brought a growing feeling that everyone had to close ranks in the common good.

For all his youthful sense of rebellion, Kenneth was strongly stirred by such genuine, non-chauvinistic patriotism. He greatly admired the brave fighter pilots of the Battle of Britain, of whom Winston Churchill had said that 'Never in the field of human conflict was so much owed by so many to so few', and he had made up his mind that he wanted to join them. It was the fashion among RAF pilots to grow large moustaches, and shortly after that traumatic Good Friday, with three months to go to his eighteenth birthday, which would make him of military age, he set out to grow his own moustache.

It annoyed his father, who had always been clean-shaven, although he remembered his own father having a moustache. His father-in-law also sported one, in the fashion of the Edwardian era to which he looked back with nostalgia. Hugh told Kenneth to shave it off because it made him look older than he was. Since that was among the reasons Kenneth had grown it, he refused.

His changed appearance led to comment and leg-pulling among his fellow workers at the bank. He was mightily pleased, though, that it attracted favourable attention from the manager's secretary, Dorothy Bestcalmer. Almost from the day he started work, he had lusted after her but she treated him disdainfully, as if he was unworthy of her slightest attention.

Dottie, as everyone called her, was a striking, fair-haired young woman with a fine body and nymphomaniac tendencies. She was rumoured to have posed for nude photographs, although nobody had ever seen any. She was also rumoured to have had several affairs, one, it was said, with the manager, Mr Mudgeon, a man with a moustache that Kenneth envied and a fine head of black hair, always brilliantined and brushed straight back from his forehead.

No one could make up their mind as to the truth of the rumours. Mr Mudgeon, regarded as a married man of the utmost rectitude, ruled the staff with a rod of iron, leading them to believe that he was incapable of emotional feelings of any sort. They nicknamed him 'Curmudgeon'.

Dottie apart, Kenneth experienced little difficulty in attracting girls and had acquired a reputation as 'a good kisser'. Apart from some breast-fondling with the more willing, that was as far as physical contact had gone. Now, he was flattered and aroused by Dottie's new-found interest.

'You want to watch her,' one of his colleagues advised him. 'She's a dangerous woman. In any case, she's too old for you.'

Another colleague advised him differently. 'She's only about three years older than you,' he said, 'and it's much better the first time to do it with an experienced woman than to fumble about with a girl who's as nervous as you are.'

The colleague concerned claimed to have 'had' Dottie but, since he was a sexually obsessed and boastful young man, no one really believed him. Kenneth concluded after careful thought that possibly he could have 'done it' with Dottie, but if so, that was likely to have been both his first and his only time with anybody. Then, to his unbounded delight, a situation arose at Dottie's instigation whereby he was himself able to 'do it' the first time with her.

Normally, Mr Mudgeon took great care to be the last to leave the bank and to ensure that everything was securely locked but, on this occasion, he inexplicably left more promptly than usual. Having secured the strong room and all other places where money and confidential papers were stored, he had departed, leaving Dottie to secure the front door. Kenneth was preparing to leave when Dottie called him back.

'Oh Ken,' she said, 'there's a small query on the Bowker account. Could you hang on a minute?' Bowker was a local florist who used the bank.

'Of course,' Kenneth agreed, but he was unaware of any query in the Bowker account, which he handled. His curiosity was aroused, together with a sudden, eager sense of anticipation.

'Now that everybody else has left, I'll lock the front door from the inside,' she said. It began to dawn on the excited Kenneth that she had other things in mind than the Bowker account.

'So what's the query?' His question was more joking than inquisitorial.

'Silly boy,' she said. 'You know as well as I do that there's no query about Bowker. I wanted to get you alone to deal with a query of a different sort. I want to find out how that moustache feels in a kiss.'

'I'll be delighted to show you,' he said, grinning broadly and instantly filled with lust. They were in each other's arms at once, and to test his response further, she put her tongue into his readily opened mouth.

'Mm! Let's do that again,' she said.

They did it more prolonged this time. He brought his own tongue into play, which left him flushed and breathless. She disengaged herself and he promptly put his hands on her breasts, trying to find her nipples through her clothing.

'Naughty boy!' But she said it approvingly. She put her hand to his groin and stroked the only too obvious bulge there. 'Nice,' she said, 'let's go into my office.'

Her office was a small room almost filled by the desk against the wall. She had pushed her chair aside and placed a folded towel on it; another towel was draped on the desk. As soon as they were in the room, she started removing her clothes.

'Don't stand there gawping,' she said. 'Get your clothes off, all of them.' He needed no second bidding.

She opened a drawer in the desk and took out a little packet, from which she extracted what was universally known in those days as a French letter. Kenneth suddenly panicked. He had no idea how to put it on.

'I'll put it on for you. It's more fun that way,' she said. Giggling, she put it in place expertly. He was immensely grateful.

She sat on the towel on the desk. 'Come between my legs and into me,' she said. He complied eagerly. He tried desperately to delay his orgasm but did not succeed and felt foolish. Dottie was not perturbed.

'Don't worry,' she said. 'We'll do it again when you're ready. Take the French letter off and give it to me.' She calmly tied a knot in the used condom to hold its contents and put it into a paper bag that was conveniently on the desk.

'Wipe yourself with that towel on the chair,' she said.

As soon as he was dry, she started fondling his penis. It erected again quite quickly and she put another condom in place. This time, coition lasted longer and made him deliciously satisfied.

'That was good,' Dottie said. 'Did you enjoy it?'

'You bet,' he said, mightily pleased with himself. He wouldn't have minded trying a third time, but she disappointed him.

'We'd better get dressed and go home,' she said. She spoke in a matter-of-fact tone as if doing no more than finalising a normal day's work.

Kenneth went home euphoric. In later, more rational moments, he would come to realise how contrived the episode had been.

Those towels had been too carefully placed, to say nothing of the condoms and the bag to dispose of them, which she had taken away with her. Then, Mr Mudgeon's departure had been unusual. Could it be that she really did have a sexual relationship with him that she used to persuade him, or perhaps even to blackmail him?

'You're late,' his mother said. 'I've kept your meal for you but it's bound to be spoiled.' It occurred to him that in the midst of momentous happenings, more mundane things continued with an awesome inevitability.

'Sorry Mam,' he said. 'There was a query with a client's account that I had to sort out rather urgently.'

If he was expecting any repeat performances with Dottie, he was thoroughly disappointed. She never referred again to their little adventure, rebuffed any moves he made towards her and simply treated him as if nothing had happened. Mortified, he took good care not to mention the episode to any of his colleagues.

Kenneth felt, though, that he had partly established his manhood and that all he now had to do was to consummate it by becoming an RAF pilot. He had visions of no end of pretty and willing girls once he was in uniform. Without waiting for his calling-up papers, before his eighteenth birthday he went to the RAF recruiting office to volunteer. Then came a profound shock: he failed the medical examination. Nothing had ever so shaken him.

'But why?' he asked the examining doctor. 'I play football and cricket and I feel perfectly fit.' He wanted to add, but fortunately thought better of it, 'And I've fucked an experienced woman.'

'I cannot say any more,' the doctor replied stiffly. 'You had better see your own doctor.'

His parents shared his shock. Vicky's feelings were mixed. In a way she was relieved that he would not have to go to war, but she was worried as to what was so wrong with his health that he could not. Hugh shared her concern, with an added tinge of disappointment. He had been looking forward to talking about 'my boy who's training to be a fighter pilot'.

'You must go and see Dr MacBrayne,' he told Kenneth. 'I'll come with you.'

Dr MacBrayne's verdict was unequivocal. 'I'm afraid you have a heart condition,' he said. He added drily, 'Don't worry, though, although it's enough to stop you going on active service, you're not going to drop down dead or anything like that. On the contrary, given the high rate of pilots' casualties, it may well have prolonged your life.'

He turned to Hugh. 'You will recall that he had a difficult birth, and I'm afraid this is one of the consequences.'

'What about my other boy? His birth was difficult too. Is he likely to be the same?'

'Not necessarily, but I'll examine him if you want me to.'

Hugh thought hard. There was an unspoken dread in his response about what such an examination might reveal. 'No, I don't think so, Doctor.'

'Very well, it's a matter for your choice.'

The effect on Kenneth was devastating. He felt that he was a failure. He shaved off the moustache. What was the point of it now? Part of the reason for growing it had been to make himself look older; now he agonised gloomily that nature would do that for him. He, who was by nature so lively, critical and sociable, became morose and unhappy. The only glimmer in what he saw as all-pervading darkness came unexpectedly from the bank manager, Mr Mudgeon, who called him into his office.

'I am extremely sorry, Hughes,' he said. He always referred to the staff by their surnames. 'I know how you had your heart set on joining the air force. A very noble ambition, but the RAF's loss is the bank's gain. As you know, members of our staff are being called up all the time and, although it won't make you happy, I am pleased that you can stay with us. I hope you mean to do so.'

'Yes, I do.' It was said without enthusiasm; he could see no choice anyway.

'Good, you are a bright young man and good at your job. If you stick at it, you could go a long way in banking.'

'Thank you Mr Mudgeon.' He returned to his place. Praise like that from Mr Mudgeon was rare and it helped, but it was a long time before he recovered anything like his old spirits. There was general sympathy and support from his colleagues, but Dottie showed no response and his former desire for her turned to dislike.

As Kenneth went through his trauma, Owen experienced the stress of his school leaving examinations. He did well but he failed in one subject. That annoyed him because it made him feel inferior to his brother, who had sailed through with passes in every subject. He was not unduly concerned, though, about the subject in which he failed because it was religious knowledge, and religion was something about which he had growing scepticism.

Religious observance was not a feature of the Hughes household, although in earlier years the boys had been regularly packed off to Sunday school on Sunday afternoons. It was an act of ritual rather than belief which seemed to be especially ritualistic and unbelievable on the mid-Lent Mothering Sunday.

On that occasion there was a special session when mothers accompanied their children in order to receive gifts from them. Mothers and children alike had to read from a supplied text as the gifts were presented and received. Vicky found it embarrassing and the boys excruciatingly so. Since the boys' pocket money was minimal in those depression years, Vicky always paid for her own gift from the already stretched housekeeping money.

The gifts had to be flowers made into posies, which could be purchased from Mr Bowker's florist's shop. Mr Bowker had himself suggested that the gifts should be in that form and from that source. He was the churchwarden and a devoted worshipper of both God and Mammon.

That was several years, though, before Owen's scepticism was triggered, in circumstances laden with paradox. He won a school prize for religious knowledge and received a copy of John Bunyan's *Pilgrim's Progress*. Gummed inside the front cover was a card to inform him that the prize had been donated by a local religious group 'To the pupils in the Bristol Council Schools who excelled in Biblical Knowledge'. That annoyed him because it sounded so patronising, coming from a group of whom very few had been educated at council schools.

His scepticism had been increased by the war and the bombing. He was not a pacifist but during his studies for the School Certificate he had asked his scripture teacher how it could be that an omnipotent power for good could allow such evil. The teacher was no theologian, he was the deputy head, a mathematician who had been drafted by the head into overseeing the religious knowledge studies. He told Owen that God had created human beings to work out their own destiny and to be answerable in the next world. To Owen, it seemed too glib, a stock answer, and he was not impressed.

Looming over all this was the question of how he was going to earn his living. He was good at drawing and had the idea of becoming a draughtman. He was particularly attracted to the idea of working for the Bristol Aeroplane Company, which employed thousands of people and produced famous aircraft.

He wrote a letter applying for a job in the drawing office and was invited for an interview. This did not go well. It was with a thin-lipped, formidable lady in horn-rimmed glasses, who was clearly no more impressed with him than he was with her. Within a couple of days, he received a curt letter regretting that there were no vacancies.

There were numerous other engineering works in Bristol. In pre-war days, they had manufactured a wide variety of products, now they were all flat out on war production. He applied to several without success; some did not even answer his letters. The break came with an application to a company which, pre-war, had specialised in building the machinery for the tobacco factories.

He was invited for an interview and offered an apprenticeship. The works manager, who interviewed him, told him that to become a draughtsman, it was first essential to have workshop experience, to gain an insight into what was practical in design, otherwise he could never become other than what was called a copy draughtsman. He talked it over with his father, who urged him to accept. To get him started, Hugh then had to sign a witnessed indenture, which bound Owen to faithfully serve his Masters, to properly and abstemiously conduct himself and to be industrious in all work set him by his Masters. They had discretion to employ him in the drawing office after the first year of his apprenticeship but it was solely a matter for them to decide. They reserved the sole right to cancel the apprenticeship if he misbehaved, in which case his father would be liable for quite substantial financial penalties.

Hugh readily agreed the terms. With his elder son installed in a bank, he wanted above all for his younger to have a skilled craft. Owen started work as soon as the formalities were completed. He had to wear overalls, which prompted sneers from Kenneth, who went to work in a suit and was at that time in the depths of misery over his failure to get into the air force. The love–hate relationship between the brothers did not change as they grew towards manhood.

Owen's hours of work were long, the pre-war working hours negotiated between the unions and the employers having been suspended for the duration of the war, whilst he had from time to time to work alternate fortnightly night shifts. Until he adjusted, it left him desperately tired. His employer's discretion to transfer him to the drawing office was not exercised and that disappointed him, but there arose a new interest to divert his attention and assuage his disappointment.

A number of women worked in the factory, the government having powers to direct them into war work, and a year or so after Owen started, an attractive, dark-haired girl of about his own age arrived. She immediately became the object of a number of young men's attention, but she did not readily respond. Owen was seized with a desperate desire to make her acquaintance but, unlike his brother, he was shy with girls and could not pluck up the courage to make a direct approach. Then, chance provided an opportunity he knew he could not miss.

Everyone was paid by the hour and had to clock in and clock out. At the end of the day, there was always a file of workers clocking out. Owen found himself immediately behind the attractive girl, who had by then been in the factory for a month.

'How are you finding it here?' he asked, screwing up his courage.

'It's all right but the long hours are tiring,' she said. She had a more cultured voice than he had expected.

'You do get used to it after a time,' he told her, near tongue-tied but desperately anxious to maintain the conversation.

'You're one of the apprentices, aren't you? I've seen you on the shop floor,' she said.

'I'm surprised you should have noticed me.'

'Well, you are one of the more good-looking boys and, unlike some of the others, you haven't pestered me.'

To his inner fury, he felt himself blushing but, confused as he was, he was still able to note that she, too, was blushing, embarrassed no doubt by her spontaneous response.

They had reached the time clock. In his confusion, he dropped his time card as he took it from the rack, fumbled as he inserted it in the machine and almost dropped it again when he put it in the rack on the other side of the clock. The extra seconds that took seemed to him like embarrassing hours and he was surprised to see that she was waiting for him. His rather flagging ego was boosted.

'Do you have far to go?' he asked.

'To Clifton.'

'Oh!' he said. 'I see.'

Clifton was very much the upper-class part of Bristol. Linking that to her cultured, although not affected, voice, he realised that she must come from a different stratum of society from his own. She sensed an air of something like disappointment in the way he spoke.

'Where do you live?' she asked, as anxious as he was to continue the conversation.

'I live at Ashton.'

'Nice part. Are you near the City football ground?'

'Yes, quite close.'

'I cycle to work. How do you get here?'

'I cycle too. Er – can I see you to the bike shed?'

An instant smile flickered on her lips, momentarily non-plussing Owen. Then the point dawned on him and they both burst out laughing. Inadvertently, he had raised reminders of jokes about randy school children doing unmentionable things behind the bike sheds. Discovering each other's sense of humour added to their mutual attraction and it was a precious moment that neither would forget. They walked happily to collect their bikes.

'See you in the morning,' he said as they went their separate ways.

'I'll look forward to it,' she answered.

He couldn't get her out of his mind. His father was not at home, being en route to Cardiff, but both his mother and his brother noticed that he seemed to be far away.

'Stop daydreaming, Owen. What's the matter with you tonight?' his mother said.

'I reckon he's met a girl,' Kenneth teased. Seeing Owen's instant confusion, he added maliciously, 'See how he's blushing.'

'Sod off!'

'Really Owen,' Vicky said. 'You know you shouldn't use language like that. And Kenneth, don't you be so fond of trying to make your brother look small.'

The tension between the two brothers was a worry to both parents, but now Vicky worried even more about Kenneth, who had become so depressed and difficult since his failure to get into the air force. He often came home smelling of drink and was clearly spending too much time in pubs and, she guessed, seeing a constant succession of girls. He always refused to talk about his activities and responded negatively to suggestions that he would be welcome to bring any girl home, from which she assumed, rightly or wrongly, that she would not approve of any of his girl-friends. If, as now seemed possible, Owen had met a nice girl, that would be something of which she would entirely approve.

The newly emboldened Owen determined to re-approach the attractive girl the next day. They had to be at work at seven o'clock in the morning, and at half past nine, when there was a fifteen-minute tea break, he went straight to her.

'I did enjoy talking to you yesterday,' he said.

'And I enjoyed talking to you,' she replied. He had, in fact, been as much on her mind overnight as she had been on his.

'We don't even know each other's names,' he said. 'I'm Owen Hughes.'

'My name is Jade Jewell.'

A bell rang in Owen's head. More correctly, a whole peal jangled discordantly.

'Oh! Are you connected with the Jewell shipping line? And do you have a ship named after you?'

'Yes, my dad is the chairman, and I actually named that ship. You know something about the company?'

'My father works for your father. He's the mate on the *Ruby* and my great-uncle was the captain of the *Pearl,* that was sunk by a German mine.'

'Oh! I'm so sorry. That was a terrible thing.'

She spoke with an obviously genuine compassion that endeared her to him, but now he was aware of sudden and unexpected difficulties.

'I'd love to get to know you better,' he said awkwardly, 'but there are bound to be problems.'

'What problems? I want to get to know you better, too.'

'Well – we do come from very different backgrounds.'

'I couldn't care less about that and, after all, we do work on the same shop floor and we both get our hands dirty.'

'Yes, but you're here only because of the war. I'm here because this is how I'm going to have to earn my living.'

She diverted the conversation skilfully. 'Did you take the School Cert?'

'Yes, and I've got six passes.'

'That's two more than I've got and I was sent to a private school.'

'I'm still studying,' he said, sensing an admiration for academic achievement and eager to impress her. 'I go every Sunday to study at the Merchant Venturers for an engineering qualification.'

The Merchant Venturers Technical College provided night school classes which, because of the wartime blackout, were held during the day on Sundays. It was named in honour of the seafarers who had sailed worldwide from Bristol in the sixteenth century to bring great wealth to the city. Their successors had brought even greater wealth through the slave trade.

'Oi! You two! Stop canoodling and get back to work. Didn't you hear the bell to end the break?' It was the stentorian voice of the foreman.

'See you at the lunch break,' Owen said hastily.

'Look forward to it,' Jade replied and they both hastened back to their work places.

Their mutual attraction blossomed. The long hours of work with the added situation of sometimes being on different shifts, plus Owen's Sundays being occupied by his studies, were daunting problems in the way of courtship. Nevertheless, they did manage to find some time to go out together. The all-pervading blackout was another problem but, in the longer hours of summertime daylight, there were Saturdays when they would cycle together into the countryside. They also went from time to time to the cinema, but there was always, for both, strictly enforced parental control requiring them to be home by ten o'clock. Farewell kisses had to be exchanged before they went their separate ways home.

Always present in their minds was the strong likelihood of parental opposition to their relationship. Owen did make it known that he was seeing a young lady he had met at work, but he carefully avoided giving any details of her background and, as Jade was a fairly unusual name which might lead to his dad identifying her, he said her name was Jean. As the romance developed, his mother suggested that he might bring her home to tea.

'Oh I don't think so, Mam. We might break up soon,' Owen said, lying through his teeth.

Jade realised that she almost certainly had a bigger problem with her parents. Questioned about her absences from home, she told them that she was going on cycling trips and occasional cinema visits with some of her old school friends, but she was conscious that they were becoming increasingly suspicious.

A year passed. Owen gave her a box of chocolates, a rare and difficult gift to find in the stringent wartime shortage of almost everything. 'You realise what day it is,' he said.

'Yes,' she replied. 'It's a year ago today that we first met.'

'You know I love you.'

'And I love you.'

'I think we ought to get engaged. Would you be willing?'

'Yes.'

'I shan't be able to afford to buy you an expensive engagement ring.'

'I don't care about that.'

The conversation, one of the most important they would be likely to have in their entire lives, was almost matter-of-fact and unemotional, but now a new and urgent dimension entered it.

'We shall have to let our parents know, and that is bound to be difficult,' he said.

'However difficult it is, we are going through with it.' She smiled suddenly in the impish way that he so adored. '*Nil carborundum illegitimi*,' she said.

That was one of the first shop-floor witticisms they had learned, derived from the name of the wheels that were used for precision grinding, which were known as carborundum wheels. It was quasi-Latin for 'Don't let the bastards grind you down'.

'*Nil carborundum illegitimi*,' he repeated. 'We'll let them know this weekend, if that's OK by you. My dad will be home, so I'll tell them on Saturday.'

'I'll do the same,' she said, 'then I'll meet you at the tech when your classes finish on Sunday.'

Owen waited until Kenneth had gone out. He did not want his

brother's sneers when he broke his news. He was nervous enough as it was and the gloomy November afternoon did not help.

'There's something I want to tell you,' he said tentatively.

'Oh yes,' Hugh responded without even looking up from reading the *Daily Herald*, now reduced to only eight pages because of the shortage of newsprint, to say nothing of the strict censorship of news.

'What is it?' Vicky asked without any great interest.

Their seeming indifference annoyed Owen. He took a deep breath. 'I've got engaged to be married,' he said in an unnaturally loud voice.

'What?' Hugh lowered the newspaper.

'Oh dear,' Vicky said. 'Who is she?'

'This is very sudden,' Hugh said. 'Who is she?'

Owen took an even deeper breath. 'Her name is Jade Jewell and she is the daughter of your boss.'

To say that his parents were flabbergasted was to put it mildly. That rather pleased him because he felt that it gave him a small measure of advantage.

'What! How do you come to have met her? How long have you known her?' his father demanded.

'She works on the shop floor and I've known her for a year.'

'Oh Owen,' his mother said. 'You've lied to us. You never told us her real name.'

'Yes, I know. I'm sorry, but I thought it better not to until we were sure that we wanted to get engaged.'

'And does she know that I work for her father?' Hugh asked.

'Yes, she's known that all along.'

'Do you seriously expect that she would want to marry somebody from our class?'

'Yes, we have discussed that and we are both quite determined. She might not want to marry just anybody from our class but she is definitely prepared to marry me.'

'Oh Owen,' his mother said again. 'You're only eighteen. You're much too young to tie yourself down – and with a girl like that – and with the war and everything. How old is she?'

'She's the same age as me. Six weeks older, to be exact.'

Hugh modified his exasperated tone. 'Your mam's right, son. You're too young to tie yourself down.' In earlier times, he had learned that his own mother had been married when she was eighteen but he had forgotten that in his bewilderment at this contemporary turn of events. He went on, 'Besides, you'd feel out of place with a family like hers. Why not give yourself the chance to meet a nice girl from our own sort of background?'

'We've been into all that and we love each other enough to overcome that kind of thing.'

'For Christ's sake boy, stop talking about "love" and face up to reality. Do you really think that Geoffrey Jewell would let his only daughter marry somebody like you?'

'It's Jade I am engaged to, not her father.'

'And do her mother and father know about this infatuation?'

'It's not an infatuation. I've already told you that we've known each other for a year. And no, her parents don't know. She is going to tell them today.'

'I bet that'll be an interesting conversation,' Hugh said. 'And when will you be seeing her again?'

'She's going to meet me at the end of classes at the tech tomorrow.'

'Well, you can tell her that your mother and I are entirely opposed to this and the quicker you both forget about it, the better it will be for everybody.'

'Whether you are opposed or not, we shall go ahead. Who do you think you are to stop us?' He regretted the question as soon as he had uttered it, knowing that, temporarily at any rate, he had lost the plot, a fact of which his father reminded him with vehemence.

'We are your father and mother and you are under age and we do not intend to let you make such a fool of yourself.'

'Oh bugger you! I'm going out.'

He left the room and the house and walked around in the blacked-out streets for a couple of hours, furious and needing to be alone. When he returned, he went straight to his room to avoid his parents. He heard his brother come home, followed by an animated conversation, although he could not make out what was being said.

Hugh did not speak to him the following morning. In his view, the engagement was impossible and he was convinced that it was a passing, youthful infatuation that could not possibly develop into marriage. As Owen left to go to his classes, his mother gave him his usual packed lunch; the family Sunday lunch would be taken later, when he came home, as it always was on these term-time Sundays when he was at college.

'Oh Owen,' she said anxiously, 'I do hope you know what you're doing. Your dad is right, you know. How could we fit in with a family like that? We'd feel so out of place. Don't go rushing into something that may seem all right now but might make you unhappy for the rest of your life.'

'Thank you, Mam,' he said 'but we have made up our minds. We both hope that once this war is over we might even see a time when there will be no more of these stupid class distinctions.'

As he was leaving the house, Kenneth appeared. 'You cunning bastard,' he said. 'No wonder they say the quiet ones are the worst.'

'Jealous because I've got a permanent girlfriend and you haven't?' Owen retorted.

It seemed an eternally long day. Normally, he was keen and interested in the lessons and he was good at them, with every prospect, after three years' study, of successfully taking the 'ordinary' level examination, which would lead to another two years' study and the higher certificate, which would be a very considerable qualification for a good job. On this Sunday, though, he was much more focused on Jade and what she would have to say to him than on the differential calculus.

Like Owen, Jade, as she fully expected, found her parents hostile, extremely so. They were a church-going family and she decided to delay her announcement until Sunday lunchtime, after church. As usual, the meal was prepared by her mother with the help of the housekeeper, a widowed lady who had been with them for many years and always joined them at the table.

Jade waited until they had finished eating, the housekeeper had retired to the kitchen to wash up and they had moved to what her parents insisted on calling the drawing room, where her father usually read the *News of the World*, popularly know as the *Screws of the World* because of the salacious court cases of which it specialised in deadpan reporting. Her mother would engage in knitting. although they both tended, after a while, to doze off to sleep. But there was no dozing that afternoon.

'I have some important news for both of you,' Jade announced.

'Really dear,' her mother said. 'And what is that?'

'I've just got engaged.'

'You mean engaged to be married?' Pearl asked incredulously.

'That's right.'

Her father, whom she had always regarded as a pompous man, seemed momentarily at a loss. He put down his newspaper and removed his reading glasses.

'And why is this the first time we have heard anything about this?' he asked in what might fairly be described as an intimidating manner.

'Because Owen and I wanted to be sure of our love before making a decision.'

'Owen! And who exactly is this object of your affections?'

'He's a boy I met at work a year ago.'

'Oh Jade,' her mother said. 'So that's who you've been going out with while telling us that it was with old school friends.'

Her father had gone red in the face. 'A boy you met at work,' he said witheringly. 'Are you seriously telling us that you've got engaged to a factory hand?'

'He's not a factory hand. He's an indentured apprentice who's studying at technical college to qualify himself to become a draughtsman and to go on to a management post. There's something else that you must know.'

When Geoffrey put down his newspaper, he had been at a paragraph in a report of a court case that started 'When her parents discovered her condition'. Association of ideas suddenly numbed him; Jade was afraid that he might be going to have some sort of seizure.

'What complications? Has he made you pregnant?'

'No he has not.' The spirited girl's voice was cold with anger. She had not expected that. 'How dare you! We have done nothing improper and neither of us ever would. Is that your opinion of me?'

'What are these complications you speak of, then?'

'His father works for you. He's the mate on the *Ruby* and the captain of the *Pearl* was his uncle.'

'Good God! A factory hand whose father is one of my employees. Are you out of your mind?'

Her mother was scarcely less shocked. 'Oh Jade, don't do this. You will be able to do far better for yourself than somebody like that.'

'The question doesn't arise,' her father said. 'The quicker you forget this nonsense, the better. As your mother says, with your background, you'll be in a position to get married to somebody better than some factory-floor gold digger who's after your money. As your mother and I have not been blessed with a son, I always imagined that you would marry some suitable young man who could eventually take over the running of the Jewell Line.'

'If it comes to that,' Jade snapped, 'I've no doubt that Owen would be quite capable, when the time comes, to take over.'

'Well he's damn well not going to. I forbid you to see him any more.'

'You can forbid as much as you like, but you won't stop me.'

'Let me remind you that until you're twenty-one, you are under parental control. As for being engaged, you can't get married without your parents' permission until you are of age. Since that won't be for another three years, it will give you plenty of time to get over this nonsense and meet somebody more suitable. And that's the end of it.'

'Oh no it isn't. Just you wait and see.'

As Owen had done, she stormed out of the house. It was getting near the time when she would have to leave anyway to meet him at the technical college. When they met, each poured out what they had experienced.

'My father is determined to make us break up,' Jade said, 'but I'm not going to let him.'

'Mine is against us as well,' Owen sighed. 'I'd like to take you to meet my mam and dad, but I'm afraid that will have to wait.' He became suddenly and unusually eloquent. 'Please, my dearest, darling love, don't let us allow them to break us up. Your dad is of course right that you can't get married without his permission until you're twenty-one. It's going to mean an awfully long wait, but I'm prepared for that if you are.'

'Of course I'm prepared for it.'

'In any case, we couldn't get married for a while because it'll be years before I'll be earning enough to support us.'

'My father thinks you want to marry me for money.'

'You know better than that.'

'Of course I do. He thought at first that I must be pregnant. Of course, if I did get pregnant, he'd have to let us get married, and help us financially.'

'Don't talk like that.'

'I was only joking,' she said. Then, the impish sense of humour they shared broke through.

'*Nil carborundum illegitimi,*' he said.

'*Nil carborundum illegitimi,*' she repeated.

Then they were in each other's arms, oblivious to the wolf whistles of students leaving the college.

The following Saturday, they went shopping and bought an engagement ring. It was only a cheap one, all he could afford. She started wearing it at once, to the fury of her father and the frustration of her mother.

Chapter 19

Jade did not wear her engagement ring to work and nor did Owen wear the signet ring engraved with his initials that she bought for him. They kept their engagement secret from their fellow workers although they became the butt of no shortage of mostly good-natured comment about lovebirds. They received no congratulations and no presents. Several months after the stormy announcements to their parents, Hugh received a handwritten letter from Geoffrey Jewell marked *Personal and Confidential*, asking if he would be kind enough to see him privately 'as soon as possible' at the company office.

They met in the boardroom, which also served as Geoffrey's office. Hugh had discussed the meeting in advance with Vicky and done his best to prepare himself. Strongly as he felt about what he regarded as Owen's foolishness and continued obstinacy, he was determined not to allow the boss to talk down to him or to belittle Owen. He did not know that Geoffrey and Mrs Jewell had also agonised at length over how to handle this difficult situation created by the daughter they regarded as misguided and recalcitrant.

Geoffrey was already standing to greet Hugh when he was shown in.

'Good morning, Mr Hughes,' he said. 'I am so grateful to you for coming to see me. Please take a seat. Can I offer you a cup of tea?' He indicated a couple of chairs at the board table.

'Good morning, Mr Jewell. Thank you, a cup of tea would be welcome.'

Geoffey told his secretary to bring the tea and the two took their seats, facing across the polished table, each wary of the other.

'The tragic death of your uncle, Captain Newforth, and the crew of the *Pearl* was a terrible blow,' Geoffrey said. 'He was the best skipper we ever had and the turn-out at the memorial service showed how widely respected he was, as indeed were all the others.'

Hugh realised that Geoffrey was making small talk until the tea was brought in.

'Yes, it was terrible and of course I saw it from the bridge of the *Ruby*,' he said.

'I found it a difficult experience reading the lesson at the service.'

'Everyone could see that you were as affected as anybody in the church, including the family.'

'At least the problem of those magnetic mines has long been solved, and we know now that we shall never be invaded.'

It was the early spring of 1944, and by then the course of the war had changed decisively. Britain was now an armed fortress preparing for the D-Day invasion of France that would re-open the western front.

Geoffrey's secretary returned with tea and biscuits. He told her to leave them and that they were not to be disturbed.

'Now, Mr Hughes, we have a mutual problem,' he said.

'I know that.'

'You appreciate, I am sure, that there can be no question of my daughter marrying your son.'

'So far as my wife and I are concerned, there can be no question of my son marrying your daughter.'

'This is not to cast any aspersion against your son, but – er – he is not a suitable person to marry my daughter.'

'Any more than your daughter is a suitable person to marry my son.'

Geoffrey was slightly taken aback. It had not occurred to him that his daughter could be described as unsuitable. 'I hope,' he said, 'that your son is not motivated by my daughter's financial situation.'

'If you mean that he wants to marry her for your money, you can take it from me that he is not that sort of boy.'

'Jade is, of course, only eighteen and cannot marry without permission until she is twenty-one. And I have no intention of giving such permission.'

'My son is the same age and, apart from any question of permission, my wife and I have told him that he is much too young to tie himself down and should wait until he meets a more suitable girl.'

'I think,' Geoffrey said, 'that in talking about suitability, neither of us is questioning the character of either of our children.'

'I am certainly not questioning your daughter's character.'

'The problem is that they both seem to be equally obstinate and determined to go against their parents' wishes.'

'I am afraid so. I must say I hadn't realised how strong-willed Owen can be. He refuses to accept anything that we say to him.'

Geoffrey sighed. 'Just like Jade. I suppose it's a wise man who knows his own children: but this cannot go on.'

'I agree,' Hugh said. 'I only wish I knew how to stop it but I can't see how; they seem to be so obsessed with each other. Vicky – that's my wife – and I are hoping that this obsession will pass. As you say, they cannot marry until they are of age. That's over two years away, a very long time at their age, so there is a chance for them to come to their senses.'

'Do you think it would do any good if I were to talk with Owen?'

'No I do not! If anything, it would strengthen his determination, but if you felt it would help if I made our position clear to your daughter, she would be welcome to come to our house.'

'I am afraid my wife and I could not give her permission to do that.'

'For the time being, we seem to be at a dead end,' Hugh said.

'Yes, I am afraid so,' Geoffrey said. 'But we have to do everything we can to discourage them and make them come to their senses.'

'That is my own and my wife's view,' Hugh said.

'I very much hope,' Geoffrey said 'that we can keep this strictly between ourselves. Nobody in this office knows anything about it. I trust you have not discussed it with any shipmates?'

'Certainly not. What's more, I know that Owen and your daughter have not said anything about an engagement to anybody at their place of work.'

'That at least seems to show some sense on their part, although how long we can keep it that way, I don't know. Now, there is another matter I want to talk about, to do with work.'

'What's that?' Hugh asked. It was his turn to be slightly taken aback.

'There's a vacancy for a mate on the *Jade*, I'd like to offer it to you. There'll be an increase in wages because she's a larger vessel. Also, of course, as she is much more modern than the *Ruby*, the crew accommodation is much better.'

'I see. When would you want me to start?'

'The week after next. Captain Portway on the *Jade* has particularly asked for you. I hope you'll agree.'

Hugh thought hard. 'All right then, I'll take it.'

'Good. Everything will be ready for you to change ships. I've already spoken to Captain Fenn on the *Ruby*.'

'I see, cut and dried.'

'No, you can turn it down if you want to and there would be no repercussions.'

'There would be from my wife,' Hugh said involuntarily, a sudden picture in his mind of Vicky's reaction if he told her that he had turned down an offer of promotion.

Geoffrey permitted himself a semi smile. 'Yes, we all have to take our wives into account.' He was very aware of Pearl's vehement opposition to the engagement and even to his having this meeting with Hugh.

But Hugh was suspicious. 'Seems strange that you should want me to go to the *Jade*. Is there any connection?'

'There is no connection, it just happens to be the vessel named after my daughter.' Geoffrey's tone unexpectedly became nostalgic. 'Jade launched her, of course. She was only a schoolgirl then and she couldn't push the champagne bottle hard enough to break it against the hull. I had to get behind her myself and push her.' His voice hardened again as suddenly as it had become nostalgic. 'I can see that I'm going to have to push her much harder in relation to this infatuation with your son.'

'Quite! And I suppose that this change of ship will be given out as the reason for me coming to see you.'

'Yes. I am sure that neither of us would want the other matter to become a subject for general gossip. But please don't think that the offer of the new job has any connection with it. As I said, Captain Portway has made a point of asking for you, and I share his confidence in your seamanship. It is coincidental that it enabled us to talk at this particular time – happily, perhaps, in the circumstances.'

'Very happily,' Hugh said drily, only partially convinced. 'Well, I'll be on my way.'

Geoffrey shook hands again. 'I can only hope that the other matter can also be worked out to our mutual satisfaction.'

'I hope so too,' Hugh said.

The war that had brought Owen and Jade together on the shop floor of an arms factory also brought Hugh face to face for the first time with one of his American cousins.

Following the death of his aunt Beatrice in Pennsylvania, he had corresponded occasionally with his cousin Abigail Gannen, one of Beatrice's eight children and herself the mother of seven. Abigail's eldest son, John, was serving in the United States Army Air Force, on the ground staff at a bomber station in East Anglia, and she was very anxious for him to use the opportunity to meet his British relatives. John had written to Hugh to ask if he might spend some leave, furlough as he called it, with them. They were as curious to meet him as he to meet them, and Hugh at once wrote back to invite him, with Owen agreeing temporarily to vacate his room and sleep downstairs to accommodate John.

Large numbers of American soldiers were stationed in Britain and their reputation was not good. 'Overpaid, oversexed and over here' was a popular description and Hugh was also uneasily aware of a Merchant Navy saying that if you passed an American ship at sea, you knew it was American long before you saw the flag because you could smell the bullshit. So his strong curiosity to meet this newly discovered American cousin was not untinged with some measure of apprehension.

Accompanied by Kenneth and Owen, he met him at the station. Kenneth wrote John's name on a piece of card and displayed it. A tall, fair-haired, good-looking American soldier spotted them.

'Mr Hughes?' he asked, going to Hugh.

'John?' Hugh asked. They shook hands. 'These are my sons, Kenneth and Owen.'

'Hi boys. Gee folks, it's great to meet you. Mom has told me so much about you and you're so kind to invite me to visit.'

'It's our pleasure,' Hugh said. 'I've waited so long to have the chance to meet one of my American cousins. Let me take your bag.'

'No way, let me handle it. Gee, you know it just kills me the way you folks have stood up to everything you've had to take. I don't think the folks back home could have stood up to all that bombing.'

It was a frank and, given their preconceptions, unexpected admission. They took to him instantly and he, who had his own preconceptions about the British, vaguely imagining that they mostly wore bowler hats and monocles and spent much of their time in obeisance to aristocracy, took to them.

It did not escape Hugh's notice that his uniform was much smarter and of better quality than its British equivalent. Nor did it escape his notice what good teeth John had. Regular dental attention was a rarity among the British. If you had a bad tooth, you waited until you could bear the pain no longer and went to the dentist to have it extracted. Such extractions were a mainstay in the work of most dentists. Hugh and Vicky had both had all their teeth extracted shortly before the war and replaced with dentures, and Hugh had not been wholly surprised to learn that George Fenn, the captain of the *Ruby*, had paid for his son to have all his teeth taken out and replaced with dentures as a twenty-first birthday present.

The Hughes took to their new-found cousin as warmly as the likeable young American took to them. Vicky had prepared a fine meal to welcome him. To supplement the stringent rationing, people were encouraged to keep poultry and Hugh had built a hen house at the end of the back garden. Many of the neighbours had done likewise and the crowing of numerous cocks was a noisy dawn feature of the urban environment. Hugh, who had not forgotten his early farmyard experience, had expertly killed one of the birds and, supplemented by home-grown vegetables, it provided a meal which John found a welcome contrast to army food, and warmly complimented Vicky.

'Better than Spam,' he said jokingly. Spam was an American product, spiced, chopped ham. Millions of cans of it had been supplied to Britain and it had become a national joke.

'We are capable of producing some of our own food,' said the sharp-tongued Kenneth, emphasising 'some'.

'Sure Ken,' John said, fortunately not appreciating the sarcastic nuance. 'I believe that before the war you folks ate fish and chips and bread and jam.'

'And a few other things,' Kenneth said, fortunately then shutting up in the face of a warning glare from his father.

'Before the war,' Hugh said, 'some people ate very well but there were plenty who did not. My brother John is a miner in the valleys and my sister May is married to a miner. They and their families had to exist on starvation wages.'

'Sure, it wasn't any different in the States,' John said.

'Tell me John, how come your family went to the States?' Hugh asked. 'Your grandmother, my aunt, went originally with her sister to Canada.'

'It was the Wall Street crash,' John said. 'My dad lost all his savings. He was a farmer on the prairie but it became impossible to make a living so he had to sell the farm. He got next to nothing for it and with seven of us kids, we were right on the bread line. In 1933, after President Roosevelt was elected and brought in the New Deal, dad decided to move to the States to see if we could do any better.'

'And did you?'

'No, not at first. How we ever made the journey I don't know. We travelled all the way on an old truck we had and went to Philadelphia. My grandmother was a widow by then, and she came too. It took weeks and we sure had a terrible time. Even when we got there, we had no idea how to survive in a big city and there were no jobs, but when the New Deal started to work, dad somehow managed to get some farmland and we moved out of Philly. By that time, we'd become American citizens.

'Did you work on the farm?' asked Kenneth.

'No, the farm's not big enough to support all of us and I guess I'm no farmer anyway. Before being drafted, I worked for the electricity company as a clerk.' In the American fashion, he pronounced it 'clirk'.

'The way your mam and dad coped, that's quite a story,' Hugh said.

'I'd sure like to get to Wales next furlough to meet the folks there. D'you think I could?' John asked

'I'm sure you could. I could get my sister in Pembroke Dock to put you up. We'll see about that later. While you're here, we'll take you to see some of Vicky's family. Her dad and her brother both live not far from here and they're anxious to meet you.'

They took him the next day to a pre-arranged tea party at Edward and Mary Newforth's. In Edward's eyes, John was suitably impressed at being in a house, now repaired, that had been bombed and outside which Winston Churchill himself had once stood. For Edward, that dispelled the suspicions he had harboured about this transatlantic colonial. Charlie was also there with Greta and their two daughters, both now growing into young women. The cold bitterness remained between Charlie and Greta, a matter of concern and sadness throughout the family, but they carefully concealed it from John.

During his next leave, he managed to fit in a short visit to Pembroke Dock. He went first to Bristol, and Hugh managed a few days off to accompany him. John received a huge welcome. Matthew, the eldest of the family, clearly remembered the departure to Canada of John's grandmother and great-aunt when he was a schoolboy. Hugh's dislike of Matthew softened as he saw signs of the kinder Matthew he had known in younger days, before he had turned into the self-centred and grasping Matthew of middle and approaching old age.

He returned with John to Bristol and there, the first signs became apparent of a growing attraction between John and Elizabeth, Charlie's elder daughter. On his next leave, John brought her a present, nylon stockings, the most popular gift given by American servicemen to British girls, although by no means always for reasons as honourable as John's. Then, presents started to come through the post and letters were exchanged which Elizabeth refused absolutely to let her parents see. Family expectation came to fulfilment on John's last leave in Britain. Nazi Germany was within weeks of defeat and John came with the news that he was to be posted almost immediately to the Pacific for the continuing war against Japan.

He visited Charlie and Greta and, in an old-world gesture they thoroughly appreciated, he formally asked their permission to marry the twenty-year-old Elizabeth, who was only too willing to accept his proposal, which she had been confidently expecting. Among her reasons was the hostility between her parents. Neither she nor her sister had any idea of the part their respective births had innocently played in creating that unhappy situation, they knew only that it had existed all their lives and that it was a blight on their own lives as well as their parents'. Elizabeth had long been anxious to get away from this unpleasant atmosphere and marriage to this attractive young American presented a not to be missed opportunity, with all the added glamour of going to a new country of which she had learned the most exciting things from Hollywood movies.

Charlie and Greta agreed to the marriage although everyone recognised – regretfully – that there was no time to arrange it in England because of John's imminent departure. However, the final end of the war, with the surrender of Japan following the dropping of atom bombs on Hiroshima and Nagasaki, made his Pacific posting redundant and Elizabeth duly travelled to America to become a 'GI bride'.

Coincidental with the end of the war came another marriage that gave Hugh and Vicky much pleasure, that of Kenneth to Joan Biggs. With the passage of time, Kenneth had recovered from the depression that had seized him after his failure to join the RAF. He had assuaged his frustrated patriotism to some extent by joining the Home Guard, which he had tried unsuccessfully to join as a boy when it was first formed, and, gradually, he had changed his boozing, wenching lifestyle.

He had done well in his work and by the end of the war, he had risen to be a senior clerk at the bank and was tipped to become deputy manager to Mr Mudgeon, with every prospect of moving on within the foreseeable future to a larger branch and ultimately becoming a manager himself.

Promotion to such seniority at such a young age had been facilitated, as he well knew, by the calling up of colleagues for military service. It had not met with approval from colleagues who were over military age but of lesser ability, as they resented his promotion over their heads. Only Dottie Bestcalmer had congratulated him. He had responded perfunctorily, suspicious of her motives.

Towards the end of his depressed period, when his innate intelligence had told him that it was time for him to pull himself together, he met Joan in a dance hall, the recognised place where boy met girl. Joan was the daughter of an engine driver on the Great Western Railway. She qualified in every way as the 'nice girl' that his parents had always hoped he might meet, while her parents thoroughly approved of Kenneth, an obviously eligible young man with excellent prospects. More important was that Joan was good for Kenneth. She played no small part in helping him away from the wild lifestyle into which he had degenerated.

With a favourable mortgage from the bank, Kenneth was able to buy a house in what Edward Newforth called the posh part of Southville, overlooking the canal that had been dug during the Napoleonic Wars to divert the River Avon and create the tideless docks so well known to his father. A little over a year after the wedding, a delighted Hugh and Vicky were presented with a grandson, who was rather grandly named Martin Royston Hugh, the middle names being in honour of his two grandfathers.

The election of a Labour government at the 1945 election with a landslide majority that took even them by surprise was received with rejoicing in the Hughes family. However, Edward Newforth threatened to withdraw his Post Office savings because 'that lot' would take them from him to finance the social security and national health service they were proposing to introduce.

Among those swept out of Parliament was Richard Mulholland-Flowers. He was not entirely surprised, although his constituency chairman, Sir Gerald Verrey-ffaire, a much less shrewd observer of the political scene, or for that matter, of any other scene, was profoundly shocked.

By that time, Gerald's moustache had turned white and he had a fine head of matching hair, but there were problems with the monocle. His eyesight was no longer perfect and he had to use glasses to read, which meant that he had to remove the monocle to wear the glasses, something he hated and refused absolutely to do in public. That sometimes led to embarrassments, as for example when he had to refer to documentation at meetings of the constituency Conservative Association. Most embarrassing of all was when one not entirely friendly member of that body, having realised his problem, began to make a habit of thrusting a newspaper at him, demanding that he read an item that had annoyed him.

Despite the passage of time, Gerald's relationship with Richard had never fully recovered from their pre-war dispute over the break-up of Richard's marriage, and relations had become even more antagonistic when Richard moved in to live with Millicent Partridge-Dove.

That had outraged Gerald and like-minded members of the association, and when Richard simply ignored their protestations as an unwarranted intrusion into his private life, some of them became so angry as to resolve among themselves that he would not be adopted as candidate at the next election. But they were thwarted when the war that delayed the election also brought other complications.

When the blitzkrieg started in 1940, Richard told Alice that she could feel free to move to Bellwood House to escape the bombing. She rejected the offer out of hand, advised by their two sons that it could be a conspiratorial move by Richard to regain occupancy of the house and install his mistress there.

Alice suffered no harm in the blitz but, in 1944, one of the first of the flying bombs launched against London and south east England made a direct hit on the house and she was killed. Three months later, Richard married Millicent Partridge-Dove in a quiet ceremony at Caxton Hall Register Office in Westminster. Gerald was caught between genuine sadness over Alice's tragic death and fresh anger at what he saw as an indecently hasty re-marriage to 'a kept woman'.

The marriage also went down badly with Richard's sons, Richard junior and Edgar, for whom it seemed the ultimate insult in their father's betrayal of their mother. Neither of them attended the wedding. Their contempt saddened Richard, especially because he was proud of both of them for having good war records. Although he had never done any military service, he was not without genes derived from several generations of Mulhollands with military backgrounds.

Both sons had joined the RAF in the early days of the war. By virtue of their social background and Etonian education, both had automatically become officers. Edgar, the younger one, became an administrative officer and served in North Africa and Italy. Richard became a bomber pilot, surviving many operations over Germany and going on to finish the war with the Distinguished Flying Cross and senior rank as a wing commander.

Richard, though, had a social problem. For him it was a sore point that so many airmen from socially inferior backgrounds had also become pilots and shown qualities of leadership, notwithstanding that they did not come from public schools. Some of these, initially given the rank of sergeant pilot on qualifying to wear the coveted wings on their uniform, were subsequently commissioned. Richard regarded such elevation of what he called 'oiks' as wholly improper. Had Kenneth Hughes, with his sharp mind, patriotic working-class background and state school education succeeded in his ambition to become a pilot, it would have been something of a revelation to come into contact with the likes of Richard and to experience the contempt with which they held the likes of him.

Although Sir Gerald Verrey-ffaire had not met Richard senior's sons, he admired their war service and was even prepared to give credit to Richard for having fathered them. As the war progressed, there were also political developments that went some of, although by no means all of, the way towards softening his hostility.

Originally, Gerald had been a supporter of the appeasement faction within the Conservative Party and in the early days of the war that had led him to serious disagreement with Richard's support for Churchill to be made Prime Minister. Gradually, though, he had come to realise what a disaster the appeasement policy had been, and by 1945 he was fervently supporting the central plank of the

Conservative election platform, that the great war leader was the only man fit to lead the country and that anyone who opposed this was at best subversive and at worst a traitor. And so it came to be that Richard was the constituency candidate in spite of all the intrigues against him.

A nationwide tour of the country by Churchill was a major part of the election campaign. He passed through the constituency, to be greeted by rapturously applauding crowds, and paused briefly to speak in support of Richard.

'Just look at those crowds,' Gerald said jubilantly. 'It's going to be a great victory.'

'That remains to be seen,' replied the more astute Richard.

He had brought Millicent to help with the election campaign, to the horror of the diehards who still opposed him. Some of them referred to her as 'his whore', the really nasty among them describing her as 'the bastard's whore'. But most of the wider electorate had long forgotten, or had never known, or simply didn't care about the pre-war scandal, and Richard exploited the situation with acumen. Millicent was presented publicly as the attractive second wife of the long-serving MP whose first wife had been tragically killed in the war. But the tactic was no more helpful than Churchill's visit.

Richard was stoical. He had sat in Parliament for almost twenty-seven years, through some of the most traumatic episodes in British history, but he felt increasingly uninterested in and alienated from political processes. He reflected wryly that he had first been elected in 1918 on the Lloyd George 'ticket' in a right-wing landslide at the end of the first war. Now, in a failed attempt to repeat the great war leader tactic, he had been put out in a left-wing landslide.

He was now sixty-one and had never held any ministerial ambitions, but being in Parliament had been no small help in his lucrative business life. As for the six hundred pounds a year salary, it had been a negligible portion of his income and he had always regarded being an MP as an investment to further his business contacts rather than a source of earnings. Business-wise, he had experienced a 'good' war. His coal, steel and engineering interests had done as well as in the first conflict, whilst the radio industry he had entered into in the depression years had paid off handsomely, not least because his company had been involved in the development of radar. He could see that the future lay in electronics and what he believed would be a great expansion in television.

He recognised that the nationalisation of coal, which had been advocated after the first war, was now inevitable, but he fully expected compensation at the market rate. It did not escape his notice that Gwynfor Morgan, who had represented a constituency where one of his pits was located, had retired and that his successor had been elected with what he regarded as an obscene majority well in excess of twenty thousand votes.

In his private life, he had achieved contentment in his so far brief marriage to Millicent, in striking contrast to what he looked back on as over thirty years of miserable marriage to Alice. He grieved over the continuing cold relations with his sons but he still entertained hopes of ultimately bringing both into his businesses. He also had visions of involving, although he was not sure how, his brother-in-law, Jeremy Hatherly, now seriously disabled and invalided out of the army.

After his posting at the War Office and as an adviser to the Prime Minister, Jeremy had been posted to the Middle East. He had fought at the Battle of El Alamein, one of the turning points of the war, and had served throughout the ultimately victorious campaign in North Africa. Then he had been transferred back to Britain in preparation for the invasion of France. Only then had his long-promised promotion to major general come through, and he had been among the first officers of general rank to set foot on the Normandy beaches. But his career and very nearly his life came to an abrupt end in the dash towards Belgium after the crossing of the River Seine.

By then, the allies had overwhelming air superiority, but it did not stop a daring, low-flying German aircraft from attacking a small convoy of vehicles which included Jeremy's staff car. He was thrown clear, shrapnel in his upper body and badly burned with his uniform alight. His life was only saved by a junior officer from the vehicle behind his own who, himself wounded although not seriously, had the presence of mind to douse Jeremy's burning clothes with a hastily grabbed fire extinguisher. Badly wounded as he was, Jeremy tried to drag his driver free from the blazing staff car. He did not succeed and had the horror of seeing the soldier die in agony at close quarters. With enemy aircraft returning for a second attack, he remained in command of rescue operations until he lost consciousness. It was a classic demonstration of his ability to inspire loyalty in his subordinates of all ranks.

Impregnated with shrapnel, disfigured with burns all over his body, his military service was over. His bravery won a bar to his DSO but, unfit for further service, he was invalided out of the army he had served so well. He received many months of surgery but he was left scarred for life. He was much moved when he received a knighthood on the recommendation of no less than the wartime Prime Minister, prompted, it was said, by his brother-in-law, then still an MP who himself had been prompted by Jeremy's old comrade in arms, Gerald Verrey-ffaire. He had to be assisted at the traditional knighting ceremony performed by King George VI, who insisted that he remain standing and not attempt to kneel. Jeremy could not help thinking how proud his father would have been. He remembered how infuriated he had been when Sir George Robson was knighted.

Chapter 20

For Hugh and Vicky Hughes, the general rejoicing over the end of the war was added to by their pleasure at the marriage and 'settling down' of their wayward elder son with such an eminently sensible and 'nice' girl as Joan. They were, however, less happy about their younger son.

Their hope that Owen's attraction to Jade would turn out to be a passing infatuation that he would grow out of had not been fulfilled. One thing they had always tried to avoid was discussing the shortcomings of either brother with the other. Characteristically, Kenneth had other ideas. Conscious, as ever, of being the elder brother, with his status now enhanced by being a married man, albeit very newly so, he felt justified in broaching the subject. He appreciated better than his father and mother that parental opposition on both sides of the disputed engagement had fired adolescent rebelliousness and increased the bond between the two young people. With all the confidence of youth unsullied by maturity, he felt that he was better able to handle the situation than the older generation.

'Well – what's going to happen about Owen and Jade?' he asked bluntly.

'I don't know,' Hugh replied gloomily, 'but I don't see how he can marry out of his class. I'm sure he'd feel out of place with in-laws like the Jewells.' The truth was that he was at least as worried about his and Vicky's ability to handle such a situation as about Owen's.

'Oh come off it, Dad,' Kenneth retorted. 'We're living in changing times. Look at the Labour government with its great majority. What about the classless society?'

'I can't see the Jewells accepting the classless society.'

'Have you spoken with Geoffrey Jewell since that first time? What was it – a year and a half ago?'

'No, I've come across him once or twice when I've had to go to the office, but he hasn't done more than pass the time of day.'

'He wouldn't try to take it out on you, would he?'

'No, I don't think so. As bosses go, he's not a bad sort. Besides, he'd have the union down on him like a ton of bricks.' Like all the masters and mates, Hugh was a member of the union catering for Merchant Navy officers.

Vicky intervened. 'I've no doubt she's a nice girl, but I could never see Owen picking up with any other sort.'

If there was a slight edge to her voice, it was brought on by still fresh memories of Kenneth's pre-marital 'carryings-on', as she saw them. She could not help glancing meaningfully at Joan, but she, even more aware than his mother of Kenneth's past sowing of wild oats, which she had so successfully put behind them both, maintained the tactful silence that she had kept throughout.

Hugh's assessment of Geoffrey Jewell as not a bad sort of employer was as accurate as his balancing view that the Jewells would not accept a classless society. But knowing nothing about the Jewell household, he could not be aware of the influence of Mrs Jewell and just how strongly she rejected any such utopian ideal.

With the ending of the wartime direction of labour, Pearl had pressed Geoffrey to contact Jade's employer, whom she assumed would be without question 'one of us', to secure her release, the purpose being to end Jade's daily contact with Owen. Geoffrey was wholly in agreement with both his wife's sentiments and her objective. He acted accordingly and Jade was given a week's notice. There had been a furious row between her and her parents.

'You can't seriously think that I am going to allow a daughter of mine to work as a factory hand now that the war is over,' her father said in response to her angry protests.

Her mother intervened. 'We didn't pay for your education so that you could work in a factory among people from council estates.'

For Pearl 'council estates' was a term of abuse. She was as much integrated into her level in the class structure as was Richard Mulholland-Flowers into his and as were Hugh and Vicky into theirs: Richard with his contempt for RAF officers who came from lower levels than his; Hugh and Vicky with their worries about their son marrying into what they saw as a higher level than theirs.

Pearl continued, 'If it hadn't been for the war, we could have sent you to a finishing school in – er – Switzerland or somewhere to prepare you for life as a lady.'

She had no direct experience of completing the education of the female offspring of the aristocracy in preparation for the ruling-class marriage market. What she said was based entirely on vague notions derived from reading 'society' magazines.

Pearl believed that there would now be young officers returning from the services and looking for wives, and that one such would be eminently suitable for her daughter. Geoffrey had vague ideas along the same lines, hoping that there might be such a young officer, preferably from the navy, who might be a suitable future chairman for the Jewell Line.

As for Jade and Owen themselves, their concern was simply to marry as soon as possible, not least because they were acutely aware of another closely looming problem, that Owen would shortly be called up for military service. With the end of the war and the perceived need to maintain large armed forces whilst demobilising millions, the reserved status of his work was ended and his call-up was imminent.

They discussed seriously the possibility of eloping to Scotland and getting married at Gretna Green but were daunted by practicalities. How would Owen support a wife? As a married man, he would receive additional army pay, but where would Jade live? It was still a time when newly married couples were often forced to live with in-laws, but with hostility from both sets of in-laws, that was out of the question. The only alternative they could see would be to rent rooms in some third party's house: an unappealing prospect. In the event, any proposal to elope to Gretna Green was abandoned. The idea fizzled out in a whimper rather than a bang.

Owen was called for medical examination and, having been declared fully fit, he was interviewed by a junior officer for a preliminary assessment of his usefulness to the army. A generation earlier, his father had been similarly assessed but now the interviewing officer was more intelligent.

'What is your job?' he asked.

'I am an apprentice engineer.'

'I take it that now the 1944 Education Act is in force, you are on one day a week release for technical college.'

'I am, and before the act came in, I studied at night school. I have my Ordinary National Certificate and am in the final year for the advanced, which I would have taken next summer if I had not been called up.'

The lieutenant realised that he was interviewing an intelligent recruit.

'I'm going to put you down for the REME, that is the Royal Electrical and Mechanical Engineers,' he said. 'With thousands of skilled men now being demobbed, we urgently need replacements. I am making a special note of your studies and the army may be able to help you complete them.'

His calling-up papers ordered Owen to report to an induction centre at no great distance from Bristol and a tearful Jade saw him off at the station. She clung to him until the last possible moment, causing envious glances from some of the other young men who were on their way to the same destination without such loving farewells.

After being kitted out at the induction centre, the recruits were subjected to an intelligence test. This was drawn up in strict accordance with the conventional wisdom, derived from the fashionable theory of the times that sustained eleven-plus segregation, that intelligence was as unalterably fixed from birth to death as the colour of the eyes and that there was no such thing as late development.

'You've done well,' an examining sergeant told Owen. 'After you've done your basic training, you'll go to a REME centre for a technical course, which I don't think you'll have any difficulties with. Don't ever forget, though, that you are first and foremost a soldier, who will be trained as an infantryman to defend your REME workshops against an enemy if that becomes necessary.'

The basic training was rough and tough and the food was abominable, but although shouted at by NCOs in the traditional army fashion, he, a conscript, was not abused as his father, a volunteer, had been a generation earlier. At least for the duration of the war and its immediate aftermath, with millions conscripted from every walk of life, the British army had become, for the first time since the early days of Cromwell's Ironsides, something of the nature of a citizens' army. The situation had not lasted long in the seventeenth century and it was a matter for conjecture as to how long it might last in the twentieth.

Owen's only experience of meeting young men from other parts of the country had been limited to his Welsh cousins. Now there was a kaleidoscope of origins and accents. There were men from north Wales who, he noted, spoke quite differently from his cousins. There were cockneys, some of whom had never previously been outside London and were convinced that the prairie started at Reading, the North at Watford and the jungle at Calais. And there were Geordies who solemnly assured him that they regarded Manchester as being in the south of England.

One squad of soldiers was kept entirely apart from all the others. They were from Eire, formerly the Irish Free State, later the Republic of Ireland, which had been neutral in the war. They were volunteers who, seeing little future for themselves elsewhere, had joined the British army, which was profoundly hated by most of their fellow countrymen. More of their compatriots had done the same during the war than the Free State government was prepared to admit. However, they had clearly not lost their allegiance to their homeland. Every evening in their barrack hut, they could be heard singing at the tops of their voices the patriotic song 'Galway Bay', which included the lines:

> For the women in the uplands digging praities
> Speak a language that the English do not know.
> For the English came and tried to teach us their way,
> To scorn us just for being what we are.
> They might as well go chasing after moonbeams,
> Or light a penny candle from a star.

Their attitude intrigued Owen. He got to learn the full words. Sometime after he had finished his national service, the song with its haunting melody became a popular hit, with the words 'the English' carefully changed to 'the Strangers'. That caused him some amusement, although not so much as the highly sanitised versions of shamelessly obscene songs he had also learned in the army that also became hits.

Home for Christmas leave, there was joyful reunion with Jade and surprise for everyone at the large appetite the training had given him. In reply to his mother's anxious enquiries, he assured her that he was well fed. He omitted mentioning the overboiled cabbage that was gritty because it had not been properly washed or the vast quantities of baked beans with melted cheese for which he had coined the name 'fucked-up cheese'.

Everywhere was drab and food remained severely rationed, but there was widespread hope for the future in that first Christmas after the war. There was no doubt, following the appalling revelations of the Nazi death camps at Belsen, Auschwitz and elsewhere, that a glorious victory had been won against sheer evil. Little was known of such events as the militarily indefensible bombing of Dresden just before the end of the war and, if it had been, there would have been little sympathy for the many thousands of German civilians who had been killed.

On Christmas Day, Jade's parents gave a party for selected relatives and friends. The guests contributed some of the food in view of the rationing. The highlight was to be the afternoon broadcast by King George VI, carrying on the tradition established by his father. It was considered to be a national duty to listen.

Geoffrey was apt to recall that 'the old King', as he referred to George V, had always sounded as if he had just had a jolly good Christmas dinner. George VI, catapulted into the kingship he had never wanted by his brother's abdication, had a terrible stammer. It was painful to listen to him but he had won admiration for the way he had faced up to his affliction, as well as for his staunchness in carrying out his duties, especially through the war.

Among the guests in the Jewell household who gathered round the wireless that Christmas afternoon, patriotic to a person and apprehensive as to how the King would perform, was a newly demobbed young naval officer of exactly the type Jade's mother regarded as a fit and proper husband for her daughter and whom her father regarded as an entirely fit and proper future chairman of the Jewell Line. Care had been taken to seat him next to Jade for Christmas dinner and then to seat him next to her for the broadcast. But Jade had pointedly avoided being anything other than distantly polite to the young man, and Pearl and Geoffrey discussed her attitude dispiritedly when they retired after their guests had departed.

'She's determined to go ahead,' Geoffrey said, 'and I begin to wonder if we shall be able to stop it. She'll be twenty-one in the summer.'

'It's madness,' Pearl said. 'If such a marriage should take place – and God forbid – she'll never be able to settle into such reduced circumstances. And we must make it absolutely clear to her that she must not expect help from us.'

'She's going to meet his family tomorrow,' Geoffrey said, 'at his older brother's house. I gather the brother works in a bank and is not long married. The parents are going to be there too.'

In both their voices there was a note of dejected weariness, as of people frustrated by a growing sense of inevitability.

The Boxing Day party had been Kenneth's idea, with Jade to join Owen and his parents at his new, so far only partly furnished home. His wife was now pregnant, making him feel a more important member of the family than ever and in a position to arbitrate in some way. Besides, he had an insatiable curiosity to meet this girl for whom his 'kid' brother had fallen so heavily.

Each of the six people who gathered at his home was nervous. Even Kenneth, beneath his public bravado, was worried about how it would go. Joan was very tense, worried as to how her cooking would compare with what she imagined Jade was accustomed to. Hugh and Vicky were nervous, and Owen was especially so. Any young man bringing his prospective bride to meet his parents for the first time could be expected to be on edge but, given the exceptional circumstances, he had more reason than most. The most uncertain of all, understandably, was Jade. She had agonised over the propriety of taking presents. It would seem churlish not to, but might it be seen as an unwelcome display of her own family's affluence if she did? In the event, she came down on the side of presents – a bouquet of flowers for Vicky, a box of a hundred cigarettes for Hugh and a bottle of whisky for Kenneth and Joan.

The presents were received with gratitude, and she made a very good impression all round, not least because of her obviously sincere compliments to Joan on the meal. Escorting her home on the bus in the late afternoon, an exhilarated Owen told her that she had absolutely 'wowed' his family. They debated as to whether she should take him in to meet her parents but wisely decided that to do so would stretch the goodwill of the season of goodwill beyond breaking point, so he left her at the door.

His parents retained doubts, even though they awarded Jade the ultimate accolade of being 'a really nice girl'. Vicky's thoughts went back to when the boys were subjected to the scholarship examination, when she had wanted them to pass but not to go to a school that would make them what she called 'potty'. She recognised that Jade measured up to what she wanted to see in a daughter-in-law – she had, for example, insisted on helping with the washing-up while the men sat around and sampled the whisky she had brought – but she worried about Owen becoming potty if he married into such a family. Hugh's doubts continued to centre more around what sort of relationship he and Vicky might have with Mr and Mrs Jewell.

Owen returned to his unit to complete his preliminary training and was then posted to a REME depot for specialised technical training. There he passed his tests well and found himself promoted to corporal. He was called in to see his captain.

'You have done exceptionally well, Corporal. The highest marks of anybody on the course. Congratulations.'

'Thank you, sir.'

'I see that when you were called up, you were well on the way to getting your Advanced National Certificate in Mechanical Engineering.'

'Yes sir.'

'Instead of your being posted elsewhere, I have applied to keep you at this training unit. With some further intensive study in co-operation with the local technical college, I think you could get your advanced certificate this summer. Do you think you could do that?'

'I think so, sir.'

'Good. Don't let me down.'

'I won't, sir.'

The sergeant who had ushered him into the captain's office and was himself a well-qualified technician told him that if he passed the examination there would likely be an additional stripe to add to the two he already had. 'Good lad,' he said, 'Go for it. I look forward to seeing you in a few months' time in the sergeants' mess.'

'I hope so, Sarge.'

His hopes were fulfilled.

Owen was due for a fortnight of leave. He and Jade were now both twenty-one. He had not wanted to publicise his coming of age to his comrades in arms but the arrival of a batch of birthday cards made it known to them instantly and led to an evening of riotous celebrations that left him somewhat the worse for wear the next morning.

He had already written to Jade to tell her that he intended to see her father during his leave, not to seek permission but to announce that he would be marrying her.

Calling at the house, he was greeted by the housekeeper who had known Jade since childhood, was devoted to her and was sympathetic to her love for Owen. Being of a romantic turn of mind, enhanced in her advancing years by reading Mills and Boon novels, she was eager to meet the young man who was such an issue of contention. The smart, uniformed Owen impressed her instantly. She asked him to wait in the hall, where Jade's father, who had been expecting him, soon joined him.

Geoffrey did not shake hands, nor did he invite Owen further into the house. Before either of them could speak, Jade appeared.

'This is Owen, Daddy,' she said.

'I know who he is. I thought I told you to keep out of the way.' He turned to Owen, 'I see that you're a sergeant. How long have you been in the army?'

'Nearly ten months.'

'That's very rapid promotion.'

'It's because I am technically qualified.'

'What does that mean?'

'In addition to having passed my REME exams, I have also just passed the Advanced National Certificate in Mechanical Engineering.'

Despite himself, Geoffrey could not help being impressed. 'That's good,' he said. 'Jade is now twenty-one, so I can do nothing to prevent her getting married, but you are aware that her mother and I are not in favour of this marriage. I believe too that your own parents are not in favour.'

'They do have reservations, but Jade and I are absolutely firm in our intentions and I do not think my parents will oppose us.'

Geoffrey sighed before responding. 'And how would you propose to maintain my daughter when you are eventually demobilised?'

'With my qualifications and service background, I would hope to get a reasonable job, preferably as a draughtsman.'

'I see, and when do you suggest that this marriage would take place?'

Jade interrupted. 'We have talked about that. We thought about having the wedding during Owen's next leave, in about three months' time. We could get a special licence and get married at short notice in the register office. After all, we've waited a long time.'

A door suddenly burst open and Jade's mother, who had been listening behind it stormed into the hall. She went straight to Owen and practically screamed at him.

'How dare you suggest that my daughter should get married in a register office! That's not a proper wedding at all! When she does get married, it'll be in our church, which we have attended for years, with the banns properly called in advance.'

'Really mother,' Jade said. 'Don't scream like that. A register office marriage is as legal as a church one.'

'Not as far as I am concerned. How dare you connive to live in sin.'

It was obviously not the time for Owen to state his own preference for a civil marriage, not only because he thought it could be arranged more quickly but also because of his religious scepticism. If I reveal that, he thought, she'll go berserk. If a church wedding had to be gone through, it wouldn't really worry him, any more than the conventional 'C of E' religious label the army had given him, and, in any case, if they wanted a lavish wedding, it would be they, as the bride's parents, who would have to pay, which, he thought, they could well afford to.

'I'm sure, Mrs Jewell,' he said, 'that if Jade is agreeable, we would of course get married in church.'

'If I can do anything about it, you won't get married at all.'

Jade moved to Owen's side and put her arm in his. 'Well, we are going to get married. Even you, Mother, must realise that by now.'

Geoffrey, more realistic than Pearl, was embarrassed by her outburst. 'As you are both of age,' he said, 'we cannot stop you. I think the best thing in the first place will be for all of us to calm down.'

Pearl showed no sign of calming down but she was at a loss for further words, so she stormed back through the door by which she had entered. Geoffrey turned to Owen.

'I'm sorry my wife shouted at you, but she really is very upset. If you do go ahead – and I can see you are both determined to – please at least have a church wedding.'

'Of course we will,' Owen said.

They all knew that the marriage was inevitable, as indeed, by that time, did Hugh and Vicky. But when Owen returned to his unit, a development awaited him that, to his fury and Jade's bitter disappointment, meant yet another delay. He was posted overseas, with immediate effect, not even with further leave before embarkation.

The captain who had been so helpful spoke to him in person.

'You are posted to Palestine,' he told him. 'There's a lot of trouble out there and reinforcements are needed urgently.'

Owen arrived in Palestine unhappy and morose over his postponed wedding and with a jaundiced view of the world in general. He was in a group who, like himself, were all newly trained. They had little perception of the maelstrom into which they were being thrown until they were met and greeted by Sergeant Major Porterhouse, to whom Owen took an instant dislike, which, even without an already jaundiced mind, was not difficult.

Porterhouse was a long-serving regular soldier nearing the end of his career and his numerous campaign ribbons attested to his extensive war service. He had applied for a commission but had been rejected, which left a heavy and permanent chip on his shoulder. After the war, he had been transferred from the infantry to the Royal Engineers, where he resented the fact that NCOs and others under him possessed technical skills that he could not match. The arrival of REME soldiers with further levels of craftsmanship made his resentment all the greater. He called all Arabs wogs and all Jews kikes.

'The wogs will try to steal your possessions and the kikes will try to kill you,' was his greeting to the new arrivals. Within forty-eight hours, they received a more civilised but scarcely less alarming briefing from their commanding officer, Major Hackensac.

'I must impress upon you that you are in a war zone where there are highly organised gangs of terrorists out to kill you, against whom you must be on guard at all times,' the major said.

'We are here,' he continued, 'to attempt, in conjunction with our friends in the Palestine Police, who have Arab and Jewish members as well as British, to uphold the British Mandate. The objective of the terrorists is to drive both us and the Palestinians out of Palestine and establish a Jewish state. The greatest atrocity they have committed so far has been the recent blowing up of the King David Hotel. Although you have only been here a couple of days, I imagine you are already aware of that.'

They were. The King David Hotel in Jerusalem, which housed units of the British army headquarters as well as of the government, had been blown up with the loss of not far short of a hundred lives, civilians as well as soldiers, Jews and Arabs as well as Britons. More than eight hundred arrests had been made but no terrorists had been found.

'The King David Hotel was blown up by a group calling itself the Irgun Zvai Leumi, which means National Military Organisation.' the major continued. 'In 1940, when it looked as if Britain was going to be defeated and before the Nazis had formulated their policy of exterminating all Jews in gas chambers, the Irgun was negotiating to try to persuade them to deport all European Jews to Palestine. They proposed thereby to establish a Jewish state that would control the Middle East as an ally of a victorious Germany.'

Blurred photographs of a bespectacled man with a moustache were handed out to the soldiers.

'This is the leader of the Irgun,' the major said. 'His name is Menachem Begin. You will carry this photo at all times. If you come across him, you have authority to shoot him on sight. I repeat, shoot him on sight.'

More than anything else, it was that chilling order that brought home the seriousness of their situation.

Accompanying the major was a young, auburn-haired woman soldier, a sergeant in the ATS, the Auxiliary Territorial Service. She had attracted at least as much attention from the soldiers as the briefing, more in some cases.

'This is Sergeant Phillips,' Major Hackensac said. 'She is our unit's liaison officer with Intelligence. She will add to what I have told you.'

'The most important thing,' the sergeant said, 'is never to forget that you are in a war zone, where we are all the targets of an unscrupulous, clever and determined enemy. The Irgun is not the only terrorist organisation and you must be armed and on guard at all times. And if you come across any information that could help in tracking down these terrorists, you must report it immediately.'

Owen noted that she spoke with a Welsh accent. When the briefing was over, he approached her. 'What part of Wales are you from?' he asked.

I'm from Swansea, Sergeant. Why do you ask? By your accent, you are obviously not from Wales. Bristol, I reckon.'

'Spot on,' he said, 'but my dad is Welsh. My name is Owen Hughes.'

'As Welsh a name as mine,' she said. 'My first name is Rhiannon. What part of Wales is your dad from, Owen?'

288

Flattered at being addressed by his first name, Owen warmed to her. 'Originally from Pembroke,' he said, 'but he spent a lot of time working in the pits, first of all, before the first war, at a place called Penduffryn, not far from Swansea. I have an aunt and uncle and cousins living there now.'

'That's interesting,' Rhiannon said. 'I also have family roots in Penduffryn. My great-grandfather was the pit manager there. It was before the first war but your dad may have worked for him. His name was William Yewsley.'

'I have heard my father speak of him,' Owen said, 'but not in very good terms.'

'I'm not surprised. Great-grandad was a hard man,' Rhiannon replied. 'My grandmother was his younger daughter. Her sister, my great-aunt, married a local Methodist minister whom my great-grandad hated, and he never spoke to her again. Her husband went on to become a Labour MP. He retired at the last election. His name was Gwynfor Morgan.'

'I've heard my dad speak of him,' Owen said, 'both about his marriage and as an MP. When my dad came back from the first war, he went to work in his constituency.'

It was as if some twist of fate had brought Owen and Rhiannon together, providing a bond between them because they both had family links with a distant village in the Welsh valleys. Normally, he had no eyes for any girl except Jade and he was proud of that, but this was not a normal situation. They were far from home, locked into a murderous guerrilla war and under abnormal pressure in what he came to call 'this God-forsaken Holy Land'. He felt an affinity for this attractive and, as he came to find out, uninhibited girl.

He quickly got to know her better. She told him that she had once been engaged but that it had been broken off by mutual agreement. She firmly declined to say any more and clearly wanted to put the matter firmly behind her. It did not seem appropriate at that stage to tell her of his own engagement.

Jade sent him frequent, loving letters and he wrote frequent, loving letters to her. But Jade was a long way off and Rhiannon was right there. He realised guiltily that the affinity he felt with her was developing into physical attraction, not least because she was good-looking with pert breasts and shapely legs. He told himself repeatedly that this was all wrong and tried to put her out of his mind, but without success.

There was only one thing to do. He must tell her that he had a dear sweetheart back home to whom he was engaged. He hoped that would help him curb his alarmingly lecherous thoughts about her and make their relationship more distant. When he told her, the opposite proved to be the case and her reaction stunned him.

'I bet you miss the sex,' she said.

'We haven't had sex,' he said gruffly. 'We're keeping that until we are married.'

'What a delightfully old-fashioned puritanical view,' she said. 'But it hasn't stopped you fancying me, has it?' She was entirely unembarrassed.

'It's not right though,' he said. 'I must stay loyal to Jade.'

'So you can,' she said. 'You and I have met in these awful circumstances and there's a sort of affinity between us. It's perfectly natural that we should be physically attracted. Sex is nothing to be prudish or ashamed about. An appetite for sex is as natural as an appetite for food and needs to be fed just as much. It's nature's way of ensuring the continuation of the species. I can respect your and Jade's decision not to indulge but, personally, I find it unnatural.'

As she came to the end of these startling remarks, a roguish note entered her voice and a roguish look entered her eyes. 'Besides,' she added, 'I fancy you too. Are we going to do anything about it?'

She was not just teasing him but twisting him round her little finger and he knew it. He made one last desperate attempt.

'I can't do anything to hurt Jade,' he said.

'Well you won't,' she said. 'We can have a purely physical relationship and not get involved emotionally. Sooner or later, army postings will force us to part company and that'll be the end of it. For that matter, we might decide to end it ourselves by mutual agreement."

'Like your engagement,' he said tartly.

She remained unruffled. 'Exactly.'

It was the end of the argument. If Owen was not able entirely to silence his conscience, he succeeded in putting it aside for the time being. The excitement of their liaison was added to by the knowledge that if a higher authority became aware of it, the consequences could be serious. But against all the odds, they were able to prevent that from happening. Even the hated Sergeant Major Porterhouse, who had a nose for sniffing out wrongdoing and an obsession for putting subordinates on charges and who came to have his suspicions about them, was not able to discover evidence to justify charging them. What worried Owen most of all was the danger of Rhiannon becoming pregnant. If that happened, it would be a total disaster on every front he could think of.

Fortunately, the army, well aware of the needs and temptations of lusty young soldiers, equally aware that putting bromide in their tea did not necessarily work, and anxious to avoid unwanted pregnancies as well as venereal diseases, made condoms readily available. Owen was initially embarrassed about going to the medical quarters to collect some, but the duty orderly was entirely casual about it. 'Will half a dozen be enough, Sarge?' he asked. 'You can always come back when you want some more.'

As Owen and Rhiannon's relationship blossomed, the military situation deteriorated and the Zionists, with growing boldness and ingenuity, launched attack after attack.

Returning to his quarters in the early hours after a satisfying session, Owen became aware of shadowy figures trying to enter the compound. As always, even when on such clandestine visits, he was, in strict compliance with orders, carrying his rifle. He challenged the would-be entrants and, receiving no acceptable response, he opened fire, thereby giving the alarm and ensuring the defeat of the attempted incursion, although the attackers were able to disappear into the night without loss.

He was commended for his vigilance by Major Hackensac. The major was a man of liberal views who knew when to turn a blind eye and he did not raise any questions as to how Owen came to be outside his quarters in the early hours of the morning. For his part, Owen reflected that had the attempted incursion been only a short time earlier, he would have been naked in Rhiannon's bunk with his rifle leaning against the wall. Sergeant Major Porterhouse was suspicious but, with the commanding officer's support for Owen and the latter's popularity in the unit for having prevented probable loss of life, he had to remain angrily helpless.

Weeks after that incident, after a night when he and Rhiannon had not been together, she came to him in an unusual state of agitation. 'Two of our sergeants in Intelligence have disappeared,' she said. 'Clifford Martin and Mervyn Paice. I know both of them. We believe they have been kidnapped by terrorists.'

A search was started immediately. It took priority over everything else, and Owen and others from his unit were involved. Nearly three weeks later, the bodies of the sergeants were found hanging from trees in a government forestry reserve. Owen was in the party sent to retrieve them. What he saw sickened and outraged him more than any of the other numerous atrocities he had lived through.

When the first body was cut down, a mine buried in the ground between the two exploded, blowing the body to pieces and bringing down the tree from which the second body was hanging. The captain from the Royal Engineers who had cut down the body staggered back, wounded and bleeding. He was fortunate not to be killed, which was the intention of those who had planted the mine.

Only later did the full story become clear. After their kidnapping, the two soldiers had been held in an unlighted cellar, shackled and with minimum food. They had been 'tried' by an Irgun kangaroo court and hanged in the cellar. The hanging was inexpert; it did not bring instantaneous death and the victims were slowly strangled before their bodies were taken to the forest, hung there and booby-trapped.

By then, the whole situation was beyond control. The British government had already announced that the unworkable Mandate was to be ended and the problem handed over to the newly-formed United Nations. Plans for withdrawal were already in hand.

Rhiannon was among the first to depart. She and Owen agreed that he would not know the address of her new posting and that they would make no attempt to communicate. He missed her but he accepted the arrangement, which was wholly in accord with their agreement from the start. Now, in any case, the time for his release from the army was drawing near and he looked forward eagerly to being re-united with his beloved Jade. Christmas came and went and early in the New Year of 1948, he received his posting back to the United Kingdom and was demobilised.

From home, he read of the ending of the Mandate over Palestine and the self-proclamation of the state of Israel, with the terrorising of nearly a million Palestinians out of their homeland and the creation of a bloody conflict that would outlive him and go on for decade after decade after decade.

Chapter 21

In his letters home, Owen had tried assiduously to convey the impression that he was not in danger. He had written regularly of hot sunshine and lovely beaches, occasionally enclosing photographs of himself and fellow soldiers in their tropical uniforms, always happy and smiling. But Hugh and Vicky had not been deceived. They well knew that he was in a dangerous zone. His safe return was an immense relief.

However, they were concerned that military service might have brought about unwelcome changes in his personality. There was no shortage of men who had found demobilisation difficult. For many who had lived humdrum pre-war lives in humdrum jobs, the war was the only really exciting thing that had ever happened to them and it was hard to settle back into civilian life.

He was met at the station by Jade, who accompanied him to his parents' house. He was wearing his 'demob suit' as issued to every demobilised serviceman and his old job was guaranteed, a vast contrast with the way his father had been demobilised. Vicky was much relieved that he was still 'the same boy' as when he had been called up. She would have been devastated if she had known of his illicit but enjoyable, not to say educational, liaison with Rhiannon. Hugh sensed that, somehow, the son whom he considered to have left home a boy, had come home a man. He put the change down, reasonably enough, to army discipline in a dangerous theatre of war, and would have been as astounded as Vicky if he had known of Owen's dalliance.

Looming over everything was the wedding that everyone knew would soon take place. Hugh and Vicky had by then established a friendly acquaintance with Jade, not least because she obviously shared their concern over Owen's safety, whilst her own parents had finally more or less come to terms with the fact that she was going to marry Owen whatever they thought.

To them, however, the idea of his continuing to work on the shop floor was anathema. Geoffrey, like Hugh, tended to a more down-to-earth outlook than his wife. He realised that Owen, with a Higher Certificate in Mechanical Engineering, to say nothing of being an ex-serviceman, which counted for a great deal in those immediate post-war years, was overqualified for such a job. He would have liked to find a post for him in his own company, but none such existed and creating a supernumerary post for his son-in-law would make both himself and Owen objects of contempt.

It amused him that he received regular letters from demobilised officers seeking supervisory posts on the grounds that they were experienced in handling men. They'll find it a bloody sight more difficult handling civilian employees than handling servicemen who had no option but to obey orders, especially in these socialistic post-war times, he thought.

Pearl echoed the same thoughts more strongly. 'These working people seem to think they've got us just where they want us because of this Labour government,' she said. To which Geoffrey's unspoken thought was: Yes, but we did have them where we wanted them for so long. For all such arguments, he felt an obligation to do something for the young man who was now unavoidably his prospective son-in-law.

In strict secrecy, he contacted the chairman of the company that owned the shipyard where the *Pearl* and her sister ship the *Jade* had been built. The result, to Owen's surprise, was that he received a letter from their chief draughtsman, inviting him for an interview with the possibility of a job as a junior draughtsman. He was asked to write a letter setting out his qualifications.

'I see you've not quite finished your apprenticeship,' the chief said when they met, 'but you already have a higher certificate. If I offer you a job, do you think your employer will release you and give you your indentures?' On the basis that you only asked such a question when you already knew the answer, he did not disclose that Geoffrey had already approached Owen's employer and seen to it that they would do so.

'I can only ask them,' Owen said, 'and even if they refuse, it will only be a matter of months before I finish my time anyway.'

'All your workshop experience was on war production – aircraft components, I believe?'

'Yes.'

'Marine engineering is very different. Do you feel up to tackling that at drawing office level?'

'I am sure I could.'

The chief was impressed. He confided to his superiors, 'This is no case of giving him a job as a favour. This young man has talent and can be an asset to us.'

So it came about that Owen, given his indentures a few months ahead of the official termination of his apprenticeship, went to work in a suit, like his brother and to the immense pride of his parents.

The question as to where he and Jade were going to live exercised the minds of everyone. Jade actually suggested that they could apply for a council house, a suggestion that nearly sent her mother into hysterics. There was a great deal of post-war reconstruction and the building of council-owned properties to let was proceeding on a vast scale, but the sheer demand meant going onto a waiting list.

Geoffrey was as hostile to the idea as Pearl. Hugh and Vicky were also unenthusiastic. Neither they nor any members of their respective families had ever lived in council accommodation and among working-class people there was a measure of snobbery against those who did.

Eventually, after much thought and discussion, not to say heated argument with Pearl, agreement was reached that there would be a joint wedding present from both sets of parents in the form of a sum of money for a deposit on a mortgage to buy a house. Pearl insisted that they must live in what she considered to be a respectable district and a modest house was found not too far from the Jewells' own home.

Preparations proceeded apace. Owen had some trepidation in approaching his parish church to arrange for the banns to be called, since none of the family were churchgoers and he had not set foot inside the church since his Sunday school days. He was nervous that he might be interrogated as to why he and his family were non-attenders and drawn into discussing his scepticism.

Fortunately, none of that happened. The church had a newly appointed curate, a young man who lived close to Owen's parents, and he went to him. The curate had a sense of public duty and a firm belief that his pastoral care extended as much to the non-churchgoers in the parish as to the attenders. Theologically, he was well ahead of his time, with serious doubts about the literality of such central doctrines of his religion as virgin birth, resurrection and life after death, whether in heaven or in hell. Already, he was on the intellectual journey that would lead to his becoming a controversial bishop in later life, as his church struggled to reconcile mythology with reality. Owen, to his relief, had no problems in arranging for the banns to be called.

There was no problem for the Jewells. They were lifelong church attenders, even if through custom and social respectability rather than belief. In their case, the vicar was older, completely set in his faith and a family friend into the bargain.

From the start of the arrangements, there had been argument over dress. Jade's mother wanted the men to be in morning suits complete with silk toppers. Owen refused absolutely to wear any such clothes, as did his brother Kenneth, who was to be the best man, and his father, who, more than any of them, regarded such dress as characteristic ruling-class nonsense, announced that, if it was adopted, he would simply not go to the wedding.

In the event, with Owen's utility demob suit, the only one he possessed that now fitted him, being inadequate and with Kenneth in need of a new suit anyway, all three bought bespoke suits from an excellent but not too expensive tailor who ran his own, one-man business. Hugh had patronised him before the war. He had a foible about dress and since the time he had been reasonably well paid, he had bought made-to-measure suits, although not frequently. Apart from smoking, it was his only extravagance.

Geoffrey was relieved over the dress decision. He possessed a morning suit but had had it for so long and not worn it for so long that he found it impossible to fasten the waistband of the grey striped trousers. For him as well as for the Hughes, it would have meant hiring a suit. He prevailed upon Pearl by a carefully crafted stratagem that, as these post-war years were still a time of austerity, it would be more appropriate to stick to lounge, or as he tactfully called them, business suits. The austerity line was what finally won Pearl over, giving her another stick with which to beat the Labour government. Naturally, she insisted on having a specially made, expensive new outfit for herself.

Vicky, together with her daughter-in-law Joan, also acquired what were, for them, new and expensive outfits. She was intensely worried about the prospect of having to mingle with a lot of posh people. The reception was held at a Clifton hotel of the sort the Hughes would normally never have dreamed of entering. Most of the two groups of guests did not mix. On both the bride's and groom's sides, there were those who regarded the others with varying mixtures of awe, suspicion, dislike and contempt.

Geoffrey, to his credit, with a reluctant Pearl firmly in tow, went out of his way to mingle. Edward Newforth received a sharp kick on the ankle from Kenneth when he addressed Geoffrey as 'sir.' Kenneth later explained to his grandfather that it was fine to call another man 'sir' when you regarded him as an equal and knew that he would address you in the same way but it was beneath your dignity to call him 'sir' implying that he was better than you.

Kenneth moved easily among all the guests and he performed his duties as best man with aplomb, making a witty and well-received speech. Privately, he reflected with some cynicism that because he worked in banking, and was now an assistant manager no less, many of the posh people accepted him as a near equal.

Another who moved easily and conversed easily with everyone was Robert Snape, who, with his wife Myfanwy, had come from Plymouth for the wedding. Robert now had a good supervisory job at the Royal Naval Dockyard and Hugh marvelled at his brother-in-law's sophisticated ease of manner. Robert had been the brightest boy at their school but he had also been the poorest. It was not easy to equate the suave, well-dressed, middle-aged man with the ill-dressed schoolboy who had been called 'ragged-arse Robert'.

Edward Newforth was now retired and receiving the modest pension provided by his former employer, together with his state pension. He was not, though, in good health. Even in his last year at work, it had been clear that he was deteriorating but, partly from stubbornness in refusing to recognise that he was not well and partly from fear of what a medical examination might reveal, he refused to take advantage of the newly established National Health Service. Eventually, however, he was forced to go to his doctor, who sent him for specialist examination. He was diagnosed as suffering from lung cancer and given only a limited time to live.

Hugh, as shocked as the rest of the family, had to consult Dr MacBrayne on a relatively minor illness and mentioned his father-in-law's terminal illness. Edward had always refused to have Dr MacBrayne as his family doctor in spite of strong recommendation from Hugh, not because of any lack of faith in Dr MacBrayne's skill but because he regarded him as a dangerous revolutionary.

'Does he smoke?' the doctor asked.

'Yes, has all his life. Worked for over forty years in Wills's and is a great smoker of their cigarettes.'

'That's why he's now dying of lung cancer,' the doctor said. 'And as I've repeatedly told you, I could cure that cough if you yourself gave up smoking. Fortunately, you've got no sign of cancer but you should count yourself lucky.'

'But we were encouraged to smoke in the army in the first war. Isn't it supposed to be good for the nerves? And it was encouraged in the last war for the same reason.'

'Yes, it was,' the doctor said, 'and between the wars it was considered fashionable, especially with one of those fancy cigarette holders, but whatever it does or does not do for fashion and the nerves, it destroys the lungs. Naturally, the tobacco companies will do everything they can to dispute that.'

Hugh went away depressed. He was too addicted to cigarettes to stop smoking. Within a few months, Edward was dead, but it was several years before Hugh was able to master the craving.

By then, there was a growing campaign against smoking, with roots in the death of the King, George VI, a heavy smoker whose death, in helping to draw attention to the link between smoking and cancer, was perhaps his final service to the nation he had served so well.

'Black ties will be worn,' a plummy-voiced courtier proclaimed over the radio, a proclamation that incensed Owen and Kenneth. They made a point of disobeying the edict, and whilst Owen had to contend with the disapproval of his mother-in-law, which he survived without difficulty, it was a more controversial gesture of independent thinking for Kenneth, assistant manager in a bank staffed almost exclusively with royalty worshippers.

The family had other reasons to remember the date of the King's death. On the same day, February 6th 1952, Hugh and Vicky's fourth and last grandchild was born to Jade and Owen. The unconcealed pleasure of both his grandfathers that it was a boy contained strong elements of what would later be called male chauvinism. Kenneth's son Martin had been followed by a sister named, not very originally, Mary Victoria, after her two grandmothers. Jade had borne a daughter, now a lively two-and-a-half-year-old, who was called Abigail Eloise.

Some argument had arisen over those names, mostly because her maternal grandmother had wanted her to be called Pearl Victoria, also after her grandmothers. Owen and Jade had rejected the notion on the grounds that it sounded too much like some minor artefact in the crown jewels or even like some sort of nineteenth-century royal jubilee, but they now reverted to what Owen called the grandfather syndrome by naming their son Hugh Geoffrey. By common consent, it was agreed that he would be known as Geoff, to avoid having two Hugh Hughes.

Several years after little Geoff's arrival and against the growing background of the anti-smoking campaign, Hugh finally made up his mind to give up. He simply stopped, and having survived by sheer willpower a fortnight of agonising withdrawal symptoms, he never smoked again. He thanked his lucky stars that, despite having been a smoker over many years, he had escaped the dangers. Even more so, he was profoundly grateful that neither of his sons smoked. What pleased Vicky most of all was the absence of the smell of stale tobacco smoke that had previously pervaded the house. As Dr MacBrayne had forecast, Hugh's cough disappeared.

Now, another important date was looming, his sixty-fifth birthday, when he would qualify to receive his state pension. It was also the date when, in accordance with the rule of the company, he would have to retire as a seagoing employee. The passing years were something to which he had given little thought. He had always been, and still was, a fit, active man and he found it difficult to come to terms with the prospect of retirement. It was a time of full employment and shortage of labour, so the government sought to encourage older men to remain at work by offering them a higher rate of state pension. So he started to look round for another suitable job.

As his birthday approached, Geoffrey Jewell invited him into the office. They met in the boardroom where they had met so much more dramatically over a decade earlier. Geoffrey was smoking a cigar.

'Can I offer you a cigar, Mr Hughes?' he asked.

'No thank you, I've given up smoking.'

'You're a wise man. I've given up cigarettes but I can't do without an occasional smoke. I've taken up cigars as they say they are not dangerous like cigarettes.'

'So I hear, but I feel much better without smoking anything.'

'I hope Mrs Hughes is well. Do give her my regards.'

'She is fine, thank you, and I will of course do so.'

Although their children were married and parents themselves, they had never got round to addressing each other as other than 'Mr'. With their other daughter-in-law's parents, Hugh and Vicky regularly exchanged visits and they all called each other by their first names, but no such familiarities existed with the Jewells and no visits were ever exchanged.

'I thought we ought to have a word,' Geoffrey said, 'in view of your forthcoming birthday. As you are well aware, we don't keep seagoing officers or crew beyond sixty-five, but we don't want to lose you. I would like to offer you a shore-based job here in the office, regular hours, home every night and with no reduction in your wages.'

Hugh was agreeably surprised. 'What sort of job?' he asked.

'I want you to be a liaison between myself and the captains and mates. Like all of us, I'm not as young myself as I used to be and I want to delegate more. Will you take it?'

Now Hugh was uncertain. 'Well – yes,' he said hesitantly, 'but I've never done any sort of office job.'

'It won't be difficult and I'm sure you'll be able to cope.' Geoffrey paused before continuing. 'The last time we met in this room, it was to discuss a family matter of great concern and then I offered you the job of mate on the *Jade*. They do say the wheel turns full circle, and in a sort of way, it has. This time, we have met here to discuss a job in the office, and now I want to raise a family matter.'

Hugh was suddenly alert and not a little suspicious. 'What is it you have in mind?' he asked.

'I hear very good reports about Owen from Jimmy Dale,' Geoffrey said. James Dale was the chairman of the company that owned the shipyard in whose drawing office Owen worked. 'As I'm sure you know, Owen has moved up several grades since he started with them. You have cause to be proud of your son, Mr Hughes. And from what I saw of your elder boy at Jade's wedding, you have cause to be proud of both your boys.'

Hugh was both flattered and relieved. He had wondered what was coming. 'Yes,' he said, 'I am proud of my boys. The manager of the bank where Kenneth works is retiring shortly and Ken has already been appointed to succeed him.'

'A bank manager, no less,' Geoffrey said, impressed. 'Of course, it's Owen I want to talk about.' He paused again, clearly not at ease. 'What I want to talk about is in absolute confidence, not to be mentioned even to Owen and Jade. Can I have your word that you will treat it that way?'

'Well, I'd like to know what it is, but I think you know by now that you can trust me.'

'Yes, I do know that. What I am going to say is something very difficult that I have had on my mind for some time. I haven't even mentioned it to my wife.'

'What is it?' Hugh interrupted, suddenly very uneasy.

'We are living in very rapidly changing times,' Geoffrey said. 'The truth of the matter is that there is no long-term future for this company. It's on the horizon that the power stations we supply with coal here in Bristol will be closing down within a few years and the signs are that the electricity board are planning to use much larger vessels than ours to supply Portishead. I've looked into the possibilities of other coastal cargoes but the fact is that small coasters like ours are simply going to disappear. For that matter, the larger, medium-size vessels that use the Bristol city docks are also on the way out. Twenty years from now, the city docks will have ceased to handle any shipping at all. Jimmy Dale's company will be gone as well.' He spoke with the air of a man who had relieved himself of a great burden that he had been bottling up inside himself for a long time.

Hugh was staggered. 'How long has the company to last?' he asked.

'About ten years, I reckon.' He smiled wryly. 'Don't worry, it'll see you out.'

'You said you wanted to talk about Owen. According to what you say, his job will be gone too. Does he fit into this somewhere?'

'Yes, he does. My great regret is that I have never had a son to succeed me. This has been a family firm for three generations, but even if I did have a son, there is no future for a fourth generation. However, I do need the help of a younger man in facing up to this situation. I want to bring Owen into this firm, say in a year or so.'

'To help run it down?'

'To face up to an inevitable situation and salvage what can be salvaged.'

'What sort of job do you have in mind for him?'

'A seat on the board at an appropriate salary. The only other director is my wife. I am the sole owner of the company but by law we have to have at least two directors. Owen would make a third.'

That really set Hugh back in his tracks; it was the last thing he could have envisaged. 'He's very young to take on that sort of responsibility,' he said hesitantly, 'and he's had no experience of any sort of management, even at a lower level.'

'Jimmy Dale tells me that they regard him as of management calibre,' Geoffrey said. 'Everything I know about Owen leads me to believe that he could face up to such a challenge and, after all, those two faced up pretty successfully to our opposition to their marriage – which, so far as I can see, seems to be going pretty well. Besides, I recall that the army gave him pretty rapid promotion when he did his national service.'

'I never expected to hear you praise Owen like that.' Hugh told him.

'Life is full of surprises and usually difficult in one way or another, but experience is a great teacher for those of us who are prepared to learn from it,' Geoffrey replied.

'What will Mrs Jewell think about this?' Hugh asked.

Geoffrey could not suppress a smile. 'A very natural question to follow on from what I have just said. I don't know what she'll think. I'm afraid that she will never reconcile herself to Owen as her son-in-law but all decisions on the conduct of the business are mine, not hers.'

There was a silence, very brief, but expressive for both of them, then Hugh said, 'I am grateful to you, Mr Jewell, for taking me into your confidence and I will, of course, not discuss what you have told me with anyone, not even my wife.'

'I do appreciate that. I look forward to seeing you regularly here at the office. Please start on the Monday following your birthday.'

After the momentous matters they had been discussing, it seemed a bit of an anticlimax, but life could be like that.

Chapter 22

After so many years when the times he worked had been dictated by the times of the Bristol Channel tides, it was at first strange to work nine to five, Monday to Friday and with guaranteed free weekends. He missed the seafaring life – the motion of a ship in all weathers, the sea air, sunsets and sunrises over the water, and above all the camaraderie that bonds all seafarers.

He was now in the only job he had ever had that required him to go to work in a suit and tie, which was considered to be something of a distinction. There was no shortage of working-class people who regarded themselves as a cut above others of their class because they worked in suits and ties, notwithstanding that they were as much wage slaves as those who did not. His late father-in-law had always believed himself superior because he was expected to wear a tie in the cigarette factory.

Not that Hugh was entirely free of such thoughts himself. He was proud that both his sons had 'collar and tie' jobs and that even when Owen had started on the shop floor in a job that required overalls and made his hands dirty, it was normal for him to go to work wearing a tie, except in warm summer weather, when an open-neck shirt was considered acceptable. It was well before 'men in suits' later reduced simply to 'suits' became a term of opprobrium.

Always interested in people, he was intrigued by his new colleagues and he soon discovered that there were much stronger jealousies and personality clashes than any he had known on shipboard. Under Geoffrey Jewell's overlordship, the office hierarchy was topped jointly by Harry Penpole, the company general manager, and Roger Meanacre, the cashier, neither of whom felt any affection for the other. It annoyed Meanacre that Penpole was paid a higher salary, which he felt unjust because it was he who had responsibility for the accounts and the preparation of the annual balance sheets for the auditors.

Both men had long service with the company and both harboured disappointment because they thought they should have been offered directorships. However, such ambitions had been very firmly blocked by Geoffrey's immutable decision that full control must be kept within the family, which in reality meant in his hands alone.

Harry Penpole was shortish and tubbyish, with an easy-going manner. He was a man grown wise from working his way up from a humble start. He firmly controlled the staff, but it was control maintained by mutual respect because those under him recognised that he not only knew his own job but theirs as well. Geoffrey had always borne Harry's competence and experience in mind when rejecting applications for executive posts from ex-officers claiming to be experienced in handling men.

Roger Meanacre had also worked his way up but had learned much less from the experience. Tall, thin and humourless, he seldom saw any viewpoint other than his own. As he grew older, he became even more parsimonious with the firm's money than with his own and acquired a nit-picking negativity that, even if he had possessed no other faults, would have made him ineligible for the post of director of finance that he believed to be his due. He was, unsurprisingly, nicknamed 'Old Meanie'.

The bane of both his and Harry Penpole's lives, and for that matter pretty well everybody else's, was the office boy, a cheeky, fresh-faced youngster not long out of school who rejoiced in the name of Justin Carruthers, which in itself was regarded as something of a joke. In addition to his non-proletarian name and irrepressible cheekiness, Justin had another handicap – he was one of those people who always found it difficult to get up in the morning and he was frequently late for work. Harry Penpole cuttingly rebuked him, 'Just because you've got an aristocratic name, there's no need to be lazy.'

When Hugh started in the office, Justin addressed him familiarly by his first name, bringing another rebuke from Harry. 'Mr Hughes is old enough to be your grandfather; you will address him always as "Mr Hughes". Do you understand?' Justin did understand and did not repeat the solecism, but it took further rebukes and the threat of dismissal before he overcame his difficulty in getting up early enough to be regularly punctual. In Roger Meanacre's view, 'the cheeky little brat should have been sacked months ago'.

After the war, in which many thousands of eighteen-year-olds had been called into the armed services and many had been killed in action, the status, earning and therefore spending power of young workers had grown dramatically. The term 'teenager' was entering the language.

It was also a time of what Roger Meanacre called over-full employment, which in his view not only gave licence to youths like Justin to misbehave but also encouraged subordinates to demand and get higher wages than he thought they deserved. He was scarcely able to contain his irritation at having to hand Hugh his weekly wage packet.

'Classic example of the effects of over-full employment,' he told his wife. 'Pension age, no proper work to do and getting inflated wages because his son is married to the boss's daughter.'

Unpleasant though Meanacre's views were, Hugh was aware that they were too close to the truth for comfort. The liaison between the seagoing officers and Geoffrey Jewell for which he had been nominally appointed amounted to very little in practice. As someone who had worked hard all his life, it depressed him that he had so little to do, and hostility among fellow workers further depressed him. Sometimes, he thought of handing in his notice and talked it over with Vicky, but the lure of the weekly pay packet and the enhanced state pension at age seventy kept him going.

He had been allocated a small table and a chair in Harry Penpole's office but he felt acutely embarrassed that he had to spend too much time sitting there with too little to do.

Harry was always pleasant to him, not least for reasons of his own, calculating that Geoffrey Jewell was moving towards retirement and was already looking forward to more time on the golf course. Since Geoffrey had no son to succeed him, it seemed obvious that his son-in-law would be brought in. Since Hugh was the son-in-law's father, it behoved Harry to be friendly with him. With the correct combination of circumstances, that elusive directorship he coveted might even yet come to him.

He had, though, wider anxieties about the future. Geoffrey had never confided in him his fears for the very existence of the company but, as general manager, he had been involved in the search for alternative work for the fleet. There had always been a small amount of such work but it was peripheral; the stepping-up of the search had seemed an ominous development, and there were other bad omens.

The Bristol docks were publicly owned by the city, and the City Council, aware that technology was radically changing sea transport, had authorised the construction of a large new dock downstream in the Severn estuary from the mouth of the River Avon, where existing docks accommodated ocean-going ships that were too large to navigate the river to the city. The new dock would be designed for the container ships that were already replacing conventional cargo vessels. No one was admitting it, but the threat of closure already hung over the docks in the heart of the city that had brought in so much wealth over many centuries and within which the offices of the Jewell Line were located.

Then a terrible personal blow fell upon Geoffrey. Pearl was taken with severe abdominal pains one evening, rushed into hospital, operated on the following morning and died that night. Geoffrey was so devastated as to be incapable of initiating the funeral arrangements, a task that was performed for him by Owen. For a fortnight after the funeral, with his worries over the future of the company hugely added to by grief, he did not go near the office.

Shortly before returning to work, he turned up unannounced at Owen and Jade's house. The two small grandchildren rushed to greet him, as they always did. He doted on them and normally he would pick them up in turn and hug them, but on this occasion he did not, to their obvious disappointment.

'Doesn't grandad love us any more?' little Geoff asked plaintively.

'Of course he does, darling,' Jade said, 'but like all of us, grandad is very sad about grandma and you mustn't worry him.'

In the children's presence, she always addressed their grandparents as 'grandad' and 'grandma'. Explaining the sudden loss of 'Grandma Jewell' to them had not been easy.

It was an early Saturday evening and she was preparing a meal.

'We'll make an extra place for you, Grandad,' she said. 'Thank you,' Geoffrey said.

Owen quickly put a gin and tonic in front of him, knowing it to be a favourite of his. They waited expectantly, guessing that he had something special to tell them.

'Your poor mother's passing has shattered me,' he said to Jade, 'and it raises all sorts of issues that I have been thinking about since her funeral.'

He turned to Owen, speaking with emotion. 'I shall always be grateful to you, Owen, for the way you stepped in to make the funeral arrangements without waiting to be asked.' He paused before continuing.

'As you know, she was the only other director of the company. We must have at least one other director besides myself. I want you to come on the board, full-time, at a salary that will be more than double what Jimmy Dale is paying you. I own all the shares but I will transfer ten per cent of them to you.'

Owen was taken aback. He and Jade had often discussed the future and concluded that sooner or later he would join the company, but this was sooner than they had expected and much more generous.

'When would you want me to start?' he asked cautiously.

'As quickly as possible. I can probably get Jimmy Dale to release you without notice.'

'I would rather you didn't do that,' Owen said. 'Dale's have been good to me and I think I owe it to them to give a month's notice.'

'Very well.'

Owen's response had arisen from the ingrained sense of loyalty that was part of his character and Geoffrey admired it. He sensed that it augured well for the future.

'Have you spoken to my father about this?' Owen asked.

'As a matter of fact, I spoke to him under terms of the strictest secrecy when I offered him his present job in the office.'

'He has certainly kept the secret. He has never said a word to me or, I suspect, even to my mother.'

'I know he is a man of his word. But there is a downside to all this that I also explained to him in total secrecy.'

He went on to explain to them that there was no long-term future for the company. There was a shocked silence, then Owen responded slowly, as a man older than his years and choosing his words with great care.

'I don't suppose we should really be surprised. There's so much changing. There are all sorts of rumours about the Dale shipyard. Like you, I don't see that we can stop it. All we can do is salvage everything we can and do everything we can for all the people who work for the company.'

Geoffrey was impressed and relieved. 'Is it a deal?' he asked.

'It's a deal,' Owen said, and they shook hands.

They sat down to the meal. When it was over and the children had been put to bed, Jade and Owen were preparing to do the washing-up.

'There's another matter I want to discuss,' Geoffrey said. 'Why don't you sell this house and move in with me?'

Surprise seemed to be following surprise. They had not expected that. There was a startled silence.

Geoffrey continued. 'The house is much too big for me on my own and there's plenty of room for you and the children, and there's the housekeeper to help with practically everything. I know she's getting on a bit now but she's fine and active – and she adores both of you and the children. In any case, when I'm gone, the house will be yours.'

Owen was hesitant. He was uneasy about taking on too much too quickly. 'I think we shall have to think that over.'

'Of course,' Geoffrey said. 'Take your time, but I do want to move quickly on the other thing. I want to make an announcement about your joining the board within the next week or so.'

Owen duly handed in his notice, more than a little nervous about what the future might hold.

For Hugh, who had been told in advance, it was nevertheless a strange experience to witness the official elevation of his younger son to be one of his bosses. The office staff had been asked to assemble in the canteen and Geoffrey formally announced the appointment.

Owen, unpractised in public speaking, had spent several days agonising over what he ought to say. In the event, he succeeded in expressing himself coherently if nervously and made a largely favourable impression. He spoke of his pleasure at joining the company in such an important role although this was reduced by the sad circumstances of Mrs Jewell's death. He realised that he had a lot to learn, he said, and he looked forward to getting to know everyone and working with them. He studiously avoided any reference to his father.

It was left to Roger Meanacre to strike a discordant note. His pent-up emotions could not be contained, exacerbated by the fact that Hugh's son, 'a young whippersnapper with no experience of the company whatever', was actually to be made a director, simply because he was the boss's son-in-law, and his father had been given a supernumerary position simply because he was Owen's father.

'What are you going to do about the fact that all the company's contracts are facing termination?' he demanded.

There was a collective gasp that immediately became an angry buzz. It dawned on Geoffrey that he had been seriously out of touch in assuming that the matter was secret. With Owen at a loss for words, he intervened hastily.

'I will answer that question,' he said. 'It is true that there is a long-term problem, but it is long-term. Nobody's job is in any imminent danger and it is my top priority, as it will be Mr Hughes', to deal with it.'

It was true that it was a long-term problem but, rumour being no respecter of truth, there was no shortage of those ready to convince themselves otherwise. Some were already looking for other jobs. For most, there would be little problem in finding other work, but among an important minority for whom retirement was already in sight and who had in some cases worked there for most of their lives, there was only embittered worry.

Hugh, the oldest among them, who had never been comfortable in his job, now found himself particularly ill at ease, with no shortage of innuendo-laden remarks that of course he would be all right whatever happened. Some of the authors of such remarks obviously wanted to incite argument but he managed to avoid being provoked. However, he was finally riled by Roger Meanacre, towards whom he had taken as much dislike as Roger had towards him.

Within only a few years of retirement himself, Roger was finally forced into accepting that his dream of a directorship was now never going to be realised. With Owen's appointment to the board, disappointed frustration turned to suppressed fury and Hugh became a special target for venting his spleen, usually through snide remarks to other people in Hugh's hearing; he never condescended to speak to him directly.

'I wish somebody would guarantee me a job until I was seventy,' he remarked to Harry Penpole, having entered his office and given Hugh his weekly pay packet.

It was finally too much for Hugh. 'Excuse me, Mr Meanacre,' he said, 'was that remark directed at me?'

'I wasn't talking to you. I was talking to Mr Penpole,' Roger replied loftily. 'But if you think the cap fits, wear it.'

'Well, I think you mean it to fit, and the first thing you need to remember is that I was asked to take this job by Mr Jewell.'

'No doubt, but nobody has the right to expect a job guaranteed for life.'

'Nobody has ever guaranteed me a job for life,' Hugh said, coldly furious. 'I believe you started with this firm, like young Justin, as the office boy and you have never worked anywhere else. My working life started as a farm boy and a miner, then, after four and a half years in the army in the first war, I worked as a building labourer and a docker before coming into this firm – and as a seaman not a pen pusher.'

For him, it was an unusually long speech, fired by what he saw as the condescending attitude of an idiot. Roger's face had become steadily redder and angrier.

'How dare you speak to me like that,' he raged.

'Because I'm sick and fed up with your nastiness,' Hugh retorted.

Harry Penpole intervened. 'I think, Mr Meanacre,' he said, 'that it might be best if you left my office before any more damage gets done.'

Meanacre opened his mouth as if to argue but thought better of it and left.

'I'm sorry about that,' Harry said to Hugh. 'I know he's been getting at you ever since you started here, but don't let him provoke you any more.'

'It wouldn't take much for me to hand in my notice.'

'Don't do that. That's just what he would like you to do,' Harry told him.

He was alarmed by the threat of such action. Hugh had a powerful friend in the chairman of the company, and with his son on the board, his leaving in such circumstances could have incalculable consequences. Harry disliked Meanacre as much as anybody did, but he did not want a situation to develop that could result in his leaving the company, possibly with repercussions affecting his own position.

Hugh felt distinctly better, feeling that he had successfully seen off Meanacre.

'All right,' he said, 'but he'd better stop getting at me.'

'He will. I'll see to that,' Harry assured him. 'The trouble is that he's got a problem. He doesn't really like anybody. He probably doesn't even like himself.'

The following day, he said to Meanacre, 'Don't you ever come into my office again with your snide remarks about Mr Hughes. I suggest that you stop your vendetta against him altogether. Are you crazy? I know you hate him because he is who he is, but the fact that he is who he is makes it all the more necessary to be at least civil to him. I suggest that in future, to avoid the possibility of friction all round, you hand me his pay packet each week and I will hand it to him.'

Meanacre had realised after the incident that he had gone too far, and agreed to the arrangement. He and Hugh never spoke to each other again. As the story got round, there was a certain amount of glee in the staff, among whom Meanacre had few friends. There was widespread pleasure that he had been put in his place and there was a distinct warming towards Hugh.

Outside the office, Hugh's life revolved round his family, his home and his garden. Now that he had regular working hours and free weekends, he was able to concentrate more fully on all three. The family always came first, with the house a close second, to provide not only his and Vicky's home but also an always welcoming place to receive their children, grandchildren and other visitors. Skills he had acquired when working as a builder had not deserted him. The house, kept spotlessly clean by Vicky, was regularly painted and decorated.

In the front, where he could still vividly recall fighting that blazing fire bomb with Kenneth on that memorable night in 1941, he cultivated an immaculate lawn and a display of flowers that was the envy of many neighbours. Behind the house, to make extra growing space in the kitchen garden, he had long demolished the wartime hen house. Its inmates, together with his homegrown vegetables, had provided a series of tasty meals.

No longer were there occasional cows gazing over the fence. The adjoining land over which they had wandered was now occupied by council houses, and land adjoining the long-defunct colliery where he had once worked was now an estate of prefabricated bungalows. The comfortable 'prefabs' were supposed to be temporary, built to last just ten years, although, in the event, they would substantially outlast his own life.

Financially, he was more secure than at any time. Until the immediate pre-war years, his livelihood had see-sawed between inadequate wages at best and sheer poverty at worst. Neither he nor Vicky had any meanness in their make-up but bitter experience had imbued both with a strong sense of thrift. He had refused absolutely to buy anything on hire purchase, 'the never never,' as it was known, and he had drilled into the boys that you never bought anything you couldn't afford; if you really wanted it, you saved up until you could afford it.

'If you don't owe money, there's no man in the world you can't look straight in the eye,' he had told them.

During the war, wages had risen significantly and he had paid off the mortgage and increased his modest savings, notwithstanding that with the heavy wartime taxation, he had become an income tax payer for the first time in his life. Kenneth, with his banking expertise, advised him where to place savings, mainly in a building society account, which was safe but brought in better returns than the Post Office savings that had previously been his only experience in investment.

It was a matter of pride for him that both his sons enjoyed incomes very much greater than his own and that Kenneth, having become a full bank manager, almost certainly had a job for life with a pension when he retired, although that would be a long way off.

Kenneth's rise to manager had followed automatically on Mr Mudgeon's retirement. Five years before he retired, Mr Mudgeon's wife had died after a long illness and within another two years, to general astonishment and no little amusement, he had married Dottie Bestcalmer.

'She's certainly moving up in respectability,' somebody said. 'No more living in seduced circumstances. She'll certainly show him a thing or two he never knew existed.'

'Oh, I don't know,' replied another wiseacre. 'I reckon they've been at it for years.'

'I bet he won't last long, though, full-time with her. He must be donkey's years older. Wonder if she'll wear a white wedding dress to show her virginity?'

Kenneth wisely avoided being drawn into these exchanges.

Dottie did not wear a white wedding dress, giving rise to further unflattering comment that was entirely predictable, her reputation having ensured that whatever she did, she was damned if she did and damned if she didn't. She gave up her job and only appeared once more at the bank, on the occasion of her husband's retirement presentation, when she turned up with a small baby. Mr Mudgeon thrived on his marriage and lived to a ripe old age.

Kenneth and Owen both ran motor cars. They had tried to persuade their father to buy one but he had declined on the grounds that he was too old to learn to drive and would not pass the driving test. They had, however, persuaded him to have the telephone installed and he had become one of the first in the neighbourhood to get a television set.

Quite often, one or other of the boys would take him and Vicky for a Sunday drive, with the grandchildren crammed into the back of the car between their mother and their grandmother. A favourite route was along quiet roads in the Severn valley, to visit one or other of Vicky's numerous relatives.

Such visits often gave rise to discussions, as they also did among Hugh's numerous nephews and nieces, as to exactly what relation various people were to each other and whether somebody was a second cousin or a first cousin once or even twice removed. Owen's late mother-in-law had rated such things highly and had tried to impress their importance on him. To her exasperation, he had shown little interest. So far as he was concerned, and so far as Jade and his parents were concerned, anybody who was not an aunt or an uncle was simply and straightforwardly a cousin.

The development of both his sons fascinated Hugh as he saw them grow from childhood haunted by poverty and insecurity, through adolescence scarred by war and danger, to manhood and prosperous fatherhood. He felt proud of the way he and their mother had brought them up.

Owen had made a shaky start in the role of company director that had been so suddenly thrust upon him. Total inexperience plus the tricky situation of his father's employment had presented what could have been insurmountable barriers but, mentored by Geoffrey, supported by Jade and showing dogged determination, he had played himself in carefully and successfully. He came to command respect from everyone except Roger Meanacre but he could live with that, recognising that nature had destined Roger never to be able to overcome his prejudices.

Shortly after Owen's appointment, the Suez crisis had arisen, with the attempted invasion of Egypt causing huge controversy and the forced resignation of the Prime Minister, Anthony Eden, the architect of the disaster. This led to an angry exchange between the two brothers. Kenneth, who in younger days had always been the most sharp-tongued critic of everything pertaining to the established order, supported the attack. That surprised Hugh, but he was even more surprised by the vehement response of Owen, normally so much the quieter of the two.

'I don't believe it,' he angrily told Kenneth at a family Sunday lunch, held as it happened in Kenneth's own home. 'You, of all people, supporting the dying kick of British imperialism. Just remember that I've seen with my own eyes what the situation is in the Middle East. I suggest you learn a bit more about it before supporting Eden in this crazy adventure.'

Hugh and Vicky were horrified that an angry row was about to break out. Fortunately, it did not. Kenneth, clearly taken aback and subjected to fierce warning looks from his wife, swallowed hard and refrained from responding. He even felt a small twinge of inward humility; it was Owen, after all, who had actually spent time in the Middle East. Those tense moments finally finished off any remains of his older-younger relationship with his brother. From that moment on, they were unquestionably equals.

If the argument qualified as some sort of defining moment between Hugh's sons, it came in the midst of something of a defining period in the lives and deaths of his brothers and sisters.

Only days later, the news came that his sister Lizzie, who had married Ray Jones and lived in Portsmouth, had died, aged seventy-seven. His eldest sister, May, at Penduffryn, had already died at the age of seventy-five, having lost her husband, John Burrows, two years earlier, a little over a year after celebrating their golden wedding. Within months, his brother John, whose forced but happy marriage to Sally had caused so much controversy, died aged seventy. Hugh remarked to Vicky that, having been miners all their working lives, both he and May's husband had been fortunate to live as long as they had.

Less than a year later, Matthew died, the last of his surviving brothers, the eldest of the family and its titular head. The news was telephoned by his younger sister, Alice.

'I take it you'll be coming down for the funeral,' she said, stating it as a fact rather than an enquiry. 'We can, of course, put you up here. Will Vicky be coming, and what about the boys? We can put you all up as long as the boys share a bedroom. It'll make it more difficult if their wives come, but we can manage.'

Alice, having 'married well', had a relatively large house in what was considered to be the posh part of Pembroke Dock. She had a penchant for arranging other people's lives. She had three daughters who had inherited her willpower, which was fortunate because it had helped them to resist her efforts to manoeuvre them into potentially disastrous marriages. Her own marriage had endured, with her husband, Emrys, commanding widespread sympathy among all their acquaintances. Her favourite reference to him was 'I never argue with him'.

Hugh telephoned Myfanwy in Plymouth and she travelled by train to Bristol and stayed overnight with him and Vicky. Kenneth drove her, Hugh and Owen to attend the funeral. They enjoyed the drive. There was then no Severn Bridge and no motorway through Wales. A ferry crossed the Severn at the location where the first Severn Bridge would be built later, but it usually meant a long wait to board it, as well as, at low tide, driving down a hazardous, mud-covered slipway. The family option was always to cross the river at Gloucester and drive on through the marvellous scenery of the Forest of Dean and the Brecon Beacons.

In the manner of such things, the funeral served as a family reunion, but there was also a large attendance of others. This impressed upon Hugh that Matthew was clearly held in high regard in the locality, in contrast to his own long-standing difficult relationship with him.

After the ceremony, mourners assembled for a 'cold collation' of ham sandwiches, tinned salmon sandwiches, cake and tea at Round Pond Farm, which was worked by Matthew's eldest son, Joseph. It struck Hugh that the farmhouse had been greatly modernised and improved, although, in the manner of elderly people visiting any place which they had only known in much younger days, he thought that it seemed smaller. Joseph made a point of approaching him.

'Thank you, uncle, for coming all the way from Bristol and also for bringing Auntie Myfanwy. We all appreciate it, and also that Ken and Owen came too.' He paused and added, 'I know, too, that this farm has particular memories for you.'

'You can say that again,' Hugh responded. 'This is where I was put to work when I left school. It's also the farm where my dad, your grandad, started work. But my memories of it are not happy ones.'

'I know that, dad told me all about it,' Joseph said. He paused again, choosing his next words with care. 'Dad was always sorry that you and he did not get on very well in later years. He really thought highly of you.'

'The reason we didn't get on was because of the way he treated you and the others when you were children, exploiting you on the farm to save paying wages.'

'I know, uncle, but none of us knew any better in those times, and at least, as you can see, he didn't do too badly. He left three farms.'

'I also didn't like the way he enriched himself so cynically in the first war, when I was away at the front. He didn't do badly out of the second war either.'

'I know, uncle, but that was the way he was made. He saw nothing wrong in it and, above all, he wanted to provide for his family – which he did pretty successfully.' Joseph paused again before continuing, 'I want you to know that you will always be welcome to come here, as will Auntie Vicky and Ken and Owen and, of course, their families. I sincerely hope that we can look forward to seeing you – regularly. There's a standing invitation for all of you.'

Despite himself, Hugh was moved. 'That's very kind of you, Joe,' he said. 'I'll take you up on that. Bristol is my home now but Pembrokeshire is where I come from and I love to visit here. As for the differences between me and your dad, you can't know how much I appreciate what you are saying. I feel that a chapter in my life has closed and that a new and friendlier one is opening with his children.'

It was a genuine rapprochement, to the intense relief of both parties.

Joe smiled. 'And besides,' he said, 'now that dad is gone, you are the head of the family.'

Back in Bristol, all too soon Hugh was seventy and finally retiring from work. He dreaded the idea that someone might have the idea of presenting him with a gold watch, 'his life's seconds numbering' as it was put in the song 'My Grandfather's Clock'. In the event, he was presented with a wallet containing an appreciable sum in brand-new bank notes, a much more acceptable and practical way of marking any working-class retirement.

By then, the Jewell Line was already well into the process of running down. Roger Meanacre had retired, which saved him the embarrassment of going to the bank to get the notes for Hugh's presentation, and Harry Penpole was about to retire. Various other staff had gone to other jobs, leaving Owen, by then firmly in charge, with problems of finding temporary staff to see things through to the end. The smaller vessels that traded into the rapidly running down city docks had already gone for scrap and the same fate was imminent for the larger coasters. The firm was not yet finished but the end was clearly in sight. Hugh worried about what would happen to Owen when it finally closed; he had nagging thoughts about the higher you climbed, the further you had to fall.

Chapter 23

The Jewell Line offices stood on the quayside within a moderately extensive area of land. In founding the company, Geoffrey's enterprising grandfather had acquired the land with the idea of having his own quay for the loading and unloading of his ships. With the docks area now being spectacularly redeveloped, quayside warehouses were being turned into shops, restaurants and entertainment areas. There were no warehouses on the Jewell land but the idea came to Owen, in what he described as 'a sudden rush of blood to the head', that it would be perfect for upmarket flats and houses.

By then, he had sold his own modest home and the family had moved into Geoffrey's large Victorian house. After discussing his idea with his brother, whose financial knowledge and experience he respected, he raised it with Geoffrey.

'The idea is that we keep the land and form a new company to develop it for housing,' he explained. 'Harbour-side houses are going to command good prices. We could build both houses and blocks of flats for rent or sale.'

'We'd have to raise a lot of money to get started,' Geoffrey said doubtfully, 'and I'm not keen on trying to sell shares to raise it.'

'I've already talked that over with Ken,' Owen said. 'He thinks we could persuade his bank to give us a long-term loan. We could then be a private company with no need to go to outside shareholders.'

By then, Kenneth was well established, well regarded by his seniors and not without influence. He was looking forward to being moved to the management of a larger branch. His son Martin, now near to his twenty-first birthday, was, thanks to intervention by his father, a bank clerk at the same bank although, at his father's insistence, at a different branch. He was not a high flyer like his father but that was not to say that he was not capable and intelligent.

Kenneth thought that Owen's idea had a good chance of success and that it would be a feather in his own cap to obtain what could prove to be a major piece of business for the bank.

'Has Kenneth sounded out the bank?' Geoffrey asked.

'Not as yet, I've only discussed it with him privately.'

Geoffrey shared Hugh's worries about the family's long-term future, not least the future of his two grandchildren. He thought for several moments. 'It might be worth looking into,' he said at last. 'If it worked out, your future and Jade's and the children's could be provided for. Why don't you set up a formal meeting with Kenneth and his superiors?'

'That's what we have in mind,' Owen replied, 'but I wouldn't do anything without consulting you. If we do form a new company, you will of course come on the board.'

'Well, I don't know.' Geoffrey was still doubtful. 'After all, like your father, I now have my working life behind me. I couldn't play any very active part.'

'You needn't,' Owen said, 'but after all your work as the successful chairman of the shipping line, you don't think, do you, that you can just be put out to grass.' He added with a twinkle in his eye, 'Besides, look at all your golf club contacts. They could well prove useful – some might even be interested in living in our new waterside development.'

Geoffrey was not a man greatly given to humour, but he laughed. 'You've got it all worked out, haven't you. Have you thought about bringing your brother onto this new board?'

'There might be problems. His bank might not be too happy about that.'

'On the other hand,' Geoffrey said, 'if they're willing to be a major financier, they might want to have somebody on the board. As it happens, one of my golf club contacts is the regional manager of Kenneth's bank. I could always have a word with him.'

'There you are, Dad,' said Owen. 'Your indispensability proved already.'

He thought what a colossal distance they had covered to bring them so amicably together. Geoffrey's thoughts were similar. The young man whom he had once despised for daring to assume that he could marry his daughter had now become a son-in-law he had to admire. He wished that his dear Pearl, who had been even more hostile towards the marriage than he, could be there now to see how things had worked out.

After what seemed interminable and frequently frustrating meetings and negotiations, the bank agreed a loan against the collateral of the land. They declined to take any shares but, not least due to some judicious golf course lobbying by Geoffrey, they expressed no objection to Kenneth becoming a director. The board consisted of Owen, chairman and managing director with a forty per cent holding, and Kenneth, Geoffrey and Jade with twenty per cent each. They agreed that Owen should be in day-to-day control because the whole idea had been his in the first place and it was clear that it was he who would be doing the great bulk of the work. Geoffrey added a codicil to his will leaving his shares to Jade.

Owen now found himself on an even steeper learning curve than when he had been co-opted onto the board of the Jewell Line.

The protracted negotiations were finally concluded and the new company was registered, under the name Jewell Line Holdings, a gesture hugely appreciated by Geoffrey. To celebrate, they met for a dinner party at the house in Clifton.

It was a Saturday evening and nobody had to get up to go to work the following morning, so Kenneth and Joan returned home late and went straight to bed. Joan awoke the next morning to find Ken, as she thought, still asleep, lying on his back. She put a reassuring hand into his and squeezed, expecting to awaken him. He did not stir, so she propped herself on her elbow to look at him. Then she could not stop screaming. He was lying there with his eyes wide open, dead. The heart condition that had failed him for entry into the RAF had killed him in his sleep. He was just forty-four.

There was a hammering on the bedroom door. It was Martin, brought from his bed in his pyjamas by his mother's screams. When she did not reply, he opened the door.

'What is it, mam?' he asked, but Joan was speechless, shaking from head to foot and only able to point at Kenneth.

Martin came to the bedside. 'Oh my God,' he said. He stood stunned, then, recovering himself with a huge effort, he gently closed his father's eyes. It was a gesture that would live for ever in his mother's memory. 'Better get up, mam,' he said.

She was still too shocked to be able to speak or to stand unaided and he had to help her to a chair.

His sister Mary, now seventeen and training to be a secretary, appeared in the doorway, also brought from her bed in her nightclothes by the commotion.

As the awfulness of what had happened sank in, she could only stand sobbing at her father's bedside. Martin pulled her away as gently as he could. With his mother and his sister clinging together and sobbing, it came to him that he was now the man in the house, responsibility cruelly thrust upon him.

He spoke jerkily in truncated sentences, getting the words out with difficulty. 'There's going to be a lot to do. I'll telephone grandad straight away. He and granny must be told at once. The first thing – is that we must all get dressed.' Even as he said that, he could not help thinking how trite it sounded in such awful circumstances.

Hugh, always an early riser, was making tea and preparing to take a cup up to Vicky, who was still in bed. He was surprised to hear the telephone ringing so early on a Sunday morning. On answering and hearing Martin seeming to be struggling to speak, he was instantly filled with foreboding.

'Is that you, Martin?' he asked. 'Are you all right?'

'Yes Grandad, it is me – but I'm not all right. Nothing's all right. We've found Dad dead in bed.'

Hugh's hands started shaking uncontrollably; he almost dropped the telephone. He had harboured a secret dread, which he had not shared even with Vicky, ever since Kenneth had failed his RAF medical examination, that something terrible could happen, but with the passage of time and Kenneth always seeming fit, well and active, he had tended to reassure himself that all must be well. Now suppressed dread had exploded into awful reality.

At a loss for words, he asked in a voice as shattered as Martin's, 'How's your mother – and Mary?' Recovering himself a little, he said, 'I'll come over as soon as I can.'

Vicky, realising that something was amiss, had come downstairs in her dressing gown and slippers.

'What's up?' she asked, alarmed.

'It's dreadful news. Ken has died in his sleep.'

'Oh no!' she said, voice choked and tears welling. 'How can our dear boy be taken from us like this?'

Hugh took her in his arms. They clung together in mutual misery. 'I shall have to ring Owen,' he said mechanically.

Owen and Jade were still in bed but, with the luxury of a bedside telephone, Owen answered at once.

'But he and Joan were here only last night. We had a dinner party to celebrate setting up the new firm. How can such things happen? I'll drive over straight away and take you to Ken's.'

Dr MacBrayne had long since retired but his successor, Dr Smollett, later confided to Martin that the doctor had written in Kenneth's file, after examining him in 1941, 'Not likely to live beyond his forties'. An unkind fate had doomed Kenneth to an early death from the day of his difficult birth.

The funeral service was conducted at Kenneth's local church. To Hugh and Vicky, there seemed to be a particularly sad irony in the sequence of events and association of ideas. It was the church in which they had been married, and it had only recently been rebuilt after being burned out in the air raid when Kenneth had helped his father to fight the fire bomb.

Kenneth, always a realist, seemed to have had a premonition of early death. He had taken out a substantial insurance policy to ensure a regular income for Joan, and all his affairs were in order. Apart from minor bequests to his two children, he left everything to Joan, her inheritance thereby including his twenty per cent share in Jewell Line Holdings. Owen invited her to join the board in Kenneth's place but she declined, saying she had no head for business.

Neither Hugh nor Vicky had ever imagined that either of their sons would die before them. They were proud of their boys, both of whom, with no advantages other than their innate intelligence, had made their way in the world in a way their parents could never have done. Hugh and Vicky in fact, had been brought up to believe that they had no right to such aspirations, but they had had visions, whether realistic or not, of both boys going on to even greater things. Now, a half of all they had hoped for was gone for ever.

Hugh's nephew Joe, son of his eldest brother Matthew, was the only one of his family in Wales who travelled to Bristol to attend Kenneth's funeral, a much appreciated gesture. It was a decade since Matthew had died and since warm relations had been established with Joe and others of Matthew's family. Matthew had worked Old Oak Farm right up to the time of his final illness, and Joe, having inherited the farm, as well as Round Pond, had moved there and installed his own son, also Matthew but always known as Mattie, at Round Pond. Joe's only brother, Oliver, had inherited the third farm, Trevill Hill, and continued to work it. Their mother, Lydia, had survived Matthew by eighteen months.

It had become a regular practice for Hugh and Vicky to take an annual summer holiday at Old Oak Farm and for either Kenneth or Owen to accompany them and to stay with their families with Mattie at Round Pond. In earlier years, the grandchildren had always been taken but they had all reached the age when the last thing they wanted was to holiday with their parents, preferring to make their own arrangements, initially a matter of some concern both to parents and grandparents but something that had to be recognised as an inevitable development.

Joe, Mattie and Oliver were truly a family of farmers. All had inherited Matthew's lifelong complaint about how difficult life was and how poor their incomes were as farmers. It did not, however, escape Hugh's notice that all three farms had been substantially modernised and improved. He, as well as Kenneth and Owen, always insisted on paying for their board and lodging and, although there were protestations that 'No, no, you're family'. the money was always accepted.

Hugh sometimes recalled the day he had run away from Round Pond Farm and how, on the journey to Penduffryn, he had looked back from the train across Carmarthen Bay towards Pembrokeshire and wondered if he would ever go back there to live. He never had, but he felt a strong affinity with the county.

Calling on what seemed to be the ever-growing tribe of his extended family – 'You must see so-and-so's lovely new baby' – became a ritual part of every holiday. Any deviation from the ritual attracted unfavourable criticism, but it took up an annually increasing amount of time that interrupted enjoyment of the countryside and the coast. He loved the beautiful landscapes and the surrounding sea always stirred his maritime instincts.

The coast, together with the Preseli Hills in the north of the county, which were always described locally as mountains, now formed the Pembrokeshire National Park. There were vantage points close to all three Hughes farms from which he loved to look on fine days across the vista of rich countryside to the distant backdrop of the hills, whilst, from Preseli Top itself, on a fine day, you could view the whole of the county and, beyond it, the sea.

Hugh and Vicky felt too grief-stricken to take any holiday in the summer of Kenneth's death, but the following year Owen joined them for the usual fortnight. He and Jade stayed as usual with Mattie and on the evening of their arrival joined Hugh and Vicky for a welcoming meal at Old Oak with Joe and his wife Myra.

'I'm sure you'll be interested to know, uncle,' Joe remarked, 'that I was talking to a very old and very distinguished friend of yours the other day, General Sir Jeremy Hatherly from Larkfield Lodge. You told me once how you had met him, when you were both boys, the day before you left Round Pond.'

'That's right,' Hugh said, 'but how did you come to be talking with him?'

'Well, as you know, my dad bought a fair bit of land from his father in times gone by. The general lives mostly in London but he usually spends the summer at Larkfield, where he has a husband and wife in permanent residence as housekeepers. When the general's here, he occasionally likes to look around what was the family estate. Except for the house, it's all been sold off – not that he's short of a bob or two. Apart from money of his own, his wife is rolling in it. Anyway, to cut a long story short, I was over at Round Pond the other day and he happened to come by.

'He asked me if by any chance Mattie and I were related to a boy called Hughes he had met there and whom he had come across again on the western front and then again in Bristol during the blitz.'

'I'm surprised that he should remember me,' Hugh said. 'All those meetings were a long time ago.'

'Well, he does, and, what's more, he would like to see you again. I told him that you were my uncle and that you were coming to stay here, and the upshot is that I am invited to take you, Auntie Vicky, Jade and Owen to tea at Larkfield Lodge, the day after tomorrow. By the way, I'm not sure if you know, but he was seriously wounded in the last war and although he has had a lot of plastic surgery, he's still rather disfigured. Don't be too shocked when you see him.'

Hugh felt flattered and delighted at being so cordially remembered by so distinguished an acquaintance, but he was nervous, and Vicky even more so, at the prospect of going to Larkfield Lodge to take tea with the likes of a general who was a Sir to boot, to say nothing of the prospect of meeting his aristocratic wife. Owen and Jade, by contrast, were thrilled and enthusiastic.

'Go on, Dad,' Owen said. 'I remember meeting him with you on that morning after the air raid, when he was accompanying Churchill. I'd love to see him again.'

At Larkfield Lodge, they were shown into a largish, comfortably furnished room. Thanks to Joe's warning, Hugh was able to contain any appearance of shock at Jeremy's disfigurement. Jeremy seemed to look out of an expressionless, artificially created face and he had a large bald patch at the front of his head, not because of advancing years but because hair could not grow on the yellowish grafted skin. It could have been a shock for anyone not expecting it, especially if, like Hugh, they had not seen him for many years and remembered him for his good looks. Jeremy did not wait for any formal introductions.

'How very good to see you, Mr Hughes,' he said, warmly shaking Hugh's hand. 'You know, I have not forgotten any of the three times we met previously, the first time when we were boys and then in terrible circumstances in two world wars.'

'I remember too, Sir Jeremy,' Hugh replied. He had debated in advance with himself as to how he should address Jeremy. Greatly though he respected him, he was hesitant about calling him 'sir' in case it sounded too subservient. Owen had put him right by telling him that 'Sir Jeremy' was the proper way to address him as a knight of the realm, without being in any way subservient. Owen had coached him further in the required etiquette.

'May I introduce my wife,' he said, 'and this is my son Owen and his wife. I think you already know my nephew, Joe.'

Jeremy greeted each of them in turn. 'Yes,' he said, 'I do already know the third Mr Hughes, if I may be forgiven for referring to him in that way.' The smile that accompanied the remark showed only in his eyes; his disfigured face was unable to complete it. He added, almost casually, 'I must apologise for my face. Jerry pilot made a mess of me. I know it sometimes comes as a bit of a shock to some people.'

'So much the worse for them,' Hugh said with some spirit, overlooking that he might have been shocked himself had it not been for Joe's warning. 'They should be grateful for the bravery of men like you.'

'That's very kind, but any bravery on my part was no more than the bravery of millions of others on the western front and in your case, if I remember correctly, in the Merchant Navy. But I am being very remiss. Let me introduce my wife, Marion. As you can see, she's a lot better looking than I am.'

The ironic joke made its point only too well. The ageing Marion retained remarkable signs of the looks, now crowned with beautifully dressed silver hair, that had made her a society beauty in her youth. She greeted each of them as warmly in turn as had her husband.

'Jeremy and I were so sorry to hear from Mr Hughes that you lost your other son last year,' she said. 'It must have been a terrible shock.'

'Yes, it was,' Hugh responded. 'He had a heart condition that took him off without warning. In a way, we ought perhaps to have expected it. Not long after Sir Jeremy met him in Bristol, he failed his medical for the RAF. He was keen to be a fighter pilot. He was terribly upset at the time but he went on in his job to become a bank manager. His death was a dreadful shock for all of us.'

'I am so sorry,' Jeremy said. 'Now you mention it, I do recall him. Lively boy and pretty outspoken even at that age in his political views. Do you have any grandchildren?'

'Yes, four. Ken's two, a boy and a girl, are now grown ups.'

Jade came into the conversation. 'We also have a boy and a girl. We used to bring them down here with us but they've reached the age when they can be pretty difficult and, of course, refuse absolutely to come on holiday any more with us.'

'I know what you mean,' Jeremy said, 'from our own grandchildren. You'll be meeting the youngest shortly. He's my son Arthur's boy. Arthur followed me into the army and is now a captain. He's on leave and spending a few days with us. He and his wife and the boy are out walking but will soon join us for tea.'

As he spoke, there was the sound of people arriving, then an obviously military man in civvies, a woman and a boy of about eight or nine years came into the room.

'This is my son Arthur, his wife Rhiannon and my grandson Crispin,' Jeremy said and went on to introduce the Hughes to the new arrivals.

For Owen, the roof might as well have fallen in. He was in shock, instantly recognising the woman he had known in Palestine as Rhiannon Phillips.

Good God! he thought. How can this happen to me? How the hell are we going to play this? He was sufficiently stunned to invoke both the deity and an afterlife in neither of which he believed.

As if in answer to his pseudo prayer, Rhiannon played it superbly. She showed no more than the faintest flicker of recognition as their eyes met. To him, it was inconceivable that she could not be finding the situation as bizarre and excruciating as he was. They shook hands in as formal a way as anyone could imagine.

'How very nice to meet you,' she said.

'How do you do.' He gasped it rather than said it.

Jeremy said, 'We're a bit of a military family. Rhiannon was in the army too.'

'Owen did national service in the army after the war. He was in Palestine when those Zionist terrorists were causing so much trouble,' Hugh said, making well-intentioned conversation in total innocence.

Owen's thoughts again went against all his principles: For Christ's sake dad, shut up! You've no idea what you could be stirring up.

'That's interesting,' Rhiannon's husband said. 'Rhiannon was also in Palestine at that time. She was involved in Intelligence. Then she was posted home. That was when we met and got married. Don't suppose you two ever met out there?'

Rhiannon was again coolly superb. 'I don't think we ever did,' she said. 'But in Intelligence I was almost as much under cover for our own forces as for the enemy.'

Owen had never felt so relieved in his life. 'No, I can't recall that we ever did meet.' He was astonished at how normal and casual he sounded.

Rhiannon turned to Jade. 'What does your husband do, Mrs Hughes?' she asked.

'He's a company chairman,' Jade replied. 'He runs a property company involved in the redevelopment of Bristol docks now that there's no shipping there any more.'

Lady Hatherly spoke to Vicky. 'You must be very proud of both of your sons, Mrs Hughes, the one who became a bank manager and the other who is a company chairman.' It could have been condescending but it was genuinely sympathetic, with no trace of condescension.

'Yes,' Vicky said. 'We are proud of them and of our grandchildren.' She looked at the young boy Crispin, who was wolfing down from the generous selection of cakes that the housekeeping lady had brought. The boy had been silent throughout, obviously bored stiff by the adult conversation. 'You have other grandchildren?'

'We certainly do. We have twin daughters older than Arthur, both of whom have children, three boys and two girls between them. We would hope that Crispin might have a little brother sometime but, unfortunately, it hasn't happened yet.'

Bet that's by choice, certainly not by incapacity, Owen thought. Bet she's making sure they're up to every sexual gymnastic they can think of but taking good care they won't be troubled with any more kids. He wondered cynically what Rhiannon's reaction would be if she could read his thoughts.

Time passed quickly and soon they were leaving. Rhiannon looked Owen straight in the eye when they parted with no flicker of acknowledgement of any past meeting. He looked at her in the same manner.

'It's been a real pleasure meeting you, Mrs Hatherly.' He had been rehearsing the farewell carefully, to make sure that he would not add 'again', which would have disastrously undone everything they had accomplished.

'The pleasure has been all mine,' she returned, 'and I hope all goes well with your company.' There was something of a hint of condescension in her voice.

'Thank you,' he said.

They parted company with both hoping devoutly that circumstances would not throw them together again. None of the others present had the slightest inkling of the melodrama that had been secretly played out among them on that sunlit August afternoon.

Owen and Jade were packing on the morning of departure for home, when Jade said, 'You were talking in your sleep last night.'

'Oh, what about?'

'You mumbled incomprehensibly, then suddenly said quite distinctly "Stop it Rhiannon, I must go now". Is that woman on your mind in some way?'

'Not to my knowledge,' Owen lied smoothly. 'But you know how daft things can be in dreams. I don't recall the dream because it didn't wake me up. I suppose she must have got mixed up with something or other in my subconscious.'

Chapter 24

> We been together fifty years
> And it don't seem a day too long.

So sang a mildly inebriated Mattie Hughes, Hugh's great-nephew, in an inaccurate but appropriate version of an old music hall song. It was December 1971 and the occasion was a splendid reception to celebrate Hugh and Vicky's golden wedding anniversary.

The lunchtime reception had been arranged with some secrecy by Owen, Jade and their other daughter-in-law, Joan. Jewell Line Holdings Ltd was starting to generate income. The old company offices had been demolished and replaced by a smaller estate office, the building of houses and a block of flats had proceeded well and there was no shortage of purchasers and tenants. So Owen was confident about paying the considerable cost of the celebration, at the hotel where his and Jade's wedding reception had been held. There was a large gathering of friends and of relatives from both families. Hugh and Vicky were collected by Owen for what they thought was going to be a lunch at his home, and were surprised on being taken instead to the hotel.

They were even more surprised, on entering the large room where the reception was held, to see who was gathered there. They were immediately greeted by Robert Snape, Hugh's friend of more than seventy years, who had been his best man at his wedding. The biggest surprise of all was the presence of Charlie Newforth's daughter Elizabeth who, with her husband John Gannen, had flown from the USA to be there.

A reasonably good meal with no shortage of reasonably good wine was served and Owen proposed a toast to his father and mother, supported by Robert. Hugh and Vicky were somewhat overcome and sat bemused. There were good-natured calls of 'speech, speech'.

'Go on Dad, you can do it,' Owen said. 'Everybody's with you and I'm right here beside you.' It was more like a father to a son than the other way round.

After what seemed ages, amid growing clamour, Hugh rose, reluctant and nervous. He stumbled through words of thanks to everybody on behalf of Vicky and himself. Seated beside him, she intuitively took hold of his hand. Suddenly, he seemed inspired and launched into a heart-felt tribute to 'my dear wife who has been such a wonderful partner through thick and thin'. He even managed a joke about the thin having been so much harder to deal with than the thick. Confidence growing, he went on to pay tribute to the two wonderful sons she had borne. One of them had sadly passed away before his time, the other had done so much in arranging this wonderful party.

His audience was as surprised by his unexpected oratory as he was, and he sat down to a standing ovation. The whole assembly spontaneously sang 'For They Are Jolly Good Fellows' and it was then that Mattie had risen to his feet to sing. Fortunately, Mattie, a member of a male voice choir, had a rather fine baritone voice and, whereas he might have annoyed his captive audience, he succeeded in pleasing them.

Encouraged by the reception given to his singing, Mattie went on to sing again, this time a popular song about 'Darby and Joan who used to be Jack and Jill'. The applause was noticeably more muted, but Mattie was now sufficiently wound up to show every sign of continuing into a full-blown recital. Owen hastily rose to thank him 'on behalf of everyone'. He was not happy at the 'Darby and Joan' reference and he could see that his mother and father were equally unimpressed.

Hugh finished up a little the worse for wear from the constant topping-up of his wine glass. He had grown up a beer drinker but wine drinking was on the increase and becoming, for the first time in British society, a classless habit. Having been introduced to it by Owen and Kenneth, he had come to enjoy it. An advantage was that sipping glasses of wine rather than downing tankards of beer lessened the constant visits to the toilet that he had discovered to be among the penalties of ageing.

Geoffrey Jewell was there, now very elderly and requiring the help of a stick to walk. Moved by Hugh's reference to Kenneth, he spoke to him about his own sadness that his dear Pearl was not able to be present. Hugh had only ever had superficial contact with Pearl and from what he had seen of her, he remembered her as a snobbish, bossy bitch, but Geoffrey's words made him aware of a mutual sense of the loss of a loved one that gave an underlying measure of sadness to a happy occasion. In all the years of their acquaintance, it was the first time they ever addressed each other by their first names.

Hugh was now eighty-one and Vicky was seventy-six. Both carried their age well but there were lines on their faces and Hugh's once thick, dark hair had thinned and greyed, and he was coming to terms with the fact that he was now an old man. He was becoming forgetful and that was what worried him most. He would go from the living room, where they always ate, to the adjoining kitchen to fetch something and then forget what it was he wanted. He would put something down because something else distracted him briefly and then forget where he had put it.

More and more, the world was becoming a bewildering place that he didn't like. His grandson Martin had introduced him to a smart young woman, had proudly announced that she was pregnant with his baby, that they were going to live together and might think about getting married. It shocked Hugh, Vicky even more so, but Martin's mother clearly accepted the situation with equanimity bordering on pleasure.

Although Hugh had growing difficulty in remembering what had happened a week earlier, he could clearly recall more distant events. Martin's announcement of a potential great-grandchild brought to his mind the sensation caused by his brother John's enforced marriage because he had made Sally pregnant. He recalled that Sally's parents had thrown her out, had wanted to have her and John publicly denounced and humiliated and had never spoken to them again. How times were changing!

If Hugh and Vicky were concerned over their grandson's morality, Owen was more concerned over his parents' living conditions. It wasn't just that the house was shabby because Hugh was no longer capable of the do-it-yourself renovation at which he had once been so good and refused to pay to have the work done professionally. More seriously, the house that had been the latest thing in modernity when built in an age of lower standards, was dangerously cold in winter. It still had inefficient open fireplaces in every room, normally with only one room heated, and inadequately at that, and the rest of the house, with draughty doors and windows, was dangerously cold in severe weather. Worried about hypothermia, Owen offered to pay for central heating to be installed but his parents declined resolutely.

'It's not healthy,' his mother said.

'It's a damn sight more unhealthy to be so cold,' retorted an exasperated Owen, but he could not move them. Fortunately, both of them were sufficiently active and had sufficiently strong constitutions and enough warm clothing to avoid hypothermia.

Apart from changes in manners and the version of morality they had been brought up to believe in, the whole world was changing bewilderingly fast. The Bristol docks, which Hugh remembered crowded with ships, as they had been for centuries, no longer had any. The shipyard where the *Pearl* and the *Jade* had been built and where Brunel's great and pioneering transatlantic liner the *Great Britain* had been built in earlier times, had long stopped building anything. The hulk of the *Great Britain* had been brought from the Falkland Islands, where it had lain wrecked for many long years, and installed in the yard, to be restored to its original condition. The once-active shipyard, where his own son had worked as a draughtsman, was set to become simply a tourist attraction and a monument to the country's industrial and maritime past.

He reached his ninetieth birthday, physically fit but developing dementia, becoming steadily more forgetful and more confused. By then, Jewell Line Holdings was flourishing; all the houses and flats were completed, occupied and sought after by would-be tenants and owners. Geoffrey Jewell had died and Owen, with his two adult children having left home, had sold Geoffrey's large house and moved to a more conveniently sized one on the harbour-side estate.

All this had only registered dimly with Hugh and Vicky. Hugh's brothers and sisters were all dead, as was his oldest friend, Robert Snape, who had married Myfanwy, the youngest of them all. Vicky's brother Charlie and his wife Greta, who had been Vicky's oldest friend, were dead. Among the numerous nieces, nephews and others of their respective extended families, there were many whom they now failed to recognise when they met them. The annual visits to Pembrokeshire had been discontinued. They no longer had any inclination to travel and had largely forgotten who was who.

There were occasions when Hugh would wake up wondering not only where he was but who was the woman beside him. Fortunately, he would regain his memory quickly when that happened but he constantly failed to recognise his now grown-up grandchildren. Vicky was more in command of her faculties and desperately anxious to care for him but she, too, was deteriorating. There were occasions when they would together make the short journey to the local post office to collect their state pension, put the money down when they got home, forget where they had put it and go back to the post office to try to collect it again. Several times, neighbours found them, either singly or together, wandering in the streets; and then Hugh fell down, badly bruising a shoulder and hip. In spite of treatment, both remained permanently painful.

With the help of Dr Smollett, Owen and Jade, deeply concerned because his parents clearly needed constant attention, contacted the local social services. They sent a representative to the house but Hugh and Vicky, proudly independent, refused to let him in.

In that sad twilight of their years, though, there came a national event that brought Hugh temporarily back to dramatic reality. It was the great miners' strike of 1984–85, called in protest at the policy to close down virtually the entire industry.

The televised pictures of riot-clad police, drafted in from outside the coalfields, ruthlessly beating protesting miners, aroused vivid memories of how he had been a miner and himself the victim of such tactics. He insisted on recounting his experiences and some of the things he had witnessed. Owen had never previously heard him speak so bitterly, causing him to wonder just how well he really knew his father.

Owen thought how true the aphorism was that the more things changed, the more they stayed the same. In a different definition of change, millions like his parents remained what they always had been, nothing more than the small change of the unevenly distributed wealth of a rich, money-dominated society. He also found himself wondering what his brother's reaction to the dispute would have been, recalling that by the 1956 Suez disaster Kenneth had already moved well away from the strongly left-wing views of his youth. Would he have been among those who had moved from the vehement left in their youth to the vehement right in middle age?

What enraged Hugh most of all was the refusal of some miners, mainly in Nottinghamshire, to join the strike. Assured by the authorities that their pits would not be closed if they worked, they formed a separate union which they called the Democratic Union of Mineworkers and worked throughout the strike. Hugh called their union the BUM, the Bosses' Union of Mineworkers. His view, drawn from his own experience, was that they would be betrayed in their turn, as they had betrayed their fellow miners and, eventually, their mines too would be closed.

But even as the great conflict moved to its inevitable end, more personal tragedy struck at home. Vicky's general health was visibly declining, with worsening dementia. She was taken into a geriatric hospital, too confused to know what was happening. Owen, Jade and Joan organised a rota among themselves to ensure that she was visited every day but Owen was the only one of them she recognised. Within a few weeks, she was dead.

With no one to look after his incapacitated father, Owen took him into his own new home when Vicky was taken into hospital. When Vicky died, they had difficulty in making him understand what had happened. He was too ill to attend his wife's funeral. She was cremated, in accordance with the decision they had made long before, when they were fully rational. Owen, notwithstanding his non-religious convictions, arranged a simple Christian service. He knew that neither of them had any strong beliefs, but since they had both been brought up in that faith, he thought it the proper thing to do.

Owen persuaded his father to live with them permanently and to sell his own house. He engaged a nurse to attend on a daily basis to minister to him and take some of the strain off Jade. It grieved him somewhat to have to do that for, notwithstanding a sardonic recognition that he was now a man of property and profit, he retained socialist views, but the underfunded National Health Service and social services were not up to dealing with the situation.

The new national ethos that elevated greed and selfishness to the level of virtues nauseated him. He described some of its supporters whom he numbered among his own acquaintances as 'the all you need is love hippies of the nineteen-sixties who had become the all you need is greed yuppies of the nineteen-eighties'. It disgusted him that the Prime Minister, Margaret Thatcher, could say that a man who found himself on a bus beyond the age of twenty-six could consider himself a failure. How, he wondered, could anybody be so nasty towards the millions who used public transport every day, helping to relieve the ever-worsening congestion on the roads.

Hugh did not long outlive Vicky. In the end, he had, like her, to go into a geriatric hospital. He had no idea where he was or why he was there. Several times, he was found wandering helplessly round the hospital. Finally, the nurses found him dead in his bed. His heart, like his elder son's – although in that case so sadly prematurely – had given out in his sleep.

He was by then a frail, confused, little old man. So very different from the rebellious youth who had run away from Round Pond Farm to become a miner. So very different from the young soldier who had marched gaily to war in 1914 and returned to woo his Vicky through one of the many long and bitter disputes in the coal industry. So very different from the mature husband and father who had faced, unflinchingly, everything that Hitler's war machine could throw at him throughout the years of the second war.

There was a government death grant, supposedly to pay funeral expenses. It had been introduced by the post-war government but had not been upgraded to take account of the vast inflation since then. It constituted only a tiny proportion of the funeral costs. Owen went to collect it from the social services local office.

'What a generous society we live in,' he said to the young man behind the glass-fronted counter. 'My father fought for this country in two world wars. We know now how much it valued him – just small change.'

He was not aware of it, but he was expressing exactly, but more articulately, the sentiments felt more than a century earlier by Joseph Hughes, the grandfather he had never known, when he buried his best friend, Matthew Davies, who had died, aged twenty, as the result of a mining accident.